AND THEN, I MET YOU

A Collection of Short Stories Inspired by an Item of World or Local News.

by
Jan Vivian

authorHOUSE®

AuthorHouse™ UK Ltd.
500 Avebury Boulevard
Central Milton Keynes, MK9 2BE
www.authorhouse.co.uk
Phone: 08001974150

First published by AuthorHouse 11/21/2008

ISBN: 978-1-4389-1424-4 (sc)

Printed in the United States of America
Bloomington, Indiana

This book is printed on acid-free paper.

Dedicated to the memory of my father,
Franciscus Henri.
He always said that I might be persuaded
to write a book.
This volume is my fourth.

AND THEN, I MET YOU

Of Satin and of Steel *(p187) – Nicole, a famed former ballerina, travels to New Zealand for an interview; a dance company seeks an artistic director. En-route she is reunited with Loualla, a friend who left the Royal Ballet to marry the love of her life. During a stopover in Perth, Western Australia, Nicole is introduced to John Poynter a renowned sculptor whose life has been in turmoil since the death of his wife in a terrorist attack while they vacationed in Bali. From the moment they meet, Nicole and John know that their lives have been changed.*

Under Blue Skies *(p311) – Anya is woken by a telephone call, on Boxing Day morning. Her girl, Josie, is on a gap year trip and is caught up in the Indian Ocean Tsunami that strikes a resort in Thailand. An unfinished conversation and no further contact leads Anya to conclude that her only child may be lost. Anya travels to London for a government briefing on the tragedy; she meets Dennis and Kate; they too are searching for lost relatives. Dennis is a recent divorcee and Kate has stayed loyal by remaining with her father. An ex wife and two children are unaccounted for. Anya has resolved to help Dennis and Kate for she believes that her life has been changed following their chance meeting.*

Strength of Character *(p381) – Frank is a counsellor to Clarissa and her mother, Rebecca. The young girl is traumatised by the death of her father by his own hand. Frank helps mother and daughter to overcome their grief, loss and anger with*

all that has befallen them and in doing so
seeks the restitution of his own well-being.

You and Me. Myth and Reality *(p403)*
—Jenny creates an alias to persuade Martin
to meet her. The Internet has proved a useful
and anonymous cover for Jenny's deceit; she
has had time to regret ending a passionate
affair with him. She soon discovers that
her tormenting remarks about their age
difference have not diminished Martin's
devotion or need of her, but, he has to be
convinced of Jenny's sincerity before he
invites her back into his life.

ALTERED LIVES

I

The gentle sun-dressed swell stretched out behind them, the surface disturbed by the foaming wake of the vessel's propulsion. To contemplate the journey that lay ahead in peace and quiet seemed impossible; the expectation of breathing in the salty tang on the air was also absent. The confined area of deck trembled and the railings rattled in their own metallic harmony; seagulls no longer followed them. Welcome, to high-speed sea travel. Taking the ferry had changed since he had last travelled on this route.

"That sailor knows peace." Joshua spoke out loud although it was to himself.

On the starboard quarter he observed a yacht moving gracefully in its own serene majesty, driven on by nothing more than the wind in its mainsail. Homeward bound, but to whom? He pictured the circumstances. Was it to a reunion with a loved one? Would the house be filled with laughter and questions about the journey? Would the helmsman have to tell of the joys and troubles that had been encountered and overcome?

"The helmsman's alone, in perfect solitude…he's got time for quiet reflection."

Had the problems of life and daily existence been forsaken for a few hours? Could he now consider them in a more vital human context, their scale measured by so much more than the lines in a personal or a business' balance sheet?

"Ja," he sighed, resting his chin on folded hands that clutched the top of the railing. "I'm going to search for that too, a different peace…and when I do I'll hold on to it, really tight."

He imagined the sailor's gains from his endeavours. Had he profited in a deeply personal way from his reliance on instinct, an eye on the weather and a keen sense of the forces that would bring him safely home? Was the person on that boat – why, it could be a woman, why think it was a man out alone – at peace with themselves? Was an inner self at rest, reassured that harm had been inflicted upon no one or the world he, or she, had briefly touched? He likened it to a communion with nature's laws.

Myriad simple and banal thoughts possessed him as he looked down at the spouting jets of water far below his vantage point. The deck vibrated at his feet as the wind-distorted announcement said that they were now travelling at forty knots! Big and beautiful the vessel might be to its creators and a twin hulled aluminium glory for its crew but he devoted all of his attention upon the yacht. He could only guess that it coasted at three or four knots; he had no idea except that it was slow…slower, quiet…quieter! It seemed restful. He wasn't the least bit interested in nautical matters but could readily imagine the solace that the yacht's solitude could bestow upon a fretful mind. The boat's rocking, rolling and pitching motion in the swell could be likened to a cradle; gentle, comforting forces were, for all he knew, at work, bequeathing peace of mind and a less-troubled soul.

"Ja," he said once more. "I'll not find such peace on this thing…the journey isn't long enough."

"Pardon?"

"What?" He was torn from his reverie and answered in a voice lacking any hint of friendly acknowledgement. The woman standing next to him continued to gaze upon the horizon.

"I couldn't help overhearing…you were talking…speaking out your thoughts." She half turned to face him and now met Josh's gaze for an instant. "Were you thinking out loud what the yachtsman in that boat might be enjoying?"

"Compared to this bone shaker?" he nearly laughed in reply. The space between them was small; he couldn't keep himself from looking at her.

"Yes," she answered. It wasn't quite a smile that she gave him.

2

Maybe, he reflected, talking to a complete stranger so publicly had broken one of her life's little rules; it's best not to get involved in any conversation with a man preoccupied, so it seemed, with the relative merits of steam power and sail. He's even talking to himself, she might be thinking behind those lovely eyes that met his gaze once more.

"It crossed my mind, only for an instant," he continued, looking in turn at her then the yacht that was already a blurry speck far away in the distance.

"It seemed longer to me."

"Yeah, okay. I was just thinking…everyone went at a slower pace not so many years ago…as nature may have intended. I once made this journey on steam ships." He emphasised the words as if to convey the progress made in travel since those days. The woman listened. "We came to Harwich by boat train, the rich in their cars…they were hoisted gracefully aboard while their owners were shown to their cabins…or was it staterooms?"

He shook his head; the true answer eluded him.

"When was that?" the captivating lady asked.

"When I was a mere youngster…my mother showed me the pictures or told me, 'Josh that's how we used to travel, before your father hit hard times'…or words to that effect." The woman gave no outward sign that she had heard him. "Josh…Joshua, that's my name."

The vessel altered course abruptly and the sun no longer held them in its warming beams; a chill wind tugged at their clothes and the woman shivered evocatively as if to make the point.

"Well," she said with a note of finality in her tone, "it was interesting to hear what you had to say. I've never done this journey before so I've nothing to compare it with or…to reminisce about."

"That's okay," Josh said easily. "I've babbled on a bit." He shrugged as if to apologise. "By 'plane is quick…this way, for

3

all its noise and bustle, you still get a sense of travel. Distance still seems to mean something."

"It has scale...is that what you mean?"

She smiled at him for the first time and he couldn't help wondering why she should suddenly do so. Don't complain Josh, he thought, it transforms her face and eases the formality of their conversation...just a bit.

"Yes...the world still feels like a big place and we get time to get used to the idea we'll be somewhere else in a few hours."

"Even if we're set on wrecking it?" Her voice was calm but the words had directness and depth of feeling that made him look at her more closely. Where did that little arresting insight come from?

"Yes!" he laughed in surprise. She had given a voice to some of his own deeper thoughts as the yacht was being observed. "I shouldn't have spoken out...like I did earlier."

She made to go, stepping away from the high rail that marked the edge of the deck. Below them was one of the main propulsion units that squirted water far out behind them and created the frothy wake. She looked at it briefly.

"It's okay...I know what you were thinking of. Somehow you seemed very involved with it all."

"For some time?" He sought to wring some admission from her. "Is that what you mean."

"Yes...that's what I mean." She gave him a slow nod to signal the end of their conversation. "Well...enjoy your trip."

"You too. I'll have to keep shtum!"

"Oh! Don't do that!" she said turning to face him for a moment. "If you don't express what you think or feel what's left?"

"Existence...at some level or another."

"Exactly," she replied, hesitating. Then her mind seemed to be made up. "Well, let's not get in too deep with all that...it's neither the time or the place."

"Yeah."

"Goodbye…Josh."

"Yeah, good-bye," he replied.

What a lame ending to their encounter.

II

The door leading into the gangway closed with an emphatic click and he was left alone once more with his thoughts.

She had been an engaging woman, with an attractive softly made up face that made her look much younger than he believed her to be. There, it had been a chance meeting between two people; they had fallen into conversation on the thinnest of pretexts; one says something to the other to provoke a deeper discussion that, perhaps, lowers carefully constructed defences or lessens inhibitions for a few telling moments. Then, you part and are left to wonder why you said what you did, why you spoke of so much and so intensely; you didn't exchange many words but they had been enough, just enough. You were momentarily hooked or in tune with another living soul. And then, it ends and you are left to wonder what may befall the other person. A few moments have been shared with a stranger whom you may never see again, or, you exchange thoughts that are unique to a first meeting. An unrepeatable union of spirits seemed to characterise such moments and to have sustained them.

"Ja! It's unlike you to get into conversation with a stranger," he muttered to himself in acknowledgement that it might well be a moment never to be repeated. "Still, I liked the look of her…so, I took a chance."

If he saw the woman again, and they talked, the pattern would be different; that was his take on it. The context would be bounded by the knowledge that the two people involved had gained of the other, scant and undefined as it may be. The words, the look of the eyes, the tone of voice, all might conform to a pattern that the first meeting had sub-consciously established. He likened it to an artist's return to his canvas. It was no longer a blank surface; outlines, form, tone and structure were already flashed upon it and now required deeper devotion.

The imagery could become a beautifully crafted and detailed picture, say a Rembrandt, or it could, to his more conformist eye have the discordant and colourful elements that seemed to trouble the observers of a Picasso. The face, the body, the setting were all captured but they all held their unique characteristics. The eyes might observe one world; the mind arranged and gave meaning to another; the mouth might speak or hint at the expression of an irrational thought or suppressed emotions.

Hells Bells! Josh! You only spoke to the woman. Why the angst or analysis of the few moments shared with her? Yes, the Picasso picture that came to his mind illustrated perfectly the discordant emotions that he now tried to understand. All that, and from such a short meeting!

The almost straight wake that frothed out behind the ship held him in thrall for a moment longer. I've got everything I need, but not everything's worked out; my life's lacking in direction now. How can someone…me, have so much, or more than enough but still feel a sense of loss or a palpable emptiness, a lack of fulfilment, in a deeply personal…yes, emotional sense?

He wandered in and then out of the Duty Free shop in a meditative daze trying to imagine that he had any need for the goods on display. Nope! He was travelling alone and would be seeing no one by prior arrangement; so, with determined steps he strode through the turnstiles by the checkouts without meeting the glances of the attendants or the security guard.

There! I don't need to smell nice for anyone now. I drink in moderation and do so only when I'm in company; the last thing I need is a sporty or fey 'yachty' garment; my cupboards are full of clothes I rarely wear. And, I certainly don't need any skin flicks as a cold surrogate for the touch of another's skin against mine.

Why is the woman I've just chatted to travelling alone? He thought of her as the code number for the door was sought on the boarding pass; it allowed him entry to the private lounge. The woman came to mind all too easily. The attentive green eyes, when they had looked upon him, seemed intensely enquiring; her pale skin had been a beauteous contrast to the tumble of dark curly tresses that held his attention when she unfastened the scarf at her throat and shaken it free. There had been no need to do so. The wind had blown it into a tantalising tangle before she had turned to look at him once more and they had exchanged a few words; a genteel sweep of her hands soon brought it to order and the silken shroud hid it from view once more. She possessed simple chic, unaffected by any mannerisms, and he had been in thrall.

He'd wanted to talk some more and blurted out his name, but the woman stayed silent on that one important detail. He knew nothing of her, not a darn thing, but her workaday beauty had captivated him. It would invite little comment from others but her perceptive remarks continued to hold his imagination.

He threw his rain jacket casually down beside him and as he settled into the seat a sigh escaped his lips; he was overcome by the need to sleep. The pace of life would ease, for as long as he chose to be away and he felt able to draw comfort from being on '*home*' soil once more. I've left work and all of the hassle that went with it behind me...

III

"Take a break, that would be my advice, Josh."

The smile was expressive and his lawyer's tone reasonable. He remembered that much behind his fluttering sleepy eyelids.

"Yeah, I hear you, Andrew."

"You've earned it…you did everything you could to hang onto the business. They came for you, uninvited…and bought you out. Be glad for one thing…you struck a hard bargain."

"It was my life's work…I wasn't about to let it out of my hands without a fight."

"Hold on to that then, Josh. You've been amply rewarded for your cussedness."

"My belief in what I did more like! I wanted to keep the business and look after the people who worked for me…with me, more like. That would be a better way to put it. At least they had their share too…it wasn't all about me. Now it's gone…the business will go overseas, thousands of miles away, the end-price will be the same only the margins will be bigger…and the costs of production lower than on our own shores."

"They wanted you out of the way…take pride from that, Josh."

"It's of little comfort."

"And the money?"

"And…your fees, Andrew?" He could play that game too. "Is that all it finally means, a few bags of money stashed away in a vault?" He dwelt on the words he had spoken but there was no malice in them. "I could give most of it to charity…or I could do good works."

"Yes, you could," was Andrew's doubtful reply, "though I wouldn't advise it."

"It might save me a whole lot in tax…only to see that wasted by some government clown."

"That's true…I still wouldn't advise it."

8

"What then?" he spoke out irritably. "Do I set up a Trust fund and see that it's spent wisely? Do I keep control of my financial affairs that way?"

"Now you're using your brain, not conceding to your emotions…if I may put it so directly." Andrew had an almost benign look as he said, "I could even help you with that ….to focus on the important details."

"At a cost!" He looked at his lawyer friend before a smile creased his tanned features. Andrew nodded. "I'll wait on that, at least for now. Let the millions…"

"Twenty five million, to be exact," Andrew corrected.

"Okay…let the twenty five million earn me some interest. I'll do as you say…I'll take some time out and get away from all the fuss and endless meetings. I'll be alone for a while and I can consider what I want to do next, for myself and with my new wealth. I don't really need it all."

"Steady…"

"No, steady nothing! It really isn't all about money…it never has been."

"Having some helps."

"Sure, it *helps* Andrew," he replied so precisely. "Only, the money won't be the answer to what's going on…" He broke off and looked somewhat startled. Andrew picked up on it.

"Go on," he prompted, out of curiosity. His client hadn't made any confessions of what lay at the heart of his personal ambitions or life's goals.

"Sorry, no. I simply need a break. It may all fall into place after that…or even, while I'm away. I may even meet someone to start a different life with."

"Sign a pre-nuptial first!"

"Steady! I'm only thinking out loud. I'm not on the lookout." They exchanged smiling glances. "Enough! This little chat…or the purpose for our meeting, it's still costing me."

"I'll stop the clock, Josh."

"Right! See that you do." He waited. "I'm going, so I'll expect a bill that shows we talked for an hour…"

"And five minutes."

"See!" He still managed a laugh in spite of feeling slightly irritated. "You're counting! See Andrew? The money hasn't quite turned my head."

But the woman he'd just met? She had, and now he saw her once more, by the coffee machine. Don't drink it lass! It's not that good. I've got a better idea, he thought.

The lovely lady turned just as the words drifted away out of mind; there was nothing for it, he would have to talk to her again, or at least try to.

"I can't recommend the coffee," he began, taking in the attentive look she gave him once more as he drew close. His voice was a whisper and she was not in the least disconcerted by his renewed attention upon her.

"It'll have to do…I don't eat or drink too much when I travel," she observed, "nor do I step away from my usual routines." She volunteered this as an afterthought.

"Oh! I was going to ask you to join me for lunch…in the restaurant."

"No," was her unequivocal reply but she noticed the flicker of his eyelids and the tensing of his lips as he suppressed his own unrehearsed response. "No, thank you," she corrected.

"Well…excuse my impulsive behaviour."

"I have." She managed a smile as a nod of her head signalled once more the end of a brief conversation between them. "I have, already."

This could become a habit, with her at least, he acknowledged later as he sat down in his seat once more. The lovely, no beauteous, lady sat a few rows behind him. He took that much in from the glance he gave towards the deck where they had first met. The salt encrusted glass was no hindrance to his view. Their second meeting had confirmed an earlier notion that had formed in his mind. He closed his eyes and played back their conversation once more.

"May I at least know your name?" she had been asked.

"Why?"

He made light of his request. "I don't usually talk to strangers."

"So we both broke our own rules," she managed to laugh. "It won't change anything, though," she finished in brutal honesty.

He took the hit. "And your name?" he repeated, "please? Talk to a stranger a little more, just this once?"

"Is it that important?" She had to look away, but only for an instant.

"Yes, it seems that it is, to me at least." He had been aware that they continued to speak in whispers by the coffee machine and she stirred her coffee endlessly as if uncertain, in spite of how she had spoken to him, whether to continue or not.

"Marianne…it's Marianne," she told him at last and stepped away but not before adding, "that'll have to do, Josh."

"Ja, okay Marianne …at least you remembered my name."

He had said it as if he was a hapless teenager who had met the girl of his dreams but she cared little, or nothing, for him.

"Oh yes…you told me twice, out there on the deck… remember?" She held his gaze for only a moment longer unwilling to reconsider his invitation. "Now, if you'll excuse me, again?"

"Yes, of course. You'd better pour that coffee away, it must be stone cold by now." He put one finger to his lips and apologised for being so bossy.

"It'll have to do." They were Marianne's blunt parting words.

He dismissed any further idea of talking to this stranger who said so little and thus intrigued him so much more. Don't do anything rash he thought or make a false step that you might regret later. How did the saying go? Que sera…sera.

He lived for now but saw nothing wrong in having expectations of a different and companionable future with someone special that he might be fortunate enough to meet, quite by chance.

IV

Marianne watched him as Josh pulled shut the self-closing door. It would have locked automatically behind him but she saw the reflective mood he had settled into from the look of concentration that he gave to this simple act.

I didn't have to say anything when I first saw the man, he could have carried on making comments about the yacht. But, he was speaking out what I could only think of to myself.

She watched him turn away believing that their brief conversation had left its mark. Josh had settled into his chair only to come to a very quick decision. Grabbing his jacket he had left the room without any further glance in her direction; perhaps he would dine on his own, after all, as he'd intended… if they hadn't met.

Leave it, let it be Marianne. She groped for her book that lay wedged against the back of her seat, finally twisting round to find it. What had he been so interested in? Not me, surely? Not so soon? Not so gently? The look in his eyes hadn't been intrusive, just questioning. Why had I chosen to speak of the boat in the same way as he'd thought of it? Josh didn't give me 'the once over', a check to confirm some mental stereotype that he might carry.

Forget it! Leave it out…don't carry on so!

I just talked to him, passed the time of day, nothing more!

Oh really?

Yeah, really!

I spoke out on the view, took hold of the ideas that he was thinking through. Funny, but somehow...I knew!

Mind you...it wasn't too difficult. I only had to see the look that he gave the yacht as we passed it to realise its significance for him.

What he thought and spoke of made sense to me...I felt it too.

Yeah, that's the truth of it.

Yes, you're right.

Yes, you're right Marianne Turner. Don't go imagining anything else. You caught his eye...only after you'd said something...it was almost intuitive...but you broke the spell he was under...only? Only, you replaced one set of thoughts with another. Josh came over and talked to you again. He could simply have left you to it, just drink the lousy coffee, girl, and get on with your life!

But, he didn't. There was no need to chat to you again, or chat you up. Only, he wasn't too good on that; he just talked and was polite; he was inquisitive too. No! He was interested...in me!

Oh well, ships that pass in the night, or some such thing. He...Josh, was open and showed no fear. And me, what about me? I was reserved and cautious. Things between people don't just happen, do they? Not that quickly and certainly not to me they don't, or, not anymore. I made that mistake once too often...it was more than enough and more than I could handle.

'That's why I'm on this frigging ferry, bumping and boring over the North Sea, travelling to Holland to God only knows what. I don't really know what I'm really going for...or, whom I might be looking for, after all that's happened. It's new and it's different...off my usual well-worn holiday paths.

I can't settle in this seat after all. The coffee was cold, just as Josh had told me it might be. Did we really chat, or whisper more like, for so long? Leave it...

I can choose when to return; I've got an open ticket and there are no plans for the return trip or the date. I'm free to do what the hell I want, when I want and with whom I want…if it gets nearly so far as that! In the meantime, there are no calls upon me, no money worries and no one to care for at home anymore. There's an echoing flat that overlooks the river; it's paid for! It's mine, all mine! The money in the bank is clean, honestly earned and there's more put by…thanks to parents who were devoted to me, their only child.

Why come into my mind…now?

I repaid them…I honoured their calls upon me to the end, their very end together. They were joyfully and beautifully trusting of each other and took it with them. Hand-in-hand we found them, on Mum's sick bed, where she had lain to pass her last few days. Dad brought her home…to her true place, her only place…there, beside him. As in life so in death.

Dad! Oh Dad! You dear man!

He'd made a pact with his inner soul and lively conscience. He administered the fatal dose to the love of his life and then took love's drug too. He must have seen it in no other way; alone, without you my darling wife, I may as well be dead. He believed, oh how he believed in an after-life!

The darling, my ever-loving father! He was bound in death, as in life, to his Beth, 'my Lizzie', and my brightest light as he was so often heard to say.

'Sparky!' he'd call out to her. Mum pretended to hate the nickname and would tap his arm to remonstrate with him, but Dad knew that secretly, perhaps, she was touched by this very peculiar endearment. That one word expressed her true and singular meaning for him, her place in his life as a happy, loving and motivating force.

I've gone with Lizzie, to be with my brightest light, with my darling Sparky'.

They had been the few words he had written on the card that they had discovered beside them. On the one side a

14

gleaming sunflower, on its reverse the heart breaking words with their unblemished and timeless devotion to a woman. He had simply signed it, 'Dad', by his own parting message for her.

Sorry, Marianne, my darling girl. Think of me and believe that it can be like this between two people.

Such unity of spirit, mind and body with another person eluded her. Such bitter tears had been shed. Caring and observant neighbours had rung her to say that the house was closed up, curtained and quiet. She had felt a frisson of venal knowledge. One was gone from her, but not Dad too, not my Dad, surely? But, yes…darling Dad too.

What would be the use of money, a home, and a few friends to her in a time of desperate and all too earthly discovery? The end was just that, the end. Morbid thoughts had filled her mind. The passing of family love had propelled her towards the ending of a relationship that pandered to her own insecurities. Hard work, a career, money to spend and possessions gathered over the years and on exotic trips now counted for so little. Her driven, acquisitive and high profile way of life needed an honest, stable and devoted, not subservient, counterpoint.

Adam, a twenty seven-year-old Omega-male was but a *'youth'*, some smiled, as her indiscretions with her live-in lover became a topic of conversation. Gamma or Omega what did she care for the adjective to describe a man whom she thought would serve as the perfect counterpoint to a successful career? She was the opposite, an Alpha woman! Wasn't that how women like her had come to be seen? Only, it didn't always feel so good to be at the top or grabbing at everything to get close to it when in a private inner life you felt so very much 'alone'.

His wayward behaviour and lack of ambition had been a blessing and a novel distraction, at first, but a seemingly insatiable appetite for copulating became an exhausting diversion from the truth. They performed acts upon each other, but they were never a couple. No one was *'at home'* to talk through the troubles of the day and with whom an inner peace could once more be discovered. She had even read of it somewhere, the words to describe the union between two people with such diverse aspirations and achievements.

Hm! What had they been called, together or individually? A *'crack filler'*? A *'relationship terrorist'*? No, maybe it had been *'dysfunction groupies'*? The labels really didn't matter when the end came.

She lacked fulfilment, a true union with another that would justify and complement her existence, as she saw it, of a successful business life and modest plenty. Yes, modest! She had learnt that from mother, the woman who found succour deep within her soul, from her one true man, and, the wealth that had been accumulated over a lifetime to secure a better giving life in her community.

Adam merely satisfied a raw physical need. What else had she shared with him after noisy and diverting coupling ended and a more argumentative, pervasive and vacuous reality returned? Nothing, or very little seemed to engage her. Absent in the man was the understanding of her, the woman, she soon realised. His parting words, incisively cruel and demeaning still filled her thoughts when she felt low. She was rich but 'ugly', successful but unforgiving of others, a lonely bitch even if she had him for company in her bed. Bonking other, younger, women was infinitely better. He had been a comforter, not a lover, to the older woman. Oh, it had been very fashionable but in her case, ultimately, and when their parting jibes had been thought through endlessly, the relationship had been unfulfilling and utterly demeaning.

Her thoughts tumbled.

Compared to your riches Mum and Dad, I merely had plenty.

I didn't see indifference in your eyes, Josh.

I was taken for a ride…on you Adam. She smiled ruefully as the man's image came to mind for only a moment. It had meant nothing, at the end, when she had finally thrown him out of the house and after honest reflection. Adam had merely been an episode in her life, until his wounding of her and the deepest soul searching began.

You saw to that, Mum and Dad…by leaving me. I had to look back on all that I went through with that man…that younger man.

Adam was still in her thoughts just then, as she gazed out of the large window at the two frothing bubbling wakes stretching far away into the distance.

I was nothing more than his comforter, not the other way round - the little shit! He encapsulated most men, no, all men that have been in my private intimate life, those that I allowed to be close to me. The passing away of Mum and Dad focussed my mind wonderfully, through all the tears. I can start afresh…without any strings; there will be no dependency upon another person except for a true love shared. That will be a very welcome and reassuring change.

The 'real man' for her would have to want the best out of life; he would pursue any opportunity presented to him…and he would possess the heart to find and make love, to her. In that alone, the emotions stirred between two people, would she wish to be equal with her man and a devoted partner.

She had thought it all through then, barely a month ago. The locks had been changed and any remaining possessions of Adam's boxed up and put away in the caretaker's store. Most important of all, the new bed was just as big but it had no trace, no mental association with the deceiving and ultimately demeaning frolics she had engaged in with Adam. The mattress had known the impress of only her body, her attractive fulsome body. She remembered the words of a lover, *'more than a handful's a waste,'* and seen to it that she kept her figure.

Am I vain and self-obsessed? Sure, just a smidge.

I have to be just now, call it self-preservation. And...was there anything else?

Yeah...I've got to get Adam out of my mind, somehow, and all that he did to me...and with me.

The coffee stood by her side, on the small laminated plastic table that divided her seat from its neighbour. Had she instinctively been united in thought with Josh? She laughed quietly to herself. Yeah, sure! The man was older, the mass of curly and almost white hair a winning contrast to his tanned and lived in face. She had seen the intensity of his stare upon the small yacht and then...on her. He was casually dressed but impeccably smart. Everything was co-ordinated for colour and style. Absent, totally, was any association with the 'dressed down' rubbish that she so often saw all around her, even at work.

He gave every sign of being at ease within himself; that was how he appeared to her. Josh wasn't copying anyone to feel at one with a monotonous world. He was different and she felt captivated by the quiet look he could cast upon her...he'd done so many times as they spoke. She too had dressed with style, to suit her idea of taste and was intrigued that she could discover such unity with a man in these unlikely surroundings.

And then...she had brought their meeting to an abrupt end.

Nothing had been said that could cause her any offence; Josh had merely sought to have company for a few empty hours and she had been disturbed by the dawning realisation that he was attracted to her. But...in spite of his easy manner and the absence of any obvious or practised introductions she'd let him know that she encouraged no further contact.

They had met, but she couldn't bring herself to admit that her response had been, *'so what?'*

Josh was nowhere to be seen. The chair he had occupied in the private lounge remained empty. What she had taken to be only an interlude between other possible meetings or exchanges between them continued.

Why yes, of course. Obviously, it hadn't gone the way Josh had hoped for.

Our brief encounter has been consigned to the past already.

There you go…move on, girl.

V

The screen showed that a few calls had been received but he still cast the mobile 'phone onto the seat beside him. There was no rush to listen to them; instead, it would be nice to get onto Dutch soil once more, of that he was certain. He could be out of the usual routine of life that had held him enchained for weeks, or was it months? It had seemed never-ending at the time.

I can put that crazy merry-go-round world behind me for a while.

"You can do what you want now, Josh."

He said it out loud, to himself, then fell silent.

So what? Where's the fun in that, when I'm still alone?

The bank's full of your money so let go and live a little, enjoy life and rush into nothing, just take your time…you've got time to think everything through and to decide what you really want to do now…rush into, or at, nothing. You can assess all the options and wait. What a luxurious and happy position to be in; enjoy it! The moment to make any decision will arrive after due process; so, what's the hurry to do anything, anything at all? Just relax…ha! When did you ever really do that? Okay, spend some time to relax…you deserve it, no mistake. You've had a hellish, hectic and traumatic few months, weeks even…a time you never dreamt it was possible to live through.

But, ja! It's all over, that frenzied time is all over, it's gone, so rest easy and enjoy life for a while.

How'd it go? Oh yeah! Chill…or, let it all wash over you.

"Yeah, sure. Only, I'm alone!" His voice echoed around the car's interior.

It was your choice.

Not exactly 'my choice'.

Oh?

I simply passed the time of day with Marianne. I broke with my lifetime's habits, or restraints, and talked to a woman I'd not been introduced to. I wasn't too formal, nothing heavy was implied, it was just? Well, it was different. It was just *'get to know you chat'* and it got me nowhere, not even a bit of company for chatty game play over lunch just to make the journey pass a little quicker. It would have been a pleasant change to be in the company of an interesting and attractive woman.

But, no, there was no way she was going to take up the offer of lunch.

She made me think though, just for a moment or two… when we chatted, that we'd found something of mutual interest and we'd move on from there; we could leave the flip-flop introductory chatter behind. The yacht, that was the moment! It was seeing it and there we were, both thinking that the sight held a particular significance. Fortunately, I spoke out…I didn't know *she* was there beside me, at first.

So what?

So…it's strange, the convergence of ideas that the sight of the lonely yacht provoked. Anyway, that's all over with. It was fun while it lasted, the thrill that maybe someone had been found in unlikely surroundings that I could spend some time with…after a decent period of introductory conversation and formal preambles had been endured. She caught the eye beautifully but it was the few words we exchanged that intrigued and then kept me with her.

Still, you never were too obvious or direct in your wooing of a woman, any woman, remember? Yeah, I have to work at it, draw them to my side gradually. It's no easy thing for me.

Sunlight glared into the car-deck as the stern loading doors of the vessel slowly parted.

At last! I can get off this thing…and get rid of those intrusive thoughts. The movie didn't help me in that either; it was crap. Why I paid to see the thing when I had a perfectly good seat, reserved and paid for, will take some explaining. Well, only to myself and I know the answer.

Marianne got to me but the interest wasn't reciprocated… or, I'm really out of touch.

He eased the car forward and out onto the exit ramp relieved at last to have something else to think about. In the warm evening sunshine he relaxed and turned occasionally to see that the car's roof retracted properly and was stowed away as he wanted. A great buy! That was how he saw it. A top of the range Saab, deep blue and highly polished, was the only impulse purchase he had indulged in after the sale of the business. It gleamed; it was richly expressive and yet it drew little attention. He drove the car quickly but not in any threatening or aggressive style, simply with assurance. He anticipated problems, concentrated and exercised supreme judgement. That's how he saw it.

"Good evening, Mr van Leeuwen. Is it a business trip, or are you visiting for pleasure?"

The woman in passport control scanned the car and gave him a cursory glance, or so it seemed. She checked the passport and held it under some infrared scanning contraption on the counter beside her seat. It's a British passport, lady…but a Dutch name.

"Pleasure, strictly pleasure," he smiled in answer to her question. His Dutch was perfect.

"Proceed," she said with a dismissive nod and followed this with a more graceful wave of her hand.

"Enjoy the rest of your day," he answered.

The lady had to smile at that. "You too, remember to drive on the right."

"It's my second home...but I'll try. Bye."

It was unnecessary easy chitchat and not something that he usually engaged in back home in England. But, deeper and unreserved instincts soon resurfaced and he was beginning to feel like a different person; business and social niceties so carefully adhered to now fell away. He crossed the railway lines and followed the road that could take him to The Hague, past the windmill at Monster...lovely name...or out to the motorways, the fast roads as they liked to refer to them here. The label was very appropriate. He was 'no slouch', as the slang phrase at home might have it, but in The Netherlands road-speed at close quarters held a new meaning. Behaviour that passed for good manners or consideration for another in the UK was seen here as a sign of weakness and ruthlessly exploited.

Welcome back, Joshua. You can find the *'other'* person in you now.

There was no sign of him, nothing. How had Josh managed to simply 'disappear'?

Marianne looked around her, at the other cars and wondered what she could gain from this futile exercise. She didn't know what car he drove.

In any case, the queues will see to it that I never see him, again.

But I'll know him won't I?

It's that mop of white curly hair! What a give-away...but I can't see that either.

Pity? No! It's a bloody shame!

I should have gone with the flow and lived for the moment.

"The reason for your visit, madam?"

"A holiday…a few days away," she looked up, smiling at the Immigration and Passport Control Officer.

I'm somewhere different, anywhere but at home with all the memories I carry around with me when I'm there. And? Oh yeah! I'm not blind to the chance I might meet someone different. It was a small item, low down on the list of priorities but it's risen to the top…thanks to that man. That man, Josh! Yes, he had only changed things, messed things up in my head, I mean. Priority one now…it's get someone into your life again, and live a 'real' life.

Just where did he get to, hide away more like?

That tells you something, doesn't it, girl?

Never mind all that now. Check the map and your notes, get on the road out of this place and follow the signs…find the quickest route to Amsterdam if you please; I want no more diversions or distractions. Just get me there! The hotel's booked and they will take care of the car. Great deal! The only problem's how to get there! She had listened to the stories from friends who'd been to the City. The traffic, the road works, the city being dug up for a new Metro! Do you really want to go there?

Yes! Maybe I should have flown after all…or followed Josh there. Leave it girl…leave it!

Someone else could have worried for me, if I'd flown. But…then I wouldn't have met Josh. Correction…seen him and chatted. I can't go on thinking I've met him, met the man. Well? Only…it seems that I've done more than just seen him.

Concentrate girl! Good, they're the signs I need!

Mind out for the cyclists! Mind who has got priority over you! Shit! They come at you from the right and think it's their turn! They just keep going! Who's wrong here…and who's right? Ha! Someone coming out at you from a road…from the right! They've got one over on you! Watch yourself Marianne… okay! You're getting the hang of this now, driving on the wrong side of the road. It's something else we didn't teach them…or they failed to teach us. Never mind.

Concentrate!

Good! The A4…Amsterdam! Here I come you city on the water!

I've got this much right…they overtake you on the inside too…lane discipline is for the faint-hearted…boot it girl! No, better not. An Audi TT it may be…with me in it…fancy free and riding the road to…where?'

"Hey! Hey! Heyyy?"

"It's him! It's Snopake!" She laughed and yelled it out.

She had to laugh at her cruel association with a name, and, she was very glad!

No…I'm girlishly happyeee!

"Slow down girl…go slower…quick! Slow down!"

She gave a little gasp. Driving slowly and talking to yourself like some kid had its advantages; well, just then it did. Nothing to get into a habit about, mind you, but seeing the guy…or his white mop of hair…beautiful white mop of hair, well it changed the day, yet again!

He's pulled out from the slip road to a service area and he's heading the same way I am!

Of course he is girl! You're on a motorway…clear you mind …and do it, quickly!

Am I in luck or what, seeing him?

I could get to like guys with white hair…well, see if I can really get to like this one guy, the one driving ahead of me.

He hasn't seen me…so what am I getting so wound up about?

Nope…no mistake, it's him all right. Now what?

Carry on, of course.

Yeah, chance would be a fine thing. I've only just met the guy. Where's he off to, I wonder?

Are you curious…or serious?

"Both," she cried out loud.

Reducing her speed she allowed the traffic to pass her by. Josh did so without a glance.

It's him all right; I might have known he'd be in a convertible; he had the tan to go with it. There's that man, Josh…al fresco in his Saab.

Keep your distance, but track him. There's time, lots of time to see where he goes…there's plenty of time to decide what you're going to do next. You calculating bitch!

Yes, that's me all right. She sighed.

When I least expect it I meet someone I like the look of…only he doesn't know it. Mind you…if he'd felt the same he would have stayed near me, kept me in sight, given a casual glance or two…he'd make no big deal of it, then…but he'd let you know he was pleased to have met you. There was no one to interfere with what might happen between you, I hope! Yes, we could both have seen what happened next…or how we'd make out.

But he'd gone!

Does a girl have to do everything nowadays? No…but it might look that way, or I'm particularly…what?

Desperate?

Lonely…already?

Uncontrollable?

Yeah…maybe all of them and none of them. I just liked the man, grey hair and all…and the look he gave me…how he looked, smart…like he cared about the things I count upon for so much in making life a little more bearable. You can have too much…except for the one thing that really counts…that *really* counts for everything. You can never have enough of someone who cares for you, and is with you in that, all the way.

It's priceless.

Mum and Dad showed me how it could be. Only, what they had was from another time, you don't see it too often these days...true love, to the end of your days. You take and you give, most of all you share. That's how it goes, or how it used to be.

Away with them! Off with you, intruding thoughts. Mum and Dad...and you, Adam, you little shit!

She shook her head and cried out...very loud.

"Now...tomorrow, and the next day! It's all about ME! ME! ME!"

And...Josh. Where are you off to now?

No, not there, Josh! Don't turn off, there! We're nowhere near Amsterdam! Josh!

"Josh?"

He's seen me. He's waving! I'll have to flash him! The lights...just the lights, girl!

She laughed now, with him, as she pulled off the motorway, possessed by a jumble of thoughts, hopes and keenly aware of the possible consequences.

Where are we going now? I can't pronounce it...I'm not even going to try.

She followed him, almost obediently, wondering when they would stop and talk to each other. We pick the strangest places to learn of each other and ask, 'what now'? Or, and more likely, just maybe, he'd ask *why are you following me*?

No, he wouldn't ask me that, would he? No. He's far too polite.

But, I would! I'd ask him! I might even tell him!

Josh? You seem to be the kind of guy to make me break a few rules, or...you're the answer to my prayers.

Yes, you may be the answer to some silent prayers.

"Are you on your way to your hotel?" she asked him with a laugh.

God! I remember every detail of his face. I love the little lines by his eyes. Those eyes! They just 'look' at you; they ask what you're all about…kindly. The little creases by his mouth, laughter lines…they must be. He's smiling so I know that's what they are. He's not old. Forget the mop of curly hair! No, I love the hair too. It lends distinction to his face. And…he's strong; he seems to have a sense of humour that pokes fun, at himself. I only heard it once, but it gave me another clue about the man.

All this…you've gathered all this from a few shared moments? Silly woman!

I shouldn't be doing this. It's not normal behaviour; he'll be thinking why is she following me, even if we did wave to each other to say 'I've seen you'. I could have simply driven on and waved goodbye…forever.

No, I couldn't have done that.

Luck's struck twice, I hope.

I've met him and now, I'm with him. Now what?

The traffic whizzed past them in a noisy intrusive drone and neither of them appeared sure if they were permitted to park where they had chosen to do so, or Josh had finally decided to pull in.

"Did you hear what I said?" she cried out.

"Yes," he answered. "I know a roadhouse, a comfortable motel. It's not far away now, in Voorschoten." He pronounced it clearly and she looked at him more closely.

"You spoke the unpronounceable!"

"Ja!" he laughed. "It's a habit of mine."

"You're Dutch?" She said it in a tone of disbelief; there had been no trace of an accent on his voice.

"No…or rather, not any more…not officially, any way."

Deep down inside, it's still a part of me, a very important part of me he could have gone on to say. But, that might be for later…or some time, soon. The woman he had left behind, or

27

so he thought, had re-entered his life. Maybe this was all meant to be. Sure, he told himself. Now who are you kidding?

"Oh!"

"I only had the chance, Marianne, to tell you my first name."

"You left me, in the lounge...by the coffee machine. I...I was left wondering where you'd gone to."

"Really?"

"Yes," she couldn't keep from saying. "Yes, really."

He took her arm, by the elbow, and drew her aside a few steps but not far. The verge fell away to a ditch, a field boundary. Cows lay in the meadow beyond chewing the cud reflectively and oblivious, it seemed, to the noise and bustle all about them.

"You'd made up your mind, I saw that much. I heard much more in what you said." He had to shout now as a line of lorries passed them. Further discussion seemed impossible. "Where are you going?" he shouted then repeated it standing closer and taking her arm once more as he did so. "Sorry."

"It's okay."

He let go all the same.

"Do you know where you are?"

"Sort of...I'm heading for Amsterdam...none of this, stopping here with you...it's not part of the plan." She shook her head to acknowledge further conversation was useless but she saw him nod. Josh had heard spoken out what had been on her mind.

"Okay." He half turned away but she grabbed his arm.

"It's not far, this place you speak of, is it?" She spoke into his ear, holding him tightly.

"No. Want to follow me? Can I persuade you to do that?"

She nodded her own reply. I've got to do this, she thought. I've got to deviate completely from my plan. What plan? Forgetting Adam, that plan, remember? Adam and all that had been associated with that life…if you can call it a *life* that I had with him. What does it say about me?

Leave it…forget it!

"Marianne?" Josh looked at her and, surprised, she took hold of the hand he now offered. "Did you hear me?"

"Yes! I heard you…and yes, I'll follow you!"

She pulled her hand free but not before his intense gaze had been met once more and she conceded that her resolve was weakening.

What is happening here? Is it that easy…or am I making out I'm easy? No…I'm not that, easy. I'm not being careful either, but I'm in a public place. I'll go and see this 'roadhouse' as he calls it. I don't think it'll be a little dump of a place. Maybe, just maybe with the right guy it can be that easy to get some help and to move on. Maybe it's that easy to get attention from someone new, someone different, someone older and someone who is…true?

<u>VI</u>

"I'm glad we're able to do this, that you agreed Marianne." Josh held out his wine goblet. "I'm glad to have met you… again."

She joined him in a toast to their meeting. He made it sound, conveniently, as a stroke of good luck and she responded by saying that an impetuous decision to follow him was now seen for what it was, a lucky break. There was no way of telling where their meeting might end he smiled.

"Unconventional as it might be?" she replied on a laugh, "for you?"

"So? You've seen that in me already?"

"Maybe I have, Josh…maybe I have," Marianne said on a reflective sigh.

"Oh well, our meeting again is all the better for that."

"It's as well that you were driving with the roof down…I'd never have seen you otherwise."

"But I saw you…so it's my gain, or may I say 'our gain'?"

"We'll see." She answered him with a smile playing at the corners of her mouth and eyes that held his gaze. She wasn't going to let the moment go again as she had done earlier, on the boat, no way.

"Yes, we'll see." Josh thought over their joint declaration.

"May I suggest, Josh…?" she began but he interrupted her with a disarming smile.

"Yes…that we meet again a few days from now? We speak first on the mobile 'phone…just to agree if we should…meet up again, or if we still want to? How's that?"

"Yes…yes, okay," she answered slowly. Did he always speak for others? She let go of the thought. "How'd you know I might be thinking that, or suggest it even…in my forward way?"

Her slight flirtatious tilt of the head made him laugh.

"I wanted it to be seen as my idea…mine alone. Why would an attractive woman in a neat little car follow me here?"

"Quite…I was asking myself the same thing, all the way over here."

"That's what I thought."

"Did you?" She couldn't be sure if he was teasing or simply playing her at her own little game. Whatever it was, it seemed to be working, this getting-to-know-you routine.

"Why yes…you followed me here," he said and paused, "instead of waving and driving on…to other people and to Amsterdam."

They again looked at each other.

"Quite." She said it in a voice that almost held regret at making her decision seem so obvious. "I'd better not drink anymore of this, had I?"

"No…or only if you intend to stay over and have dinner with me. You missed the lunch I hoped I might share with you.

Anyway…you'll beat the rush hour by waiting a while longer if you still decide to travel on."

"Yes, that's an idea." Marianne looked at her watch. "It's early evening…their rush hour?"

"Yes, still rush hour. So, Marianne? I'll leave it to you."

He gained the attention of a waiter and asked for a menu. The terrace of The Golden Lion was busy; the dining tables, set under striped parasols that flapped on the breeze, were a chosen haunt for diners enjoying the evening sunshine. The setting put everyone at ease, or so it seemed to him and Josh smiled at her.

Marianne felt strangely discomfited by his gaze, as if he was willing her to come to a decision and this time of his choosing.

"I'm going to make a call…I need to change my plans," she told him uncomfortably pleased that he was taking the lead now. Only, it had been a while since that had happened to her and she wasn't ready for it, not this quickly.

"Sure?"

"Yes Josh! I'm sure!"

She spoke vehemently as she looked over at him. This time no smiles were exchanged between them. That man! Yes, that man, Josh! He's got to me…and he bloody well knows it!

"Okay, I just wanted to be sure."

"Don't look so pleased with yourself, Josh!"

"I'm not. I'm pleased for both of us…no harm in that, is there?" He gave her a teasing quizzical look then grinned. "We're both in this together…we didn't plan it to happen this way, but…it has. I, for one, am very pleased about meeting you…again."

"Josh…" she began but stopped.

You charmer! she thought flicking him a glance. He simply waited for words that never came and instead poured out some more wine and put the bottle back in the ice bucket placed nearby on his side of the table.

"Marianne?"

She looked away. Christ! Things don't just happen, not like this and not to me, not to me they don't, or do they just for once?

"Yes," she finally said, "it's happened, us meeting again. It wasn't on the plan, *any* plan at all…and I'm still going to Amsterdam."

"I know you are. Don't change a thing."

"I won't, not until tomorrow Josh, not until tomorrow."

"I know."

"What do you mean, '*you know*'?"

He shrugged and gave her that phlegmatic teasing grin as if to say they had fallen into this happy arrangement together.

"That you'd better make your call while I confirm that you to have a room for the night. I'll pay…no discussion."

"The place is busy."

"There's room Marianne, believe me, there's room. I know this place and they know me. I've messed up your arrangements…so, the least I can do is pay up."

"And tomorrow, what then?"

She felt as though she was losing her grip on events. It was quite ridiculous. She didn't talk like this to strangers, or with others. She didn't go out of her way and follow them to some roadhouse and sit in warm sunshine and sip on a good white wine, or two. The hotel was clean, the waiters and waitresses moved quietly and with assurance and no-one seemed to rule the place; there was no major domo, just well-practised routines and all of it to be found in what others might snootily call a 'budget hotel'.

"Tomorrow, I go into The Hague and you set off the other way…where you always intended to go, to Amsterdam…to a swank hotel and to new people."

"We split."

"Yes, Marianne…we go our separate ways."

VII

"Goodbye Josh."

"No, 'tot ziens'…until we meet again, Marianne."

"We'll see," she replied curtly, in a way of speaking that wound him up, just a little. He'd have none of it.

"There you go again."

"Yes, Josh." Instead of looking at him Marianne made sure she had everything. "We'll see. You've got your plans…"

"And you've got yours…I know. We talked of it, only a little mind you." He crouched down by the side of the car and looked in at her. They had met again at breakfast; she had been late or, as he said gallantly, he had been early. "I'll call you as we agreed…I haven't misheard that too, have I?"

"No." Marianne started the engine and looked behind her ready to move out. "Yes, call me and we'll take it from there, if we can."

She gave him a bright smile but thought to say no more. *'Give nothing away'* she couldn't help thinking. It wasn't quite a game being played out, more a case of being sure of how it might be if they did speak or meet up again.

"Right…well, mind how you go…Marianne. I'm glad you stayed…" He waited for some acknowledgement of his remark.

"Yes…it was different."

So, that's it, nothing more?

Josh stood up and away from the car, just enough to make it easier for Marianne to reverse out of the parking space by the steps that led to the hotel's main entrance. He gave a casual wave and looked after her as she left him at their first meaningful rendezvous. A bag had been left on a settee in the echoing reception area and he collected it, sure now of what the day held in store for him. Something was happening, in his life, as a result of meeting Marianne but he hadn't quite worked out how to play the game of 'hello-and-goodbye' they had fallen into.

I've no idea what the rules of this particular game are, not really, even if I did suggest it. He whistled softly, content that there was someone very new and attractive to think of and hear from…if he didn't call her first.

The machine spewed out the ticket and he sauntered onto the deserted platform; no railway staff were to be seen, anywhere. That's an automated railway system for you, just trains and their drivers, he hoped, at the very least.

His mobile played its' little tune and he hummed along for an instant…he'd met a tender woman…had she stolen his heart away, already? Marianne, you ain't seen nothing yet. The tune had caused some amusement with his closest staff members amongst the team that had helped him sell the business and worked themselves out of a job. Still, they had been amply compensated for their efforts.

"Hi." He recognised the number only too quickly. "You're calling *me*."

"Hi…yes," was her soft reply. "I thought I'd tell you…I've arrived. The directions you gave me were perfect; the time it's taken unreal."

He could have told her that too.

"So, what now?"

"I take in the sights," she began breezily, "then, I'll check out the shops…maybe, do the canal boat trips and learn a bit about the place. It's all like I told you," she went on, "like I said it would be last night, Josh. I made some plans, remember?"

"Yes…okay. Meeting me changed nothing?"

"I didn't say that."

"No. I did. I was just thinking out loud, if it was that way." He scuffed a shoe lazily over the platforms' slabbed surface while he listened and thought of what he might say next. "Thanks for calling, Marianne…for letting me know you've arrived safely."

"I have…the hotel's just great! I can get just about anything I want here."

Don't I just know it, he smiled.

"Good, that's Amsterdam for you as you'll find out. Mind how you go."

"I will. What are you going to do, Josh? You never said."

"I finished dealing with a few business matters, a few e-mails…on the laptop."

"I thought you were taking a break!"

"There are breaks…and *breaks*."

"A real break, Josh!"

"I am. Now…I was going on to say I'm visiting my only relative, a cousin on the van Leeuwen side. Then…I'll come back here…hire a bicycle and head off for the dunes. It's a break from routine," he went on enthusiastically. "I'll have a day or two out in the sun…and there'll be no more work worries…none at all."

"And no more e-mails!" he heard her laugh. "Forget that modern way of keeping touch!"

"Yeah…I prefer listening to a voice."

"Josh?"

"Yeah, okay…I'll keep quiet on that."

"We wait and we see…remember?"

"Yes. Now…this is my plan…I'll be out in the sun under big clear skies and I'll relax. You've probably noticed how high the sky is here."

"Josh…" she said slowly wondering just what he meant.

"It's true! Look at the paintings…the Dutch Masters! It's an unmistakable trademark of their work and the country!"

"I…I…hadn't really noticed."

"Marianne." He said her name slowly, on a sigh, as if disappointed in her. "I could show you if you'd only let me. The sky's just huge here!"

"And no where else?" she teased.

"Let me show you then, you disbeliever!"

"I've told you…we'll see. Now, off you go…enjoy the day."

"In the sun…"

"You don't need it."

"Oh yes I do, Marianne."

And I'd like you to be here, woman, to help me get over the last few weeks. Last night, our dinner for two was only the beginning. A few days in the dunes or on the beach will be a perfect chance to unwind after all I've been through. But I'll be alone…at least for now.

"Well? I've said hello…I thought I'd ring you, just to say I've got here…and to thank you for your company over dinner."

"Gladly done…I'm glad to have met you…really glad to hear your voice now."

"Josh?"

"Marianne?" What now? He'd told her simply that he was pleased she had called him, in spite of the calm arrangements she had made only a few hours ago.

"Josh?"

"Later maybe! I've got to go! My train's arrived! I've left the car…I'm being milieu friendly!"

"Whatever that means! Bye Josh…will you take care?"

"Sure…and will we speak again?" he asked hurriedly. "Will you take the call?"

"We'll see."

Marianne was gone; she simply rang off.

"Yes, we'll see, Marianne. You can count on it," he said in a barely audible whisper.

The train's doors closed with a thump of their rubber edges against each other and locked behind him. Woman, we're heading in different directions…at least for now.

The light was dazzlingly bright, reflected off the clean walls of the courtyard, and the roofs perfectly outlined against the clear blue sky. Marianne gazed out of the window at the scene before her, acknowledging as she did so that the peace offered by the hotel and its setting, among many of the oldest buildings and canals in central Amsterdam, justified its cost.

Josh is further away from me than ever, was an intrusive concern that distracted her from considering the surroundings and luxury of the hotel that had once been the Town Hall. It was entirely suited to those seeking refinement and attention to one's every wish.

She could hear the excited chatter and laugh of the guests in reception waiting for the guides that would take them on the afternoon's tour of the City. Nearby, there was enough to be seen for no one to feel any immediate need to join the crush on the main thoroughfares that could be found a brisk fifteen minutes walk away.

Her luggage, such as it was, had been taken to her room and there it remained, unopened. Staring out of the window she recalled once more the conversation she had with Josh before leaving him.

'We'll see what happens', had been one sentiment she had spoken out and now she remembered how he had not taken to her remarks; they were intended to show that she would follow her own star and decide upon any continuing contact.

I could have been more open about us meeting again, or not. Instead, I made it sound as though I wasn't too bothered, one way or the other. Was that Adam's meaning, his remarks that I wanted to be in control of everything and yet need someone by me, on any terms…well, almost any terms? It was more a question of finding someone real, someone to help me be who I am.

And who is that?

Someone independent. Sure, on the outside…but deep down the question still gets asked, *'who's there'*?

Someone useless when they're on their own, that's who.

So what the hell am I doing being here *on my own*, in a plush hotel and all that goes with it? Some comfort blanket!

You know why you're here, alone. All of your friends, or those that you can really count on, are spoken for and couldn't get away. They're all hooked up with someone, not officially just intimately, and with no real commitment from what you hear them say. They use all kinds of words to describe their arrangements. They've got 'partners'! How I've come to hate the word...probably because I haven't got one. Oh, I had a guy...Adam, but there was no union of minds as well as our bodies. It's begun to matter to me now.

And where are you? In Amsterdam, on your own.

And where's Josh?

He's miles away, out there...out there, somewhere... somewhere I'm not. He's alone too...to all intents and purposes. I only guessed that bit, but I can read the signs. He wasn't casual; there were no easy words to seduce something from me; that's a change from the usual way of things as I hear it said.

Where's the bloody thing got to? She scrabbled for the mobile 'phone in her handbag.

Forget it! Don't ring him. You'll only come across as an obsessive if you call him again so soon. The 'phone nestled in her hand with the screen shut, then opened out, then shut again. Damn it! The number was keyed in from the memory dial-up.

I can't stop myself! I can't stay here, on my own. The number rang...and rang...and rang until she thought the messenger service would cut in.

"Hi...it's me again," she said on hearing his 'hello'.

"Hi...it's Josh again. What's up? Has something happened, Marianne?"

"No," she answered, reassured by the concern in his voice. "No...and then again, yes."

"Meaning what, *exactly*? I'm no good at riddles."

"Tease." She said it without thinking.

"Am I?"

Did she have to spell it out? Probably; she might even find it useful was the distracting thought that now came to mind.

"I haven't unpacked. My stuff is in the room and here I am...ringing you, from the lobby of the hotel. I can't explain it. I don't understand it at all."

Is that honest enough for you, Josh?

"Would you like me to come to Amsterdam and help you understand?" He was light and attentive at the same time. "I could be company and we can see the sights together...and, you can tell me what's up."

She laughed out, nervously. "And have you see me make a bigger fool of myself? No...." she hesitated. Was that really what she wanted, for him to stay away from her, again?

"Is that a 'no' as in '*I don't want you to come over to see me?*'" he said quietly but in a clear voice, "or could it be, '*no, stay there because I can't quite follow what is happening or believe in something new...or, that it's happened quite so soon?*'"

She felt herself shaking and leant against the casement of the window.

"Why do you...where do you get such understanding from? Where?" she replied challenging his perceptive remarks. Were they perceptive or merely an admission that they had each found something in each other to make separation a ridiculous and wasteful pretence?

"I have eyes, Marianne," he said simply. "If you want me to just say 'thanks for calling' I will."

It sounded pathetic and touchingly simple on the lips of the man she carried a mental picture of. It sounded so believably honest and she understood him; she had seen Josh's look upon her to know they weren't empty words. He hadn't made any attempt to make a pass the previous evening; at one point when she had used the ambivalent phrase '*we'll see*' he had retorted 'que sera...sera'. They had even laughed when he had turned the phrase on her, saying 'we'll *wait and* see'.

"I want to come back, Josh…to Vorskooten or however you say it! I want to come back…no strings, no promises and no touchy-feely antics. I just want company." She gasped in her breaths as a means of expelling her chasing emotions. He said nothing. "There! I know I said 'we'll see'…only, I didn't mean it in the way I wanted the words to sound, I'm beginning to realise that now."

Josh spoke, at last. "Sh…sh, Marianne!"

"No! You've heard how it is…mixed up and spoken out like a kid!" She felt the tears come to her eyes. Oh God! Not that too? What an emotional mess I'm in. I need one good man, a real one, who's not afraid to tell me how it is…how he really feels about me. "Sorry…"

"Don't be," he answered soothingly. "If I can be of any help…just ask me. Got that?" He spoke it out simply, so directly, that all she did was listen.

"Uh huh."

"You're not a kid by the way…and you don't need me to say it, but…things have happened. So, you're like me…we're here to get a life back…one way or the other, together or separately. I may as well tell you that much." He paused, and then chuckled knowingly. "You're forever young, by the way."

"Silly…silly…silly words, Josh," she said before pausing. "They don't make it any easier for me. I'm confessing that I shouldn't have left you earlier. The fact is I didn't need to…or want to. I just felt…I had to."

"Enough…enough now, Marianne, over the 'phone. Keep the room reservation for a day or two. Just come back and talk…spend time here with me if it helps and if you want that?"

"Yes, I want that. I'm no good on my own at the moment or not over here."

She suppressed a groan. What the hell am I doing making all these confessions…and to him, to him! Josh! He's still a stranger! And what does he do? He talks as if he can help me out and he's known it all along!

"And why should you be on your own? You've met me." It all sounded beautifully simple and totally persuasive as she heard the laughter in his voice. "I'm asking you once again, Marianne…come back here and meet me."

"Josh?"

"Marianne? Just come back and be with me? I promise to behave…there'll be no 'touchy-feely' antics." There, it was his engaging chuckle once more. "I've got an idea…come back and enjoy some two-wheely frolics instead? Do it and forget all about any other reasons…just be impetuous. I haven't felt like this in a very long time. Do it! Just be here with me…just do it!"

Her mood lightened upon hearing his enthusiasm and certainty that the right decision had been reached. She was hooked by the words used in Josh's bubbly chatter.

"Yeah, okay…for both our sakes then. Where are you now?"

"Wandering around the city, The Hague…I'll tell my cousin I'll come over later in the week. It'll be okay…we speak regularly. Come on now, Marianne, make ready!"

"I will…only, I won't be back for ages Josh, if this morning's traffic is anything to go by."

"Forget that…leave the car! Take the train…it's easy. I'll meet you at the station, here! Just call me when you know your arrival time. You get your train from Central Station…by the way. You could walk it from the hotel you're at." He gave a laugh as if he recognised a hint of where to go might be of help to her. "We can go back to Amsterdam later in the week and collect your car and other things. Remember, keep the room reservation."

"It'll cost."

"Let me worry about that, Marianne."

"It's still going to cost."

"There you go again!" he said in laughing admonishment. "Never mind all that, Marianne…to me it's worth every cent, or is it Euros?"

"I hate the money too! So, it's that simple, is it, Josh?"

"Yes Marianne, to me it's that simple. We've met…nothing else needs to be complicated…not to me and certainly not now. We've only *just* met."

"It's a bit crazy…all of this," she replied with a note of wonder in her voice.

"Yeah…but it's a different take on life. See you soon…and, don't forget to call me."

"Again."

"Yes Marianne…I'm not tired of you doing so, not a bit."

The scenery flashed by the window, a flat landscape with a huge cloudless sky above, just as Josh had described it; he had omitted to speak of man's intrusion, the pylons and the monolithic buildings that passed for architecture, but she forgave him this small lapse in detail. She had '*seen*' precisely what he meant and imagined the rest.

How remarkable and so refreshingly different had been his candid admission that she had been in his thoughts. It dispelled, somewhat, her unease at having rung him, twice, only to confess how it felt to be out of his company.

I'll see, she thought now, what I can share with him.

VIII

"Is this allowed?" Josh smiled.

Marianne nodded as he took the shoulder bag and held his hand out to her. In his embrace she felt calmer and pressed her face to his lips to meet each kiss, to her cheeks. That was it! No more! There was no brush of his full lips to her mouth; no advantage was taken of the moment or deeper solace offered.

42

"It's that simple, is it?" she asked him, smiling, and looking into his eyes. They met her gaze unmoving as if in a trance.

"Yes, we're together and we can talk…we can say what needs to be said or to be forgotten."

"Or put away in the past," she said on reflection and broke free of his clasp upon her but Marianne continued to look at him.

Josh was casually dressed; the white polo shirt with three navy blue bands at the collar and on the cuffs to the sleeves fitted perfectly. He carried little surplus weight around his midriff and the faded jeans with the webbing belt did not seem incongruous on a man of his age. She had noticed the penny loafers too. The whole image was taken in once more as she walked towards him on hearing Josh's soft call to her and she caught sight of him at the top of the stairs. He had come to meet her on the platform and it felt natural and spontaneous.

I'm with him, she thought in reassurance. That's all that matters to me right now.

Josh held open the car door and threw her bag casually onto the back seat.

Where's he taking me? He's behaving as if he's done this often enough not to be fazed by it.

"To the beach, that's where," he told her when she asked. "We're going to a place with another unpronounceable name - Scheveningen." He waited for her to respond but she remained silent. "Okay…you could at least try."

Marianne pulled a face and grinned. "I won't…like so many more of them, you'll have to help me with the *'unpronounceable'*."

"You'll get the hang of it, in time…and with a bit of practice. Now, if you agree I'd like to go out into the dunes… while there's still time." He glanced at her, fastening his seat belt as he did so. "You've dressed for it, so what do you think? Do we take a walk along the sands or is it to be a leisurely cycle ride? It will set us up for dinner and you'll see something of the locals too…the street artists and musicians come out in the evenings and entertain the crowd…I want to leave the car somewhere and just set off."

"A walk along the sands, okay?" She held out her hand and Josh took it, only for a moment. "Nothing too organised…just an easy time of it."

"Sure…we just take a break from usual routines. That's why I always come back here."

"That's what I thought." She pulled back her hair and drew it into a pigtail before letting it flounce to her shoulders catching his gaze upon her once more. "Still okay?"

"Yes…everything's still okay."

"And I hope it'll get better, Josh."

His voice held a soft tone of admiration for he found her voluptuously beautiful. He had taken in, by a single glance, a woman, and a fellow traveller on the windswept deck of the ferry. Now, dressed in cropped black trousers with a studded belt that hung loosely against her stomach Marianne was once again a new woman to his eyes. She had changed; he had expected her to do as she had told him and *grabbed a few things, stuffed them in a bag and got on the train*'. Instead, her short sleeved soft pink top complemented perfectly the lightly tanned skin to her arms; they had a fleshy fullness that he restrained from touching. Even her flat soled tasselled pumps added to her delightful and, seemingly, relaxed image.

She touched his hand again, as it rested on the gear lever, and turned briefly to look behind her. "No-one's waiting for us, are they?"

He took the hint.

"No. I told you about large skies…over the fields and the sea…they're stretching out to meet it. A picture by van Ruisdael comes to mind…just a beach with the dunes behind them, a few people walking alone. Or…there's another. The tide's out and in the foreground is a boat, very Dutch with its rounded stern and bow…fishermen are unloading a catch under a large sky with clouds, drifting lazily in a breeze…high up. The sun's setting on a perfect summer's day…a pennant hangs limply at the mast head…"

His voice trailed off and he looked away, concentrating on exiting from the station car park and driving west, towards Wassenaar and the main road. Woods, secluded houses and then…the dunes and a mental image of the world he had described.

Marianne waited until they had settled into the light traffic passing along the tree-lined road. "Who painted that one…the picture you've just described?"

"I've been rattling on!" he laughed in reply. "I was trying to remember! Silly isn't it, a favourite and…Mesdag! That's it…he's the one!"

She gave him a softened smile. "Which period was it?" Marianne could tell it was a deeply held interest for him.

"About nineteen 'hundredish'…not really sure. Van Ruisdael was a little earlier."

"By about two hundred and fifty years…"

"You know?"

"Don't be so surprised!"

"I'm not…or rather, there's so much to know about…why remember a painter of a very dated style?"

"I know of certain ages…or periods in art history. I don't know the detail, like you obviously do."

"I have an interest…a financial interest in some of the work. I donate funds for restoration work…or to buy pieces, modern work too. I'm not so old I can't see merit in recent craftsmanship, an eye for a setting and colour! Colour and brilliant light!"

He drove too close to a car in front of them and Marianne had to deter him from saying any more.

"Later, tell me later, Josh."

"Yes, okay. Wait and see?"

"Don't tease…don't remind me of all that," she laughed tapping his arm in admonishment.

I'm glad she called me, again, Josh thought, watching her for an instant as Marianne settled back in the seat and closed her eyes; the sun was on her upturned face and the wind in her loosened hair. He had picked the right moment to drive to the coast, before the rush hour frustrated easy consideration of the scenery so particular to the Dutch coastline.

"I want to share some of this with you…no, all of it," he said but in a voice he hoped she would not hear.

Marianne gave no sign that she had except to put her hand on his once more and locked her fingers with his.

She was drifting, on a daydream…

Here she was with a new man in her life talking about art and of a world that held its own fascination for him. She felt touched that Josh should speak to her so soon of sights that moved him. I'm part of this emotional journey and I'm wondering…where do these way-marks take me? Only, I don't know if I'm ready to face the changes in my life that may follow our meeting. It seems so soon…it's so intense, already…it's so utterly different.

I don't know what he does; we never spoke of it, or rather he never said anything about it to me last night. He joked and said disarmingly, I'm unemployed.

I just blabbed it all out…my job in the City, a girl made good or some such egotistical rubbish. No! It's not rubbish…I'm proud of what I've achieved in someone else's world, in a so-called man's world.

I competed, really struggled for all that I've got, so, why take up with…? Out of my mind! Away with you, Adam! I don't need these memories coming to the surface and haunting me. I don't need you, Adam! No, I don't…I don't! I really don't!

Someone else has found me, a real person…clever and open, maybe too open in what he shows of his feelings. And yet? Can I allow myself to believe that in meeting this man I may find myself again…the real me? Can I do that, with him?

"I'll wait…and I'll see." She murmured languorously; then, her eyes flicked open. She sat up and looked about her. The car was stationary, and she was alone! The sun was lower in the sky. I'm alone!

"Josh? Josh?" she called out.

"Easy!" he laughed softly. "I'm here…I'm here."

"Oh!" she gave a cry of surprise.

Josh raised himself to look at her and smiled, his head cradled on his arms as he rested against the door. "You fell asleep…that's the effect I had on you…so, I've been sitting here in the sunshine, or what remains of it."

"How long, how long for?" She was dismayed at what had happened.

A hand touched her cheek, then, Josh withdrew it. "Not long…not long at all. I simply didn't want to wake you."

"Did I say anything?" She made it sound light-hearted but the question held a dreamy recollection.

"No, you looked thoroughly at ease," he said, sitting back on his ankles. "I didn't dare to disturb you."

Marianne saw now that he had changed into some shorts and was bare foot; she took it all in, his altered and casual appearance, once more.

"Look! Look," she called out and pointed before standing up to grip the edge of the windscreen. "Look at the big sky… look at the sun on the clouds!" She turned to him. "It's like you were saying…isn't it?"

"Yes…yes it is," he answered smiling in surprise at Marianne's excited outburst.

"Come on then…show me!" The door opened abruptly and Josh managed, just, to skip out of the way.

"Yes…come on. It's that painter's moment…the sun's on the clouds and the blue sky still peeks through from behind them."

"Very poetic…very descriptive," she said following his gaze, upwards to the changing colours of the clouds in the sunset.

"No, not me…"

"Mesdag's portrayal of the scene, then?"

"Yes."

"We'll just have to go and see it, the real thing now…the painting, later this week," she finished after a pause. I didn't do anything quite so simple, so innocently pleasurable with Adam.

"Come on, my lady of the ferry. First yachts…now sunsets."

"Yes, whatever next?" she whispered.

IX

"Do this one thing for me?" Josh asked of her as he held a small digital camera and waited. Someone would soon come along and he would ask if a picture could be taken. "A memento of a walk along the beach."

Marianne drew patterns in the wet sand with her toe and waited. "Aha!" she heard Josh exclaim and looked up.

"He'll have to do," he remarked as a gangly youth in nothing more than Bermuda beach shorts trotted towards them, his skin wet and glistening with sand. A longhaired dog rampaged through the stilled waters of the foreshore with loud joyous barks. Following a brief conversation and after various poses had been tried, assessed and discarded could they see, on the small screen, what they chose to be the definitive picture of them together.

Josh smiled and looked very relaxed; his face was turned towards her but Marianne did not meet his glance and instead drew windswept hair from her face in a seemingly theatrical gesture.

"Okay, thanks…your dog needs you, I think." Josh spoke out to the young guy.

"Gladly done…have a good day, what's left of it," came his reply and he gave them a wave. "Hier, Teef!" he called out to the dog.

Josh laughed, disbelieving the call he had just heard.

"What? What did he say?" Marianne asked looking at him then at the man who was again jogging through the lazy tumble of surf, the dog barking and chasing in large leaping bounds the stick that was being thrown for it.

"Here, bitch!" Josh told her in a quiet voice as they stood still, shoes in hand and the water lapping at their feet.

"Oh…oh!"

"It's not what you'd expect to hear…and certainly not in England," he said noting how Marianne clenched her lips together. She was no longer at ease, he saw that. "It's a different take on life…maybe that's the best way to explain it."

"Yeah," she acknowledged in a flat voice. "Shall we go? I think I've seen enough…the sun's glow isn't on the clouds anymore…and that guy did the rest."

"Did what…did what, Marianne?" He came to her side. "Hey? What's the matter…tell me?"

Marianne moved away, not with the lazy contemplative strides that had kept them close as they spoke to each other but with a new and definite purpose; it was to leave this place and its darkening views.

The sun was but a glow on a hazy horizon and the magic of a few moments earlier had gone, completely.

"What's happened…what is going on behind those lovely eyes of yours? Tell me?" Josh asked her as he brushed the sand from his feet and legs as he stood close by. The walk to the car park had been brisk and purposeful.

"We saw a man and his dog."

She didn't turn to look at him and instead settled into the car seat and pulled the door shut sulkily.

"I didn't mean that Marianne…what's changed your mood?"

"Going to the beach," she now said bluntly.

"Right." Josh said it with a hint of sarcastic reflection in his tone.

"Please, don't say 'right' like that," she flared and then…a smile broke out on her face. "What are you doing?" Her laugh came suddenly.

Josh visibly relaxed. "That's better…"

"Are you dressing again for dinner?" she went on and peered at him.

"Of course." He wobbled, only for an instant, as he pulled on his trousers and fastened his belt, making sure that he was presentable. "You're dressed up…I was a mere beach bum by comparison."

"You'll do." She looked him over as Josh sat down beside her. "Can we get a drink? I think I need one now…maybe more."

"Sure, we've earned it." Josh leant across and opened the glove compartment, searching for his glasses. "I need them sometimes," he explained on seeing her study their effect on his appearance. "Is everything settled, again?"

"Not quite. 'Here bitch!' They were only two words," she muttered waving her hand as if to dismiss any further recollection or association that they had intrusively conjured up.

"Forget them," Josh said as he drove out of the parking space. "Forget them, there's nothing kind or loving in them to our ears but the dog knows no different. The tone at least was friendly."

"That's true," she reflected. "Now, I really need that drink and something to eat, I'm famished."

"You look well for all that." He smiled an obvious compliment. For him it was true; an attractive, firmly voluptuous and engaging woman sat beside him. Only, the

50

mood swings had to be understood and the reasons behind them discovered.

"Concentrate," she replied giving him a weak smile. "Think you can manage that?"

"I'll have to try," he smiled back. "Now, tell me…about them, the words? I have to ask."

"Do you Josh? I thought we were going to forget them?" He heard a harder more authoritative tone.

Okay, maybe I deserve that.

"Easy," he said.

"No, Josh. Tell you about what? We've only just met… known each other for a couple of days or so. Things clearly aren't so simple, are they, after all?"

Marianne looked away and rested her chin on a clenched hand as she leant on the door's windowsill. They drove slowly, cruising the route into town looking, she assumed, for a place to park. I've walked quite enough for one day, she thought, and I'm in no mood for interrogations.

"You closed in on yourself, suddenly…out there on the beach."

"Look!" she snapped turning on him. "Enough! Enough questions or I get on a train…again!"

"Oh, really?" he shouted. The car stopped abruptly and Marianne gave a cry as her hands reached out for the dashboard. The seat belts gripped her firmly and Josh saw a fulsome distracting shape for an instant. "No, you look! The beach…the scenery and sky…me just being there with you? All of it was great, just as I hoped it would be…for you! Then? Wham, all change! Just be straight, direct…and honest. Do that for me, will you?"

He had yelled it all out in one energetic burst of anger; then he relaxed, expelling a deep sigh of breath.

"Josh?"

"For God's sake…no mine," he smiled ruefully, "just tell me why a man and his dog have ruined the end of our day, our first day really together?"

"Something was said…"

"Not by me…"

"No…no!" She tried to grab his hand for a moment. Oh shit! She thought as Josh withdrew any prospect of her touching him. I'm coming across as one mixed up woman. "I'm a jumble of memories…all too recent memories," she murmured.

"What?" Josh hadn't heard her, clearly, above the noise of the traffic.

"Nothing…"

"*'Nothing'*! To hell with that for an answer! Buzz off!" He waved at a car to pass them as they heard a hoot. They were still parked at the side of the road. "You were saying?" he pressed with a harder edge to his voice.

"Something was said…it ruined the moment, I'm sorry." She ended in a whisper. This is all too heavy, so self-obsessed… I know that, and…it's too soon, far too soon to go on about… the reasons I'm in this place, this country. Maybe I'd better go, leave him here after all.

"Revived memories for you or brought back a memory of someone?"

"Yes! Yes!" She met the unrelenting stare of Josh's eyes but noted that the set of his lips showed no anger, merely patience. I'm in his spell…is that where he's taking me, a moment where I can tell it all? "Yes."

"Want to take it out on me?"

"No, of course not!" She was relieved that he had driven on, he'd have to think of something else for a while. Underneath, that smooth tanned skin and kind words, is another man. He's trying to help me, allow him that much, Marianne.

"Good," Josh winked at her. "It'll all blow over, all of this…and we can be friends. I hope?"

"Yeah." She wasn't about to let the moment go. I'll find something out about him for a change.

"Has anyone been in your life where some words, just a few, bring back memories or have their own peculiar association?"

"Hurtful association do you mean? Is that what this is all about?" He glanced in the mirror as another hoot of a car's horn interrupted. "You can buzz off too…I spotted it first!" He had found a parking space, miraculously it seemed to her, and she saw the irritated stares of the occupants as the car passed them with a noisy flourish.

"Well?"

Josh answered at last. "Yes, people have been in my life. There's no one now, there hasn't been for some time…in fact, there hasn't been anyone for quite a while."

There! She'd got that out of him. "People? People? You make it sound so cold."

Her remarks didn't provoke him.

"That's how it was in the end, some time ago now," he answered. "There has been no one to make a difference, a vital difference to me or my life."

He stared at her for a moment.

"I'm quite prepared to speak of it, or, you can ask me if it matters to you…after only a few days of knowing me. I prefer to deal with an open hand, Marianne…with you, especially. I know that much, already."

"Josh…" she bent her head and twisted the silver rope bracelet on her wrist, thinking. Have I ever been this way before, in the early stages…during the very early stages of a relationship? It's almost as though he's saying listen and know this about me, then decide if you want to go on.

Josh sat back casually in his seat and reached over to press a button. A hum announced the closing of the car roof and Marianne watched as the frame fitted tightly against the windscreen. Next, the windows closed and Josh turned on the air-conditioning.

"There, the day's shut out. Now, dinner and a drink or two." He reached for the door handle beside him.

"In a moment" Marianne touched his hand in restraint. "I don't know what to tell you...where to start."

"Remember what you said? 'Wait and see.'"

"Okay."

Nodded smiles of agreement were exchanged as they got out of the car. In a gesture of easy companionship Josh took her arm as they began to walk along the promenade.

Suddenly, they had become just another couple out together for the evening.

The restaurant proclaimed that it was special; the prices on the discreetly lit menu board revealed much to potential customers who hesitated at the top of the stairs to consider its attractions. Steps lined with lanterns led from the promenade down to a terrace below; it lay sheltered behind glazed windbreaks; soft yellow umbrellas offered beguiling seclusion to the tables decked in cloth, not paper, and candles in fluted holders flickered in the evening light.

The very place, Josh had thought on seeing it and the intimate atmosphere that beckoned to them. It was busy, not crowded, and their table offered a fine view of the darkening beach and the sea. In the distance the bright lights of the pier held their own fluorescent fascination.

Money can't buy me love, had been another thought but the environment had to be created for a soft word and to confound any denial that a bond was forming between them so soon.

Marianne had taken his arm as they walked, chattered about inconsequential things, commented upon the street traders and expressed surprise at the eclectic tastes in music that was performed along their route. She had come to the same conclusion as he had on finding the place to be 'alone' with him. A meal had been shared and the intensity of their afternoon had been replaced by lighter conversation.

"You're making love to me," she smiled over the rim of her glass and met his gaze upon her once more. The coffee hadn't been touched, but, he had a weakness for the chocolate accompaniment and she slid the small silver wrapped confection across the space between them.

"Oh, ever so slowly and politely…we're in company after all." His fingers touched the skin of her throat in a moment's caress. "Someone, sometime has to help you let go…I would like it to be me."

"Josh?"

"Yes, Marianne?"

"Is it that simple?" She gave a happy disbelieving laugh as he drew his chair closer and on hearing his matter-of-fact way of talking to her now.

"This is…I'm going to kiss you."

"Gosh! Is it that time, already?" It became the briefest pleasurable meeting of their lips.

"Uh huh."

"Knowing me," she said taking his hand and gripping it, tightly.

"Knowing you."

"Uh huh…when?" she heard herself asking.

"Soon, Marianne…soon."

'*Soon*' became later that evening, much later, and followed laughter filled moments, captivated by Josh's extrovert nature. It was a wonderful revelation; he was light on his feet and spared her blushes as he impetuously took her in his arms and they danced, on the promenade. Live music came from a small bandstand and the crowd bobbed, but his exuberance was difficult to ignore.

"Should we?" she laughed looking about them but unable to escape the hold he had upon her, so, she followed his steps. The wine had made her light-headed and overcame any instinct to be restrained. Josh's enthusiasm and a departure from routine behaviour made up for a moment's embarrassment; he had cast his spell upon her.

"Josh! Should we?"

"Oh yes!" he murmured at one point as the tempo moderated, just a bit. "I don't do this…very often," he continued in a gentler teasing voice. "You've made me forget some inhibitions that I'm good at keeping, but…only in England."

"Really? Who'd have thought it?"

That's what being alone for too long does for you, he could have said. Work had ruled everything, but life could change so quickly and this time, now, he wasn't intending to miss out, or let a beautiful winsome woman, who had miraculously come into his life, just leave it again.

People stared at them, looked at each other and concluded, why not us too? The band played on as the sense of an impromptu party spread through the crowd and others joined in.

"See? We're no longer alone…see what you've done?"

"We have…you have."

Josh smiled and shrugged his shoulders in feigned apology. "Carry on?"

"Oh yes, lead on," she urged, smiling up at him. Any remaining reserve that they may have felt, at the speed with which they were drawn to each other, seemed to vanish.

"I will, Marianne…forget everything…think only of what may be."

"Yes," she had told him and danced, rarely free of his touch upon her. "All this…and so soon!" She couldn't help herself from telling Josh in the simplest terms.

She was unable to disguise her bewilderment on meeting him and finding a common cause. A prevailing thought had been, I can truly be myself and give full expression to how I feel, unrestrained by convention or the prying eyes of those that know me but who watched every social move I made. From Josh she had heard that he had travelled to his home country to grow accustomed, once more, to an altered life but for which there had been 'some' compensation. He had said that much and then fallen silent on the subject.

Could she dare to believe it? She had found her own 'sparky'! He was older, but she was drawn to his vitality, his spirit and intellect; he loved art and spoke knowledgeably but not quirkily about it.

Above all else, right then, he only had eyes for her; she felt appreciated, wonderfully alive and close to him in mind and body.

"Soon is now, Marianne." Josh whispered as he opened the door to his room and turned in response to her hand on his shoulder.

"I…I can't keep myself from touching you," she said. "I've met you…I've found you."

It was the briefest of caresses in acknowledgement, once more, that a bond had been formed between them, so unexpectedly soon, and despite the intrusive recollections of other times. She was only too aware of the wonderful contrast of Josh with another man from a former existence.

"So soon?"

"Josh!" she cried out but their union remained unconsummated.

"What is it?" Fleshy it had been, yes, but their frolic was not the success he had hoped for. I *am* out of touch.

"You're trying to make *'love'* to me."

Josh remained in her moist and clammy embrace.

"And I'm sorry not to be succeeding." Marianne looked up, and seeing his teasing smile her lips trembled.

"I'm sorry…I have to do this." She clenched her eyes shut and the tears flowed, in a gentle trickle over her cheeks. After an indolent teasing release she held him to her. "We're still close...so close, so soon...you lovely man."

Desire ebbed away, gradually, in spite of their lingering kisses.

"There will be a time...a better time." He breathed slowly. I thought I knew a thing or two was but a momentary observation that he made, to himself.

"You're not to blame...it's not what you think."

"Strange as it may sound," he observed and just about believed, "I'm more concerned about the emotions behind this than how it works. Let me help you to let go of whatever it is from your past that's holding you back? As you told me, earlier...I've met you. That's how it is for me too."

X

Marianne gasped in simple pleasure.

The water douched over them and pricked their skins. In his tight embrace she remained, her face lifted to meet any kiss that Josh might yet offer. He was unashamed and his attention constant. She had offered no explanation for the previous night and a sought after release from the memory of another's touch upon her.

"You're a lovely man," she said once more against his lips and held Josh tight, her arms wrapped around his neck. They just stood there, in the shower and stroked skins. "The Ferry Company should have warned me that I might meet someone special."

"Ask for your money back if not completely..." he was interrupted by her kiss. The water beat on their faces until they had to break free with gasping laughs.

"Don't say it! Don't you dare! I've met you. There's satisfaction enough in that for me."

Josh could only nod his reply before he attempted to open the door to the cubicle. "Finished?"

"Yes."

She clung to him briefly until the water eased to a stop and he opened the cubicle's door to reach out for the towels. Marianne stroked the tightened muscles of his shoulder but could not restrain him.

"Wrap your beautiful body in this," he said at last in a low voice as he drew the towel about her and fastened it at her breasts. "How's everything now, my lady of the ferry?"

"New, and very different." She could have said more but Josh had turned away, slipped from her sliding hands over his skin.

He stood at the basin now, naked, lathering his face in the old-fashioned way with a sable shaving brush. That was the only concession to past routines. A modern razor was now in hand and he began to shave.

"Is everything okay?" he asked with a questioning tilt of his head and meeting her gaze upon him in the mirror. He stopped shaving at the sight of the lazy lovely way her hands ran through her wet hair.

"Yes…yes," she nodded vigorously and took the hand he held out to her behind him but maintaining eye contact. She clasped his waist and he, encumbered by her hold upon him, bent to splash water on his face and washed away the residue of lather.

"For me too."

"I'm taking in every moment we can share," she said with lips pressed against his skin in wordy kisses.

"Money can't buy this for me," he said turning to face her, "know what I mean?"

"Josh…"

"I've got it…money, but no job. I've got money put by… my lawyer didn't want to believe me when I said it counted for so little, that it was all but worthless…when you can share simple moments like these."

"Softee…"

"Your fault…"

"You'll get cold," she smiled at last, after they had been in a silent embrace.

"There's a remedy for that too…take off the towel?" He put his hands to the wrap of cloth at her breast. "Your skin on my skin, very close…share our body heat…let's try again?"

She met gentle, provocative kisses. "Soon…soon, Josh."

"Yes…okay, or, wait and see. Before we know it we'll have a few of our own little by-words." He relaxed his embrace then stepped away from her. "C'mon, dress quickly now…and, join me for breakfast."

He sat alone on a rattan chair in the sun, with a glass of orange juice in hand, listening as the number rang out.

"Edward! I'm returning your call of yesterday! It's Josh van Leeuwen!"

"I understand perfectly, Josh. You're away…you're distracted."

"No…I'm engaged."

"What!"

"Take it easy, Edward," he laughed imagining the look of surprise on his lawyer's face. "I'm actively engaged… relaxing."

There was an audible sigh. "Okay…okay. I'll have to see the funny side of that even if it is early in the morning…for us here in England anyway. Besides, things don't happen that quickly."

"Don't you believe it!" Josh made his reply sound light and carefree. You've got me to put up with Edward, you poor chap! Poor nothing, not at the hourly rate you charge! I suppose even this call will cost me.

"What time is it?" Edward asked needlessly. "Oh…right. It's half past eight here so…nine thirty your time. I should have known, you've been at work for ages already. Old habits still clinging to you?"

"Something like that...I was just checking my inbox. I'll switch the thing off again in a minute. I'm really not addicted to these mobile 'phones like so many are...or happily dragging a laptop around everywhere, both like some baby's dummy...you're lost, quite inhuman if you don't have them constantly in use."

"You're in a minority," Edward chuckled.

"Yes, I suppose I must be...or getting to be that way." He considered Edward's remarks for only a moment as his thoughts turned to Marianne, a charming distraction from all that his lawyer wished to discuss. Calls such as this had to be quickly dealt with; he wanted to devote all his attention to her and felt relieved that there were few to be answered. "What have you got for me, Edward?"

"Money...in a word, money. The deal's done, all wrapped up. The money's in the vault, so you can relax and turn off the 'phone. I thought I'd tell you in an e-mail...I know you read them, even when you're away."

"True..."

"But, I thought by word of mouth was better...the human touch."

"Very considerate of you."

"There's still e-mails to read...I sent you some. Most important one is to ask when you're thinking of coming back."

"No idea."

"None?"

"No...none. One minute I'm supposed to be enjoying myself...which, I am incidentally, then the next minute I'm being asked when I'll be back at work. What work, and who's asking?"

"Clients...companies that need your skills."

"And contacts..."

"Yes...but mostly the very skills and attributes that you got someone to pay so much money for."

"Remind me again? How much was it? I can't remember…"
He gave a laugh.

"Don't start that again! 'It's only money'."

"From where I'm sitting it's just that. Any ideas I've still got I'm keeping to myself for now…and the money can stay in the bank."

"People are still asking after you…you can't fall over the edge."

"Yeah, well said."

"You sound disappointed in all that's come your way."

"On the contrary!" Josh sat up and laughed loudly. Although two tables away from his nearest neighbours they still looked over at him. He mouthed an apology with a smile creasing his face. That did the trick, winning smiles in return. "I'm really not at all disappointed. It had to happen sometime and I've had a few days to think it all through. I now have an opportunity to be distracted for a while…and, I'm not going to let it pass me by."

"Okay…we've spoken about some of the things I called you for. Enjoy your break. When you return there are people who want you to worry about more than just the P & L Account. That'll be a change!"

And a lovely change, a delightful passionate person who has caught my fancy; is now coming my way and she is looking out for me.

"I've got to go Edward. Thanks for taking the call. Speak to you soon…I've had no breakfast, but I can do something about that now."

"Lucky chap. I suppose it's breakfast on the terrace somewhere out in the morning sunshine?"

"Precisely…now, goodbye Edward."

He pressed the key with the little red telephone icon. Off! Yes, I'm off to be with a new woman in my life. That's what I hope for now; it's *'so soon'*, as Marianne keeps reminding me.

Somehow, I've got to overcome her doubts or concerns that seem to re-surface when we least expect them.

"You look wonderful." Josh stood up to greet her and drew back a chair from the side of the table.

"Thank you," she was able to reply before meeting a soft kiss.

"You're my 'belle de jour', Marianne."

"Very gallant…and that is a language I do know," she smiled back at him. "Are there many belles?" She had wondered often enough why there was no one in his life to claim him, a man for them alone.

"No, I told you…there aren't."

He made it sound far too serious and relented under her watchful gaze as the 'phone was laid down on the table once more.

"Work? Were you catching up on some work?"

"No. I was just tying up some loose ends from a former life. The 'phone's off now so there won't be any interruptions." On impulse he touched her cheek. "I'm glad to have met you…the sun's in your hair…it catches the colours beautifully." He looked at her and smiled. "Stay there…wait a moment!"

"Josh?" He had taken his 'phone and switched it on again. "Not a picture…not with that?" she asked smiling.

"Oh yes…it'll be beauty in my hands," he winked mischievously, "all of the time."

"Flatterer…only, don't stop." She took a sip of his orange juice and looked at their surroundings. "We should have breakfasted on the terrace, like this…the last time we were here."

"Yes, only the circumstances were very different then." His chair scrapped on the slabs at their feet. "Now, what can I get you?"

"Whatever you choose…something light? Fruit say, some croissants and lots of coffee. How's that for a starter?" She rummaged in her shoulder bag that had been placed on the table. "I suppose I'd better do what you've done...check out who's been trying to reach me. I left this off most of yesterday... I didn't see the need for it after we met again."

"No...and I'm glad you did, on both counts." He leant on the arm of her chair looking at her. "Shall we promise each other that they will both stay off all day...after we've checked their in-boxes through?"

"Yes...promise."

By some fluke or extreme good fortune she noted how her pale yellow slip dress matched for colour his loose open necked shirt. For her the instant of seeing him at the table had prompted the thought that they were a couple already. She shook her head as the words came to mind once more, 'it's so soon, far too soon'.

There were messages; the 'beep' alerted her to that intrusion but she was unprepared for the contents of the message board displayed in perfect clarity on the small screen. The tally showed twenty calls, but only three numbers were repeatedly shown as she scrolled down the list. They were all recognisable. Two were from her closest friends, curious, no doubt, on how she was 'making out'!

'I'll not tell them that! They'll...they'll say...that's quick! Or, so soon?' She could just imagine the gossipy and laughter filled chatter over the airwaves.

And then...and then she saw it, Adam's number.

There had been several attempts to make contact.

I erased it! I erased the number, didn't I? I must have done...must have! It would have been...should have been, the first thing to have been done...to erase any visual reminders of him and that past life. It was a start to the healing process and a change in my life, the first step in my search for a very different life with a very different man.

She looked at the screen, her mind chasing conflicting thoughts and emotions.

Even if I hadn't done that vital thing…making that break, denying myself the sight of his name or number on the screen when he called I would have remembered that little omission, wouldn't I? I'd remember that I kept it on the list…just in case. NO! NO! There was to be no turning back, no reprise of former times!

I'm here to forget you, Adam! I've made up my mind …and I'm following through on it. Go! Away with you!

No, it's not that easy. I found that out, in spite of being with Josh throughout the night, my skin against his; we were joined but we weren't as one. How he yearned for that the lovely man and something held me back. No! I won't allow your memory to hold me back…not you, not memories of you Adam!

She turned her face to the warming sunshine and closed her eyes for what seemed only a moment.

No, it wasn't easy for me to forget, even with Josh's loving attention, his patience and his restraint, his wonderful desire to share a blessed heated impulse with me. Had it ever been like that before, tenderness and passion for me? No…only I couldn't so easily forget, after all, your touch on me, Adam. They're like invisible shackles and I need to be set free, completely free of them…even now…even after being with Josh, so intimately and so soon.

She whispered these contrasting and violating thoughts of what she wished to know of Josh, and felt a strange gratitude that he had not yet returned. She might be provoked to say hurtful things and all because that man Adam still retained a vivid place. I've still got my memories of you, of us she now whispered.

Oh Adam!

The frequent calls that we made to each other, or answered during those early days of our relationship. There was the excitement and discovery of a new passion, the expressions of a deep physical need at the time when we had first met. They seemed to fill every moment of our day and we lived for them and them alone. But, I soon realised…that I couldn't discard the truth. It wasn't 'love' that we felt or what I would wish to know of it.

You seemed to crave and to meet in me a baser instinct.

Why ring me? Why haunt me with these memories when we've split up…I've put you in my past? Why call we, why do so now when I've found someone different, so very different… someone so new and different from your plain ordinariness. Why call me and leave those intrusive memory-chasing messages, Adam?

Oh yes, I know why, Adam. You were selfish and arrogant in your belief that I needed you, still, in spite of everything that was said and done when we parted.

I don't need reminders, especially now. I'm trying to forget who I was or became when I was with you, Adam and that lovely desirable man Josh is going to help me find the person I really am.

With you I was just a silly woman! I was seen…I found out later, as a 'silly' and 'older' woman. But it was an observation of me that was quickly shattered. I saw to that! I was older, but I wasn't silly! I simply believed in a love between two people. It could happen…it should happen, at least once in our lives, just to show us how it could be.

The daydream persisted; she recalled so much of what had been endured and held her 'captive' in a relationship with a *'waster'*. At the time, emotion had displaced all reason. And now?'

I'm so lucky! I've met someone…I've been found by someone so very different from you, Adam…and, it's so soon. I've met someone different who won't put me through what I had to endure…in the last months spent with you when I went through emotional hell and degradation. Yes, that's how I looked upon those wayward moments with you, Adam. I felt like a lost soul and had to get away.

Thank God! I've been so lucky…and so soon!.

Josh is not like that! I've found him!

We've met and somehow something has happened! I can't believe it, even now. It's soon, so soon and I am not going to tell anyone of what I have found, so soon!

What a cliché, but it fits my situation. I'm going to live for the moment…or, live one day at a time. I'm going to live and to learn of that man…that man, Josh!

<u>XI</u>

"Oh! Josh!" She gasped and opened her eyes in shock, staring up at him. The telephone that she clutched so tightly in her hands was cast onto the table with a soft thud.

"Yes, it's me, Josh." He gave her a bemused smile. "You seemed to be miles away…in another place. Are you okay?"

"Yes…I am now." She held his hand as he offered a reassuring touch to her cheek.

"Good…I've brought you a small selection as you can see. Just loads of fruit, croissants and some jams…they're for both of us. The honey's for me. Oh! I've also brought a large cafétiere. Is Madam content with that?" He adjusted the collection and took the cups that were precariously balanced at the edge of the tray. Then, he looked at her once more. "Sorry…I'm chattering on. You were distracted…but then, I wouldn't have seen the sun in your hair. You seemed lost…"

"Yes…yes! I was." Marianne held out her hands once more and her grip tightened as he took hold. "Come closer…please, kiss me?"

"Of course I will." The frown she had at first seen left his face and Josh smiled now. "What's up?"

It was a gentle and fleeting moment of tenderness from him. He pulled a chair close by her side and sat down; nothing further was said; he tended to her, poured out coffee and set the cream jug down before her. They sat so still that crows, young and with glistening feathers hopped close-by, flapped their wings to rise up and perch on a nearby seat waiting for scraps to be thrown; they looked about them with turns of sharp beaked heads and black staring eyes but they were ignored.

"Josh…I…I…" Marianne stuttered.

"Is it off? Have you turned your 'phone off?" he asked in a flat voice.

"Yes."

"Have you seen what you needed to know and switched the bloody thing off again?"

"No…and there were messages I'd rather not have known about."

"They're a bloody nuisance," he said vehemently under his breath, "most of the time."

"Yes." She clasped his hand once more and their fingers entwined. "Yes, they remind you of unfinished business…or, in my case what I want to forget and leave behind me." On hearing this softly spoken confession Josh took his 'phone out of his pocket and switched it on. "Josh? Now what?" she said leaning against him.

"Wait and see. I won't be too long." He pressed the keys and drafted his message. Satisfied, he scrolled down a list until he found the number. "Send…it's a little different from a message in a bottle."

"Josh?"

He had stood up and prepared to leave.

"Answer it when you're ready. There's no rush…I'm here, quite near." He kissed her cheek then almost sang out to make the words sound easy and carefree. "I've forgotten something… back soon."

Marianne opened the message.

'U r with me…me. If u can and you dare, believe in something else with someone new. 2 me u r beautiful…but u need to hear it from someone u can believe in. Make the journey, please? It cld

be special…and yes, IT'S HAPPENING, SO SOON! Josh…the ferryman.'

Message deleted, deleted, deleted. Erase, erase them; there, all of Adam's messages have been erased. Unread…unread… unread. My life can change, so soon…soon…soon.

This time Marianne made sure that there was no trace on the hand-held messenger of the man in her former life. Was he a former 'love'? No, Adam was never quite that and she had no intention of going over old times to convince herself that she had been justified in her decision to end the relationship.

I'm not even going to recall some of the better times with Adam, early times, unrecognisable times from those I had to endure towards the end of our liaison. If I did it would be destructive and it would strike at all that I am searching for now from a new life. That's why I left England…that's why I am here. It feels like I'm on the edge of a new life, already…so soon on a new life's path, with a man I have yet to know in the deepest sense that can be enjoyed between two people.

I still hurt enough from all that Adam said to allow his memory to regain its suffocating grip on me. I'm with a new man; I've met Josh. I've been in a naked embrace with him, so soon after our first meeting. From that moment on I corrupted any previous emotions I may have felt for Adam; but then, he had left me long before our parting truly came. Last night I forsook any sense of propriety; Josh and I, we seduced each other, and…I loved every minute of it! Life will soon be changed…it will be altered, of that I have no doubts. There will be no return to how it was yesterday, or the day before that, or…the weeks and months before, when I was with Adam. But then, that partnership was more in body than body *and* spirit.'

That lovely man, Josh! He knew how it could be between us before I did.

She said the words to herself and cast the 'phone into the chic shoulder bag.

He's gone and told me, in that cryptic but understandingly gentle and persuasive language.

'If you can and you dare'.

Well, I dare! But do I believe that it can happen so truly and madly, so amazingly soon?'

"I've found you, Josh," she said touching his arm.

"Yes…it's becoming a habit of ours, parting and then finding each other." He looked from her to those about them in the small area set aside from the main body of the restaurant. He did not react to the softened look that Marianne gave him. "If I stay here any longer I'll want to grab even more to eat and I haven't even started on what I brought out for us."

"Josh, listen…please?"

"Sure." He gave a little gasp. "The birds! The birds, Marianne! They'll be feeding off our table. Quick Marianne… sauve qui peut!"

Josh slipped out of her grasp and walked out into the sunshine.

"You needn't have worried." She spoke and clutched a fold of his shirt to lessen his pace.

"No, I see that now." He turned to the waitress and thanked her for watching their table. Marianne marvelled at the speed in which he could change from one language to another without a pause to reflect or compose what had to be said first in his mind. He leant over the table. "The coffee's gone cold I suppose? No, it hasn't!" He quickly released the grip of his large hands on the cafétiere.

"How can you think of such everyday things when you've just sent me a caring and thoughtful text message?"

"I'm giving you time and space. I also want to try and get away from the stress and angst that keeps coming between us…it's exhausting. I'd like to help and do something about it, if you'll let me?" He waited until they were again seated at the table before continuing. "Last night…us dancing and being together? That's how I would like us to be…to grow together, over time…whatever it takes."

"If I dare?"

"Yes…learn and love a little. We grow together and believe in loving, a lot."

"Where did you learn to say such things?" She put her arm through his and pulled them close to stare unblinkingly at each other for an instant.

"Sorry…if it sounds a bit, well…soft."

"Don't apologise…I haven't heard it said that way in a *long…long time*."

"I told you, Marianne…I have had time to think, on my own. There's been no one else for a *long time* in my life." He repeated her words with the same inflection upon them.

"We both dare to try, is that what you're saying to me, Josh?"

"Something like that." He nudged her, playfully. "Now, breakfast and the rest of the day together…us, together. We've had more than enough disruptions. It's time to enjoy ourselves."

"We wait and see."

"I couldn't have put it better myself." He looked at her and took hold of the cloth necklace that matched for colour the pale yellow slip dress that she wore. A white diaphanous blouse with its billowing sleeves was an eye-catching contrast. "I'm glad to have met you and…to have been with you so close. Don't allow anyone in to spoil what we may have found." He had drawn her closer by a gentle pull on the necklace and stared into her eyes. "Is it a deal?"

"Yes, it's a deal. One last thing though, to put your mind at rest."

"Sh!"

"No." She would have her way and moved to escape his fingers as they tried to press her lips into silence. "I've deleted all the intrusive messages. The 'phones off. I'm with you…"

The rest of the line had remained unspoken "I'm with you, in body and mind."

Adam's attempted calls and messages had seen to that. She would have to rely on Josh to sustain her and to help in the consignment of that past relationship to its rightful place. It had merely been an episode in her life; that was what she kept reminding herself. It had not been a life with Adam the loss of which should be mourned.

I think I've got that right; she leant against Josh's shoulder as she sipped on her coffee, lost in thought. The sun was warm and a new day keenly anticipated with a man who dared to speak of her renewal, with him…so soon! Mother and Father had a wonderful life together…I need to find one that helps to make my own come close to its pattern.

She held the coffee cup in one hand; with the other she held Josh's arm and felt reassured by its warming strength.

"Penny for them?" she asked.

"Come to Amsterdam?" Josh replied making a feeble joke. "It almost rhymes."

"No cycling in the dunes? No two-wheely frolics?"

"Fancy you remembering that."

"I liked the idea…the way in which you suggested it. I thought, 'here's a guy who knows how to treat a lady a little differently'."

"Oh, I see." His hand discreetly caressed the soft skin of her thigh. "So soon?"

"Yes, so soon." She took his hand preventing any further exploratory caress concealed by the tablecloth. "Behave… maybe it will be all the better if we do wait?"

"Yeah, okay." He smiled in mock resignation. "The lady of the ferry has decreed that it be so."

"'Que sera…sera'. Isn't that what you told me Josh?"

"Yes…I know other words but you'll have to come along with me to see them. They are the title of a picture…a painting, and…you'll only see it in Amsterdam."

She nodded. "Where are you taking me?"

"To the pictures."

"Very funny," she looked skywards in mock despair.

"It's true! Art and pictures. A gallery first then a late lunch in a quiet café by the canal-side somewhere in Old Town...." He too looked skywards but saw the darker broken cloud drifting above them on the strengthening breeze. "I hope the weather holds until we get there. It's not how I want you to see it, in the rain. There should be light, the cobbled streets look so much better with the sun through the leaves of the trees and the sky and house gables reflected on the water...drifting clouds...so, the scenery changes all the time...they're moving pictures, and they're free!"

He rolled his eyes mocking his exuberance at the thought of it.

"It's fine, poetic...you make it sound magical." Marianne touched his face with the back of her hand without turning to look at him. "You romantic...it's also near my hotel."

"Precisely, I thought we'd go there. Call it love on the run, in a manner of speaking."

"And what do you feel about that?"

"We're together...we wait and see. I want to take you to the exhibition...Baroque Art, by two of its finest but very different exponents. One is from the Low Countries, the other from its birthplace.

"Rembrandt and Caravaggio? I've seen the advertising flyers.""

"Exactly. What do you say?"

"Yes...yes! I was going to do that, it gave me something to look forward to."

"On your own?"

"Yes," she answered softly, "until I found and then met someone who gave me a better idea." She turned and kissed his cheek. "Isn't that right, mister ferry-man?"

XII

They sat facing each other, by the window, on the top deck of the fast train into Amsterdam. There would be only one stop, at a "double decked" station that she remembered for its modernity, as so much seemed to be in The Netherlands.

"I'm not planning to make this journey too often," she told Josh. "I'd like to stay put in one place and completely relax. Will you let me do that?"

"Sure, after today." That was all he said on the subject. "The exhibition of Baroque Art doesn't last much longer so it's a chance to see thirty pieces of work, the best to be brought together in one place for a very long time. We can both compare the styles and the subjects, the emotions and engagement of the characters with each other...and, all of it's in paint!"

"And up here." Marianne touched his face then his forehead, leaning forward to do so. "How have I come to meet you...who ordered it?"

"Sh!" he smiled. "We promised...we'd ease up a bit. Remember?"

"Yes, I remember. Only the pictures will stir things up again."

"That's what they're meant to do...you never quite get bored or feel the same about them or the image they create in your mind's eye. You come back to them and something new appeals to you, to your senses, to your feelings." Josh sat on the edge of his seat and Marianne copied him so that their knees touched.

"Will I have to kiss you to make you shut up for a moment?"

"There's an idea! But...I'm too old to misbehave like that in public." He sat back and smiled at her. "Such a bore...a lover of art and a would be lover of...hm?"

"Sh!" Marianne held an index finger to her smiling lips, but no one paid them the least attention. "You were talking about emotions...all of it captured in paint."

"Yes."

"Why the Van Gogh Museum? It seems a strange place to hold the Exhibition." She held up a promotional flyer for him to look at. "I was sent this."

"There's a tenuous link, but it is there all the same," he observed after reading the few printed words; well-known paintings, masterpieces of the genre, had been cleverly used to capture the imagination of those considering a visit.

"Oh?"

"Yes, it says that Van Gogh was an admirer of Rembrandt."

"You don't see it in his work."

"Don't you?"

"No, or not to my eyes." Marianne held up a bottle of mineral water before taking a few sips. "Want some of this?" She wiped the neck of the bottle with a clean tissue.

"No thanks, Marianne." He spoke softly and smiled before moving to sit next to her again. "You don't have to do anything like that, wipe the bottle. We share…share everything…got that?" Their heads touched as he leant towards her.

"Ease up you said."

"Yeah, that's what I said…maybe, I didn't quite mean it." He winked before moving away from her.

"So, you were also telling me, or about to tell me, about the relative merits of Rembrandt and Van Gogh." Marianne half turned towards him in the confined space offered by the seats. "I want to hear what you've got to say on the subject. It'll be a distraction for you…and me." She tilted her head and smiled. "Yes?"

"Ja? That's how you say it around here."

"Give it time. Now…you were saying, about Rembrandt and Van Gogh?"

"What do I know?" he replied shrugging amiably. "I have an opinion and a liking for their work…even if they are distinct and separated by the centuries. There is beauty…a bit raw in

Van Gogh's case. But there's skill none the less. You see it in his choice of colour and attention to detailed brush strokes.

"And devotion?" Marianne prompted. They could talk as if they were quite alone in the compartment. Josh did not look at anyone but her.

"Yes, that too. We've only got Rembrandt and Caravaggio to compare. See?" He eased the leaflet from her grip and set two pictures together, along a fold line, holding the paper between the thumb and index finger of each hand.

Wonderingly, Marianne caressed his fingers. "You're very strong...you have loving hands," she whispered.

"They're not artist's hands...I can't draw to save my life and I don't play music. I'm useless in that way."

"I know of other qualities...other skills that show devotion," she answered suggestively.

"Each to their own."

"Yes...something like that, Josh." They exchanged glances and laughed softly.

"I think I'd better change seats again. There's no knowing where this might lead to."

"Oh yes you do, Josh."

"Okay...in time." He held out his hand across the narrow space restored between them. "Now...there's one picture that I want to see; it's very appropriate in the circumstances...it's in the title, even if it is not always quoted in full. Do you know which one I mean?"

"No." She watched him as Josh let go of her hand and sat back once more in his seat. "Tell me something more...of Rembrandt and Van Gogh? You keep being distracted."

"Hm...oh yes," he considered for a moment. "They each brought intensity to their work. Rembrandt possessed supreme artistic skill in his detailed emotional portrayal of all that possessed the minds of the characters...I keep looking at that picture, the writing on the wall in 'Balthazzar's Feast'. It seems so simple...yet it provokes deeply intrusive thoughts. And then, at the opposite extreme are the raging emotions that you see in the brilliant colours and weight of the many brush strokes that make up a Van Gogh. You think it's simple…almost inexpert, just daubs of paint, and then you come in closer. The picture is a mosaic…made up of little brush strokes, heavy with paint or the lightest touch. Then…the light catches the work, each ridge seems to light up and the picture comes alive. No one recognised the gift until years after his death…poor man! That was what he was…in everything but talent!"

"Phew!" Marianne laughed. "You seem so involved with it…you feel the emotions that make up the pictures."

"Yeah, sorry."

"No! Please, don't say sorry, Josh."

"Okay, I won't!" He gave a little shrug. "I can go on a bit, though…only I don't dismiss so quickly or easily what the pictures stir up in me. They provoke thoughts that are still so relevant, even today. You just have to look, understand and think it all out…you ignore some of the messages some would say…at your peril."

"You've brought them alive." It was how she felt and all she could do was look at him; she marvelled that out of such clumsy opening conversations between them on the ferry a caring and sensitive man had emerged. She had found Josh again, quite by chance…on a motorway! None of her friends would believe it.

The train swayed gently as it went over some points and those around them busied themselves getting ready.

"Centraaal Stationnn, Ammsterrrdam!" the driver announced in his own quirky style.

"You'll see them…real soon now, paintings and all the moving pictures…all of them reflected in the water. They're constantly changing." He held her hand in a loosened grip for an instant. "Look! The Old City's to the right and the harbour and the way to the sea, the new way…is to the left. The two were cut off from each other in the nineteenth century by this modern temple to travel. They can't leave the place alone, constantly messing about with it…now they're working on a metro station…all that modern stuff under an ages old city."

He gave Marianne a glance and fell silent on seeing her indulgent smile. The shadow cast by the domed station roof plunged the compartment into near darkness and fellow passengers began to clog the narrow gangway between the rows of seats.

"You're my guide," she told him as they waited patiently for the throng to disperse. Be my saviour remained an unspoken thought.

Tickets were bought in a clapboarded pavilion and tourist office. On the tram they looked out onto the crowded streets; it was if the world had descended upon the city and everyone was oblivious to them. They rattled noisily past a melee of backpackers, day-trippers with their shopping bags, and excited new arrivals, visitors with their wheeled suitcases. The throng was likened to a human drift moving purposefully along the pavements. Few looked up to see the sky and the changing architecture of the gables; the shop fronts and pavement cafés held their own tawdry fascination.

The museum was set at the edge of a small park, a quieter haven to enjoy or to study, according to preference, the creative output of two Old Masters.

"I wonder what everyone here thinks of it all, the works on display?" Josh read a few lines of the guidebook but felt more inclined to study the posters of the paintings that they would soon be able to consider.

"Are we heading straight for this piece of work you so wished me to see?"

"No, in my opinion that's for later…but, you decide. There's so much to see…major works gathered in one place and brought here from all over the world. To be here is special… and, I'm glad to have you by my side for company."

"Josh…" She met a gentle kiss to her cheek and saw the smile of gratitude on his lips.

When, at last, they came upon Rembrandt's work they were startled by the light cast upon the faces of the king and his guests. The collection had so far encouraged the onlooker to study the detail of gesture and expression captured in portraits or a biblical scene; but, they had all been set against a darkened, or faintly lit, backdrop. The contrast between those works and the scene now before them was startling.

"There!" Josh sighed out on a wondering sigh.

"Balthazzar's Feast. The message in it's pretty clear…"

"It sure is…the *'writing's on the wall'*."

"'You've been found wanting,'" Marianne said, adding, "are you sure I'm not supposed to be reading something more into all this?" She squeezed his arm playfully, just to make her point.

"No, or not unless you want to…it's your choice. I came to see the paintings…that they hold an important or perceptive meaning for the onlooker is a compliment to the skill of the artist. You have to stop…let your mind go blank, in a manner of speaking. You could say it's…"

"Closing out all other thoughts and concentrate on the work before you? Look…really look and wait for the association of image and thoughts to appear?" she added helpfully. "Distractions aren't allowed?"

"Yes," he winked in acknowledgement. "That's how I go about these visits…they seem to be reminders, in paint…on the canvas, of what is going on in everyone of us."

"Enjoy them, Josh…don't go getting in too deep. You're only with me…"

"It's enough…and, don't dismiss the ideas." He broke free of her hold upon him and took up a new stance, to study the picture before them once more.

"Okay…only, don't close me out."

He stood silently beside her and reflected for a moment.

"Yeah, sorry...okay. I'll lighten up...just a bit."

"Promise?"

"Yes...I promise." He took hold of her hand and kissed it. "I've got to say...all that we've seen and this picture especially are not a moment's composition...they're not like some picture in the tabloid newspapers...they endure, the image and the thoughts they bring out in anyone who looks at them."

"I know...I understand."

"Do you?"

"Yes," she whispered and touched his arm to retrain Josh from moving on too soon; it would be easier to offer an opinion given his deference to the setting, the Art, and those about them.

"There isn't the gaudy, trashy and sensational innuendo in the work. Rembrandt has for me captured the moment brilliantly...it's deep significance to all who look at the script."

"Which is? Tell me..."

"Goblets spill their contents...Balthazzar's right hand grabs at food, his hand is almost closed...he has what he wants! With his left hand he protects what is dear to him...but the posture, the look on his face and of those about him, his companions...they all speak of a deeper emotion. They've been caught out...over indulging, all of them...but your eye is on one man...Balthazzar. He dominates the foreground. The painting is about him, and him alone."

"And? What else? There's something else that makes me look at it differently." Marianne gripped his arm tight. "Stand still for a moment!" Her tone made him meet the stare she now gave him.

"Go on...you tell me."

"There's only one hand...by the writing on the wall. There's no immediate threat...it's as if it is disembodied...it's all in the words and the brilliant light that shines from them." She gave him a smile as if embarrassed to have succumbed to his way of interpreting the picture so deeply. "Sorry...you've got me at it now!"

They laughed and gave each other a nudge in acknowledgement.

"We'd better behave."

"When? Now?" Marianne looked at the picture once more. "Sorry..."

"No, don't apologise...if that is what the image tells you, or makes you think, hold on to the thought." He looked from her to the picture and fell silent, his eyes drawn to the words and then he moved from them to the figures in the foreground. "You've made me realise, or helped me to see again two pictures, both on that one piece of canvas." He drew Marianne closer to his side. "Thank you...I'm glad to have you for company."

"Josh," she replied slowly. "It's a different medium...simply of its time."

"Compared to my newspapers idea...is that what you mean?"

"Yes. They are the modern way...they have a particular immediacy but are the messages so very different? Someone does wrong...they are exposed by the media and it happens very quickly. Rembrandt was of another time, that's all...and fewer people saw the message. That picture? It was intended to be seen by a select few."

"Unlike some newspapers, you mean?"

"Don't be so snooty! They have a place too."

"Okay." They stood in front of the picture talking and more intent on what they were now discussing than the merits of the work. "The papers have transience, they're all about immediate consumption...tell the story and move on. There's no moral value to any of it. On one page there's a story to titillate, on the next a criticism of someone's behaviour. It degrades. None of it lifts the spirits or makes you think more carefully...this picture succeeds in that, brilliantly."

"Sure, it's made me think." Marianne tugged on his arm. "Let's move on, otherwise we'll be here all day discussing each picture...there's so much more to see and do."

"You won't see them together like this for a long time...if ever again." He loosened her hold upon him and began to move on. "There's a message in each of them."

"Wait!" Marianne hissed. "I asked you to wait!" Josh turned.

"What?"

"Is there some connection I should be making between the picture and what's going on...in my life, say...or in yours?"

"Soft now...and no, it's not in that picture alone."

"Where then?"

"Stay close...I want you to see another painting," he said before pausing to look about them. "This is not the place to talk of any significance I might attach to the works, for either of us." Josh moved on once more but Marianne was soon at his side.

"That's convenient."

"What is?" he asked on a sigh.

"Saying what you just have and then closing down any further discussion of it."

"I'm merely saying art can mirror life."

"Not mine, Josh. I haven't seen anything here to remind me of that...not one piece...and I'm not going to try and keep up with the pretence."

"I'm not pretending and the pictures have their own implicit way of telling a story or illuminating a truth. For me, the thoughts that a picture may provoke...by what is seen and felt, later, that's what counts."

"Are you sure?"

"Yes, Marianne."

"Like the '*writing on the wall*'? One relationship's finished so move on to the next?" She stood facing him, very close. "It's not very subtle. Why not just tell me what you think?"

"It would be a cliché."

"I…I don't follow?" Her brow furrowed for a moment, then she smiled. "Right," she said slowly. "I get it. A picture…paints a thousand words?" She tapped his arm. "My brain's going to hurt if I have to second guess everything you're thinking or hinting at."

"Don't try so hard."

"Don't patronise me, Josh."

"Fine," he sighed out in acknowledgement of an honest opinion about him and his views.

"Is it…*'fine'*?"

"Yes, it is. Now…maybe the next painting will spell it out…come with me, Marianne, please?" He tilted his head in the direction they should now take. "I'm sorry…I have my pompous ways. I'll lighten up soon."

"Promise?"

"He's not beautiful, the face is plain. He's not a vision of Cupid as many would wish or expect him to be."

"The title of the painting says it all. Caravaggio got that right…and so much more."

"Cupid is the messenger, is that it?"

"Yes, that's it." Josh looked from the painting to Marianne. "Love Conquers All, or as the painting's entitled, 'Amor Vincit Omnia'." He waited to see if Marianne would respond. "Cupid isn't supposed to be beautiful or handsome…the artist is making you think beyond what your eyes are telling you."

"So, it is all in the emotions conveyed you mean?"

"Yes."

"But the saying goes on doesn't it? The whole message is, *'Love conquers all, so concede to love…or yield to it'.*" Marianne smiled. "So? Is that why I am here? This very overt message should be considered while we stand here, together?"

"What do you take me for?" he smiled disarmingly. "I'd just come out and say it, or ask if you would consider the idea."

"And?"

"And, will you? Will you consider the idea...better still, believe in it?" He put his arm about her waist. "And, don't you dare say 'we'll see', I've had quite enough of that for a while."

"Decision time? Is that it...and so soon?" she laughed out another of their little sayings. "Is that what you're asking me?"

"No, not exactly."

"What then, exactly?"

"I'll tell you over our late lunch. Then, I'll bring you back safely to that swank hotel of yours."

"It's not 'swank'," she interrupted.

"It is compared to my unpretentious roadhouse."

"Then what?"

"I leave you."

"Leave me?"

"Yes, I leave you. It was what we agreed...on the first day. We said that we would have time apart."

"We've had them...I have. I told you! We got together... took a walk along the beach...we did all that, and more because I couldn't...or rather didn't want to be on my own here."

The painting before them was forgotten. She had misunderstood the purpose of the visit and the return to Amsterdam, together, completely. There had been a particular and seemingly undisclosed significance for him that Josh had only now revealed to her.

Love conquers all. What is Josh telling me, that he knows it is so for him already, after a few days...so soon? That really would be a trick! How does he know, how can he be so certain and so soon?

"I know you didn't want to be here on your own…but you're not, not anymore. We're separated, only for a few hours, a few days."

"Days? Days!" All she could do was stare at him and held onto his arm possessively. Others looked at them for a moment as her voice rose then fell, just as quickly.

"It's not so long. We've met…that's the important part of the story." He held one hand out to her. "Come? Come with me for walk, outside in the sun? We'll find a place for lunch…or a drink."

"Or two…"

"Yeah." He walked easily, holding her hand and smiled.

"Did you always have this in mind…to bring me back and then, leave?"

"No."

"Say something more…will you? Explain to me what's going on in that head of yours, please?"

That beautiful head with its laughing and expressive eyes and that teasing smile to your lips. I don't know…I still don't know…I still can't work out if you're just saying these things to tease me, or to win a concession from me. I'm wavering, but I'm not going back on the feelings I first showed you last night.

"We take some time to reflect," he answered gently. "I visit my relations and become a dutiful cousin for a while and spend time with a dear cousin. Then, we meet again and see how it is. We haven't rushed into anything else. We've found each other…shared tender moments…unexpectedly soon. I don't want to rush you into anything more."

She stood on the steps, outside the museum's entrance and simply stared at him. Josh stood below her now, looking up. Without taking too much in, they had simply walked through the remaining exhibits engrossed in what they had to tell each other and out into the sunshine once more.

"Ha! Very funny! What have we been up to these last few days? It's been a rush," she confessed, "headlong, in my case. I've made a break with a past that still haunts me. But, I'm not looking to return to a life that was so utterly different to what I see before me now…it started on the ferry! It started that soon!"

"Yeah. Now, let the idea settle."

"Josh, it has…believe me."

"Then there isn't a problem, or there shouldn't be. You have some time to take in the sights…or the shops here. Then we meet up, again."

"I'm not going to make a habit of it."

They had taken only a few steps before he embraced her.

"Amor vincit omnia?" he asked.

"Et nos cedamus amori?" Marianne replied. "We concede to it?"

"So? Shall we?"

"Don't make me say it!" she smiled up at him. "We'll see."

XIII

"Gotcha!" The words were uttered with a gloating and laughing satisfaction. "I've gotcha, at last!"

"Adam!"

She had left her 'phone switched on for a call from someone very different and special. They had spoken once; she had called just to check that Josh had arrived at his hotel, 'their hotel' he had corrected her when she asked him.

"I was beginning to think you were avoiding me…deleting all my calls like that." Adam spoke quickly to prevent any interruptions. "How are you, Marianne?"

"You woke me up." She rested her elbows on raised knees as she sat in the large bed. The spare pillows had been arranged beside her, a shape to lie against and serving as a reminder of how it might be again, quite soon.

"There was a time when you didn't complain," Adam confided.

Besotted fool that I was.

"Wwhhy call me?" she stammered and then, holding the mobile 'phone away from her ear checked that a finger was close to the 'off' button, just in case. She checked the alarm clock. "Why call me at this time of the night…three ayem?"

"Because I'm surprised…just a bit, that you weren't even tempted to call me…to see how it was going."

"I wasn't in the least bit 'tempted'."

That's better, she now thought. I'm not going to let him get to me…if I can manage that.

It soon became clear why he had rung her. To chase after you and to admit that I made a mistake; is that what you mean? She listened to him talk with the arrogant bravado she remembered so well…when Adam knew that he had caught her unawares and unprepared. It gave him an edge, an advantage that she knew he would exploit. Not likely…and I'm not going to admit anything close to how hard it was for me to fill the hours when I was alone.

"After our time…I reckoned you might have given me a thought…how it was…what we said and did to each other. Instead…you deleted my messages, unopened. Have you really changed so much?"

His words held a practised rhythm that were deliberately meant to drip, slowly drip, to provocatively drip pervasive recollections of them together into her wakeful mind.

"Yes I have…I'm fine…we're fine, Adam."

She would try to sound detached in spite of her wildly beating heart; she could feel it in her throat and the sudden light-headedness that overcame her. I've just left one man…a dear man to me now, only to be pursued by another.

"We?" Adam asked her now. "You're fine...I'm okay, though you can tell...from my call...that it would be better... if I had you near me again."

"Sure." She made her reply sound cold and disbelieving.

Adam spoke on with a heavier invasive tone. "So, is the 'we' you refer to, is it really meant to be 'us'?"

"No, don't even think of it! Don't delude yourself! You know it doesn't mean that, not one bit."

"You're alone," he reasoned. "I know that you're alone Marianne...I know that you're alone because...I asked Maggie."

"Maggie? Maggie?" She really listened to him now.

"Yes, Maggie!" He mimicked her voice. "What's the fuss about? You and I, we used to get it together...now you're alone...and lives have to go on, somehow."

Margaret Antrobus was a friend, but she wasn't one of those to have left numerous messages for her yesterday. What did she really know about how her life had been turned upside down by the man?

"Yeah, Maggie." Adam paused then said quickly, with a soft revealing laugh and with the clearest certainty, "we bump into each other...more than occasionally. You're alone again...I was told that...and you're in a strange place." He paused once more to let the words bite deep. "But at least, where you are you can be seen to...you can find what you're after. Am I right?"

"No...and I don't have to listen to any of this." Only, she did nothing to end the call.

"True," he said with breathtaking confidence, but then Adam knew her, far too well. "Only, Marianne...we're talking of things that may still matter, to you at least."

"Don't count on it...there's no need for me to speak to you about anything or...my new life, without you Adam."

"Maybe...at least we've had time to see the rights and wrongs of what happened, on both sides."

"The wrong's on your side, Adam…just yours. I've had plenty of time to realise there was little that was right between us."

Memories of them together intruded.

"I'll have to believe that…or try to. Have you found someone to make it as good as we used to have it…or made it happen?"

"I don't need to listen to any of this, Adam." She would have to break the monotonous repetition of her answers, spoken as if to herself and in a tone that did not conceal the effects his words had upon her.

"No," he said slowly and in teasing disbelief that she meant it. There was a long silence. "We're finished…" he continued with an understanding of how to seduce a further confession from her by simply saying a few words in a voice that trailed off and fell into silence. Seeds were scattered…

"Yes…utterly finished."

"But…you haven't forgotten."

"It's all in the past Adam, the distant past…all that we really had is in the past, and…it wasn't that much. I know that only too clearly now."

"You haven't forgotten…otherwise, you would have hung up by now."

"I knew before it ended, I ended it, that whatever it was we really had…there was no future in it, unlike the one I now see."

"You're alone…gone away to be alone. Why do that?"

"I'm not alone…and there's a future."

"You're talking to me…you're still talking to me." He received no answer but waited, for teasing, intruding, and thought provoking moments. "You're still there Marianne, I know you are. Do you remember," he said wistfully, "how it could be between us? That's what I miss…really miss."

"You found *it* with others…do you *remember* that?"

"Yes, I do" he replied in a cool matter-of-fact voice, "you never let me forget."

"Too bloody right!"

"Easy! It's over...isn't that what you've just said?"

"Yes."

"Still, we had our moments...with others it was never quite as we found it to be."

"That's not what you told me...I was just a *bitch* to you!" She screamed out the word, then gave a gasp of surprise.

Josh...Josh! Memories of that word brought me to you! I needed your touch, a different wondering touch...to help me dispel pervasive thoughts of another man. How undeserving he, Adam, was of me! How abject my behaviour had become with him! But Josh? You have offered me the chance for renewal...the beginning of an altered life, with you or thanks to you and your attention to me.

"Marianne?"

"What...what?" She couldn't even utter his name now yet felt that she had to endure this last wounding and masochistic moment, to rid herself of the hold he still had upon her.

"There were times Marianne...and I remember them all too clearly...when you liked to call out to me...remember? Or...were you too high on what we were doing?"

"Shut up...shut up!" she moaned in a deep exhalation of breath. She didn't want to hear it. Why remind me of that past life? Why do so now?

"I'm helping you to remember, your times...with me. We had our glorious moments. Remember them?" He fell silent, knowing quite clearly that memories would surface, slowly. "I thought so. Is the guy you're with now making all that we had seem so dirty to you? It didn't come across like that to me...at the time!" He gave another knowing laugh. "We shared those moments often...do you remember? Hours, it seemed...of slipping and sliding...resting, then slipping and sliding some more."

"You're crude...you're cruel...and you're out of my life, Adam."

"But still in your mind, as you are in mine."

"Liar...cheat...betrayer!"

He ignored that one. "I'm the guy that really made it happen for you...it's what you kept saying to me...remember?"

"No Adam, I don't remember that bit at all...and you're so wrong, totally and arrogantly wrong."

"I don't think so! I heard the yells...I had the scratches and the bites to prove it...sometimes, where the sun don't always shine." He chuckled at the memory of those moments. "We had very good times, Marianne...I miss them...I even miss you."

"Quite, you *even* miss me...how shallow and truly pathetic you are. Be yourself...with *others*!"

"Maggie then? She's younger...and fitter than I imagined."

"Bastard!"

"Bitch!"

"Cruel...deceiving bastard!"

"Bitch!"

"I'm going..."

"Here, bitch!...Remember that?"

Marianne gasped and took her finger from the button that would put an end to this mental and vocal torture. "Cruel... cruel! So demeaning."

She had never thought to despise him as she did right then.

"We shared the moments, remember what we said? '*Take me, take me right here.*' That's what you said so often...and I only had to say, '*here bitch, now!*' for you to come.'" He laughed at the mental torment that his words would inflict upon her.

The tone had changed; it was one of command, a call that she had all too willingly succumbed to, on many drunken occasions. How can I forget that? Josh? How? How can I forget

I could behave like that, once…and, so very recently? But…but the death of two loving people changed my life and my hopes for it. I was no longer blind to the truth; I felt stronger and faced reality. My eyes were opened and a myopic nightmare was suddenly over.

And then…I met you, I met you Josh, and I knew that life could change. I simply didn't think it could happen…an altered life, and so soon!

"I…I was so right," she said with all the strength that she could summon to make her last reply to his call, she hoped. "I've listened to you just to make certain that I was so right to end it. I've learnt from another…someone I've only just met… it's soon, very soon, but I know one thing. It's not what you do but how you make another feel as a person that counts…for everything! The other person is not an object to play games with and to take pleasure from. You won't understand…it's being as one in mind and body with another person in the deepest way possible."

"Very profound…but it's not what you used to say to me, Marianne…how you've changed…or is it to excuse…to yourself…what we used to share…so often?"

"No…we didn't share anything that was meaningful, or in the least bit *special*."

"See here!" Adam yelled.

"No…no! Not any more! That was my biggest mistake, after keeping you for so long, thinking that we *shared* something. Now, go and play your evil games on someone else. I've had enough, but at least by taking this time to talk to you I've got you out of my system…totally. You're small, in so many ways and…in a way that you can do little to put right."

"Bitch!"

"Yeah!" She laughed now but with trembling lips. "I found out recently from someone new that you're small, really *small* in a place where the sun don't always shine! Bye, you evil *'little'* man…for good!"

Such language! Such hurt! Such wordy rejection of what they had taken of each other in pursuit of pleasure. She had given voice to or listened to such awful and demeaning memories.

She threw the 'phone against the quilted headboard and fell back onto her bed, crying now with large heaving sobs. She had endured the last minutes in one vengeful effort, upon herself, to rid her mind of that younger man. Compared to Josh he was ignorant and cruel; she had inflicted a mental torture on herself by listening and being reminded in Adam's own words of the depravity he had been so capable of. She felt humbled and shamed by the experience and what she had been a partner to.

"Get going!" she said into the coverlet, gripping it tightly, before saying it again and again as she stood up.

"Get going! Get going!"

Her shouts filled the room as she packed; she tore at the clothes that had been put on the hangers and threw them into her case; the contents became a jumble of garments. She didn't care! She'd do anything now to get going and to go back…to go back to Josh. Go back and find him so that she, with his help and loving attention, could find herself. It was so old-fashioned, so against all that her daily life at work and the magazines would have you believe was the 'modern woman'. She suddenly cared nothing for it, nothing at all! Like Josh and his story of money, he had it but it couldn't buy the one thing that mattered to him…to them both.

"To us!" She shouted again.

"Soon…so soon…to us!"

The tears continued and she sobbed with relief.

I didn't say all that I did tonight when I split from Adam. But, I have now! Yeah, the man got to me, he took his pleasure as I did; he reminded me how it was between us, but I sought so much more. He failed to make me a whole person, body and soul. I deluded myself for too long so that now, when a real man comes into my life so unexpectedly I don't know if I should believe it.

"It's so old-fashioned!" she cried out as she zipped up the bag, checked she had everything and went to the door. She gave the room a farewell glance and stepped outside.

That night's reception staff was reassured; no criticism was implied by her choice to leave at such an odd hour; their establishment was wonderful they were told as she settled the bill. Soon, driving along the wanly lit canal-side she felt calmer. There was the outer self, the person shown to the world, and then there was the inner soul, the human spirit that only she knew how to tend.

I've known it all along and had constant reminders, even in those 'squalid' times with Adam of how it ought to be, only with him what I truly felt and sought was wasted. He was an aberration and I've paid a heavy price to learn my lesson or to be reminded how it could be, with the right one beside me. It involves a true partner, a fellowship, call it a union of spirit that dear mother and father held onto even after death.

"I have to believe in it…I can believe in it…I have to dare and believe it will all work out, me finding my way, with Josh."

XIV

The traffic lights were all set at amber, winking a warning that extreme care in relaxed out-of-hours circumstances was called for. She drove carefully and marvelled at how the route was recognisable, in spite of the turmoil of thoughts that possessed her. Josh would be asleep; she had not called him in her wish to be on the road and heading back to where she could find comfort.

Every moment spent in each other's company seemed to be driven by force of immediate circumstance; they should seize an opportunity. During the sea crossing he had left her, uncertain of her feelings or interest. She had seen him, on the motorway; they had parted once more only to be re-united; one event had been the genesis of others. She could not account for their good fortune; she simply seized the moment and believed in benign providence.

So little was known about him, where he lived apart from a place name; no image of 'home' for him could be conjured up as she drove south. He was unemployed yet he had money; its possession held no mystery for him. Josh had even told her, so soon into their relationship, that all the money in the world could not acquire what he now sought.

The roads were clear; even that observation held its own significance as she took in familiar landmarks that he had noted for her to help find the way when she had first travelled this route...to get away from him. Her feigned indifference of that moment had deserted her, so soon after her arrival in Amsterdam.

"I'm going back, for this one last time...I'm going back. No more separations!"

There he was!

There's Snopake, that lovely man, Josh!

The electric window hummed and she called out to him as he jogged along. What a time to be up-and-about, it was only six thirty. I know a different kind of exercise and it's far more companionable she told herself.

"Going my way, Mister?" she laughed out looking at him then at the road before her. The car had slowed to a crawl.

"You're early!" he called back and gradually eased off his jogging pace.

"You know me." The engine was stilled and Marianne got out of the car and ran to him. "It's not a moment too soon...I wanted to be here with you and nowhere else!"

"I have to admit," he said holding her face in his hands and simply staring at her, "that I had trouble sleeping. It didn't seem right to be alone anymore."

"Me too. I've finally woken up from a nightmare."

"We'll have to show each other how it can be. Will you join me?"

"Yes! Yes! Yes!" she called out laughing once more and with her face raised to meet his kisses as if in sublime jubilation that she had found her true man. "You know what they say? 'Amor vincit omnia'."

"So soon?" he smiled before he kissed her once more.

Marianne nodded her reply against his lips and held his sweaty body to her.

"Show me how it can truly be," she was able to whisper, at last. "Don't stop until I tell you."

"As if I'd do that, lovely lady."

Josh broke free from her embrace and beckoned for Marianne to follow him.

☙

LOVE CUTS DEEP

I

"I can't help you, I regret to say." The consultant gave her a considerate smile. "These preliminary consultations serve one important function, to tell a prospective client whether we will undertake certain elective procedures or not."

"You just come right out and tell me don't you…Neil?"

She had seen his name on the door to the consulting room; now it was proclaimed with the lettering neatly picked out in gold on the mahogany stand placed before him on his desk. It was all very swish and to the point.

"Yes…I'm sorry to put it like that, but…yes."

"And…it's my choice, so I can do what I want and where I want."

"That's true Mrs Nance." He closed her file. "It's your choice where you seek treatment…and it's my decision whether I can be of any help."

"I heard you the first time."

"Okay," he said giving a little smile on hearing her direct way of speaking.

Marla Nance was the name neatly written on the label. On the inside cover was a digital photograph, on glossy paper. It showed no blemishes, no disfiguring marks or lines to warrant a closer look or examination. There was nothing to all outward appearances to keep her with him. She didn't take the hint that their consultation was over; he would have to re-phrase his dismissal of her case. It was the least he could do; at the hourly rate he charged it had to appear that he remained attentive to her call for help to the very end of the allotted time.

"The transformations that we achieve here," he felt obliged to continue and re-opening her file, "are often medically demanding and may involve invasive surgery and therapy quite different from what you believed we undertook at this clinic."

"I had invasive therapy from my husband, of a sort…only, he wasn't invasive often enough."

Marla gave him a fixed grin but her remark failed to shock him. There! She saw that lovely soft smile again but his eyes asked of her, what's a looker like you doing in my place?

He would have to respond with vernacular turns of phrase.

"We don't do that kind of surgery either...new fangled danglers, new breasts or enlargements. We don't undertake cosmetic surgery of that kind at all."

"So, what *exactly* do you do here, Neil? I took it from the information handed out that your clients could find the treatment they required or wanted *right here*, in this clinic."

"Not *'wanted'*, as I think you mean it. No," he went on calmly, "no, we *mend* broken bodies not perceptions. I try to rebuild self-worth in my patients...or referrals, after accidents or to restore broken spirits after a physically and psychologically shattering event has been suffered. And then...if we can, we help to mend or alleviate the distress and discomfort of deformities...let's call them accidents of birth." His eyes scanned the voluptuous attractive woman seated before him. "If I may say so, Mrs Nance, you suffer none of these justifications for being referred to me or to us here."

Her file was closed and this time he placed his hands upon it to reinforce the decision he had reached. He met her gaze for an instant.

Marla looked over his shoulder. "Who's that little boy, in that picture?"

"What? I mean, pardon?" The question had the desired effect, changing the subject completely.

She could study him for only a moment, take in the slender face, the neat close-cut dark hair and the smooth skinned lightly tanned face. Sure, he was older but the difference between them wasn't so great. He wasn't what people in her line of work called handsome, but then they preened themselves to meet an image others had of them, or they believed would help them to fit in. Neil wasn't like that at all, not this man, the doctor.

He seemed at ease in that respect; he didn't put on any act now that he had a 'model' sitting before him. She'd simply put that down on the registration card, under 'occupation', to justify...no, to *explain* her attendance at the clinic.

"Who's that little boy, in the photo...there on the shelf behind you? Is it your son?"

Neil turned in the swivel chair for only an instant; it was an automatic reaction to a bright enquiring stare.

"Yes," he answered unable to resist a moment's small talk.. "Yes...and what about you? Do you have any children?"

"No...and I don't have a husband either." He hadn't sought that item of information but on impulse she decided to volunteer it. "It's one of the reasons I came here...to rediscover the trick." She looked from him to the photograph; Marla would see only a fleeting likeness with my son, Neil thought. Jamie, my boy, had taken after his mother.

"How old is he, your son?"

Neil closed his eyes tight shut for only a second and held his breath before exhaling slowly.

"He would have been twenty this year. He...Jamie died shortly after that picture was taken."

Neil stared at her. I was a youngster when the boy had been born to me. What did I know then? I was still learning, of life and love, of sharing and of giving to others.

"Oh! Oh! I'm sorry." Marla met his unwavering look upon her for an instant.

She relaxed and forsook the rigid posture she had held herself in since her arrival. He could be made to talk of other things after all and she'd have to find a way to persuade him or others in the clinic to help her '*get sorted*'.

"Don't be. It's my concern, and mine alone. His death provoked me into doing this work...mending broken or injured bodies, not egos." He stood up and turned away to stare out of the window, remaining silent for a moment longer. "I'm sorry to have spoken to you like that...so directly."

"You told me the truth...even if I didn't want to hear it all, Neil."

He faced her and gave a gentler smile. "I'm sorry not to be able to be of any help. I can write and advise you who may be able to undertake the cosmetic procedure you're seeking...but, as you know it carries a cost."

"That's not a problem for me...it's the results that count."

"I see. To me...and from the brief conversation we've had it is not what I see on the outside that should count for everything, at least not in your case."

"It's about perceptions...about how others see me. That's why I'm here."

"Really? So, it's not about how you see yourself? Wouldn't that be a fairer, or more honest, thing to say or admit to?"

"Up to a point! Now, there's no sense in talking anymore if there's nothing for you to do about how I look."

"Or feel...don't forget that," he said trying to coax Marla to think through all of the reasons for her attendance at his weekly assessment day.

"I'll start with how I look, got that? It's the reason for me driving over here, why I came to you...to your clinic. The rest may follow...*will* follow," she finished with greater certainty.

Neil looked at her again with unmoving studious eyes.

"You have a natural beauty and fulsome attractiveness...if I may put it like that...which has been your genetic inheritance," he said at last and to her surprise. "You...you are who you are. Don't change or tamper with anything because of some passing fashion...that would be my advice. It's something you can take away from our meeting."

"Yes, I hear you. Only...only my husband exchanged me for a passing woman he fancied. So, it's my decision. What I do may get me the attention I've lost and I don't need from him. Those days are over, long gone."

"Yes," he said slowly, "it is entirely your decision, only think carefully about it. For what it's still worth, in my opinion it would be a shame to meddle with what you've been given and cared for." He saw Marla's smile brighten as if it had been a while since she had been paid such an open compliment. He walked round his neatly ordered desk and as a prompt for Marla to leave him. "I'm sorry to be unable to find a special remedy that might be of help to you."

"I'm not asking for any special remedy, Neil…just do what's needed, by my reckoning!"

"Okay," he almost sighed. "I've given you my answer on that. Now, is there anything else?"

"No…we've talked," she observed briskly. "I didn't like what you had to say but I've got the message…or your take on things. I should go carefully…have I got that bit right?"

"Yes, you're right." He opened the door of his consulting room for her. "It's your last chance…any more questions before you go?"

"Yes, tell me what happens to the case notes, the pictures and everything? You took a few."

"I can destroy them all and…I'll only keep a card to record that we met…and that after one consultation it was decided you couldn't be helped."

"I can be, only it's not going to be here…it's a shame. That's what I think."

"True…that's true."

"Yes, and I'm sorry for that." She held out a beautifully manicured hand. "Well, good bye. Shred all the papers… simply keep the card. Will you do that, just for me?"

"Yes, of course, for you…and any client. They only have to ask."

"And I have." Marla checked again, just to be sure nothing had been left behind, next to the chair she had been seated in. "Well then…it's good bye?"

"Yes, it's good bye. Let me know if you need any names that I can refer you to?"

"Yes…I'll speak to my friend, the one who brought me to see you. Goodbye then, Neil. Lovely name by the way…it's also very posh. Neil Allman-Brown, it sounds very grand."

"What's in a name, Marla?" he smiled and looked unwaveringly at her.

"Okay, okay." She waved her hand but not out of impatience or to swat away his remark. She returned his smile. "You've told me once before, or are you making me admit it? Beauty's only skin deep?"

"I couldn't have said it better myself," he laughed.

"But you did."

"Maybe. Now, please excuse me…I have to prepare for my next consultation."

"Take care, Neil."

He met her gaze as he held the handle of the door to his room.

"I will…usually it's me who says that to a patient. So, you take care with what you decide upon…it's you that counts, Marla, you the person not just how you look. Okay?"

"Yeah, okay…very deep, what you've just said. Do they all get to hear it…everyone you meet here?"

"No…or in different words. Everyone's special."

"I'll remember that."

Her reply indicated that she'd think about the words the man before her had just spoken. She hadn't heard them said in quite the direct and honest way he had done; it was as if he'd been speaking to a child but she knew precisely what he intended by the manner of his talking. He was communicating, expressing what he felt person-to-person, nothing more. He wasn't trying to lecture; he was speaking out what he felt, making a simple observation as he saw it.

Still, she couldn't keep from thinking, Neil's a doctor… correction, a consultant no less, so he probably spoke to everyone like that even if he did make it sound special…just for me.

II

"Well? Will he see to you or not?"

Betty came right out and asked her, before they had even stepped outside the doors of the clinic. Marla walked briskly to their car before answering.

"There's a thought, the touch of class to my skin." She looked at her friend but shook her head. "No…it's the wrong clinic, but the right guy. Closed in on himself though."

"How'd you work that one out?"

"What he said, and what's happened to him. It didn't take much more to figure it all out." Yes, her questions had caught him unawares.

Betty rattled on.

"They do private work too, girl! Where've you been all this time? You just need to ask the right questions…the clinic's the legit face to the world, a front. Settle on the right deal and they'll do it for you, quick and discreet if that's how you want it."

"Got experience of it all, have you?"

"Well, no…" Betty looked crestfallen. "So?"

"So I don't think he's the kind of man to do 'trades' and get won over. I saw it in his eyes and heard it in how he spoke to me. Neil's very different from the blokes we mix with…"

"Oh? Tell me more?"

"No. It's done with." Marla opened the driver's door to the 'wagon' as she fondly called the four-wheel drive vehicle. "It's not about quick fixes and an easy earner for him."

"Principles got in the way, did they?"

"You could say that…he also made me stop and think."

"Not too long, I hope?" Betty asked with only conversational concern. "You've been goin' on about these changes long enough."

"I want it done right! Let's leave talking about it…for now, okay?"

"Yeah, okay!" Betty pouted in annoyance at the turn the conversation had taken. "He really got to you, the doc, did he?"

"You could say that."

"And?"

"If I drive maybe it'll stop me thinking and talking about it…and of him, that Neil fella."

She'd do that, drive the wagon, in spite of the turmoil of thoughts stirred up within her.

"Its as much *how* he said things to me as *what* he said that made me think twice."

Betty sighed. "I hear you, girl…I hear you."

Marla fired up the engine. "I hope so. Now, where to, *girl*?"

Neil moved the picture to the top of a small bookcase, to a spot that he could observe but a client could not pay heed to when they spoke.

The picture only prompted questions, like Marla's of a few minutes ago. Wrong! Marla asked it straight out; there was no preamble just the wide-eyed stare on Jamie's image then onto me. And what did I do? I blabbed out all that worked on me at the mention of my boy's name. She really got to you…your usual reserve simply vanished.

Yes, fool!

Still, she's brightened my day.

He looked at the digital picture of her once more. It seemed a shame to shred it and to dispense with an image of fulsome womanhood in a clinging dress.

I've done the right thing, saying 'no' to her. Why mess with her form in the hope that I will help her find what she's looking for? The knife, some suction, any treatment wouldn't take away the hurt from what truly ails her. Rejection. Sure, I could lift and firm, reduce or remodel the press of flesh so beautifully and engagingly wrapped within the close fitting dress she had worn.

There! I can't erase the picture of her in that dress! And...

I simply can't imagine what other passing fancy would have so beguiled her husband that he should leave her. She'd made a flippant comment but I knew Marla was trying to relax or keep herself from telling me all about an errant husband who'd fancied someone else's body, not hers, or not enough... so, she almost said the first thing that came into her head.

The record card was removed from behind the pictures of Marla and he flicked the staple into the waste paper bin nearby. She was different, oh yes; Marla was not like his usual patient. He had been honest with her, to the core; he mended people, like the helpless and tragic victims of accidents or of birth; he strove to make good the legacy of a deformity as far as his skills and their creators allowed. He could do something innovative and offer by his own hands an emotional palliative for what had befallen those who came to the clinic and to see him.

He had two like-minded partners, both female and as dedicated to their surgical skills as he was. They brought conviction to the smallest acts of making good what God, a cocktail of genes or fellow man had inflicted upon those referred to them. But for him it was an escape from a suppressed and mostly unspoken reality, a truth about his deepest self that Marla's few words had exposed, all too briefly. He had almost lost it, taken in by the engaging look of her eyes and Marla's direct speaking. And then...there was the mass of blonde hair and those earrings! They hung so engagingly, those glinting crucifixes on thin chain, first visible then concealed by each twist of her head.

There was none of the modesty or restraint that he would expect from someone who wore a religious token. Religion seemed so far removed from the life he imagined of her. She had her own faith, a belief in the body beautiful and the maintenance of a beacon of attraction to man's eye. He had tried to make her think of other reasons for one person to love another, or for her to love herself and respect what she had been given and nurtured.

Fool! Why go and tell her it was the inner person that counted for everything, well, almost everything, when what she really wanted was to feel comfortable again with her looks? Marla wanted to feel at ease within her own body but you go and ask why mess with what is eye-catching to someone else's eye, the right person's gaze upon her? It's only your opinion. She came to see you and to part with her money…and, what do you do? You persuade her to think twice! Morality over venality, was that it?

Yes.

It had struck a chord, faintly in her and more strongly and believably in him though God did not enter his own reckoning too often. He had seen enough over the years of what men, and women, could do to each other; he hoped that he had mended a few souls in the course of his work and its aftermath. Only so much was within his skills to make good.

Why meddle with that woman's body, Marla's body, that beautiful and attractive body? It was her choice, you said so only you had to offer advice. Was it professional or personal, the source of your considerate words?

He took the file with him and met his next appointment.

Yes, he answered the practice secretary, destroy the file, only keep the record card.

The rest of Marla Nance, what she looked like and sought to change, that's stored in my memory.

III

The caller was insistent.

"I've waited two days! There's been no letter, no e-mails and no 'phone calls. Nothing! Not a damn thing! I had expected Neil…Mr Allman-Brown I mean…I'd expected him to have called or written to me by now."

"I'm sorry for the delay, Mrs Nance."

"Marla…let me speak to him, can I do that? Please?"

"No, I'm sorry that's not possible. He's in surgery…away from the clinic."

"So? When *can* I speak to him?"

"I can let him know that you called Mrs Nance."

"Just call me Marla…Misses is out and Nance is my married name…only I'm not married anymore, or soon won't be."

There, she'd gone and blabbed it out. May as well, I've got to get used to the idea.

"I'll let Mr Allman-Brown know that too. In the meantime I will see if the list of clinics he suggests you refer to can be sent out. I know he always wants to send a letter with such papers…"

"To show he cares?"

Amanda the duty receptionist waited before giving her reply. "Yes…it's also a case of being polite. Now, if you'll excuse me, Mrs Nance? There are other calls I have to answer…I'm holding back the tide on my own at the moment." She gave a reassuring laugh.

"At least you're busy…so, you can turn my business away!"

Marla wasn't sure her closing remark had been heard. Still, she'd got the thoughts that had provoked her irritation at not speaking to him out of her system.

"Hey!" The silken robe was drawn tighter. It's not so late… it don't matter how late it is she thought on hearing his 'hello'. She knew it was Neil, *'the man who feels'* as Betty teasingly called him.

"I'm ringing to say that a letter and a list of helpful and very good clinics is on its way to you." He sounded business-like and had quickly dispensed with the social niceties of greeting.

"Are you annoyed with me…cross for chasing you up about the list?"

"No."

"Good." She could answer bluntly too, only, it didn't last. "I merely wanted to follow up our meeting…Neil."

"And there I was thinking that was my job," he replied with a soft chuckle.

"Or mine…I haven't forgotten what you told me."

"I gave an opinion, Marla. That's what you pay people like me for. You can now decide what to do, you will have my letter very soon." He gave a yawn and followed it up with an apology on its fading breath. "Sorry it's so late, only I came back to the clinic and found a note saying that you'd called."

"I didn't make it sound that urgent."

"No."

"Why call me then?" Here we go again, she thought, one word chitchat or wordy to-and-fro between us.

"I simply wanted to…and to clear up any concerns you may have."

"You know what they are Neil, you wrote them down in my file."

"Shredded…it was cut to pieces, all of it, just as soon as you left…and as you wanted it to be."

"Everything?" She was at it now.

"Yes, everything…just as you asked. Remember?"

"Pictures and all?" She couldn't help but lift her voice. This may go on for a while so she settled back against the headboard of the large bed. Wasted, them silk covers if you're on your own. Calm down, girl.

"Why yes."

"Oh!"

"Oh what? I still have a memory you know, even at my age." He gave a laugh, "Sorry."

"For what? For having a nice laugh?"

"I'd better go, Marla," he answered in a deeper and more serious voice; he had been reminded of the purpose for his contacting her, no doubt. "My call seems to be changing…"

"From a purely doctor to patient call….to something else, you mean?" She was delighted that Neil was now simply chatting to her.

"Yes," he said with a sigh, "something like that. Now, I really am going."

"Back to home and family? Very cosy…I'll appreciate your call even more now."

"I didn't say that, did I?"

"No…no…no you didn't."

"Cosy for those that have such an arrangement."

"Yeah." She felt unusually compliant, taken aback by the sudden change of mood and his tone. So quick the change, from light to dark, hard and business like to soft and close…or, closer.

"Bye Marla. You'll have the information you're after soon enough."

"Don't hang up!" She sat up and yelled out his name. The line was still open. "Neil? Neil?"

"Yeah?" he said after a moment's pause.

"Sorry. It's none of my business…or rather you aren't. Thanks for calling me, Neil."

"It's okay." She waited and listened…is that all he's going to say? "Marla? Don't speak out everything that comes into your head…not to me….or not yet. Will you do that for me, please?"

"Sure...yeah, sure." She answered with deliberate calm. "Anything else, before you go?"

"No," he paused, "not particularly."

The line was quite still.

"Neil...are you still there?"

It would take some time to get used to his manner of speaking or dealing with her, if there was to be any time allowed to them or any relationship developed out of these fractured exchanges.

"Yes...I'm still here."

"What else did you have to say?"

"I've spent a long and tiring day mending a young girl's face and chest. The poor girl had no other options available, her beauty' was smashed by a boy showing off in a car. He drove into her...but got away with it, walked away from the crash. He'll live with the knowledge of what he's done. She will have more to cope with...and that's what I do my best to help and overcome...the legacy of a few seconds of madness."

She heard him yawn, long and deep. "Neil?"

"Sorry...sorry about that. I've rattled on long enough."

"No, it's okay."

"Yes, it's far too long. Sorry once again for making my call so late. I'm knackered, totally done in...I'll have to go. Take care in what you do, Marla, and of yourself, promise me that at least."

"Neil?"

"Yes?" She heard the stifled yawn once more.

"Sleep well?"

"Thanks...yes, I will thanks." He laughed ruefully. "Not for long though, I'll soon be back in theatre."

She lay back on the bed and closed her eyes, recalling all that she could of how the man looked and how he talked to her. Neil just said things that she just knew would come back to mind at the oddest times. He has his ways...*just* has his ways. They're so different from what I find out in the men that enter my life, then leave it just as quickly.

"You can fix people just by talking to them Neil, can't you?"

"It's been known to happen," he replied evenly. "Telling some people they're beautiful…or as nature intended isn't always part of the day job…it's not a skill that I have developed too much or use often enough."

"You're wrong Neil. You have used it…that's why I rang, that's why I called you."

"Oh! Oh, right…I see! Well," he chuckled, "I'll have to keep practising 'til I get it just right."

"Do you understand what I'm saying?"

"Yes Marla…I told you the truth. Don't be so surprised, or…are you?"

"Yeah, you could say that." A confiding laugh escaped her lips. "You'd better not say anymore or I'll keep ringing you."

"And that would never do," he said in mock seriousness, "would it?"

She couldn't help smiling at that. "Don't push me!"

"I won't. Just think it all through. I didn't say all that I did because you might become a patient or a client of this clinic or of someone else."

"I know, and that's what's so crazy about it all."

"Yeah, but that's life for you. What I said to you was a simple truth…don't mess with what you've been given, blessed with even."

They were his last words. She had listened as Neil thanked her for listening to him and sharing his thoughts on the day's work. He endured torment of his own she surmised from the expectations of the young girl he had so tenderly spoken of and in response to the anxieties of her parents. She had worked it out before he told her; the question they might all ask was, 'who would be restored to them' by his hands and gift of knowledge?

You've treated me differently and made my day. There was no pain or discomfort, and I still see the same person in the mirror, but for a while you made me feel like another person, someone I don't allow to be seen.

"News Girl! Great News!"

Betty's excited voice distracted her from the divorce papers scattered over the table. What passed as her breakfast had been left untouched.

"Really?"

The lawyer's letter had spelt it out for her. Reading between the lines it was more of a 'carve up' than a settlement or sharing of the marital spoils. Still, she thought easily, the house is mine and all paid-up. Take it and the cash, get on with your life was what the lawyer man had told her; it was no good having your name constantly in the newspapers, *'the seamier Sunday rags'* as he had described them. Still, they had served a purpose; they'd got her the payment Eddie was so reluctant to agree to. A few hints to them on where to lift the odd stone to see what crawled underneath had done the trick. Eddie soon paid up.

He had cursed and used language not fit for a lady's ears but she'd won her share. Messy, and not the way two people would normally behave towards each other, not after all that they had endured in the wake of his dodgy business deals. She sighed.

"Yes, really," her friend said doubtfully, wondering about the lack of interest held in Marla's voice. "What's happened?"

"Skin work is it? Is that the news you've got for me?" She made it sound as if she wasn't too bothered by all that Betty had to tell her.

Her friend cursed.

"What's up? I thought you'd be chuffed with the news…at least it's brightened the start to my day."

"Good. I've got effing divorce papers to deal with, that's what's up."

The modelling and 'skin work', her words for the calendar and magazine features, was not as it used to be. It was not like the early days, her younger days, but those times had taught her something that would last her fading looks. The doctor, that man Neil got that bit right. It's whom I am that counts now and I make of my looks what I can, to suit the passing of the years.

"Are you still there, Marla?"

"Yes, just dealing with a few things…in my head." Leave it, don't tell Bettina what's bothering you; it's my look out now what I do and whom I do it with. It'll have to be someone special and new, out of the usual crowd of folks I end up with. "What've you got girl?"

"Work, for both of us. Your idea has come off, the mag' liked it. Gerry's rung me to say there's a preliminary shoot in a couple of weeks. He'll call you later about it! Just think, quite a few grand for the pictures!"

"Yeah…"

"Well! Thought I'd tell you! Gotta go girl! Gotta get the body checked over and soothed…there's only one man to *really* do that for me."

"Freddy again?"

"Yeah Freddy. I only need a couple of hours with him to feel a whole lot better about myself. I'll be ready for the shoot after a few sessions of his special care…and oiled up hands of course."

"Mind how you go then, Bet…" She couldn't quite join in with her friend's good humour.

"Not with Freddy, not with him I won't, no chance!" She gave the happiest laugh Marla's mood seemed to allow.

"Okay…I hear you."

"Bye! Gerry'll give you the details of the photo shoot…you mind how you go too! See you soon!"

She was gone.

The lawyer's letter and all the sundry papers were swept up and stuffed into a bulging tagged envelope. She wrote 'Sorted' on the outside next to the label that read 'bust up', smiling at the choice of words. Bettina was unaware of the settlement she had reached and the taking to her heart of the words to move on. The diary was not filled with new assignments so the 'shoot' was a useful start to a new life, a life to be lived alone…for a while at least. And why not do the session? It bought some time; it offered an opportunity to think through if any cosmetic meddling with her figure could be endured. Neil, that doctor Neil, seems to have got to me; she reflected on the possibilities.

"Misses Nance?"

"Yes, Misses Nance…" for only a few weeks more. She answered hesitantly not recognising the caller's number that came up on the screen of her mobile 'phone.

"I'm calling on behalf of Mr Allman-Brown."

"You mean Neil?"

"Why yes," came the discreet reply. Amanda on reception there wouldn't know how she had got on with him. "I was asked to call and see if our list of suggested clinics was of any use to you…it's merely a courtesy call to follow up our letter of a few weeks ago."

"Well, out of courtesy I'll tell you that I've been to see a couple…no, three! They were on the list. I haven't decided on anything yet…I've been far too busy tell him, uhm…on a special piece of work." Call it my swan song, she thought. "I'll have to see how things are after that and over the coming weeks."

"Thank you, I'll pass on the news."

"Such as it is."

"Yes…thank you for your time."

"And thank you for calling…" She could get used to this politeness, this gentility of dealing with one another; it hadn't been a strong feature of the 'shoot' that had just been completed.

"I'll let Mr Neil know."

"Mr Neil?" Marla laughed, "Mr Neil?"

It was Amanda's turn to laugh. "Okay…yes, that's how we call him…when we speak to clients if they address him by his Christian name."

"Never mind me…I'm sorry to keep you. Thanks for the call, and my regards, to Mr Neil."

"Yes, I will…we're used to doing things in a certain way," Amanda felt obliged to explain. "We can't get too familiar."

"I understand you, thanks. Still, give my regards to Neil." It was probably not done and far too familiar but she would put the message out there, let it sink in with him.

"Will you let him know when you have decided on a clinic? We don't need to know the details of your treatment, just where you have decided to go. Neil…Mr Neil, he will want to have it recorded on the card. It simply completes the picture…that's what he said to me."

"Ask him to call me if he *simply* wants to know, will you do that for me?"

<u>*IV*</u>

His desk was meticulously tidy; files awaiting his attention were neatly placed at its centre. He was accustomed to a quick review of the case notes or referrals for treatment on the evening before a new working day. But, this late afternoon was different; he would merely prepare for the coming week; there were no patients or clients to see tomorrow. His Friday was to be a rare day off, so he could plan for a long weekend and make the best of it.

The diary was quite clear he noted, flicking the pages just to make sure; there were no dinner parties to attend, no drinks do's, and no lunches. He could catch up on some sleep and follow a relaxing and diverting pastime. There would be no voices, no chirruping of mobile 'phones, no cars…just silence and the glorious stillness outside the canopy. Gliding - he would seek that peace to recover his emotional sense of equilibrium and reflect, briefly, upon all that he had achieved or reached out to and nearly grasped in the past few days and even weeks. His mind would gradually clear to leave him with a palpable sense of deep relaxation. It would be a satisfying end to times spent devoted to his skills that he hoped would be of help to others. Such times took a physical and mental toll upon him.

His patients could not see this; he controlled himself and suppressed all that moved him until he was out of sight, away from company and prying eyes or gossipy mouths.

High above the ground, soaring and swooping, drifting along or propelled by unseen thermal currents he was quite alone. Only…only he *'knew'*, he sensed keenly the presence of another by his shoulder and he would be stilled. He was unconcerned by his companion's attendance upon him. He was closer, loosened of any earthly ties and nearer to Jamie, his only boy. Yes, he was encased in a contraption that brought him skywards, a man-made device that defied gravity and brought him closer to the spirit of his creation, the product of an earth-bound union with a woman. She could not accept the lot that he believed was theirs.

Annie had a life to live and a duty to her kind as she saw it, to bring life into the world, to conceive and nurture a child. They had found each other and loved; there was innocence, a heartbreaking ignorance of one inherent and potentially terminal genetic defect in them both. They consummated their union joyfully, became doting parents only to be torn apart on account of their son's genetic destiny; their Jamie was to pass from this life to the next with merely the fleeting touch and kiss of doting parents to his skin. Their boy had been taken in the 'blink of an eye', that was how it had felt to them. He had mourned Jamie's loss and been forsaken by a wife who chafed at and finally broke with the ethical bonds that he lived and practised medicine by.

Oh yes, he could understand another's motives all too clearly, to seek the conception of a healthy child and too follow a path that did not lead to the premature death of an innocent ignorant life if a defect was discovered. In Annie's case that 'choice' was not to accept their lot and remain childless or having to face the termination of a life, of only a few weeks, until a viable human being was conceived. It had been for the best only he couldn't bring himself to fully accept the reasons for the choice that she had made. He had been discarded in the determination of another's life, Annie's.

The telephone message was held in his stilled hand. Amanda's note, in clear and beautiful handwriting had lain on the top of the files, under the glass paperweight. The name written upon it and the number were only too recognisable.

'Marla Nance said she would answer your call if you simply wanted to know which clinic she was going to attend. Sorry,' the postscript said, *'they're her words not mine! Enjoy your weekend. A.'*

It's the sort of thing Marla would say, he thought as he tapped the edge of the note against his fingers and thought over what he might do. The woman was so economical with her words and the sentiments she expressed…so utilitarian in her outlook. Was that it? Had he read that into her request to be treated at the clinic so many weeks ago? Yes…or, possibly. To refuse her request had been his immediate instinctive and morally founded reaction. Oh yes, Marla was undoubtedly utilitarian in her outlook. Give thanks and bless the hands that feed you or looked after you, don't thank those that made you…or was it Him? Him, the God that Jamie was now, hopefully, entrusted to.

He gave a deep sigh.

Your father and mother had been of no real use, Jamie. They cared and they toiled, helplessly, but you died...the operation failed. The life giving slice and mend did not restore you to us. We lost you...I lost you...and because of that I found a new purpose to my life. I mend people now; I restore and bring to them a healing touch as best as I and devoted helpers can achieve with our knowledge.

Another sigh escaped from his lips.

The views I hold are unfashionable in a seemingly God-less world. I know he's near me, my Jamie's closer to me when I am freed of earth's shackles. Ignore gravity and a man-made contraption...my glider, for a minute!

So, what am I to make of an attractive woman, Marla? Is she shaped as nature intended or has she followed the fashion, the utilitarian ethic of an earth-bound life by believing it's 'all about me', it's all that we, as humans, can expect to experience. So, if I want to pay you...go on! Help me to become another person, or help me to feel that I am, at last, the real person I am supposed to be under my smoothed and tucked, firmed and cleansed skin.

Compared to my Jamie she has everything. I simply told Marla that I treat the sick, in mind and body, the really sick or injured. I don't go in for treating those with misplaced envy or excess, or deformity, unless their lives really depend upon it. No, I don't tend to their God given but all too human shell because they don't like what stares out at them in the mirror.

I also have my beliefs and a code of practice that I *have* to follow; the fact is I don't talk about them. Well, not too much...or unless I am provoked into doing so by a lovely shape that seeks perfection.

So Marla Nance, I can not help you in that way. It's an altogether different type of care and attention that you need.

The note with her number was put to one side. Later, I'll ring it later. First, I need to clear my head of this introspection and re-discover normality. Ethics and the inner self are only a part of me, of any one, even of Marla Nance. The body beautiful is only a vessel...it's what I said to her. What it contains should be beyond measure.

"Amanda left me your message."

"And?" was her unconcerned reply, "have you simply filed away my card? I told her that I haven't found anyone to help me."

"You will Marla, there should be no rush...I was talking of your well-being and I meant it. You'll find the right clinic to put your trust in...and, to undertake the procedures you are looking for."

"I know," she said interrupting him, "I know all that. I read about it too. I found the right clinic and the right people; only, they seem to have a hang up about me...or its what I want them to do for me that gets to them. It seemed to get to you."

"Yeah, I know what you mean. Scruples can get in the way."

He spoke easily, thinking that he had been around long enough to know what his work should mean to him.

"What? You don't believe in helping someone like me. Is that it?"

"No Marla, that's not it at all. I help where I think it's needed." He fell silent to allow his reply to register. "Tell me? What have you been doing since I last saw you...since I sent you that list of names?"

She made him wait now.

"Working," she said at last and quickly. "I set up an assignment for people that I know and for myself. It's a specialised type of work. You prepare manically for a few weeks because the people that pay you are a bit picky on who they want. So, it's been a busy time."

Neil heard the lightness of her voice as if she was bored to tell him of it.

"Good…and what else?"

"And nothing…and it's finished with, Neil…it's over and done with."

"What now?"

"Nothing or rather something else…I move on to something else and hopefully very new. I really haven't thought it all through yet…there's things to deal with and people to clear away out of my life…I've got to get through all of that first."

Yes, she would spell it out, as much for his benefit as her own. She was surprised he had called for a chat. She hadn't left the message with any expectation of Neil ringing her at all. She'd left it simply to 'wind him up' and his reaction was unexpectedly soon and not as she imagined it might be played out between them.

"It's late Neil, to still be at work."

"Yeah, and it's becoming a habit to ring you so late. Truth is I didn't think you'd be in to answer."

"Well, I am and I did."

"Yes…is everything in your life settled now?"

"Yes," she replied in a voice that left little doubt of her certainty. "Will that go onto my card? Will it read '*divorced*'?

"No," he answered with a soft sigh that she could just make out. "I'm sorry you had to go through all of that. Breaking things seems so easy compared to the other side of it…making good."

"I wouldn't know. It seems I've got a lot to learn, again. Got any ideas, have you, where I should start?"

"Sure…I've been there and done it."

"I know…sorry. It was a bitchy thing for me to say. It's far too late to talk about it now…some other time, maybe?"

"Yes. Tell me, Marla?"

"Hm?"

"Do you like flying?"

"Yes…as long as there's a drinks trolley and at least two engines." She joked but her tone held a hint of her wish to hear more about why he'd asked.

"Have you ever been gliding…been in a glider?"

"No. There's only room for a hip flask…and it's self service."

"Yes, very true."

They both laughed.

"Why? Why ask, Neil?"

"I…I wondered if…if you'd keep me company? Spend some time with me at the gliding club…I'm inviting you to keep me company…I'll take you gliding, we leave everything behind for a few hours…we can be together, just the two of us."

"No…it's nuts! Do you think I'm nuts?" She continued to reply as if nothing would persuade her to do such a foolish thing, but…she couldn't quite disguise the faint possibility of being persuaded to change her mind.

"No…and don't keep on at me about clinics and changing the way you look."

"Oh! Oh?"

"Do I have to spell it out for you…yet again?" He gave a laugh that unsettled her for only a moment.

"No. Why ask…why ask me out?"

"You answered my call."

Good one, Neil. "Meaning?"

"You're at home."

"So what? It's late…and it's not all fun what I do, to get by."

"Okay…no," he acknowledged. "I've never asked…"

"It's written, simply…on the card."

"Tell me…simply, it's better that way."

"You don't know or haven't guessed? You haven't sussed yet why a person like me should come to your clinic…your recommended clinic by the way, a place of discretion and understanding, to get some help?"

"No Marla. Maybe I'd better think it through to discover just what it is that you do and that makes you come to me."

"As Bettina would say, 'where've you been mate?' only she'd say 'girl' to me."

"Where've you been, Marla?" His voice now had an interrogatory edge.

"In the mags…" She stopped herself from blabbing it all out then, after a moment's thought, she decided to get it over with. "Pics, in the papers or the mags…with my kit off, simply that, that's *all* I do…nothing more."

She held her breath and waited for a dismissive voice to reply but all she heard was his measured tone as if Neil was taking stock once more.

"I see."

Or imagine, she could have added helpfully.

"Only…only the work's getting less, is that it?" He continued, "so, you come to me or ask for the names of clinics in order to prolong the life that you lead?"

"It's the only life I know Neil…and I'm not embarrassed or feel any need to explain it all or the *'why'* to you, not a single bit and definitely not at this time of the night."

"No…no quite." He waited for only an instant. "You will explain it though, won't you?"

"Yes."

She spoke to him in a softer voice now. He had maintained his interest and called, in spite of her less than forthright confessions of her work; he seemed not to be perturbed.

"Yes Marla?" He was drawing her in once more.

"Are you…are you shocked, disappointed even in me, Neil?" She felt compelled to ask him. It was the second time that he had spoken of the motives that lay behind her quest for change.

"No."

"Say a bit more, for Christ sake! Don't go using one word answers on me, not now!"

"I don't embellish the truth."

"Then tell me what you really think, Neil...do that for me, will you? Tell me *the effing truth*!" She sighed. It was all she could do to keep herself from yelling out in a language others of her acquaintance might be inclined to use.

"Yes! Yes I will! Don't change! Don't ask me to change a beautiful thing!" he said vehemently, and it sounded as if he did so under his breath, provoked at last by her taunts. "That's what I really think...that's why I thought it worth calling you...even at this time of the night, and even after a long day!"

"Oh! Oh Neil!"

"Forget it...forget what I said. It's your life! I keep repeating myself...from where I stand, and looking at all that seems to motivate people...it's all about well being...only, it's also about chasing your inner self by meddling with what's on the outside. If that's what you really want...do it! Only, don't keep leaving messages that make me want to talk and answer your questions."

She heard him curse.

"I'm not going to forget this call Neil, or anything else you've said to me."

"Marla," he sighed, "just care for what you have, please? Simply...simply be glad for all that you've got. It's priceless, and...and to me it's beautiful."

Silence fell between them but they were still in contact.

"Neil?"

"I've said too much...I've said far too much, Marla."

"No...no, you haven't."

"Yes, I *effing* well have!" He spoke it out in a poor imitation of her accent, laughing.

"Tut, Tut!"

There was no response merely the hiss of a disconnected call. Neil had gone.

"Hello?" Marla answered in a half-awake stupor and looked at the alarm clock on the bedside table. "Hello?" she said again, falling back onto the pillows in dismay at the time of this 'phone call.

"It's me, again...Neil." There was just the hint of an apology in his voice.

"I know...only you call me at odd hours, Doctor Neil," she observed calmly and with the hint of a disbelieving laugh.

"Yeah...I'm sorry," he acknowledged but went on without a pause. "I'm sorry for swearing earlier."

"I've heard worse, Neil."

"There's no real excuse...I shouldn't have said what I said in that way."

"I forgive you."

Neil took in how she had spoken. "Have you got my number?"

"No, but you've got mine. When I get yours maybe I should call you at, what? Oh yeah, one thirty in the morning."

"Got a pen and paper?"

"Soon will have...what's the rush?"

"None," he said. "Got it handy now?"

"Yes...yes I have, *now*, Neil."

"Good...this is my private number." He spoke it out slowly and waited between the groups of numbers he gave precisely and in a clear voice. "Got that?"

"Yes Neil," she mimicked a theatrical voice of obedience, "I've got that down."

"Good, thank you. I can sleep now...I shouldn't have hung up on you. I'm sorry."

"Apology accepted Neil. Count yourself lucky that I picked up the 'phone…again."

He gave a little laugh in acknowledgement of the tedium of having to do so.

"Thanks…yes, I am lucky. The offer to come out on Saturday, it's still open. You'll be safe, flying with me…and you'll live differently for the day. Say that you'll try something new and that you can be somewhere else."

"With someone new…with someone else," she reflected in a whispered reply.

"That's another way of looking at it, yes."

She remembered their earlier conversation only too vividly. "No one's ever said that what I had was priceless…"

"Life is Marla," he observed without any hint at condescension in his tone. "I learnt of it from someone so much younger, from my Jamie. He was only two-and-a-half when he was taken."

She didn't know how to respond to that and instead thought of other things they'd spoken of. "You said something else, do you remember that bit too, Neil?"

"Yes…it was only the truth, and it doesn't always have to hurt to hear it."

"No, but where I've been and some of the people I've been with, beautiful is only a word…nothing more. It's used to get a concession…"

"Let me show you then, Marla? It's more than just a word."

"Yes, show me Neil."

She couldn't remember that she'd ever spoken to anyone in quite the way he was encouraging her to speak now. It was too simple, too bloody normal; it was so nice to simply talk and not feel that *'he was on the pull.'*

"Good night, Marla…I'll call you tomorrow, late morning." She heard once more a stifled yawn.

"Okay…but`call my mobile. I may be out, Neil. There's something I need to deal with…something I want to change."

"Okay…it's a deal. Night, Marla…I really need some sleep."

"You and me, both then…at least I can now."

Late mornings for them were going to be different, clearly. Neil rang at nine-thirty.

"I'm barely awake, Neil" she said in reply to his 'good morning, Marla'.

"I'll call back."

"No! Stay there."

"Yes miss," he teased. "Have you thought anymore about the gliding?"

"Yes…I'll do it! I may as well go to extremes, just this once."

"Great!" He seemed boyishly happy.

"Not doctor's speech now, is it?" She had to laugh at the simplicity of Neil's remark. "Great!"

"What you see isn't always what you get," he observed calmly.

"Only teasing…just a bit. Anyway…it's far too early in the day for all that deep stuff…get me?"

"Yes, okay…that's me for you."

"Are you, Neil?"

"We'll have to see…we'll meet, we'll wait and see, won't we?"

"Yes."

"Right." He said it as if he knew their conversation was almost at an end. "May I call you later to make the arrangements for tomorrow?"

"For our date?"

"Yes okay…put it like that, '*for our date*'," he laughed.

"Yes…you may call."

"Bye then."

"Yeah…bye Neil…catch you later?"

Think on it Neil, my doctor friend. I'm beginning to like the man that you are…as far as I can tell from what you've said to me. Your line's a little different from what I'm used to…

<u>V</u>

There, that's one reminder of the past out of my life. I've ditched the wagon, Eddie's over-the-top present. Now, I'm going to change how I look, it's the right time to make a break with the past…my days as a topless model are history, or they soon will be.

The sporty little Peugeot was parked up at the front of 'Sandy and Damon', the hairdresser's salon she had heard so much about. 'Coiffed by a Queen' was how Bettina had described sessions there with her usual direct and hilarious wit. No matter what their tastes or diversions were, one of them would help to change her looks.

Neil had called her; he'd woken her up more like. Early morning's for him were nine thirty, apparently. He called her again, within an hour to settle things and no doubt his mind too. The arrangements were made and he had helpfully given some ideas on what to wear, unprompted. The man clearly thought of everything, and of her; he must have done 'cos, if she was interested, he'd take her to dinner after their day…at the end of their first date. So, he had suggested, bring what will make you comfortable in the evening.

"Just think it over, Marla", he had told her.

"I already have…we're going out, you've got me as your date" she had affirmed to him once more.

"You won't regret it, I'm sure…I'll see to it, Marla."

He could say such considerate, simple things.

Whether I wet myself with this gliding caper or not, I'm going to go through with it and see the man for what he really is. Why's he bothering with me if some of the things he's already said aren't meant to be taken seriously? Neil's different, he's someone new, he's someone to start a new life with…well, he can help me cross the line and take the first few steps. I'll decide on everything else and everyone who's going to be in that new life with me at some other time, later, just not too much later.

Neil told her to look out for the white stucco fronted house along the Woodstock Road in Oxford; just turn left at the roundabout, before the garage on the inner bypass north of the city. She remembered. Betty had driven her wagon, last time, as she was taken over by nerves at going to the clinic and a first meeting. So she'd driven along the motorway, just as Betty had done, and relied on memory; it was becoming a habit heading west and away from London and work; drift out to the sticks, away from home, a home town called Beaconsfield. That place was no great shakes she told herself, not in comparison to where she now was.

There! There are the gateposts Neil said to look out for.

Perfect, I got here without a hitch. The drive was the easy bit. I'm out on a blind date; well, that's what it feels like. I've only met the guy once…and here I am, going to his place! I'll remember what he looks like won't I? Yeah, sure I will, but I've changed. How much more will I have to do, or rather change in my life because of what that man, Doctor Neil, has stirred in me? I've had the time to think and he's made me look at myself again, twice, three times…over-and-over.

I went to consult a surgeon, a knife man and what do I get? Who am I going to see? Right…a man who's doing my head in! Why? I don't know…all this and I've only met him once. Get a grip girl, as Betty would say, only…only first dates are always special. You live in hope and believe it will be different this time. Bet on it girl!

My God! There he is…there's Neil! Get a grip, girl.

Yeah…he's different, oh so very different!

You're going to be okay…you can trust him.

We spoke several times…often enough, girl.

He didn't try it on…you chucked him a few comments and put down some bait…and still he didn't say anything flash. Oh no. All he did was ask if I'd like to scare myself…what's the word? Leave it. Oh yeah, scare the hell out of me…would I like to go out with him and be scared, shitless.

There, not lady's talk is it? I said it anyway, but only to myself. It's what the people I usually hang out with would say.

If I get through today, and whatever else follows, we'll both have learnt a bit about each other. So, is this what a girl's *really* gotta do to have a good time on a first date with an interesting and oh so different bloke?

I'll check I've got everything…my sunglasses and mobile 'phone. They're almost a part of me, I'm lost without them. The hair looks great, my natural blonde and no more tarty blow-waved frizzy wavy curls. Gone they are. Now, I've got a stylish cut, to the shoulder and still enough to put in two pleated strands to keep it special, to frame my face and still look a bit 'glam'. I feel great…the workouts for the shoots helped, they did the trick. Yeah, not bad for a chick of thirty five, or so, a chick who used to get her kit off to get by, but a chick who's got a new life to live…with a caring and devoted guy, that's when I find him.

The time's come to move on, girl…to step up a notch or two. The past is just that…yesterday.

And Neil? What do I make of him? Have I found the right guy already? Has it happened so quickly that neither of us really knows it yet? Too late now, girl! Here you bloody well are at his place and about to go up in a frigging glider to find out if you can both get past first base. And Neil? What do I say or do about him? He's probably wondering where I've been and who with…only, the image hides the reality. That was Freddy all the way through, mean and unpredictable underneath the cool exterior and the ready cash. He knew where I earned it but I never quite figured out what he was up to…or whom he was *in* to…well, not until he chased off with some girl. Yeah, that's it, some young thing to practice on…again.

Yeah, the image hides the reality. Only, I didn't say that, Neil did! That man said it all, that man, yes that doctor Neil. It was clever and he's asked me here to find the real me or for him to get to know the real girl.

The body's just a vessel…

"Hi…welcome, Marla. I'm glad you've made it…"

His smile said it all. It's going to be okay.

"Hi, yeah…thanks…I found you."

"Yes…and that's a relief." Neil grinned at her as Marla smiled at the intentional double meaning to their exchanges. "The first bit's over…meeting up, like this."

"Yeah."

"Come in…bring your bag. We're not expected at the field until one. So, we've got time. May I offer you a drink?"

He was so polite and formal that she simply followed. "Yes…yes please. May I have a coffee?"

"Sure."

"With a tot in it?" She tilted her head in enquiry, "and with a spoonful of sugar?"

"Sure." He wasn't fazed by her request at all. "It'll be okay…the hardest part is over." Marla gave no reply and simply stared at him "For me it's us meeting up again…for you it's doing something crazy…and on a first date!"

"That's just what I was thinking," she said smiling at him again as if Neil needed reassurance, only she was the one who felt awkward.

"You'll be fine…"

"Yes…I know. I talked myself into believing that to get through the day I'd have to get the gliding thing over with… after that everything else will be easy."

"Quite." He held a hand out to her and she clasped it for only an instant. It was their first touch. "Wait and see…that's what we agreed Crazy things first…then dinner, to say thank you."

"I don't want to wait too long, mind. I've never even sat in a glider…flying in one is something else again!"

"And there's no drinks trolley."

"Speaking of which?" she asked.

"Yes, quite! Make yourself at home." He stopped at the doorway. "I'll join you, coffee only. I have to fly the thing, remember?" He looked at her with stilled eyes.

"Everything okay?" she quizzed.

Neil's look made her feel self-conscious and she raised a hand to her hair.

"Yes…everything's fine. I heard you tell me that you had to make changes…and I see that you've changed how you look." Neil did not finish the compliment his look upon her conveyed.

"It's what I do, Neil."

"Did, Marla…it's what you did. That's what you told me."

"Yeah, right…only some things stay with you…I've learnt to adapt…to get by…in a new situation…I've got to choose who to be with. Now," she said in a determined lighter voice and thinking she'd made enough confessions for a while, "what about that coffee?"

"I'm going. I just wanted you to know that I've noticed who you are now."

"I've seen your look, Neil, so…I know."

There was an absence of clutter; the house was filled with light and space. On arrival she thought it to be an old and dated place but Neil now guided her to a sun-filled living room that looked out over an immaculate garden He put down the tray he had brought from the kitchen and came to her.

"Wow!" she exclaimed. They stood by a floor to ceiling window that created the impression that the room and the garden were at-one with each other.

"I don't do it," he said in reply to her unasked question. "There's so little time."

"And this?" She gave an airy wave of her hand to take in the whole room.

"Yes," he shrugged almost in apology but it was a modest acceptance that it was all to his taste and his idea. "I picked a nineteen-thirties house and put modernist furniture in it...and a few inherited bits. It's my home...the pictures are all my purchases...and the glassware." He looked at the items then at her. "I like shape, style...and colour."

I'll bear it in mind, she thought. There, he was looking at her again.

"Neil?"

"I'm glad you plucked up the courage to spend the day here."

"It's no big deal," she answered, far too quickly.

"No...I guess not."

"I didn't mean it to sound the way that it did."

"No," he acknowledged with a smile. "Here's your booster...with a coffee afterthought."

"I don't think I'll need the booster after all...you seem in control, of everything."

"What you see Marla," he laughed engagingly as their eyes met.

"Isn't what I get? Thanks...thank you." She took the coffee glass in its silver holder from him as her mobile 'phone trilled. "Damn it!" She exchanged an apologetic glance with him before pressing the answer key. "Fine...yeah, I found it...no trouble at all. Yes...it's great...gotta go...I'll call you sometime, soon." She listened but held Neil's gaze upon her. "Tomorrow...make it later tomorrow. Bye...yes...bye, girl!"

She took a gulp of coffee and looked at the glass for an instant. "Hm…that's good. I need it."

"Everything all right?"

"Fine…'twas Betty…checking I got here." She met Neil's gaze upon her once more and looked away for a moment. A hand brushed her hair as if in harmony with a decision she had come to. Tell no lies…don't hold on to many secrets and don't evade the issue with half-truths. "Neil…it's like this, she was simply checking that I got here and I was okay."

"And…are you?"

"Yes," she said drawing closer to him. "I'm very okay."

"Good." He saw that her cup was empty and took it. "Now…lovely as you are you'll need to change into something more practical and less worrying if it gets dirty. It's not going to be first-class travel…and there's no silver service."

"Oh!" she gave him a look of surprise. "What ever gave me that idea?"

I can't help it she thought; I like just being with him. He talks normally to me; there's no act and he says what he means…that's the impression I get. Jeez! He's so different from the others I meet.

"Come?" He held a hand out to her and she was surprised by the spontaneity of the gesture. "I'll show you to the guest rooms."

"My bags are still in the car."

"Of course…we forgot to bring them in. I'll get them. Keys?"

She handed them over and waited as a zipped leather bag and matching suit cover were brought in to her.

"If madam would like to follow me I'll show her to her rooms."

I'm not staying she thought in a panic and wondered how to keep the note of unease from her voice as Neil led the way.

"You've gone to a lot of trouble."

"Sh! And no I've not. You are my guest…you're company for the day."

She saw more light, more pictures, more touches of his simple taste, colour and love of shape and form. The walls to the staircase and landing were painted in a soft discreet yellow, so soft she thought it to be white emulsion on the flocked decoratively patterned wallpaper. There was such brightness that the light enhanced and brought a unique clarity to the glass objects on display.

And then…and then she saw it, a picture of Jamie, a smiling happy face with wide-eyed pleasure and a hand held out as if he knew that he was the centre of attention. He was not alone in the picture.

Neil had opened a door and passed through into the room beyond. "Marla?"

"Here." She replied from the landing.

"It's Jamie…as you know. He's with my wife…my ex-wife." He spoke from inside the room and they looked at one another through the doorway. "She's remarried…she lives in France now…she's had twins…twin boys…and everything's fine…they are both healthy."

"She let you know?"

Daft question, girl! But, how do you tell someone you said you loved that you'd rather have healthy or unblemished kids…with some other guy?

"Yes."

Neither of them had moved and she looked at the picture once more. The woman's expression was not hard or calculating but to her eyes the smile was not heartfelt or spontaneous. Jamie's was altogether different. He was blissfully ignorant of the circumstances in his life and let all of his spirit shine out in a brilliant smile and through bright, beautifully rounded eyes.

"Lizzie wanted me to know…she had fulfilled her idea of destiny…as a woman."

And that she could live without him after all.

"Yes…" she whispered to herself. Neil broke the spell.

"Quick now, Marla…please? I'd like to get on with our day…our few hours together. There's not a moment to lose."

I'm with you Neil, she thought…but not *'simply'* with you, not any more.

VI

The field was a rundown and very shabby Second World War airfield on the top of an escarpment that looked out over the Vale of the Red Horse. For him it was of no consequence or concern. The location offered a choice; rely on thermals to soar high above the Warwickshire countryside or take advantage of deflected air, to gain height from ridge lift and soar for hours.

"I won't bore you with the technical details," he had told Marla, "simply enjoy the flight and the stunning views."

The day was bright; broken high cloud drifted way above them and the breeze tugged lightly at their clothes. He had timed their arrival perfectly and now supervised the last minute flight preparations.

"Look after me?" She now felt the need to ask him as Neil bent down to check that she was correctly buckled in. He would occupy the instructor's seat behind her and she gave voice to the thought that she was entirely under his control.

"Of course." He delighted in her perfume and Marla's softly tanned skin that contrasted beautifully with the cropped sleeve cardigan that she wore over a charming vest whose collar was trimmed with diamante'. "You look wonderful…even if this is your dressed down look."

"Thank you," she smiled up at him. "I'm wondering what I've been talked into."

She had said it many times as they drove through the countryside, over narrow and winding roads to get to the field.

Now, the aerotow aircraft started its engine, a waft of smoke drifting away on the breeze. Neil took his seat.

"Are we setting off now?"

"Yes," he soothed, "there's not long to wait. Soon it'll be peace and quiet…beautiful light and silent views."

"You'll hear my heart beating."

"Still…you'll soon be transported…to another view of the world, believe me." He leant forward and touched her neck with his fingertips. Marla started. "Don't be alarmed…I'm close by."

"I won't be…I'll try…if you say so." She moved her head under the lightest caress of his reassuring touch and watched as the canopy was closed and heard their fastening close them in. "No going back now."

"Soon it'll be just you and me," he offered reassurance over the simple intercom. "Don't be frightened and, please…don't touch anything unless I say that you can. You may see or feel the controls move, but, don't worry…it's quite normal."

She gave a little cry as the jerk on the tow cable indicated that they were setting off on an adventure, just the two of them.

"I'm not going to forget this first date in a hurry!" she managed to joke with a quavering voice. "No way!"

"Good…now shush Marla, just for a few moments. I need to concentrate."

The wheel beneath them rumbled and thumped over the roughened runway surface and its uneven joints. Neil watched as the tow aircraft rose before he eased on the stick, lifting them gently off the ground.

"Wow!"

"Yes," he laughed. "Now, it's nice and steady for a while." The ground fell away beneath them very quickly. Neil felt the lift of the air under the wings as he trimmed the 'craft, enough to maintain his level behind the tow aircraft.

Marla sang and waved her hands, as much as their cramped space would allow. "I'm leaving ...on a sail plane..."

"Don't know when we'll be back again," he responded singing in tune. "I know that much of the song at least. You okay...girl?"

"Yes, doctor. Tell me, when is the fun to begin?"

"It has, earlier today...and...now we're flying."

"Neil..." She sighed but couldn't look round at him.

"Okay, I won't tell you how it is." He spoke lightly. "Look out to your right. You'll see down below the fields where the battle of Edge Hill was fought in the Civil War...sixteen forty something. To your front you should be able to make out Stratford upon Avon...behind us is home and Oxford. And above us...above us is..."

He fell silent.

"Heaven and the sky," she finished for him. "Infinity!" She raised both hands; they were held out to him, behind her head. "Neil?"

"Yes?" He took hold of one hand that she held out behind her as she spoke to him. "Are you okay now?"

"Yeah, I really am...Neil."

A voice interrupted them over a crackly radio link. "Tow release in five...count from five...five...four...three..."

Their forward momentum slowed.

"We're really on our own now, Marla."

He had released his hold on her hand and taken full control of the glider. The aerotow banked and flew past with the towrope streaming out behind it, marked by fluorescent yellow and pink tell-tales.

"What now, doc?" She couldn't help a silly giggle.

"Ha!" he called out. "We circle on the air, maintain our height until you feel at ease...and then," he chuckled, "why then, you can try it. I'll just say, 'you have the ship'...okay?"

"No way! No way!" she yelled out and held a hand up to him once more. "Hold it! Tell me you will fly it...all of the time!"

"Yes...yes," he soothed with a soft laugh that she could just hear. "I'm only offering you the chance to try...when you're quite ready."

"Later...much later...some other time, Neil."

He leant forward as far as the seat straps allowed.

"Marla?" His hand touched her cheek once more, just. "It's fine...relax and enjoy the view and the stillness. Heaven's above and the earth's below. The feelings never change for me when I'm up here...only, I've got you for company now, special company. It's that simple."

"Nothing's ever '*that simple*'," she murmured.

This little adventure, the man sitting behind me, the different life I'm looking for...it's different already but it sure isn't simple, taking it all in so quickly. Things, life...maybe me, they're all changing and it's far too quick.

"We'll see," she heard him say, then there was near silence and the gentle suspension of her belief. She had been taken out of her usual circle of friends and pastimes; a strange exhilaration caused by her fear of being so intimately dependent upon him now possessed her but the gentle rise and fall of the glider wrought its own soothing effect. She felt happy but restrained herself from the noisy chatter she knew she could so easily lapse into when her usual cares had fallen away.

"Neil? Talk to me?"

He had no way of knowing how long he had been in a state of reverie; he remembered Jamie's small hands and how he twisted his father's hair as he sat on his lap listening intently to a story being read out. In spite of the thoughts that had possessed him they were subject to other imperatives, the need to control and fly the glider.

"Yes…I'm here…I was thinking…I'm back with you now." He took hold of the hand that she offered to him. "We'll gradually descend and I'll take you along the ridge, along Edge Hill…we'll ride the wave of air for a mile or two…there's a lovely windmill to look at, by Compton Wynyates and we'll bank there…turn and head back to the field, for a landing."

"Are you sure?"

"Yes…we've been up here for an hour…I don't seem to have been very good company…I lapsed into day-dreaming."

"It's okay Neil…I gathered you were on a trip."

"I'm clean," he laughed. "I'm sorry to have been so involved…and not to have paid you more attention."

"It's not been a problem…I've been taken out of my usual routine too…I spent enough time thinking and wondering about today. Now, I've seen it for myself. You're right it's a magical place to be. Thanks…for asking me, Neil."

"Gladly done…I shouldn't do that though, it's not very doctorly behaviour." They had touched hands for only an instant once more.

"I forgive you…and you're not a doctor right now, not here and with me. Anyway, I stopped being frightened a while ago."

"Good."

"It's like you said it would be and you've kept your word… you've looked after me."

Her words sounded so simple but they gave a true expression of how she felt. Their moments together had been different from how she had imagined them to be; now they held an altered and deeper significance for her.

Marla refastened the headscarf, tying it in a fashion reminiscent of a Fifties film starlet. She waited in the car and thought through what she had shared with him. Neil had performed a series of manoeuvres just to show her the versatility of the glider, his skills as a pilot and to also offer an insight into the forces that had kept them airborne. Now as she waited for him, and looked around her at the unfamiliar and grubby surroundings she could only smile at the anxieties that had possessed her during the previous evening and more recently, that morning. They had been dispelled by his first touch, the attentiveness to her and the seemingly uncomplicated demands he had made upon her. He had been moved to very personal and intense communions once more and unbound from anything that she could then offer. He had excused his behaviour only once, in a touch to her cheek and soft words of explanation.

Now, back on firm ground she had seen the man once more; he was a guy who had sought her company and who lapsed into easy chatter. Yes, the chat would become easier still and they'd grow accustomed to each other. He hadn't tried it on at all, or if his touch meant anything it seemed to express an easy delight with her company.

Yeah, right! He's a man...do you believe what you've just thought out, girl?

He's different!

Yeah...he's still a man! They're not that different, one from the other!

That's Betty talk for you!

I'm the one who's here! I'll listen to my inner voice that tells me he's *different*...Neil's not like the others I've known... or, been with.

Just maybe they would discover that they had no sides to their characters and that they could speak it all out. Girl, you know that really would take time...and that really would be a change in your book! You haven't got that many names written down in your life's book, but your first time out with Neil, your first date, it had been okay. So far it has been more than you expected.

He was the doctor and she the showgirl. Correction! The ex-showgirl. It seemed that the distinction was going to matter...even more now.

VII

"Call me, when you get home?"

It had been the only thing that Neil had asked of her before she left him. The hour was late; he had been charming and attentive company throughout the day and evening. They had walked arm-in-arm, a novelty in itself for her, past the Colleges of the University and taking in all of the noisy, boisterous student life and the bustle of the historic core to the city. Neil had entertained and made her laugh with some anecdotes about his work and the jokes that did the rounds, he smiled, on medical matters. So, any concerns that Betty may have had for Neil 'coming onto her' had proved groundless.

"Yes…I will," she remembered saying, "thank you for everything. It's been different, quite a day! I feel as though I've been in a spell for a few hours."

Yes, she remembered the words spoken only too clearly. A soft embrace, a kiss as a token of thanks or deeper appreciation of what they had shared would not have been refused, even if it had been their 'first date'.

But, he had surprised her.

Neil had simply said, "Step by step."

He had kissed her hand, in an all too formal gesture but it had been accompanied by a tender look of his eyes upon her; it was the only admission he could offer that the day had been special for him too.

"Keep it simple?" she had said in response to his gentle touch.

"Yes…it's a word that keeps cropping up in our conversations, but…it's not that simple, is it?"

"No." She had agreed with him after all. 'Step by step'. She hadn't believed it possible that Neil's words would resonate quite so strongly within her too and his unhurried attentiveness welcomed.

A cliché sprang to mind only it seemed entirely appropriate to their circumstances. He had said it differently but the intention of his thoughts remained consistent; he would continue to be true to himself and she discovered, after such a short acquaintance, to her too.

There were to be 'no quick fixes'.

She shook her head, to free her mind of Neil and what they had said and done during the day. She had to concentrate. The mobile 'phone had been cast aside onto the car seat beside her. That girl, Betty! She would insist on calling her when she least expected it.

"Haven't you got anything better to do at this time of night?" she had laughingly enquired of her, "or someone to do it to?"

"Yeah…but, I still have time to think of you Marla, my friend."

"Okay…thanks. It's nice of you to do so." She hadn't fallen for the gossipy introductions. "I'll tell you all about it tomorrow, come over and keep me company?"

"Right, until then girl! You take care now, hear me?"

"Yes, I will. Thanks…thanks for calling me."

"It's nothing. Where are you?"

"Getting some petrol…never know when I may be needed again." Betty's call had kept her from getting out of the car.

"That so?" Betty quizzed eagerly now. "Seen the signs, have you girl?"

"No!" she laughed. And yet, over dinner with him, with doctor Neil, I was just wishing and hoping, thinking and praying…like some young thing, on a first date! At least she'd called him, just before the turning off the motorway, to say 'nearly there, and thanks once again for a lovely day' and to hear him say 'goodnight Marla' as if he really meant it.

Are you happy?

Yeah!

That's how I feel.

I've had a tiring, happy and such a different day!

I've met and could grow to like this special man.

He's Neil…

Could it be that he's not simply my Doctor Neil anymore?

Home was nearby but the need to stop and talk to Betty, if only for a few moments, had compelled her to pull in at the garage. You never knew who might be watching you driving and using the 'phone. She pushed the silk scarf back and adjusted the knot by her throat, shaking her head as she did so to loosen her hair. She pulled the small lever by her seat to release the filler cap. Under the glacially bright lights of the petrol station's forecourt she noted a dirty pick-up van with a woman at the wheel. She paid no further attention to it and began to fill the car's tank, looking at the counter; the sound of laughter made her turn, only briefly.

Two young women, slovenly dressed in comparison to her own close fitting tailored suit that had drawn a fulsome compliment from Neil, came towards her then veered off to get into the van. It's engine spluttered into life before the vehicle jerked into motion. She had noted the women's spiked hair, the glint off the many jewelled skin piercings that disfigured their faces, and the momentary challenging stares. Then, they had disappeared from her view.

"Got all you need, luv?" the elderly man behind the counter asked in a friendly conversational tone of voice as he took the credit card from her.

"Yes thanks…and I'll take these packs of chewing gum too. Add them to the bill, please?"

"Right you are. I'll be packing up soon," he went on as he fiddled with the card and the reader he had to push it into. "Just got to wait a while longer…then I hand over to my replacement…I don't stay out on late shifts no more." He gave an expressive shrug of resignation. "That's if he ever turns up, mind."

The receipt was handed to her once she had punched in the PIN number and the till settled up.

"Thank you."

"Ok," he smiled jovially and in a sign of pleasure to have ended his evening's shift serving a smart lady. "Mind how you go."

"I will...good night." I'm not usually so talkative or chatty in a place like this she thought and opened the door. She gave the man a smile before stepping outside.

The newspaper rack caught her eye; there was a supplement, a magazine insert to one of the tabloids lying on the ground and she picked it up. Curiosity got the better of her and she hesitated, flicking through the pages. A caption on the front had made her stop with a frisson of recognition as to its contents. 'Beauty and Grace...our girls now', the words spelt out. Angie, one of the other girls chosen to feature, smiled from a corner of the page.

"So soon?" she whispered to herself and looked at the date printed on the cover.

"You're one of them!" a hard voice snarled.

She looked up, startled, and threw the magazine to the ground. She was confronted by the two women whom she had seen earlier. Now, they stood close by, far too close, and stared at her as the way to the car was blocked.

"Don't know what you're on about. Sorry..." She made to brush past them.

"Not so fast!" The voice was unforgiving. "We recognised you...the face, anyway...just now...and from the mag you've just ditched. Best place for it! In the dirt!"

"Got your clothes on now!" the first woman's companion added. "Tits are tits! Only...you sell the idea of so much more!"

"I don't know what you're on about...let me go."

"Yes you do...and there's no where to hide from it...not now."

Marla felt a strong hand restrain her. There was no time to escape the slap...and, then...the searing pain. She screamed and tore herself free raising her hands to her face. Wet stickiness! Then…she saw the blood, her blood…smeared over her hand and the frilly cuff of the lovely silk blouse that showed off her figure. Yes, she'd known only too well how to interest the eyes and mind of Neil, and, she had been guided by different motives too that evening. The man was so *very different*…he had made her believe in herself, her deepest self. Easy had not been his treatment or expectations of her.

"Let me go! You've made a terrible mistake…let me go!" she cried out. "Let me go!"

Only, there was no escape.

"Not yet, lass!"

Teasing and scornful derision were now accompanied by strong hands that gripped her clothes as she attempted to get away into the relative safety of the shop. Instinctively, she raised her free arm but could not avoid the zealots staring eyes or the slashing cuts that she felt traced across her chest. This time she screamed in blind terror and disbelief.

Her assailants now eased their hold upon her and stood back, as if to admire their handiwork.

"What have you done…why? Why?"

Trembling hands could only clutch at the rent and stained fabric of her blouse and jacket. They had been too thin to offer any protection.

Blood! Blood! Her blood seemed to be everywhere!

My blood…it's everywhere!

"Why? Why do this to me?" she moaned. "I've done you no harm."

It sounded weak and pathetic. Her attackers weren't done with their final wounding and tormenting task, taking turns to humiliate and degrade her.

"Bitch!"

"You whore!"

"You're a disgrace to womankind!"

"Not so pretty now are you?"

"Slag! Who's to want you now?"

"Flash them tits at other sickos, not the types you always flashed 'em for!"

"Tart!"

"Bloody tart!" one laughed.

They left her as Marla stumbled to the ground.

All she heard was a scornful laugh and then the banging of the door to the filthy and tatty conveyance that had brought her assailants and a wounding nemesis. It had happened in seconds; it seemed like a rape by word and deed, the ruination of her life, a nurtured self-perception and the shattering of her nascent hopes for a different future.

"Lass? What's up, lass?" The word sounded mournful on the old man's lips.

She heard the gentlemanly attendant call to her from the doorway. You poor man, it wasn't your fault.

"I'm here...I'm here," she croaked and began to sob uncontrollably, looking at her hands and then her bleeding body. "I'm cut! I'm bleeding, all over!" She could not restrain her wailing recognition of what had befallen her before... nothing, just darkness and oblivion.

"He'll have to help her now!" Betty said through gritted teeth. Amanda tried to restrain her.

"He has. Mr Allman-Brown has already been in touch with the hospital."

"Oh. Oh! When was that?"

"I am unable to say, exactly, and I can't find out for you. Mr Allman-Brown's in theatre...he won't be disturbed. I can't contact him."

"Process...bloody process and forms, I suppose?"

Reception's empty, thank goodness, Amanda thought as Betty let fly with her emotions.

"Yes," she answered calmly in spite of the provocative remarks the woman had made almost from the moment she had swept in noisily from the car park and asking for 'Neil'. Where had these two women come from and into all their lives?

"Yes, process…but it helps us to get through the days and to get our work done properly…more important still it helps our patients and clients in the best possible way that we know."

"I'll have to take your word for it," was the tart reply.

Amanda didn't know the woman's surname. "Yes, you'll have to do that. Now, Betty…if you'll excuse me, please?"

"Right…"

"What you have told me is useful. I will pass on what you've said of Mrs Nance's condition to Mr Allman-Brown."

"Neil…Neil," she cried out. "To Marla he's Neil…Mr Neil if you must know."

"Yes…I know." Amanda smiled for the first time at her. "She's spoken of him like that to me, too."

"Okay," Betty gave a smiling sigh, "it's a little joke. Marla told me all about it." Betty's lips quivered as she fought back the tears. "She's so hurt…Marla's hurt so bad. Her beauty's cut…just cut…cut to pieces! He's got to help her…he simply has to."

"I know, Betty," Amanda said gently now. "He's only heard about it and talked to a consultant where she is. The news came as a great shock to him…and to me. I remember…"

"That's all she's got! That's all she has now…memories! Memories and pictures of how she once looked!" Betty couldn't remain still and paced the floor of the small consulting room Amanda had felt obliged to take her to. She seemed like a caged animal and paced the floor, on the point of nervous collapse. "When's he back? When can Neil be talked to? When can he be asked to restore Marla…give back her great…great looks?"

"I can't tell you that, precisely…and I can't stay with you like this, not…not for much longer."

"Marla and me? We're close...she's my one true friend in all the 'shit' we have to live through...or put up with in our work. Only...only a man didn't do these things to her."

"No," Amanda agreed quietly and reflected upon the meaning of the words just spoken. She had heard the story from others; they had seen the reports in the newspapers, and pictures of Marla Nance's fleshy beauty. They weren't the sort of pictures she came across in her newspaper, but then, naked flesh held few if any secrets for her anymore.

"Who'd do such a thing to their own?"

"I can't answer that Betty, I can't begin to tell you." She sat down beside her and held Betty's hands for an instant. "C'mon? I'll fetch you a cup of tea...or a coffee."

"I need something a hell of a lot stronger than that, girl!" She began to cry. "That poor girl! Poor Marla!"

"Yes...I'll get you some coffee...it's the best I can do now."

"Okay...thanks," Betty whispered. "You're a mate."

"Yes," Amanda laughed as much to cheer up Betty as to acknowledge the meaning of the words just spoken. "Yes... we're girls, all of us together."

"Yeah...some of us, anyway." Betty looked up and smiled. "Thanks...I've been a heap of trouble...I had to come here, felt I had to...silly girl, eh? Only...only she asks for him especially...she said he was quite simply the *only man* to help her."

"Simply?"

"Yes! He was *simply* the only man...it could only be doctor Neil for her." Betty looked at Amanda once more. "Marla said it was a special word that they had used to describe what they had between them."

"He's...he's a doctor, nothing more," Amanda replied in a thoughtful voice.

"Don't you believe it! He's going to be her helper."

"Her saviour?"

"Yeah!" Betty sat upright and punched the air. "Yeah!" She gave a brilliant smile and wiped at her eyes. "Brilliant! It's a brilliant word, Amanda girl!"

"Easy…"

"No! It's a brilliant word. Yes! Neil's going to be her *saviour!*" She couldn't keep herself from smiling. "Wait 'till I tell her…tell Marla."

"I'll get you that coffee I promised you," Amanda said, acknowledging the improvement in Betty's spirits by her smile, but she could not allow her to imagine that a single procedure might resolve the torment presently endured. "I still need to say it Betty, go easy on what you say…more importantly how you say it."

She closed the door behind her and remembered only too clearly Neil's comments soon after they had all met Marla for the first time. They had smiled at each other and admitted that they had seemingly shared in a new experience; it was that of voluptuous loveliness in a clinging dress seeking of them the repair of a perceived imperfection.

"I can't do anything to improve that woman's appearance or others like her. They should be only too glad and give thanks to their God or their loving earthly creators for making them so attractive."

She sighed.

The man she worked for was light and of an easy humour but his deepest self sometimes found a more public voice. The time had arrived for Neil, once more, to become a devoted re-creator and restorer of an all too earthly body and mind.

VIII

He had taken the unusual step of travelling to collect her, accompanied by a nurse. The hospital had been telephoned and he had spoken to Paul Harris, the consultant assigned to her case, hours before they set off.

"There's no time to lose. May I have your consent to transfer Marla Nance to the care of my clinic, in Oxford?" he had asked.

"She's of a mind to discharge herself…Marla is a very determined lady. She wanted your clinic to treat her. I'll get her notes ready for you."

"Thanks."

"Think nothing of it…we had a shock though."

"What has her treatment been so far?"

"Light dressings and wound cleansing, that's all. She and that friend of hers, Betty…they work together, apparently… they were both very insistent that your clinic attended to her. Have you met Marla Nance? Do you know of her case?"

"There was no case for treatment, Paul…none to speak of. She called upon me two months ago. There was no case to be treated," he said again thinking how quickly life and circumstances could change. He remembered another occasion only too vividly. This time he intended to be fully involved.

"I'm sorry Neil, for having to say it. There is now."

The case notes were clutched in a tight fist as he studied her; Marla read no signs of the emotions at work in him. Her face was swollen by the bandaging; tufts of the lovely blonde hair that he had looked upon only hours before poked pathetically through the swathes of lint.

"I would have liked it better if we had seen each other again with me looking my best," she mumbled and smiled with quivering lips.

Her eyes! They were so stilled and imploring.

"I'm here now…I've come to take you back to Oxford. We're going to help you, Marla." He bent down to listen as she whispered a reply.

"You are going to help me, Neil. Just you…no-one but you."

"Step-by-step, others have skills that I can call upon. I will always be there. You can count on it."

"Betty told me something else."

"Oh…what was that?"

"You're going to be my saviour…can you believe it?"

"I'm going to try, Marla…to mend your body and mind."

You're not just a patient anymore he thought. You're a friend; you're a special friend.

"You saw me at my best."

"No…I believe that is yet to come and with my help, Marla."

"How can you say that? I'm cut to pieces!"

"I saw another person, too."

"Bull shit!"

"Mind…"

He released the hold she had taken of his hand; her grip had been unrelenting as she sought to draw strength from him, the look upon her and from the words of reassurance that she had expected to hear from him.

"Are you like this with everyone who comes to you?"

"Yes…those who have been treated by me have been changed. I've told you. Now that you're in my care and that of my assistants I have to treat you like any other patient."

"Oh really?"

"No," he whispered, "but I'll have to try."

"Let's get real. I'm a Customer…I'm a paying customer now, Neil!"

"No! No! No!"

He shook his head vehemently and stepped away from the bed that she lay upon, awaiting his examination and that of a colleague, Anne-Marie Gericault. Between them they were to reassess the severity of her injuries and the steps to be taken for the reconstructive treatment she required.

"This is business, Neil…don't go kidding yourself or me that it's anything else…not now." There was a hard edge to her tone; a cold-voiced bitterness at what had befallen her. "We had a brief spell outside the usual arrangement. But now? Here we are in our little compartments once again…you look after me and I…or my insurance company pays the bills." She gave a little shrug. "Life's become that *simple* again."

"No it isn't, '*simple*', not any more."

"Think on it, Neil!"

Why am I being so hard on him? I can see that he cares for me.

She turned her face away and stared at the window and the diffused light that came through the cream coloured net curtains. Her well-known, frequently trodden life's path had been briefly forsaken; she had been with a man of whom she knew little, nothing in fact. She was still ignorant of the deeper details of his experiences but she knew the person, divined from his attentiveness that there was a deeply caring spirit within him.

Neil would restore a resemblance of her former looks; that was the reason she had turned to him, unafraid to have him see how her features and body had been altered. Hers was damaged flesh. He had seemed ignorant of her true vocation, the work she had done and the provocative performances in front of cameras to give a vicarious thrill to the observer of a fleshy, but cold unresponsive image of her as a person.

The man had ignored it all and sought to learn of her as Marla, simply Marla! He had seen the reality and somehow known of her dream to be thought of as just another person. At first she had attended at his clinic as a prospective customer; now, she felt a deeper association with him. A bond, far more complex than a doctor to patient relationship allowed, seemed to have developed in the few hours she had spent alone with him.

She turned to look at Neil.

"Sorry…for saying what I did, just now."

"Let me mend you, Marla…make you who you are, again."

"Changed…"

"Yes…but still…beautiful."

"Oh, Neil." Tears welled in her eyes and she raised her unbandaged hand to him in search of a restorative clasp. "May I do this again?"

"For a moment." Neil held her hand and they gazed in silence at each other before he loosened her grip and walked to the door.

"Hi."

Amanda had changed into a surgical suit and waited for him to step aside.

"I'll clean up and prep…shall I?" she said to him, before flicking an inquisitive glance at each of them in turn.

"Yes…I'll talk to Anne-Marie…back soon." He turned once more to speak to Marla. "When I return we'll have a brief chat about the treatment we propose to undertake…the first stages."

"Treatment you will do…just you, Neil."

"Yes…I will do." Once anaesthetised, Marla would be oblivious to everything. So, he gave her an understanding smile in agreement with what she had asked of him. "We are all here to help you get through this…and afterwards. Have no fear."

"You don't do you?"

"No…no, I don't. This procedure is simply going to be special." He did not smile or look serious; his features merely displayed a profound conviction in his belief at the outcome of his work for her.

Marla laughed softly. "Nothing's simple."

"This time it is…the doctor and patient know exactly what is being sought."

He gave a slow wink to Amanda and left them without another word. The outcome rested entirely in his hands and this time another's precious gift would not slip from his grasp.

A surgical robe was drawn loosely across her body and was tucked neatly by her sides. A bonnet concealed Marla's hair and the light dressings had seemed a waxen blemish to her tanned skin. Her eyes darted from him to Anne-Marie, then to Amanda before they were stilled and looked at him once more.

Neil held her gaze for an instant and gave a soft smile.

"Time?" she asked.

"Yes, it's time...it's time to start mending you."

The word felt strangely inappropriate, mending what had befallen or struck at her loveliness. But, he thought of the word differently. He was making amends for what others had done to impair the eye-catching and fleshy beauty of her. He sought, nonetheless, to explain his choice of words.

"Anne-Marie and I are going to restore your looks...today is a beginning, an important first step. Anne-Marie will make good the damage to your breasts, the two skin lesions and cuts. I will treat the damaged skin to your face...it will be a slow process, Marla...one that may involve some light reconstructive and restorative surgery and...it will mean the taking of some drugs if the steroid creams we intend to prescribe do not help... as we hope."

Marla nodded and said nothing. She simply lay back on the pillows and closed her eyes, opening them only to see if he would continue to explain what she had already heard from Amanda they might undertake.

"What I...Anne-Marie...all of us wish for is the minimum of scarring...the reduction of the risk that scar tissue will form. If that happens our work will take longer."

"How long?" she said suddenly as her eyes opened and she stared at him. Anne-Marie answered, on Neil's nod of agreement.

"Much as we would wish to reassure you and to be definite we can not be...we can not be precise about these things.

A great deal can be achieved over six months, in twelve the improvements will be even more noticeable."

"Too long...too long! Much too long!" Marla cried out in distress at the thought of being cooped up, out of view and stuck in her home like a prisoner in a cell, her own form of solitary confinement while her looks...some of them, blighted and disfigured, were restored. "Who'd want to see me, anyway?" she mused as if they weren't in the room with her, "who'd want to see me now, like this?"

"You will have care...support and help," Neil began but Marla swatted his comments away with a dismissive sweep of her hand.

"So what?" she flared. "So what? My looks...I've lost them, my shape and my unmarked...my unmarked skin!" She tore the robe free and lay before them half naked to their view, the bandaging holding the rent flesh an angry red vision to them all. "Gone! It's all gone...taken from me...taken!"

Neil let the moment of drama pass before answering.

"You're here with us...in our care now, just as you asked," he said considerately and pulled the robe back to cover her nakedness. He continued in a firm and authoritative voice. "We will work together to help you."

"You go home and shut out of your mind all of this! You have distractions! Me? I'll look in a mirror and...and I'll see myself as I am now...like this!"

"Easy...easy now," Amanda intervened as Marla attempted to pull open her robe once more.

Anne Marie assisted in calming her down.

"You won't look like this for long...believe us, please? We can achieve minor miracles, so...help us to help you. Above all we have to wait and see...so look after yourself in the post-op period, it will be the best medicine that any of us can recommend to you...after we have done our work to help you."

She stood on the other side of the bed and now looked at Neil. Overcoming mental turmoil and securing this patient's acceptance of the task that lay ahead in her reconstruction, to almost unblemished loveliness, would take time. An image of the person they once were, in outward appearance, and clung to in their mind's eye had to give way to another, bestowed by man's touch, skill and devotion.

"We have time Marla…after we have undertaken our initial work to restore you, to offer help with the consequences of all that has happened. We have done it before…rebuilding pride in how you look and restoring a belief in yourself, your worth to others." Marla listened to Anne-Marie speak but she fixed her gaze on Neil.

"I've only got you to trust and believe in," she said. Marla did not avert her gaze upon him. "I remembered what you said to me when we first met, you mended broken bodies…"

"Not perceptions…" he finished for her.

"Yes, that's right."

"I've got to do both now. I have in Anne-Marie a first class colleague and partner in my work. Look on both of us as friends. We are here to help. It's…it's our…" he looked over at Anne-Marie who smiled softly.

"It's our calling, Marla. That is what Neil was going to say."

Rarely did any of them, she, Neil or their partner Margaret admit to their deeply held motivation to offer succour; they all possessed a unity of purpose, spirit and the belief that the patient should see this openly and with little sentimentality.

Neil watched the effect Anne-Marie's words had upon Marla. She had listened attentively but suddenly held a hand out to him as she began to weep.

"Make me whole again?" she said over trembling lips. "I did no one any harm…I didn't hurt them like I've been hurt."

"Sshh, now…enough. We've talked enough." He squeezed her hand for only an instant and let go. "We will make you well, again."

With a nod to the others he prepared to leave but stopped and turned to her once again.

"I don't say this to many patients," he said before pausing and reflecting for only a moment. "All of us here who are going to help you have learnt something new. I know I have because of your visit to us…to me. The vessel, all that you are on the outside is stricken, but only for a very short while. The beauty it contains and that it still shows lives on. We…all of us, here, will work to make you feel and look complete again. Believe in us and help us to help you, Marla. Now, I must make ready."

His lips were clenched together for an instant before relaxing in a trembling pant. He had never seen the look that Anne Marie now gave him but they held a deep understanding of his motives to help this woman. He closed his eyes in acknowledgement of her consideration.

She had seen his startled look for only an instant and recognised the association he had made with his son. The link had been made unwittingly and provoked by the words that Marla had uttered to express her own fears and hopes.

Make me whole again…I did no one any harm.

Anne-Marie had read a deeper significance in the words he had uttered and the look Neil had given but they had had vanished after the first phrases were spoken.

"I'll join you in theatre, Doctor Neil," she said formally. "I'll help Amanda make ready."

With those words still in his ears he left the room.

IX

'Heaven Can Wait' the card said.

The handwriting was neat, perfectly formed, and meticulous; the writer had intended the message that

159

accompanied it to be read, quite easily. She had detached a small envelope and put it in her handbag; it was for her eyes only.

"Marla! It's unsigned...dohhh!" Betty exclaimed in frustration. "Who'd send you a whopping great bouquet like that and not sign the card? Message's a bit weird too. Do you understand it?"

"Not really," was her evasive reply.

"Very odd," Betty continued, the possibilities intrigued her. "It doesn't give any clues. It doesn't even say 'love from'...'or sorry to hear what's happened, get well'...there's nothing!"

Marla was no help and not in the mood to debate the matter for too long with her.

"Don't fret girl, you know what? It's just bound to be one of my admirers, one of the many that read the mags and rags that I've appeared in."

"And you may yet do so," Betty smiled.

"Wake up girl! Wake up!" Marla grimaced and eased back on her pillows and exhaled loudly. "It's over...all of that's over. It's well and truly over. I'd already made up my mind before this lot happened...when I had my few lovely hours with Neil."

Betty bit her lip to stifle any immediate response. She fiddled with the ribbon that still held the bouquet tightly together in the vase.

"Other work may yet come your way...our way. Wait and see, Marla."

"No. I'll have to find a different way to live...only...only I've got to dare myself to look in a mirror again before I can even think of doing anything again. Any modelling I do will be with my clothes on."

She thought of the words on the other card, the one for her eyes only, sent by Neil. It had been put in her bag, on the shelf of the tall bedside table. The words had been easy to remember and deeply personal. They had offered a glimpse of

160

the other man and a confession. 'Everything…even heaven, can wait until I can look upon you again. The beautiful outer vessel holds the real person I wish to know.'

"We both need a good man, Marla girl," Betty opined brightly and met her friend's look with a smile.

I've found him…I think I've found him, already, and he's found me, Marla thought. Only, we've come from opposite ends of a social scale that counts for nothing…or almost nothing these days. It's whom we are that really matters, who we spend our time with and love. But, those looking in from the outside and saw us together would probably think it unbelievable.

And that's the crazy part, the bit that makes no sense to me at all. I go out looking for a doctor to make me feel good in myself again, take a knife or whatever it is to make me right and he did it without a touch. He didn't do anything! There's been no touch that really said I fancy you; there's been no physical sign to say I want to make love to you; he didn't offer a kiss to demonstrate or convey any attraction to me.

But I knew how it was for Neil…before I got cut! I'm even more certain of it now.

Neil simply showed me, aloofly some might say, that I was in his thoughts. He'd sent the flowers, sent cards, one of them with special words…how do I say it? Yeah, lofty words to express deeper sentiments. Oh yes! The guy's so very far from the image of the man I thought might, one day, replace Eddie. That man was an emotional vagrant compared to Neil. My 'ex' is shallow, so lacking in real feelings or concerns. He's drifted from one relationship to another with heartless and casual ease.

Betty said she'd passed the word but Eddie has made no effort to contact me.

Yeah, the flowers could indeed be from anyone, but I know that only one man has the depth of feeling and the courage to write what he has and to admit, in a few words, how he feels. He's even scribbled out a drawing!

She laughed out loud then grimaced. "Yow!"

"What's up girl?" Betty enquired.

"Nothing, I was just thinking of something I read."

That man! He had drawn some twirly lines in a conical shape; they looked like bandages. And then, he had drawn a butterfly and coloured in a few parts of it! She had got the message, only too clearly. Out of ugliness, a temporary phase, out of that was created beauty. 'Heaven can wait', that had been the clue.

There had been no need to read on although his doodles on the paper had caught her eye and reinforced the message, as if that was needed! The intensity of feelings had been simply expressed in a few words. At any other time, an earlier time in her life, she would have scoffed; she would probably have laughed off the sentimentality of the moment and the writing on the card. But I've had time to think over what had made Neil express deeper emotions in his own quirky way. It had been a heart-breaking event, brought upon someone who held a place in his life, already.

Was she really such a person?

Could it really be so?

Things didn't happen that quickly between people...and certainly not to her or anyone of her acquaintance. Betty would be scornful and speak out some crude explanation that summed up most of her experiences with men.

She'd say Neil, deep down in his kindly heart was probably no different; maybe, he just knew a few tricks that would broaden her own repertoire when it came to it, later, and after they had tired of one another and moved on.

"Well, there's no clue in the card...who they're from, I mean," Betty babbled on. "Still, they brighten up the place while you're here."

"That won't be long...I've only got a few stitches."

"That's for starters..."

"Don't you think I know that?"

"Sorry! Sorry…girl!"

"It's okay…I may as well face up to it!" Marla gave a teasing smile at the unintended poignancy of her remark, but she had spoken out with trembling lips. "Dohhh! See now what you've gone and done?" She gave way to tears. "Sorry…sorry."

"It's me who should be sorry…for saying something stupid."

"Leave it…forget it? It's the truth…I may as well hear it. I have to face up to all that's happened…and whatever it is that Neil has been able to do for me."

"Well, when you're back at home I'm going to be there to help and boost you…keep you bubbly and see the girl again that I really know."

"My life's changed…it will all be changed…everything."

"What's changed, Marla…on the inside?" Betty asked her now as she sat on the edge of the bed and looked down at her friend.

"I've had time to think…it's as if everything I've done in my life or what I've achieved has been squashed into a few hours…a few photo shoots and lots of time in between…that's how it seems to me. I've also had time to think about what those women said…"

"Slags…that's them in a word."

"Never mind all that! I've had time to think over what they said as they cut me. They made me realise…I don't need that way of making money anymore…my time's past…and I don't regret, too much, what I've done while I had the chance. At least no-one got hurt by what I did."

"Too right! And you didn't deserve any of this…" Her look upon Marla showed a deeper sentiment on all that awaited her in the weeks ahead. Betty fell silent.

Marla clutched at her friend's hand.

"Someone thought so…that's why I've ended up in here, slashed to bloody ribbons."

"Someone's mended you…"

"Yeah…I owe him…Neil did it for me, for someone different in his life."

X

She was alone with Neil for a few moments. Betty, bless her, would soon be taking her back home, to an empty house, an altered perception of life and as far as she could remember no commitments in her diary.

A single item of luggage with all that she had brought to the clinic lay on the bed and Neil's bouquet of flowers was again carefully wrapped. Obsessively, she had checked and re-checked that nothing had been left behind. Neil's card was safe; she had made sure of that. Life's memories were made of little items like this.

"May I call to see you?" he asked.

"Doctors? Making house calls? Whatever next?" she smiled. He was immaculately dressed, in a dark blue suit with a light blue shirt and a patterned silk tie; she admired the attention to detail with a practised eye. "Will I see you so smartly dressed next time?"

He gave a little bow of the head in acknowledgement of her remark.

"Hm, I can't think of any medical reason why I should do it…but, you know me?"

"Hardly…but I'm learning."

"Okay…you know something about me," he smiled. "So, you'll know that I can make an exception in your case."

"Thanks. I'll have to think it over, mind you," she spoke out in all seriousness. "I can't receive visitors looking like this, now, can I?"

"I'm your doctor…a special visitor, then…but, okay," he replied with a note of acceptance to his voice.

She stood closer and touched his arm. "The wrapping… the case," she said softly, "it has to be taken away or broken open…"

"To reveal…the butterfly?"

"Yes, something like that," she managed to smile. "I want to make sure that I'm ready to see you again…and others."

"You will, when the dressings and the small sutures have been removed…then, I'll see you again."

"Stop teasing me…you know exactly what I mean, Neil."

"Yes, and you know exactly what I mean, Marla." He held out a hand to her. "I've always seen the butterfly, even now."

She did not take hold as he had hoped and Neil let it fall back to his side before he drew away.

"Step by step, Neil…it's what we agreed."

"Yeah, I think I remember that bit," he answered looking at her with a sweep of his eyes. "Look after yourself?"

"Sure…"

"Call Anne-Marie or me if there is anything…anything that bothers you? When I next see you so much will have again changed and I hope that will restore your belief in how it will finally be for you. Life won't be as it was before…it can't be…but in one respect what we have been able to do for you will be a start, an important stage in making you feel complete again."

"Betty's taking me to an empty house…"

"But your life won't be empty…you have a good friend in Betty and from what she told me many more…"

"She talks too much…"

"Cares for you, Marla."

"Yes…okay, true."

"So, maybe, in time, you will see me in that way too."

"Neil," she said softly. He had made a special journey to see her and in the expectation that perhaps a unique, an intimate bond might be recognised between them. "Closer…

come closer for a moment, please close the space between us? I'm leaving soon."

"Yes, I know…but I don't go for the obvious routine."

"Don't I just know it!" she interrupted laughing and now looked at Neil fondly. Conceding to that simple emotion did not mean any prolonged commitment or an enduring friendship.

He looked unwaveringly at her with stilled and unblinking eyes.

"I'll tell you something else before you go…or we are interrupted. I wanted to tell you that there's been no one else in my life since Annie. When I see you again…outside of any clinic visits, I hope that we can talk?"

"Yes."

We'll see how it goes she thought and gave him a smile that disguised the tumult in her own mind. Assisted by Anne Marie he had attended upon her; now, salvation was in her own hands and she would have to get through the coming days and weeks, somehow, on her own.

She occupied her own homely comforting space; sure, it felt as if she was cloistered away, but the telephone rang frequently enough to dispel any sense that the world or friends had forgotten about her so soon. Eddie, her ex had even called. He had surprised her and was full of the easy chitchat and conciliatory words that she had become used to. It made for a happy contrast with the last time they had spoken and the scarcely concealed animosity of their exchanges. They were emotionally and legally separated now, at least that was what she had thought and kept telling herself.

Memories of Neil and how they had been together and spoken to each other again came to mind. The almost chirpy bubbly repartee that had been her experience with Eddie contrasted with how she was with Neil. It was so very different…so very far from her world with its recognisable boundaries. There she felt at ease.

Because of my divorce…I've merely closed the door on one life.

With Neil, I've looked through an opening door to another, but I've taken care or stayed alive to the differences between us.

Nice and attentive isn't the only guide to the man. Is Neil truly free in spirit, like I want to be again?

She didn't rightly know and had wondered if she could summon up the determination or the interest, after all that she had said, to find out what really made up the man, that Doctor, that Neil Allman-Brown.

"Hi," he said softly, as if in a sigh that acknowledged that he had waited far too long before travelling to see her.

"Hi, I'm glad to see you…I'm grateful that you've taken the trouble to come over here."

"I…I had to," he confessed all too quickly.

Marla had been asked to return within a week of her treatment to have the sutures checked and cleaned. But, the impulse to call upon her had been too great to resist, besotted creature that he was. The thought crossed his mind as Marla welcomed him. Yes, okay…okay! He had to admit it; it had been a long time since he had felt so engaged by a woman. Some, no, many would say it was a baseless sentiment. Image was overcoming sense and reality.

He had grown up, hadn't he?

These juvenile infatuations were of the past, weren't they?

So?

She's a 'looker'; so what?

You want more of someone than the attractions of a fleshy and bountiful outer shell, he thought. Yes, that's true, but the woman had called on him to change that and improve upon her appearance still further but to his practised, manly eye there had been no need. Until…a few days ago.

Someone had desecrated the person and the image he had formed of her. They were likely to get away with their misdeeds. Marla had told him that everything happened too fast that night. It all remained an agonising blur; the wanton heartless sculpting of her face and body by loveless hands had absorbed her mind.

"I've done everything that you asked me to do. I've looked after myself and resisted the temptation to look properly at what you've done for me. I haven't touched this little lot." She pointed to her face and the dressings that covered the wound.

"You can now...and again tomorrow. Anne Marie and I will remove the bindings. You will have no more swathes of bandages to hide behind."

She looked at him with startled eyes.

"You're honest, I'll give you that much, Neil. You're hard even...I haven't felt that I've been hiding behind them at all. I've been waiting...just waiting to get better, here in this little prison of mine."

"Yes...yes, I know." He shook his head at the realisation of how insensitive his words would have sounded. "I'm sorry...I should know better than to say such a thing. I have experience and people have told me often enough what goes through a patient's mind after they've had reconstructive care."

He fell silent. I've been alone, really alone for far too long, he thought. I've lost any real sense, it seems, of saying a gentler word to someone who is close to me or to whom I'd like to be closer.

"Penny for them?" Marla asked as she impulsively touched his chest then drew away just as quickly. "May I do that? May I say that I am glad the doctor's called upon me?"

"Yes...we're alone."

"Would you be in trouble if they...the authorities knew?"

"No…or rather I'm not even going to think about it. I rang you on impulse, there are medical reasons or justification for coming here. There are post-operative reasons too…call it care, or anxiety to see that what I have wanted to bring to you will be achieved."

Marla laughed softly but touched her face. "Oh! I've still got to take care when I do that!"

"It all helps…and it's nice to hear your laugh again."

"No more heavy words, Neil? Just tell me that you wanted to see me. So, you came over."

"Okay…I've been rumbled." He smiled in acknowledgement of the obvious. "You did say, before the op, that all we had was simply a doctor and patient thing."

"That was then," she answered, "and as I've already told you, nothing's ever simple, not for me any way."

"It never was," he smiled; his reply had been amiable enough.

"See me without the bandages, on my face and here," she said pointing to her breasts. "We can then see how the patient and doctor thing has worked out, or how I as the customer feel about what's been done to fix me…to set me up somehow for a new life, whether I wanted it or not…or in the way it's worked out."

"And before? What about the time spent with me before it all happened? Did that count for anything?" As he spoke he became preoccupied with a small case that seemed to hold all that was needed in the way of surgical instruments and dressings. The case was opened but little removed from it.

"Yes, but in spite of what we said…your flowers and your visit now…we need to think it all through, at least I do." She spoke evenly as if a process of appraising all that they might learn of each other had begun.

"Fine," he said in a cool tone of acknowledgement as he looked about the room. "Is there a stool you can sit on? I need to examine your face and our treatment carefully."

"Through there. Come?" She crooked a finger beckoning to him. They did not speak again until she was settled in the kitchen, a modern delight of tiling, wood cabinets, glass and crisp lighting.

"Your scent's wonderful," he observed as he began to lay out a few instruments but left their wrappings in tact.

"I still put it on, for myself at least…but thank you, for noticing."

She watched him take off his jacket and cast it casually to one side on a worktop, the keys in his pockets clacking on the surface. Neil then began to wash his hands in slow sensual sweeps before he pulled on thin latex gloves; it was an act that held its own momentary appeal for her.

"Let's have look? If it has gone as I hoped I might be able to remove some…not all, of the sutures. A lighter dressing will help," he smiled, "with your looks."

"I'm expecting more," she said in a very matter of fact voice, "a lot more."

"I know, and so am I…of your looks I mean. The burden's on me…to be your saviour in that respect at least."

He began to ease the dressings from her cheek as he talked, working gently and stopping to look in her eyes and in doing so to enquire if she was discomfited by his gentle steady progress. Marla gave no sign and saw him offer a satisfied smile and a gentle nod of appreciation.

"What? What?" she asked in an excited voice. She grabbed at his arm as Neil gently turned her face from him to study his handiwork. "Is it okay? Is it as you wanted?" she asked with a rising note of interest and anxiety.

"Oh yes."

In the time that had elapsed since their last meeting the wound had closed neatly; only a thin line could be discerned, a healthy pink in colour and with the faintest suture markings on each side.

"Well?"

"Have you got a mirror? A hand mirror? In here?"

"No…there's one in the cloakroom." She made to leave the seat only to be gently restrained.

"Wait."

"I've done that! Let me go there…I'll be able to see it for myself and judge your work."

"Not in there." Neil stripped off the gloves as he spoke. "I'll bring it in here…may I do that?"

"Please yourself," she answered flatly noting as she spoke how Neil's eyes narrowed on hearing her tone of voice.

"No, I'm doing it to help you. It's also a slightly cleaner atmosphere in here."

"A lot cleaner, Neil."

"Take it easy, I'm not having a dig at anything."

Marla shifted on the seat. "Just show me what the damage is…or is likely to be? Will you get on and do that, please Neil?"

"Sure," he said in a clipped tone and without looking at her.

"And?"

Neil held out a gold painted ornately framed mirror. "Observe madam…the wound has healed even better and quicker than I dared to hope. You've done as I asked of you… and behaved yourself."

"Yeah, for far too long." She gave him a smile but he made as if he had not fully heard the reply she had given; instead he placed the mirror on the worktop in front of her.

"Turn round…that's it, just to face the mirror for a moment. I'll explain what we could do next."

"I could take my blouse off and you could look at the rest of me. How's that?"

"No…that's for another time and for someone else. I came to see your face, what it is that I know and remember. Anne Marie will attend to everything else, tomorrow…or is it the day after?"

He shook his head in annoyance but thought it was of no consequence. She would be back at the clinic soon enough. His wait for Marla's restoration would not be long.

"Check me out Neil? Reassure me…help me sleep better by knowing it has all come good, all of your work. How my face is repaired is only one part of what I need to feel. What my body needs to feel…and I need to know, is that I will be complete again."

"And I've told you already. There's more to it than just the outside." He paused for only a few seconds. "Now? Sit still. I'm going to see if I can remove a few of the stitches." Some cleansing spirit was dabbed onto her skin before he snipped at a tiny knot. "Ready girl?"

"Uhhuh." She nodded, felt the latex against her skin and grew tense. "Take care."

"Of you? Yes."

"That's what I meant," she replied after the first suture had been gently eased from her.

"I know. I should take care of the outside, what I and everyone else can see. Others…Betty for one, can help you to complete the restoration of the inner you."

Marla looked at him now and pursed her lips as if out of consideration for him and what she was to say.

"That's what I reckoned. I've had time to think it all through. In spite of what we've done I can't believe in anything more than a great doctor and patient thing between us."

Her voice fell away as Neil resumed his work and she moved in response to a touch upon her face, a gentle tracing of the wound, from her ear down to the point of her chin.

"Still! Be still!" he said harshly. Their eyes met and he gave a slow nod. "Okay…I hear you."

She closed her eyes to blot out the image of him for a moment. "We're too different, Neil."

"We're both alone." He did not stop in his slow gentle work, so carefully and almost tenderly performed. "We're both alone, for now at least."

"Yes, but there could be others, Neil."

"Are there others, possible others in your life?"

"No," she answered softly. "But, there are people…men who live in the same fashion or show world as I do"

"Have done!" he intervened adding more emphatically, "you have done. I thought it would all be put in the past, especially after all that you've been through."

"The cuts? They made me think of other ways. Some may remember, many more may see me do work along similar lines but modelling, doing discreet promotional stuff. A bit of makeup, hide the neat little line you'll have made of the cut…and I'll be back, somehow and somewhere. It pays…and it gives me some control over my life again."

"You'll adapt, is that what you mean?"

"Sure, it's no big deal. I'll move on."

"Are you sure? Are you sure it's where you want your life to go?"

"It's an option," she answered casually. Neil put down the small tweezers and stood next to her leaning against the worktop.

"There's…there's another way."

"The prince…and the showgirl?"

She gave a little enquiring smile. This kind of easy chat suited her. She had rehearsed how to speak to him the next time she saw Neil and if he should ask for a closer relationship between them, or to explore the possibilities for them getting together. It had even occurred to her too as her emotions to find a place in his life vied with others, those that meant a return to the society that she and Betty knew so well.

Her friend had simply told her to get Neil to fix her, to make it right again and for her not, at all costs, to get drawn into a heavy relationship, or ties and any commitments. No girl, not yet! She'd just been freed from all of that. So, live a little and maybe love a lot; find a guy to make you feel right again…that's what Betty had told her. And…she had slowly come round and agreed with her. She'd been to a clinic to get fixed not to get laid!

That Betty, she knew how to choose her words.

That Betty, she'd just come out and told her that Neil was a guy to mend her, not a guy for her to think of as one she owed any particular fleshy favours to. Was she tempted to think like that of him? Sure, he was strong and good-looking, but…he took his time. Being deliberate and slow was fine…only, say something to let me know it was heading somewhere I needed to be, and soon.

That girl, Betty! She just told it to you straight. Don't go getting into any sentimental kind of bind with the guy, that way you avoid making mistakes. You've made a few of those, girl, and you've become a victim. It was time to take control for a while and see who was out there.

There's no rush; that was how Betty had put it and how she had finally accepted it. But, the man was with her now and he cared for her. How did the saying go? Oh yes, 'I can't get my head around it'.

But that man, Neil, my doctor…my doctor Neil. He had a way of saying things that just made me stop and think where I was going or aiming to go. There were other ways to decide on him weren't there? It was no good relying on some instinct that you felt well up inside you just because he was different and caring. He gave; he just gave without wanting anything obvious in return. He'd said it all along…step by step. I couldn't find anything wrong in that. I knew that I didn't have to look for any faults in where he was coming from, or how he chose to come onto me.

There's only so many ways to tell a girl, a woman, that you fancied her. But Neil, he'd found a way. He had mended her. Oh shit! I don't know what to do or say. I'm all screwed up…yeah, how I wish I was, 'all screwed up'! They could decide on a few important emotions there and then…on them silk sheets I sleep on, alone.

The man interrupted her moment's thoughts.

"No, it's not the prince and the showgirl. It's just you and me."

He looked at her with stilled eyes. Absent for now was the livelier interest in them that she had seen on his arrival, the pleasure on meeting her again so evident. He had made it seem so simple, to care.

"I kept an open mind," she blurted out. "I hoped that it might all turn out so different."

"Well, at least I've seen you and found you so much better. Your life is saved." He took her hand and kissed the knuckles, just once.

"Neil…?

"Take care…see you tomorrow?"

"Yes…you too. Mind how you go."

Their exchanges sounded banal yet strangely truthful to her.

She watched him clean up and wrap the instruments in some tissues before placing them in his bag that he snapped shut emphatically, as if the task she had set him was almost complete. He had been in her company for less than an hour yet she felt that they had exchanged so much.

"Anne Marie will be impressed with how you are doing. I'll let her know and tell her to expect a new woman!"

The door closed behind him with a click and he then heard the sliding of the bolts. The light over the doorway illuminated the brick and stone paving of the entranceway for only a moment. It was long enough for him to settle back in the driver's seat of the little coupe' that they had driven in to the glider field only a few days, a week, however long ago it was.

The sky above him was cloudless and maybe, just maybe, he would see some stars when he got clear of the town lights and the fluorescent orange glare that illuminated everything except what he held most dear or sought to be reacquainted with.

"Oh God! Why now…why here?"

There was nothing he could do in the time and space allowed to him. Contra-flows on the motorway were not the place to behave like a 'tear arse', as some would describe the driver's actions of a careering vehicle heading towards him. He recalled in an instant that the studious observance of certain rules and limits had been expected of him and in particular by his inner self. What others did for themselves alone could hurt you.

"I'm near you!"

He called out to Jamie for terminal solace, only once.

The stars were bright against the darkened heavens as earthly bonds fell away.

ை

Robert In Perpetuam

A story to mark the 25th Anniversary
of the Falklands War.

Emily stood alone, waiting...waiting until she was quite alone.

"Robbie, it's your Emily. I'm here with you now, at long last. You're never out of my thoughts...I can't forget you."

Her words were carried away on the wind as two small wooden crosses were pushed with trembling hands into the finely raked and tended gravel spread around the simple gravestone. Its beauty was an evocative remembrance of a man's sacrifice for another.

"I...I love you still my darling man, even now...right here, in the freezing wind! I'm all wrapped up in my warm clothes but the wind here is something else! It just cuts into you. It's as well I've got a scarf to cover my greying hair. Yes, I stopped being blonde some time ago but I don't care; I've kept it in the style you always liked. I'm old, some say, but that's only what they can see. I know who I am, Robbie...I'm still your girl...I'm young, on the inside, and your love and memory keeps me that way...time has stood still. I've not grown old...just...just as you never grew old, with me beside you...to hold and love you.

You see? No one came close to filling my life as you did, Robbie. I stopped looking at anyone else after I met you and I haven't since...since you were taken from me...when you were taken from us!

Yes, us!

I knew...I felt deep down in me that it wasn't a surprise to you when our son was born. You see? I've felt you near me even if you're in a special place now.

I just know that you have seen him, our lovely boy, Robert. I had to name him after you...I just had to...and you know why? It was because I wanted to keep saying a name that clicked with me...to express a name that brought so many memories back to me...of you, my darling man and of our times together.

We had fun, didn't we? We had a great life together on the base, with other men and women who were part of the team, the Army family who took pride in all that they did, for the Battalion, for each other as comrades in arms, and, for their country.

You believed in what you were tasked to do and you prepared me for what you had to face...you didn't have to spell it out, or go into any detail but...you told me, quietly, of the ultimate sacrifice that you might be called upon to make. Yes, you told me so bravely that you might have to die for what you believed in and trained for...looking after comrades, your mates and for us, your kith and kin.

Darling Robbie, your memory lives on, even if I'm thousands of miles away across an ocean and your body's here in a military cemetery...among the crosses 'row on row'. I can't remember who wrote the words, but they click with me. I've seen them here...your cross on the simple stone...and, I've also seen relatives stand by them back home...and at all those cemeteries, across The Channel of men who died in other wars. A loved one, lost, is not forgotten...you're not forgotten, even if I've been without you so many years. You're precious to me, still! My memories don't fade...someone wrote about that too and, silly me, I can't remember who that was either.

Never mind, you know what I mean, don't you Robbie?

From my cruise ship, just as you must have done from a landing craft so many years ago, I saw these beautiful islands and thought...how lonely...so lonely, but so recognisable as some parts of a wilderness back home would be. You couldn't have seen a final resting-place, like this. It's so cold and windswept, so wild and desolate, with no trees...it's so wild and empty...there's a view towards a hill...I can see an expanse of endless ocean, and...I can look up and see heaven touching an endless sky.

Don't laugh at me, Robbie! I've had a long time to think about all I want to tell you, now that I'm here beside you once more. I looked up at the endless sky so often on my way down here. I stood on deck and just looked up and I wondered where you were...among the stars.

You're there now in what I imagine as heaven, a place of peace and tranquillity. Robbie, you played a part, got mentioned in despatches. Your CO wrote me a lovely letter to say how proud he was, and the Battalion, on account of your bravery and selflessness in action and tending to others. I can't imagine, or want to know or torture myself again with thoughts of how they found you.

Oh God! I want to remember you as a strong and handsome man, so loving and devoted. You would have been a great dad. You are a great Dad, thank God!

Only, I nearly lost our boy on account of the news I got about you. I had Robert early, far too early some said, but I looked on his birth so differently. I was given consolation or God sent me help, in his own way. Robert had to come and nuzzle me, comfort me at my breast when I knew you had gone from me, forever. That's how I looked on his birth, my darling, darling man. I found relief in his small frail body; he was so dependent on my love and attention, just as I had found it with you.

You're lying here Robbie, under this sodden ground, and yet I'm close to you...so close. My flowers will bring some colour to this barren cheerless place...a foreign field, a haven that has a raw, start of the world, beauty about it. Only, it's not home...our home for me and for you.

Home is *'our cottage'*, that's what I named our house, just that. I haven't moved on, as it's the place where you last spoke and loved me...so tenderly. It felt as though you knew that our parting was meant to be this way.

Sorry, I'm sorry. I need to speak it all out now, my darling man...I've become a bit weepy."

She sighed and drew deep breaths for comfort. The small wooden British legion crosses had her name and their son's neatly written upon them. The wood and the writing would fade but her memories of him would endure…

"I have to go soon, after waiting so long…such a long time to be here. I saved and got by somehow until I had the money to go on a cruise of remembrance, for that's the reason for me being here. I wanted, just once, to be with you, here, in body as well as mind.

The sights, the sounds, the laughter and the feelings of unreality didn't distract me…or take my mind off the reason for why I'm here, Robbie. It wanted to be with you again, for the last time in this worldly sense because I don't want to travel any more. I've been with you and now I'm leaving the cruise. I've had enough. I'm flying back home…not via Argentina, you'll be relieved to know."

Emily looked about her but she was afforded privacy and could speak out every thought that came to her as she knelt by Robert's gravestone, the unit's emblem beautifully carved on the stonework above his name and rank.

"See? I'm talking to you here, in the wind and chill as if we're so close and holding hands like we used to. I'm simply touching the place where you now lie and drawing some comfort from you. Can you sense my presence too? I hope so, my darling man. You were so good at offering me reassurance that, somehow, you'd get through the invasion and the fighting to regain our possessions.

And now?

You wouldn't believe the changes this place has undergone since…since you left me. The war made a difference; a small jewel in the crown has been buffed up. And still the Argies lay claim to this place. So I pray, I pray that other women won't weep the tears that I have done for the love of their lives…in places such as this.

I'll have to do a lot of that…praying and hoping. We still get into things and have to really wonder, 'why'?

Many will say your death and those of so many others was 'worth it' or a 'price worth paying'. Maybe, but we...the country, had its pride then. Now, it's a lot of talk and your kind is no longer about or recognised for what they really do. You served our country, our friends and neighbours honourably. Your memory, your pictures are all about me at home; a few of your things keep you alive...in my heart and wakeful mind.

Only...only, something died in me when the news came that awful tear drenched day. I became a widow, bereft through war of the man who was meant to be my lifelong soulmate. Well, so you are Robbie darling. Only now, and since the day you left me, you rest in my heart and mind, but dead...dead to my softened wondering touch.

Happiness now is your son...he's away from me, at work, but he's close. He's devoted, as I knew you to be. He does it out of instinct; I don't ask him to attend on me. He feels a bond; it's strong and I love him for it, just as I loved you...love you still.

I see you in our Robert. Thank God you left me with him as a comforter.

I feel you near me in spirit. I often wake in the middle of the night and speak to you in wonder.

Are you with me again, my one true man...my Robert?

That's what I say.

Or, I might say, 'have you come to see me again, have you come to be with your Emily?'

Oh yes, we speak, or I do because...because you're close, you're so near to me at times like that...I wake up and I know the reason why. That's how your visits are for me; that's how I know you're near me. There's a bond between us, Robbie, and it won't be broken, it can't be. You see? There's a silver thread that keeps us together...as one, between this world and the next.

That's my life's little secret. I know of it but I keep those feelings to myself. Folks either feel that way or they don't. I

183

feel…and I know of it, Robbie, my one true man. I believe you're in an afterlife and so, one day, I'll be beside you and I'll hold you close. We'll smile…we'll be together and have no cares."

She stroked the surface of the gravestone to reaffirm the bond to her man.

"Robbie, rest in peace…you're my Robert in perpetuam… I got the Latin bit from some book or other. Yes…you're my Robert, forever."

"I love you…love you…I miss you…miss you."

Emily stood up, felt her knees creak, and drew the jacket about her body as a wrap of comfort and in a clasp that sought to restore an inner strength.

"Thank you," she said to the guide, as the little gate in the dyke-stone wall that surrounded the small cemetery was closed behind her. A final glance was cast upon the headstones…row on row.

"It's quite okay, Emily," Fred answered giving her an understanding smile. "The time is yours…yours alone."

"Yes…yes, mine alone."

Emily's determined face and lively, tear filled eyes met his look upon her.

"For many, this is hallowed ground," Fred continued, prompted by the woman's tears.

"Yes…to my man's memory and so many others. I wish my husband wasn't so far away or that he had gone to make good what man had done unto man."

A ray of sunshine pierced the clouds beyond them and glittered upon the endless ocean.

Of Satin and of Steel

I

Nicole, your reputation lives on!

Can you believe it?

You were recognised, and in such unlikely surroundings!

You were on a flight, to Dubai…so, far away from your usual haunts.

And here you are…the desert kingdom has to be seen! You've read so much about the place or you've been told about its attractions.

How could you pass through without seeing the Emirate City for yourself?

Exactly! Explain that one, if you dare!

Everyone 'who is anyone' seems to come here or has an investment property as a conspicuous hideaway amongst a well-to-do elite.

But not you, you're here for a very good reason.

It made no sense exhausting yourself when a brief stopover for a day or two might be the ideal preparation for the onward journey.

Oh God! It's hot out here…I can't keep still.

Oh, I was certainly persuaded that it was a good idea coming to this place…until, that is, I left the aircraft.

Now…I can't bear it.

The heat! The heat's intolerable!

I could go back into the comparative cool of the 'plane and wait, only there are other passengers pressing up behind me to get off.

So…I'll just have to put up with it…accept that I'm not going anywhere for a while longer.

Why fret or worry? There's no sign of the transfer bus… just miles and miles of concrete…with an aircraft parked here or there and the terminal way off in the distance.

Try and relax, you're a visitor passing through en route to a new opportunity, so be prepared to endure the trip alone, just this once. Your friends back home were helpful; they just came out and told you that the flight 'down under' would test your resolve.

How right they were!

"Never mind Nikki," they said, laughing. "Long-distance travel has changed...the flying boats stopped long ago...the trip doesn't take nearly so long as it did then."

"In a time when there was a sense of style," you remember telling them.

"And considerable noise and discomfort."

Yes, they'd reminded you of that too and you had to agree. Still, you clung to the belief that it seemed so much more romantic, then.

Oh well, Nikki, desert heat and hazy horizons beckon, if the bus ever shows up.

They were pervasive thoughts soon interrupted.

"Goodbye, Miss Nicole." She was acknowledged for one last time.

The stewardess, Margot, was formal and polite; a beaming smile had been the outward sign of a deeply felt pleasure to meet Nicole Gorrin-Eyre...ballerina. Well, a former ballerina, or to some a 'danseuse' who had become a principal. She took no exception, in the early days of her career, to the deprecating label of 'danseuse'. Grace, sublime technique and emotional intensity in a performance had won many loud calls of her name, some years ago now, to soften any hurt or insult that the word may have provoked at the time of their utterance.

Deeds spoke louder than words.

The overused phrase was appropriate to her circumstances; she strove for perfection and followed the example set by her peers, in the Kirov and Bolshoi ballet companies whenever they could be seen. Whether she had been admired or not, the corps de ballet had an ambitious talent amongst its members. She could never be described as a conformist, although she acknowledged the heritage of dance and interpretation so many artistic directors sought of her to sustain. No, instead she had thought of herself as a creator loosely bound by tradition and with every intention of developing her art.

She strove to instil new life into the work she lived for. Now, and whenever the opportunity arose she choreographed; a suppleness of body and mind persisted so younger women, and even male dancers, could be shown exactly what she sought. Devoted, some said passionate, involvement was a description often given to her presence in rehearsal rooms; for her the only remaining ambition was to bequeath a vibrant legacy.

"Thank you for all that you have done. The flight was a pleasure."

These parting words had been spoken in all sincerity; Margot had made it possible without any of the other first class passengers believing that she was receiving exceptional treatment. Margot knew the secret – to care for many, but devote your self discreetly to the few. Margot Bourdain the name badge told her.

"You only have to ask," Margot smiled when drinks had been served during the flight.

The young woman possessed a fine, even memorable, first name that soon brought to my mind a ballerina of peerless quality…to my eyes at least, yet in Margot Fonteyn I also remember a woman struck by personal tragedy.

Still, to be on a stage with Nureyev and dance a pas de deux with him, now that would make up for some of your unhappier moments, surely? Never mind that now. Leave it…

"Stand and wait, wait…wait," she said to herself and tapped a foot irritably on the metal decking of the steps.

The heat, in the middle of the night was unbearable and a glance at her surroundings indicated that they were nowhere near the passenger terminals. They would all have to wait…yes, just stand, fidget and wait.

What else did I say?

Oh yes. "Enough…I've had quite enough, thank you."

Her hand with only a slight and discernible tremble had been held over the glass. That much could be remembered. Champagne was a favourite but it would never do to drink more than two glasses before dinner. Service in the curtained off First Class section of the aircraft had seemed more stately and serene...so I had to behave accordingly.

Anything else? Oh yes, an envelope had been left with my name neatly written on its face; it lay within the folds of the napkin. Inside, there was a simple note written on light blue paper:

'Forgive my intrusive request, please? I have been honoured to see you and to be of assistance. I was at Covent Garden, in 1986, to see you dance in 'Swan Lake' and was captivated by your interpretation. It has remained an enduring memory. My father took me, as a birthday present. May I have your autograph, please, to keep with the photograph I still have from that night?'

Yes, in a small touching way my reputation endures with some people, still.

◆

I'm on my way, again. Farewell, until the next time.

She closed her eyes and settled into the gently reclined seat; through the headphones Rachmaninov's Piano Concerto could be heard yet the music was not the distraction she hoped for, even if it was a favourite. The aircraft banked before setting its new course and she chose the moment to gaze out of the window at a desert scene far below.

Dubai had been a revelation and thought provoking; without any cause for complaint, of anything, the hotels' guest questionnaire would make pleasant reading for its management; she had completed it with scarcely a second's thought. The staff had been attentive, not obsequious, and proclaimed a devoted change from what she often endured elsewhere. At home, back in England, she might encounter the condescending smile of an apparent servility, ill conceived as the notion of service to the customer may have been in the giver's mind.

In a Jumeira Beach hotel the men and women aimed simply to attend to every need or request made of them. The grand, not sumptuous, surroundings were spotlessly clean and created a cool oasis in a desert that was all too visible but unrecognisable close by her window. It would have been easier to observe the hectic panorama from a hot and very dusty balcony, if she had chosen to step outside into the heat of the day.

Elsewhere lay the world she knew or was more accustomed to seeing and at ease with. Close to the hotel, construction sites had prevailed upon the view; from her vantage point the men appeared small as they stepped from the grey buses that had brought them from their employer's camps. A blue overall and white hard hat identified an army of workers, uniformly dressed for an offensive to transform the area. Buildings towered over the hotel, truck engines beat a noisy rhythm and cranes swung their loads high over her head. Amber warning lights flashed and hammers beat a staccato rhythm.

The margins to the swimming pool and the hotel's garden offered some of 'natures' solace, but not too much. Outside there was no greenery, no vegetation save for the stunted growth of palms, encased in hessian sacking to protect them, and placed by a developer to break the angular vista and vertical lines of monumental structures. Modern design vied incongruously with Muslim traditional architectural form; alien vernacular styles more at home in Europe, Italy in particular, drew further attention to glaring inconsistency. Terracotta roofs to a parade of shops shocked the eye in a mingle-mangle of designs aimed at providing a more human street scene. She possessed conservative tastes in such matters and had quickly concluded that the developers had failed; everyone and everything was dwarfed by the monolithic structures created all about them.

It seemed as if Bedlam was being built in front of her, around her, and eerily over her. She marvelled at the views yet a humble human scale was absent from her perspective; man was but a small essential to the vision of a new land. No simple explanation could be found for her reaction to all that could be seen, so, it was easier to concede that without man's ingenuity and organisation none of the creative work would have been possible. The determination to transform the landscape was admirable but images from the silent movies came easily to mind, of factory work, of men and women tending machines, but who was in control?

"That's the impression I'm left with," she remembered telling her friend, Loualla, over a clear mobile 'phone connection before discussing the onward journey.

"You don't sound very relaxed, Nikki."

"No, I don't fell like that at all…fortunately, the feeling will pass," she confided.

"You can be sure of that, right here with us."

"I can't wait to be with you," she had answered before going on to admit, "but, I had to visit this place, just to confirm my impressions after all that I've read about it."

She was in an unaccountable and fearful awe of a locale where a night and a whole day had been spent. Her stay was thankfully brief. Not my kind of destination at all she had quickly concluded but the critical thoughts and dislike were premature. She accepted that much. They were sentiments she encountered in her work often enough but she had witnessed something unique and inspiring.

The Emirate Kingdom was being transformed yet it was into a world that she could not fully recognise as offering any comfort to her own inner self. She had tried but the predominant thought was of fakery; the desert home intended for so many people felt contrived and quite out of place. The word 'globalisation' was often heard; was this really the product of well-meaning aspirations she so often had to listen to over the radio? There was 'sameness', a lack of a unique distinguishing mark, that would set all that had been seen apart from any large Western city. Man was in control of this narrow strip;

for some, a green swathe had been fashioned from the desert sands not far beyond the boundary of the concrete and steel oases linked by a wide highway.

"But, were you impressed?" Loualla had still asked in an effort to wring a grudging confession from her.

"Frightened I think would be a better way of putting it." Everywhere she looked, or had travelled, a view more recognisable had been disclaimed, and all of it achieved by the sheer scale of development. "I thought of home comforts...the relief to be found in my 'ancient' home and a sense of place."

"Well, I hope you'll feel at home here with us," she was told affectionately and with friendly reassurance. "It will be quite wonderful to see you and to talk face-to-face instead of on a telephone...with the world between us."

"Yes, and I need to be with you, Loualla. Wonderful as it is...to someone's eye, I need to be away from here. It's modern and a testimony of what the human hand and mind can now achieve."

"But?" Her friend picked up on the doubts she continued to express.

"But...it all feels so remote. No one seems to live in the places I've seen or driven through. There they are, these little oases of new buildings...modern creations, but I see no beauty that I can relate to. I simply get an impression of *'money after more money'*. Where will it all end?"

"Soft now," her friend almost purred. "Come to us...you'll be restored!"

There, it was the heart-warming laugh that she had heard as the humane counterpoint to what must have seemed the irrational observations she had given voice to.

Yes," she sighed.

"We need to see each other again!" Loualla consoled.

"Oh yes! I'm all right, really I am," she observed somewhat defensively now. "I needed this diversion...if only to remind myself that in dance, so in architecture. Creativeness does not necessarily mean a complete rejection of the past, of a historical legacy. Diaghilev is not forgotten, is he? They're not bored with Petipa's choreography for Swan Lake, are they?"

"No," Loualla replied with a sigh, reacting to the serious even depressing thread that ran through their conversation. "Nikki?"

"Yes, Lou?"

"Get on that plane! Have a drink…have a few! Then, think of all that awaits you…what we've got to talk about and catch up on, to remember, and what you're going on to do."

"Creative dance…the new fashioned from the old, inspired by the past but not enslaved to it." She brightened. "Theatre… art, colour and music!" She had felt calmer. "And there's you to be with…it's been so long, so very long!"

"Yes…you'll find a home for your thoughts down here with us."

"Yes, another home for my thoughts and memories."

"Be the girl I know, Nikki."

I had to laugh at that one, she remembered now.

"Deep down, yes."

"Don't change that, don't you dare, and not when you're here with us!.."

"No."

There's a desert not unlike like the one I saw being transformed outside my hotel bedroom window. There's a little desert in my mind…no, in my life.

I'm alone.

I'm alone, but I find ways to skirt that inner wasteland by passing through more fertile and comforting margins that I call my work, a few close friends and family. Work, creative and expressive endeavour, fills the many hours that another might share with a loving companion. There was a time I closed my eyes and danced a solo; I 'listened' and communed with a partner that I knew was nearby in a dialogue of sensory contact, communicating our emotions in silence. And then, with our touch upon each other renewed, we performed a pas de deux. Our union of mind and body transcended all that had gone before. Then, each moment on the stage was a provocative reunion of mind and body, emotionally moving and joyously physical.

But who fills my life now?

I'm alone and old…older and living alone.

I'm on a voyage…off on my travels.

Once more I am setting out on a journey, filled with hope. It is an all too recognisable journey that is work and creativity, the re-interpretation of the old to create the new, the vibrant and the colourful, the expressive and the joyful. It is soft, recognisable as being human and sentient…therefore, it must lie somewhere in all that I witnessed in the desert oasis. My art should have been of help to me in reaching an understanding of those scenes. The true legacy of the 'old' is that it provides an enduring foundation to all that is innovative.

I have learned to improvise. Musical tastes and new compositions sustain my art and prolong my association with it for I would be 'lost' if I were to stand on the outside of the dance world and look in. Approval may not follow until time has passed and a less emotional and visceral assessment is made possible. I have always been prepared to listen when reflective criticism is offered rather than the heated dismissal of new ideas.

Someone stood close by.

"Yes, I will have a glass of champagne after all."

She had been lost in thought and the stewardess gave a soft smile as if in recognition of her remoteness. Have I really drunk the first one so unaware of it? I must have done.

How I wish for a creation in my own life, my all too visible life that also sustains me, the woman…the girl, as Loualla would have it! It's not much to ask even at my time of life, or is it? We all need someone…one, just one with whom to share a really close union, close of skin and to the eye, to the voice and mind, a kindred spirit that binds and does not hold captive or represses the inner self.

II

"Would you like some coffee?" Dinner was finished and cleared away.

"No, thank you…but, I'd like some more champagne please, if that's possible?"

"I'll be along in a moment…I'll serve the other passengers. Is that okay?"

"Yes…fine." Conversations were kept brief.

In a while, refreshed, she settled once more and pressed the button on one arm of the chair. Relax, you'll soon be in the company of friends. Let the mind wander. Go on. Rest…rest. Dismiss any intrusive thoughts. Play some music, there's enough to chose from. Clever you! You've worked out the technique for tuning in to the entertainment system.

Her eyes fluttered, then they were closed.

"I'm thinking of you," Loualla told her when arrangements had still to be made for the trip, "so I called."

"You read my thoughts, I was about to call you! I'm coming your way! Can you believe it?"

"When? When?" It was a happy enquiring reply. "Make it soon!"

"Yes! I am…I'm making it very soon!" She had picked up on the infectious happy laugh of her friend. "Soon…is in just two weeks time!"

"Great! Bloody marvellous…sorry. I can swear a bit when hubby's not around."

"Say it then!"

"I will!" Lou paused. "What the heck…I've got an excuse to swear. You're coming here, and so bloody soon, girl!"

"It'll be just like old times!" They shared in a friendly harmony of anticipation at the news.

"Yes!" Lou exclaimed, "and there's no 'fines' tin! It saves me a fortune." They had both laughed some more. "Visit us on your way, do that for me please, Nikki?"

"Yes…I have absolutely no intention of a fly by."

"Good. Andrew would call it *'touching base'*…but that's too cold and impersonal."

"I quite agree. It's a bit condescending too…that's how I would take it." She had gone on to say, "I'm thinking of you, dear, so I thought I'd call…ease the conscience that I am away enjoying myself somewhere, without you…maybe?"

"Steady…"

"Okay, I know it is heaven as far as you two are concerned."

"Close…I struck gold."

"Lucky you…Lou!"

"Yes," came her slow response inviting an admission. Time had passed and Loualla had not shared in any secrets of her friend's other life.

"Apart from me the house's empty…it has been for quite a while now. I make up for it in other ways…in my creative life." I have a body still aching for release, even from age's bonds. I have to look after it although the years have taken their toll, so slowly that it often goes unnoticed. "I can still show an audience how I feel or how the music affects me…I have no choice, Lou. I practice and exercise all my movements so I can maintain some agility. I have to! Everyone I work with has to be shown the old girl can still do it…creakily sometimes and it hurts later! I'll admit that much to you."

"Let me see you…soon. I can't imagine you the way you describe yourself at all."

"I can still make them gasp…"

"Men?" Loualla teased.

"Chance would be a fine thing," she chuckled. "No, the company I work with. I play an active part…demonstrating moves if they're too new…or they're too innovative. I even do it on my own, in front of the mirrors."

"You deserved everything…you had such devotion. We all knew that you gave of yourself in the roles you danced, Nikki."

"They still seem surprised, even now, but…I know no other way. Those that follow have to know the art has to re-create itself to stand any chance of survival. That's my opinion."

"You made them gasp Nikki…you were wonderfully inventive…even suggestive."

"It couldn't be otherwise…I expressed all that I felt or the music and the story inspired within me."

Oh yes, she remembered everything.

Emotions had to be conveyed by her grace and agile movement, by timing and an expressive touch. More, there could be the hint of a caress but flesh was only aroused in the observer's receptive mind. Yes, I played a part on the stage, inflamed emotions by the hint of passionate physical love between two people. It was for the audience to infer its consummation.

"You gave everything, I remember that too…in every role."

Loualla's fallen into my reflective mood only she could not be told, or guess, that I never met the man who I could say counted for everything in my other life, my inner self, the life off-stage and out of the public's eye. To admit that would be to confess to a dependency on another and I have never felt that, or, not yet. To do so or even hint at it, for real, would be to surrender my individuality and all that burned within me…and still does. The creative flame would flicker and I might be dependent upon another to sustain it. I haven't met the man who could distract me off my life's path, such as it is or has become as I've grown older.

"I'm still here, Lou."

"I was beginning to wonder. Is life getting to you...are you so closed in on yourself?"

"Not particularly..."

"What's that supposed to mean?"

"There's been no one special in my life for quite a while...I seem to inspire intense emotions in others by what I do or encourage others to portray through dance. I haven't found it for myself...I'm leaving it a bit late."

"Nonsense, girl! There's time...it just has to be the right one, the right man. We can always talk about it when you're here." Lou's voice hardened for only an instant. "If I'll let you...there's plenty to distract you here. You never know," she added with a soft chuckle, "you may meet someone new, here on the other side of the world...right here in Perth, WA, and away from your usual haunts."

"Yes, there's always that" she said doubtfully before thinking 'what, and to be torn from all that is familiar'?

"Still, my creative instincts haven't deserted me. I've been lucky. I'm travelling your way because I've been asked to commemorate the opening of a new theatre dedicated to ballet and dance in all of its expressive guises."

"Well then, think of nothing else...and be happy here with us for the short time you can stay. You're always welcome. Besides...we can still talk of anything, can't we, in spite of our separation? Nothing's changed there, has it?"

"No...and you're right," she answered after a moment's thought. "I really need this break from my life's usual routines."

I'm alone was the pervasive thought as she pressed the 'off' button on her mobile 'phone. I've been asked to collaborate upon a ballet, the depth of my involvement has yet to be decided upon; it suits my present mood perfectly and my life doesn't depend upon it, in any way. Through a staged musical narrative accompanied by dance I can concentrate upon all that moves the human spirit...there are two central characters;

other dancers in the company will each portray what is good and evil within us. And then, there will be periods of silence, the dancers held in a single spotlight as if to affirm that each living soul is unique.

It is but the outline of an idea; I have yet to meet the company and the musical director...and they've got to meet me, creaky old me they may come to say. Shush! You're not creaky...slower and more stately in your movements that's all, still lithe and graceful, slender of form. Yes, the face is lined but you have the happiest of smiles! That's what they keep telling you, those you trust and who are close to you. The hair's a bit greyer, but it retains its silken vitality...you've cared for it as you have of yourself. Your clothes fit you beautifully as if they were made to suit someone only with the grace and ease of movement that you possess.

Age shall not weary me...at the going down of the sun... and in the morning.

Where did that thought spring? Oh yes, I'm telling myself I'm not creaky.

Hm! I'm even thinking of Grandma, 'alone' for so many of her days, wed to one man and his memory. She told me about him, lost at Ypres in 1917. Poor woman; did they recognise her man, when they found him? Probably not, just a name on a disc tied to his body.

Away, you awful thoughts!

Her eyes trilled.

Somewhere beyond her wakeful consciousness, the fasten seat belt gong sounded.

Turbulence, they were told; it's better to be secure in your seat.

Yes, be safe in your place. Could it also mean know my place and be free of emotional turmoil? Once more, I'm on a journey of discovery and hoping for my renewal.

I have some pills...to calm me down, but vowed that I wouldn't take them...unless it all became too much to bear. As

Lou told me, being somewhere else might rid me of depression and the knowledge that on more than one occasion I thought I had discovered a kindred soul and I opened my heart to him.

I held out my arms only to hold a ghost.

You should be thankful girl; you had the uncomplicated love of thousands who saw you dance, embrace, step softly and cavort in the arms of so many leading male dancers in a very public arena.

Be glad of that!

Believe it's enough!

Give thanks, rejoice even that life's spotlight was on you for a few short moments and that acclaim more than outweighed, almost silenced, the rude invectives some directed against you. That's how life can be in the world of dance or in the more prosaic endeavours that others call *'work'*.

For me it has been a life of bliss and sorrow, vitality and considered movement; my ageing body may bear witness to the passing of the years but I have glorious flights of fancy, fantasy and dance. For me, that is my true belief, my religion if others want to see it that way! The body may be rooted now as it never was before, but the will and energy to pursue a fulfilling life is as strong as ever!

Can it really be said that I was a danseuse made good? God no!

A ballerina, then? Oh yes!

Finally, she drifted into sleep as the ocean passed far below her.

III

"Nikki! Nikki!"

The joyful uninhibited shrieks were in time with the wave of colour that greeted her, a large bouquet under stress from Loualla's exuberant calls to her of welcome.

"So long…it's been so long!" Nicole gasped as she was embraced, meeting the quick fervent kisses to her cheeks with a laugh and responding as best that she could. Loualla's scent was instantly recognisable and she noted, with a pang of regret, how soon she had forgotten its pervasive presence.

"Yes! Yes!" Loualla laughed leaning back to look at her for an instant. "Let that be! You're with us…you're here with us, at long last! I can't believe it, you're here." She blinked back tears and half turned retaining her grip on Nicole's arms. "Andrew?"

"Close by," he said.

Her husband stood a few steps away allowing the two women their happy and noisy rendezvous. He knew how it was, how it used to be, between them.

"You both look wonderfully unchanged," Nicole smiled as she held a hand out to him and slipped from Loualla's grasp. She met his unaffected kiss to her cheek.

"There's time to take a closer look," Andrew laughed, nodding his own agreement with Nicole's remark. "Lou keeps me young in mind and body. There's little time or energy left to grow old with her." A loving smile met Loualla's gaze upon him.

"Ever the charmer," Loualla said answering him fondly. A hand brushed her husband's arm for an instant in acknowledgement of what he had confessed to. They began to walk.

"Welcome to Perth, my dearest friend. I'm so glad to see you again. I've almost counted down the hours." Tears trickled down her face now as she spoke and she laughed out of feigned embarrassment. Andrew kept himself discreetly behind them and watched the women walk arm-in-arm through the busy concourse exchanging gossipy giggles.

"Forever loved, that's what you told me," Nicole whispered; her head was bent closer to Loualla's so that a confidence could be shared.

"As you are Nikki."

"Not like this...not like you two."

"Shush now...not the time or place."

"No." Thank goodness I popped a pill Nicole thought. She squeezed her friend's arm. "I've flown away from all that...that self-obsession, at least for a while."

"Shush, I said, Nikki. Your room's fixed up. You may even hear the sound of the surf if you leave the window open or the door onto your balcony...it will soothe and work it's own magic upon you. Besides all that...I've so much to show and tell you about!"

"Hm," Nicole answered in mock reflection. "How will I be able to sleep...?"

"You will! There's no sign of builders or noise of that sort, anywhere!" Lou tightened her grip on Nicole's arm and laughed, raising her head for an instant of disbelief that their reunion had finally taken place. "I'm so happy to see you! I've bored my man rigid telling him of all that we went through and did...in pursuit of our...our..."

"Our calling?" Nicole finished for her.

"Exactly!" came a bright reply. "I said as much to my darling man. That's how I saw it too...nothing else had the slightest appeal for me."

Loualla met the softened gaze and acknowledged her friend's smile.

"Okay...okay, until my man came along and changed me."

⁕

"Shall I brush out your hair?" Loualla called out following a knock on the door. It remained closed until an answer was given.

An hour had passed quickly since their arrival. Nicole had bathed, eased her stiffened limbs by means of a long soak in a miniature 'pool' that occupied the en-suite bathroom and she was now stretching her limbs. It was a habit interrupted by a long flight and a disinclination to do anything so energetic in Dubai's heat and the confines of a hotel bedroom.

"Give me a moment or two?" she called out grabbing at her underwear as she did so; it was of stark white satin with lace trim and a shocking contrast to the orange quilt laid over the large double bed. White sheets and pillows, with orange scatter cushions brightened the room. Here, it seemed a perfect setting and she felt quite at ease.

"Drink? Like a drink...some champagne maybe?" Lou paused for only an instant then gave a little laugh. "Lots of it?"

"My favourite! You haven't forgotten!"

"Oh no. Of you, of us together, I remember a great deal." Lou's voice was heart-warmingly affectionate. "I'll soon be back, Nikki."

Nicole only had time to slip on a loose fitting camisole blouse over her slacks. The hems dragged, just, on the highly polished wooden floor. Slipping her feet into homely flat-soled suede pumps, trodden down at the heels, she called out once again as the door was gently kicked to announce Loualla's presence.

"Come in!"

"Not easy, girl! I've got my hands full...I don't want to spill a single drop!"

"There!" Nikki laughed on opening the door.

"Say no, to me brushing your hair...it was just an idea," Lou handed over a glass and began to sip on her own eagerly. "I need this too, by the way."

"Oh?"

"Girlish excitement on seeing you...Nikki."

"That you should remember brushing my hair!" It had become a habit of hers; Nicole had never prevented the moment's relaxation that her friend's simple task offered after performances that drained her emotionally and physically.

"No," was the soft reply. "I never forgot how we could talk in the dressing room after the applause had drifted away…"

"And the audience had gone into the night."

"Yes." It had been a small and uncomplicated act of friendly intimacy between the two women. "Give me the brush Nikki…have you still got it, the silver one? Have you kept the brush with the lovely engraving on the silver handle? It was Dutch…wasn't it?"

"Yes…it was a present from an admirer."

"And?"

"And it didn't last. You'd been gone a few weeks by the time that finished." They exchanged glances before Nicole gave a hollow laugh of admission at the memory of that affair. "Nothing's changed after that particular situation…not for me, anyway."

Loualla took the brush held out to her. "Tell me if it helps? Andrew's in the theatre."

"Theatre?"

"Yes. That to you and me would be the TV room and library, at a stretch. Here it's called a 'theatre'…it's a bit grander, and certainly larger than what you may have back home."

"I haven't the space…and I try not to spend too much time alone at home." She clutched Lou's arm. "Tell me to shut up with this introverted nonsense?"

"No…or not if it helps you to unwind, to let go for a while. I'm a good listener, remember that too?"

Dearest friend, Nicole affirmed to herself once more; how I could find a way again if I had you near me, just to talk things through and to share my hopes or fears with. The brush moved lazily, starting at her brow and drawing the soft strands gracefully down to her neck. Two braids, which leant distinction to hair touched with grey, had been loosened and the tidy mantle was now drawn clear of her fine-cheeked narrow face. Lipstick no longer gave her mouth its own smiling vitality; with others she could put on an act and conceal with complete conviction all that moved her. The image so often concealed the inner reality.

"How I've changed since we last met," she smiled at the reflection in the mirror before them.

"Tell me what I've been missing in the years since we last saw each other and I did this?" Loualla's measured voice, in time with each stroke of the brush, seduced further comment from her and Nicole shifted on the seat.

"I've been alone, I've not danced with anyone except to demonstrate in my own creaky way now what it is to be a ballerina. Then, no two moments on stage...no performance was the same in every detail...it couldn't be, not in my mind or in my heart...I had to respond to the music, the emotion carried on the air from unseen eyes and breaths. It was never a performance but a communion. I had a partner...a partner..." her voice trailed away before she shook her head. "Stop...stop." She felt the first tingle of tears and closed her eyes. "Sorry... sorry."

"Nikki?" Loualla put an arm about her and embraced the trembling shoulders. Her cheek touched. "I had no idea...why keep all this from me? Is there no-one to share these feelings with?"

"No...no!" The reply grew stronger as Nicole took hold of herself once more. "Continue...please, continue." She said it to encourage the more purposeful resumption of the brush's touch. "There has never been anyone to talk to as I could do with you...no one."

"The years will fall away...we'll make out as if we've only been apart, not separated for so long."

"Do you do this for Andrew, your man? Brush his hair... massage his skin to ease him?"

"Occasionally, it has to have a certain context." Lou's voice hinted at regret. "You know men..."

"I thought I did."

"You know them, Nikki," Lou persevered. "To share is to be seen as weak…concede to nothing, or only if you're alone. Don't admit you have a softer side to your character."

"Conceal the inner man?"

"Yes, it's something like that."

"Well, in the short time I've been with you two again, I can see that he shows you the inner man only too clearly, the man that loves you…it's in his eyes. There it is, the emotion's expressed in every glance…it's that obvious to me." She reached up. "I'd forgotten how close we used to be, in our own particular way…forgive me, Lou."

"I have…I do. These last few moments have told me so much. You've withdrawn into yourself and…it's not like before, when you prepared, mentally, for a performance."

Nicole sighed then nodded her head with eyes closed to stem the tears once more. *I've got to get hold of myself…what has come over me?*

"I've travelled so far to see you…then this." She gave a wobbly smile in spite of the mood she had succumbed to.

"Nikki…"

"I have friends…but I'm alone like I've never been before. I…I can't help it."

"C'mon girl! I think a decent night's rest will be the cure for this…or go some way to help you. It's all been a bit much… travel and reunions." *Journeys through happier times* she could have added, *and the lost love of others.* "You're tired, not beaten…you're strong. And," she said with a happy smile that Nicole could only respond to with her own, "you're here, with us. So, anything's possible!"

Nicole studied herself in the mirror and began to make a plait of hair. "I'll be along in a minute…we can finish the bottle of champagne together."

"Good idea! Andrew can make our supper." A doorbell rang, echoing in the hallway outside the room. Loualla put the brush down again with a glance that showed the memories it stirred within her. "Who can that be? No one's expected…I made that much clear to Andrew. Tonight was for the three of us to be together and to enjoy our reunion."

"And I'll be good, from now on…I'll be happy, I promise."

"I'll see to it, do you hear me, girl?" Loualla touched Nicole's arm for only a moment of affirmation.

"Oh yes. I'm on the other side of my world, who else can I turn to?" She caught her friend's acknowledging wink of eye and laughed. "That's what I thought."

IV

She walked towards the sound of laughter; it came from the room that Loualla called their 'day's living space' and Andrew, correcting her, called it the 'family room'. Her bath had been of temporary comfort; she felt the grip of fatigue overcome her once more; sleep and a concession to the effects of being in another place would work their own magic. Her moccasined feet trod noiselessly on the polished surface.

"Nikki!"

"Yes…me again." She laughed and twisted the empty glass by its stem as she held it between her fingers. "I've come for a refill."

"And we're ready for you," Andrew smiled and brought a full glass to her. He took the empty one and gave a teasing theatrical bow. "Welcome, once again."

"Thank you."

She was aware now of three pairs of eyes upon her but felt drawn to meet those of John…John Poynter as he introduced himself without waiting for the others to deal with the formalities.

"Hello, I've heard so much about you…from Lou-Lou here, so much that I simply had to call."

"Goodness…" She hadn't heard her friend called by such a name before and was met by a shrug of the shoulders.

"See what I have to put up with?" Lou smiled.

"Now," Andrew intervened, "a welcome toast. Stay with us, be happy and good luck on your trip down under."

"Thank you," Nicole raised her glass in response to them.

"Go much further and you'll fall over the edge." John stood close by. She had felt his gaze upon her almost from the moment she had entered the room. "I've brought you a small welcoming gift…I'll go and collect it."

"Oh!"

"Artist to artiste," Loualla offered by way of an explanation. "It's his secret, take my word on it…only I hadn't reckoned on him bringing it over now."

John soon returned with a box and placed it at Nicole's feet. "Am I glad I don't live too far away…I wouldn't have been too happy if I'd dropped it." He stood up before her. "So little time…so, it was the best I could do, in the circumstances."

There was no label, no fancy wrappings, and the gift was concealed in a large box the contents of which might grace the local supermarket's shelves. She could even make out crumpled newspaper that served as padding.

"Cornflakes," Nicole laughed on reading the print on the box. "Australian ones, I take it?"

"Yes, locally crafted," John smiled back. "Now, " he went on "what I've made is an interpretation…my perception of what you do…of your art."

"The inspiration? It was drawn from…where?"

"A photo…photos that Lou showed me…Andrew and I had to look at them and listen to the commentary…and some music. After that I had no choice, I had to make something."

"What do you do?"

"Later…I'll tell you later. Call what I've made a welcoming commission."

He crouched down at her feet once more and began to tear at the corners of the box until it lay opened out, flat on the polished wooden floor; its contents remained tightly wrapped.

"You won't need this now. When you've unwrapped the rest I hope Lou-Lou will let you put it on the table." He beckoned for her to kneel down beside him. "Come? You do the rest, Nicole…it's best that you pull at the paper here…it'll be easier…and don't worry, it won't break so easy."

She saw the craftsman's hands, strong and broad fingered, the nails clean but uneven. The skin to his left hand was scarred and the middle finger was only a stub. On looking at him more closely she noted that the backs of both hands were scarred, the twisted tissue passing under the cuffs of his denim shirt. She felt attracted to the face of a man who seemed perfectly at ease and who, for now, dominated all that passed between them.

"Have you suffered for your craft?" she blurted out. Her glimpses at his hands had caught his eye.

"Direct…aren't you? I wasn't told the whole story about you." John stood up looking at Andrew and Loualla before taking his glass from the table; they met his gaze impassively as if they had seen the fulfilment of some plan. Two friends of theirs, complete strangers to each other, had met and they were on hand to arbitrate if the need arose.

"Yes…in a manner of speaking."

"No, in what you say…there's no lead in."

"I'm in Australia…"

The others laughed at her easy observation.

"I'll have to think on it…in case we meet again." John crouched by her side once more. "Now…go on, open it, please?"

"Yes, get on with it, girl…then we can all settle down for a real drink," Loualla chipped in. "I've asked John often…what have you spent so much time on?"

"No time at all…some work comes to the eye and is easier to create than another."

"And this?" Nicole held a paper fold and delayed tearing it open.

"Creative inspiration…out of nothing more than a black-and-white photo or two."

"Of…me?" She spoke in a slow and wondrous voice.

The unremarkable wraps of paper were soon drawn away to reveal a double helix, in glass, evoking immediately the slender pirouetting form of a dancer. The shape seemed to float before a 'curtain' of wood and glass worked into clever waveforms that offered either a view to what lay beyond or closed off any deeper perspective. Even the ends of the glass form, where the dancer's feet could be imagined, John had delicately etched and worked upon the surface.

"I'll put it on the table. It's not supposed to be a floor piece."

John noticed a frown of concentration on Nicole's face and waited. He had sought to understand, or interpret, the art of the dancer and how the eye's observation of movement might awake deeper emotions or deny them.

Instead of speaking, Nicole studied the piece as an 'audience' might observe the figure. John had even raised the beautifully coiled glass above the mock stage floor; the 'dancer' seemed to float. She closed her eyes and, absorbed by memories of a former existence, her imagination took hold for an instant.

"It is beautiful, complex and yet so simple," she said at last and looked first at John then at her two friends. Little time seemed to have passed but so much had been experienced. "The transition from light to darkness or the other way about…you have captured it wonderfully. It speaks to me of so many emotions…or…" She stopped talking as if none of them would wish to hear of it.

"Go on...go on!" John urged with a laugh. She had seen him nod as she rattled off her initial impressions of his work, his gift.

"It speaks to me of emotions...but the choice of material, how you have arranged them to make the complete piece of work, it signifies, to me, also the light and dark side of the human character." Her voice trailed away once more and she waved in distraction for her glass.

"Here..." he had found it. "You're interpretation's on the mark...what I sought to convey in the piece."

"I think she likes it, John." Andrew smiled at them.

"I do...I do like it. A sense of movement has been captured in the glass...the texture's wonderful...I love the discreet colours within it." She couldn't stop herself from making these observations as the piece was studied; her feet moved noiselessly over the floor. "Tomorrow morning, with a bright pervading light...the sun...it will come alive of its own accord or in the observer's mind." She gave a little grunt of self-admonishment. "I'd better shut up now, I seem to be going on a bit." There was only a moment's pause. "It has life even in this poor light," she concluded and pushed back her hair in a single movement, as if collecting her thoughts once more on her surroundings and the company she had been brought into.

"I don't look on sculpture as a static object...it may be fixed to the ground but it has to draw the energy of life, its own life, from the surroundings it is placed in."

"It's how you were, Nikki...how it was on stage!" Loualla was captivated. "I think it's wonderful, John...so much style and grace in a small work."

"Of art...it's art!" Nicole cried out and looked at them all in surprise; her voice had trembled. "I don't know what else to say about it!"

"That you'll keep it safe...it's unique. No copies have been made. It's unique...one of a kind."

"It's about you and your work, Nikki," Loualla smiled at her. "What you brought to so many…your light and your grace."

Nicole slid her fingers over the glass helix, its surface smooth and sensually turned to depict the pirouette of a slender shape.

"I don't deserve this from you, John," she said suddenly. "You've gone to a great deal of trouble."

"Yeah…but it's all been worthwhile. I know that now… now that we've met." John spoke in such a matter-of-fact tone of voice that Nicole really could not believe it was simply a gift to her, from a stranger. "The motivation…or creative impulse, if you like…"

"Was what?" Nicole interrupted sharply then gave him a look of regret.

"The chance to meet you. The pictures were an accurate portrayal…for me. There seemed no artifice…I didn't feel that as an onlooker I was being conned."

"You saw all that? In the photos I showed you?" Loualla intervened.

"We only saw some pictures, John" Andrew chuckled but misunderstood.

"*Only* I saw something else," John said with a hardening of his voice. "Something quite different is what I saw…I saw someone else," he added in a voice so low that his intention must have been for Nicole to hear it alone. He made no more fuss and simply began to gather up the wrappings and the flattened box. Crushed together he put them under one arm.

"I'm going now. I didn't mean to interrupt your evening for too long. You've got things to talk about…to catch up on."

"One more drink, John?" Andrew ventured. "Stay a while longer?"

"Yes, do that for us all?" Loualla looked over at Nicole but she now sat by the table where the work had been placed and simply stared. She gave the appearance of being on the edge of sleep.

"Thanks...some other time." John moved and stood by Nicole; she took the hand he held out to her. "Enjoy your visit...and, if there's time," he said squeezing it gently and then releasing his grip. "Ask Lou to bring you over to my place. You're welcome to see where and how I made it. There's no mystique involved when you see that."

"John," Nicole smiled at him for his modesty, "all of my instincts tell me that I can't agree with what you've just said. The mystique lies in the creative impulse...its fulfilment in your eyes and hands."

<u>V</u>

"Catch you soon, mate?" John said. "Look after the ladies."

"Sure," Andrew answered, "mind you, I reckon they'll do that for themselves...just talking."

"Okay. Ring the mobile...it's the best way to keep in touch. I don't know where I'll be."

John leant out of the Land Rover as he spoke, the window slid back to make room. Others had plush, carpeted, leather seated utility vehicles, 'utes' some called their prized possession. To him, the vehicle was a tool of his trade and not a status symbol. All you could say was that it was old but immaculately looked after; it was a motor that fulfilled many functions. Carla had made sure that he kept it that way, cleaned, washed and regularly, even lovingly, maintained.

"Just like you my darling," his wife used to say.

But...she was dead, gone from him now for a couple of years; no one came close to filling the void in his life, night or day. She was in his mind, living by his shoulder or on the air. He had never reckoned, much, to the idea that someone stayed near by, or with you when they had moved to the 'other side'.

The explanation was simple. No one had taken hold of him and all that he had come to live for like Carla had. She was his life's love, an inspiration and creative muse. Most of all she had been his daily devotion, the girl who had managed to keep him in thrall for thirty years…a lifetime of change.

Yeah, he'd changed from a struggling sculptor and artist, or handyman in desperately lean times, to a recognised creative genius, but with a small 'gee' he frequently corrected.

It's no big deal, he always said and what those who heard him called disarming modesty, for a 'hard man', only he didn't think of himself as a 'toughie' any more. He lived, breathed and felt like everyone else, only he didn't show it too often and certainly not to strangers.

"It's work for some, to me it's a hobby."

Most folks couldn't follow what he was talking about. Good! For him his real job had been tending the love and basking in the companionship that he found so naturally and unpractised with Carla…his only girl, his darling wife…his lost girl, his dead wife.

She hadn't been sick; there had been no struggle through an ailment that she finally conceded to at her life's parting moment. Oh no! She had travelled with him to a place where they could be happy and safe, a holiday place where they could both check out local art! They could learn some more on how to sculpt in stone and wood, from craftsmen eking out an existence in rudimentary shelters but their minds open to every idea.

I'd only been gone a minute, seconds…moments too long but just the moments needed for that bomb to do for her and so many others. Man, I was hurt…beyond dying! I lived on with that, the knowledge of how we'd been torn apart, forever. I hurt where others couldn't see. I was busted, deep down, but I kept it hidden, hidden deep to think on it when I chose or I couldn't keep them out, the memories and the love I have, still, for my girl…my Carla.

I couldn't do a goddamn thing!

Getting burned and losing a finger was one excuse I took hold of. Losing the will to go on for a long, long, time was the other; I couldn't find it...the will to create a frigging thing. Nothing touched me, hurt me or lost me to others like her death, my Carla's death. Christ! No, it wasn't a death I could be reconciled to, she...she was killed! Why, and for doing what?

Where was the sense in any of it? Tell me that! A voice seemed to scream it all out inside his head. It seemed like everyone there lost a loved one; the faceless cowards didn't give a damn for native or visitor when they threw the switch.

His fists gripped the steering wheel and he felt like bellowing out his despair, only...only he'd seen a new light come into his life, or better still he'd heard some words that gave him hope.

"Come back inside...stay a while longer...join us in a drink?" Andrew smiled as he stood by the window now.

"Thanks, but no..."

Andrew's voiced concern. "You okay?"

"Yeah...I was just taken back for a moment, or two."

"I understand," Andrew said now his smile drifting from his face. "I hear you...you know where we are if you ever want some company...no appointment's necessary, you know that, I hope?"

"Yeah...cheers, you're a mate Andrew...you both are."

He had seemingly sat with the engine running as the thoughts pressed in, gutting him and bringing tears to the eyes. No one can see what's at work in me so to hell with it. I'm alone in here...with you Carla, with your memory.

"Sure about the drink?" Andrew's hand rested on his arm for an instant of friendly concern.

"Yeah." He let the word out on a sigh. "I'm going...see you all soon."

"Yeah. Remember, John? The door's always open..."

"Yes, thanks. C'mon on now...it's not far, girl."

John spoke in a tone of affection to a machine that repaid him with uncomplicated reliability. The vehicle was backed out of the driveway and, with an uncommon crunch of the gears he set off.

"I'm glad to be here. Goodnight Andrew." Nicole waited in the picture lined echoing hallway until the door was closed.

"Good night, Nikki." He met the kiss to his cheek. "A new day tomorrow in a different part of the world for you. Rest up and you'll be fine."

"I'm counting on it. Mind my piece of Australian art for me, please?"

"Sure…it's original and genuine."

"A one off. It's unique," she heard Loualla say now.

"Yes. I've never been given anything quite so exceptional before."

"Well, you've prompted the artist to show his true character again…John's a dear friend to us."

"Oh?" Nicole turned yawning out her reply as she did so. "Sorry."

One hand covered her mouth, too late.

"Tomorrow," Lou answered. She stood arm in arm with Andrew and smiled. "More of that tomorrow."

"Yes…'night."

Nicole's feet moved silently over the polished floor; all she could make out were the murmured exchanges between her friends as they walked away.

◈

"You took your time getting back to us."

Lou settled against Andrew on the sofa as she spoke, slipping off her shoes.

"Yeah. John was lost for a few moments…so I stayed with him while he worked it all through. I know the signs…I just haven't seen them for a while."

"Tonight made him think...the days before obviously have too."

"Oh?" Andrew's lips brushed Loualla's hair and kissed her temple.

"I knew the meeting with Nikki would matter to him... only I didn't reckon on it being quite so soon."

"Oh?" Andrew said again picking up on Loualla's pensive way of speaking. "You expected all of this to happen?"

"No...but I changed my mind when I heard he was at the door...then here with you," she corrected. "I knew something was up when he broke out the present...and the way he just looked at Nikki."

She spoke now with a tone of wonder at the 'piece' he'd left for her.

"Nikki won't forget that in a hurry...now..." Andrew whispered in a breathy caress against her skin, "talk of something else...better still...let's do something else...?"

"She's supposed to see it as a special gift," Loualla went on, undeterred. "Weren't you paying attention to anything tonight? Hmmm?"

"Just you darlin'." His hand stroked her side, underneath the thin lambswool jumper.

"Easy!" She conceded for only a moment before the progress of his hand upon her was stilled. "I meant, did you see John's attention to her, how he looked at Nikki? The gift was meant to be so much more...so much, so much more. He even told us...its creation was easy."

"Spontaneous."

"Right...right! Good word, lover!"

"Did you 'plan' all this...their meeting? It was goin' to happen...only, the timing was a shock?" He spoke in between their soft kisses. "Is that why you talked...so much about her, to us...to John and me?"

"No...not exactly," she said slowly.

"Meaning?"

"Nikki has something that John needs…that he's missed so badly since Carla left him…she's got creative intensity. It needs to be devoted to something more…"

"To someone…that's what you really mean."

Loaulla simply nodded. "Maybe."

"The flame doesn't burn so bright all of the time, Lou Lou."

"Don't call me that, please? John's got away with that for far too long. You have other names for me…" She conceded to a lingering kiss and a renewal of provocative caresses. "Soon," she whispered. "When the flame flickers…when he's lost and doesn't know what to do with his talent that's when John needs someone to be there…to offer comfort and a different consolation."

"And Nikki? What about her?"

"She's different…intense, like Carla could be only she is more like John in the way she keeps working…just to be busy, to distract her from parts of her life that are empty…or gone that way. She went on talking earlier…about being alone. Then…suddenly, when I saw them together, when I saw what John had made I knew something was happening…right there in front of my eyes. I couldn't have planned it…I couldn't have come close. It just seemed to '*happen*'."

"Easy girl, they've just met!"

"So?" she answered as if her explanation was simple. "John needs creative inspiration, encouragement and loving criticism; he only gets that with his other life filled by someone. Carla meant everything to him…you've got to admit it…we've not seen him do work like he showed us tonight, not for a long time."

"He's been quiet," Andrew agreed. "It was something small and very special…even I could see that."

"Yes, when he's quiet…when the flame's not so bright then John…Nikki too, that's the time they need another's touch to keep them right. They need to find a different happiness during those quiet spells."

"Their low period," Andrew knew the words. Lou spoke them often, of herself and the role that he played in her life. "You think everything was started by those few photos you showed him?"

"Exactly. I can't see any other way." Lou broke free of his embrace and standing up held out her hands. "Now...make love to me...we've got all night."

She felt overwhelmed by thankfulness that she had Andrew, a partner with whom she could share her life. What a glaring contrast with her two friends; was it emotional and sentimental nonsense? It didn't seem like that to her. They were some of the reactions she could imagine in others or what she might read about in some magazine. Close up, she could realise all too clearly what might be at work in John and Nikki. Of her friend, asleep in a room close by she knew more; Nikki confessed to her 'aloneness' openly. She was soft. John was altogether different, hardened by experience and with a character that would not openly reveal too much of his real self.

But she had seen his other side...and Carla had told her of it too.

The spontaneity of the gift, its creation from the smallest 'glimpse' of Nikki's character, from photographs, said so much more of the inner man. To borrow a phrase Andrew often used, it was a 'win win' situation; two people meet at a defining moment in their lives. Whatever John had been shown of Nicole the result had been to reawaken a creative impulse that might yet restore the man she and Andrew had befriended so many years ago. Then, the patch of bush had been but a wilderness with a cabin set among the gum and Eucalyptus trees.

How their lives had changed; how John had transformed the place he had shared with Carla; how he had loved and lost a wonderful woman; it was a cliché but it was very appropriate to his circumstances.

As for Nikki, well she yearned for enduring companionship in the later years of her life and had yet to find it with her one true man. I'm not puzzled by Nikki's search at all; I'd like her to fall in love and be completely possessed by another's attention upon her as I have been.

If they can find each other I'll merely be a witness. How the next few days unfold is up to them, entirely. But, I know how Nikki and John have lived. They might even say…I was lost…and then, I met you.

"That's how it was for me, Andrew…meeting you."

"A special moment?"

"Yeah…"

"And now…?"

"Many more…with you, oh so many more…special moments."

VI

John got out of the car to open an old farm gate, the roadway leading to the house beyond faintly illumined by small, low intensity, lights recessed into the rough rock and gravel surface. He likened it sometimes to an airfield runway, only it followed a meandering course through the trees and native shrubs so lovingly planted and maintained over the years. Parrots squawked nearby, their night time's roost disturbed for a moment. Small animals roamed the 'park' as he often called the grounds within which a home had been built. Close to, water features soothed and gave a cooling atmosphere; patios adorned with sculptures linked intimate wooded glades to a well-kept garden that surrounded the house.

The rest of his domain he left wild, unkempt, just as nature intended. He had never felt the least inclination to put man's stamp upon all of it. Carla had even come up with the idea of creating a conservation zone linked to the bush beyond the boundary markers and a rickety fence. By doing so they could keep at bay the acquisitive hands with wads of cash that sought to turn their 'park' into another pricey housing lot or two…or many. They regarded it as their own space and money wasn't everything. That's what they kept telling each other…but that was then.

The timber shack, their original home remained; it had been spruced up and modernised to become his studio, the windows opening out onto the bush beyond; it overlooked carvings and sculptures set amongst the trees; they all remained as a testimony to his craft. Stone, wood, glass and unforgiving metal were all materials that he favoured, not one to the exclusion of another. He took no risks; the furnace remained unused in the dry season, during months of the year when a bush fire would destroy in seconds all that he possessed. Instead, he sculpted; manual crafts were relied upon to occupy the hours and bring to life creative ideas.

He parked by the Norfolk pines that on the hottest days still cast their shadow over the front of the house .The dogs barked their noisy welcome home.

"Easy, girls," he laughed out to them as he opened the door to the house and they rushed out to investigate if he was alone. Satisfied, they sought him out and nuzzled his hands.

"Home, I'm home girls…settle down now."

Unquestioning devotion and affection were offered and received from the two Cocker Spaniel bitches. They belonged with him, a decision they had soon reached after Carla's leaving; he fed them after all. Megan and Holly never roamed too far; they knew the limits to their territory, the tended garden and patios nearest the house. He had only to call once, 'stay close', for the girls to come to heel as they followed him to the studio along the winding path through the 'bush'; this wilderness, compared to the immediate surroundings of the house, was home to other creatures.

"There's work to do and so little time," he told himself. "There's so little time."

✦

Preparations for the evening and into the night were complete. The bubbling homeliness of the percolator had finished; John filled a thermos with coffee, put some thick slices of bread on a plate, piled large chunks of cheese on top and then spooned olives into a bowl as a savoury accompaniment.

Whistling, he carried this simple meal to the studio. Sleep, he had soon realised upon arriving home, was out of the question. He wasn't the least bit tired and felt, for the first time in many months a familiar and welcome creative buzz coursing through him. He sensed a creative restlessness that had to be satisfied...sleep was for later.

"Things are going to change, John boy," he said, putting into words the thoughts that now preoccupied him. "I've got that woman...Nikki...Nicole...to thank for that."

Sure, he could summon up the image of that svelte woman quite clearly in his mind's eye; he had no trouble with that at all. Tired or not, she was a 'looker', no mistake. The photos he'd seen of the woman had captured her perfectly. He had been provoked by them into producing a small piece of his work, a demonstration of his craft, as much to welcome her as it was in recognition of a step he had been compelled to take en route to his own restoration.

For reasons that could not be explained, if he were asked, Nicole's eyes revealed to him a secret life that she lived through. Upon meeting her he had dispelled the intrusive thoughts that Nicole 'lived out' her days in the hope that she might yet discover fulfilment with a life's companion, someone she had still to meet. Loualla had given him a hint to what was at play, only once, when the photos were shown to him; Nicole was 'only involved with her work', when an appointment could be secured. The trip 'down under' was an expenses paid but speculative venture. And yet, in spite of the uncertain future,

Nicole's look upon him had brightened and her parting words so reflective of his own thoughts.

The mystique lies in the creative impulse…its fulfilment in your eyes and hands.

As for him? Well, being alone after all that he had shared with Carla had wrought its' own changes.

So what?

So, Loualla had spoken in graphic and often gossipy detail about her friend, her remarks interwoven with serious observations on the dignity that Nicole brought to the roles she had been called upon to portray. Often, so the story went, the emotional intensity reflected her off-stage life. Loualla didn't have to 'spell it out', she had said just enough to bring to mind thoughts of bygone days when the woman he had so recently met was in her artistic prime.

So what?

Nicole lived, she was sustained, by memories of her past, a glorious past as he had been told of it, but it was a receding past and yet she was still compelled to look for opportunities to prolong a creative and fulfilling life.

So what?

I'm a fellow traveller, that's what…and that's who I am.

I work hard at what I know and love the most…just like Nikki.

I like the sound of her name, that way's the best…the other's too formal. I'd like to see the woman really let go, let the real woman shine through, once more.

A reason could soon be found to run down the clock, as he had often put it, and to work through the night. Only, the urge and the need to do so had deserted him, until now, or up to the moment when Loualla had shown him the pictures. Inspiration and devotion to his craft had been re-discovered, as if by some miracle! He'd been told that the person featured so brightly within them was coming to the place where he worked and lived.

Get that!

A kindred spirit or a like-minded beautiful vision was to enter his world. The 'creative impulse' still lay deep within him; the light had only been dimmed. He had heard other artists speak of it, the deadening of any creative impulse until something changed you or someone came into your life and you felt rejuvenated.

The fatigue and lethargy of lost moments simply fell away.

A few moments in Nicole's company had justified the making of a votive piece for her. She was a 'looker', no mistake, but the woman with those beautiful shining eyes looked out upon the world as he did; she saw everything as a source of inspiration and, considered closely, of infinite wonder.

"Thank Christ! I've met her!" he yelled out and laughed. The sudden noise made the dogs bark and run over to him. "It's okay girls...I've met someone special. I know it!"

⁂

"The place's tidier than it's ever been."

John wandered about the studio gazing occasionally at the outlines of the trees that could just be picked out in the soft light from the room. The bread and cheese was consumed heartily and the dogs followed more in hope than expectation; they would be out of luck but their tails wagged none the less; a morsel might yet fall to the floor for them to scrap over.

Until he had brought himself to create Nikki's piece the studio had been cleaned up, the rubbish generated in the making of so many failed 'pieces' or 'works' carted away and the tables cleared and wiped down. It would be cluttered soon enough after worthy endeavour, he mused, once a new project took hold of every creative instinct within him. They had done so before and would do so again, he was quite certain of it now. The pictures of a younger Nicole had inspired him; they had provoked an almost feverish impulse to work; he had looked upon beauty and grace, wonderfully captured in simple photographs. The woman possessed them still in her slender form, on her smiling face and in those wonderful eyes; the kiss of grey to a garland of braided silken hair enthralled him. He sensed a youthful vitality held in check by deeper restraining influences.

He had been overcome and felt quite unable to give expression to his feelings by any other means than to create a small sculpture. He had gained so much more from the experience; he had tidied everything away! The studio was not pristine in its tidiness, just ordered, and he drew comfort from the realisation that he could live with the change from the companionable bustle, the mess, and often the noise that had been the prelude to a blossoming of a creativity with Carla. He had grown accustomed to reflective quiet and the realisation that no longer would he have to work with the debris of the past, real or imagined, about him. He had his memories. Mess was no longer to be endured as an accompaniment to a creative mind overcome by the turmoil of endeavour, at least not for long.

"I've changed...I had to." He sipped on his coffee and lapsed into silence once more.

I've not gone back on a promise I made to myself, I haven't returned to old and comforting ways. I can find life again, as a sculptor and artist. It all began with that statue...and those pictures! Life's new again and all because of a stranger, a vision that entranced me and then became real.

The statuette had become a potent symbol of renewal.

And, Nicole doesn't even know what she's made of me.

Thoughts came to him as a drawing pad was taken off the shelf and a stick of charcoal scrabbled for in an old lidless cigar box, close by.

His hand moved quickly over the rough weave of paper. No conscious thought was required. The creative process 'happened', its conception described as the work of another; he simply had no idea, in any detail, how the best moments of creative energy had been passed. Upon their conclusion all that he felt was elation, an intense and painful joy gathered from instances that he lived for – apart from the loving of a woman with its vaulting singular intensity.

Yes, I've been possessed and now I can consider what has happened; I can see the effects of my mind's *'possession'* by another, albeit temporarily. Nicole had spoken so profoundly yet the language had been so simple, so prescient of his renewal.

The mystique lies in the creative impulse…its fulfilment in your eyes and hands.

❖

The sketchpad was laid to one side as he slumped on the stool, breathing slowly; he sought the recovery of a wider consciousness of his surroundings. As the outline of a new work was studied he knew where his muse and the reincarnation of his art resided. Nicole's words had breathed new life into him; the lines and swirls on the paper depicted movement, the continuity of life and the revelations of a light that had been shone into the darkness.

With Carla he had been able to speak of his deeply held beliefs in the enduring quality of art, high art some might say, and not the easily consumed kitsch that so often confronted him. They were not the subject matter of everyday conversation or the happy to-and-fro of human exchanges; such ephemeral pleasantries flew away on the wind. What he spoke of and sought was a continuation of his art's sustaining ideas and images, a reflection of that moment's taste or a commentary upon what had moved the creator of the work. The best of the physical arts, in paint and sculpted form he was convinced, endured.

Poor Nicole!

He could only imagine the torment of ideas and memories that she experienced. Her craft was temporal; dance, the portrayal of emotions was a fleeting pleasure and to his eye, finite. It could not be recorded, for the secret lay in the immediacy of sensation whereas in his craft or that of the painters, colour, texture and shape, context and perspective they all continued to provoke the imagination of the beholder. Each work of art possessed its own unique interpretation or recollection of an idea.

All of these emotions sprung from *'the mystique of the creative impulse'*.

Nicole, dressed in satin, had lived for sublime moments on the stage.

All that he knew and felt was crafted in steel or carved from stone; it was the soft set against the hard and immovable, the fleeting graceful movement accompanied by sound in contrast to an enduring, visible and tangible legacy.

My mind's buzzing…it's in a creative whirl!

Woman, what have you done to me?

VII

"Hello, John?"

The voice was bright and wakeful, arresting any other intentions than to listen. He knew who it was on the 'phone.

"Yes, good day, Nicole."

"I'm not disturbing you, am I?"

He gave a soft reflective laugh. "No, not at all."

If only that were true.

"I wanted to thank you, once again…for the wonderful sculpture. It has a life and beauty all of its own," she said quickly. "I've had time now to really look at it…marvel, more like, at what you've given me."

He had no intention of interrupting her, just yet.

"The light has brought it alive, just as you said it would! All that, from a few photos!"

She had an engaging soft laugh; he was momentarily distracted from giving any reply and tried to memorise every nuance.

"Yes, of you," he said at last. "They weren't just any photos as you told me yourself, remember? The mystique lies in the creative impulse."

He waited.

"It's almost the only thing that I remember saying last night, John," was the direct but soft voiced answer.

"You said something else. You said that you might come over and visit me, if you had any spare time before moving on. Remember that?"

"Yes, I remember that too."

"And?"

"Will I do it?" Nicole paused for only a moment's reflection. "Oh yes, I'll do it. I can't refuse your invitation. I want to see where the sculpture was made."

And all I want to do is see you again, John thought.

"Crafted," he said needlessly and with a hint of arrogance in his tone.

The word held little meaning for him nor did it truly express the trouble he had gone to in showing off his skill. An example of conceptual art was how some observers might describe the piece. If so, it was a new label. See? It was all coming back to him, his self-belief and conviction that on his work no label could be hung that said it all, about him or to describe the outcome of his creative impulse. He shuddered at the thought, 'what you see is what you get'. Art was not so easily understood if you aspired to be at the 'cutting edge' or 'innovative'. He was irritated with the clichés that came to mind as he spoke to her.

"Yes John, that's how I could see it now, only the word 'crafted'? It's too easy."

"Oh?"

"Yes!" She gave an embarrassed laugh. "What a conversation to be having at this time of the morning! I only rang to say 'thank you'."

"Accepted," he replied flatly but with no intention of letting her leave remaining thoughts unspoken. "You were saying?"

"Yes...yes," she stammered, only for a moment. "I meant that 'crafted' is too easy a word to describe what you've created..." Her voice fell away once more then an idea seemed to come to her. "It's too meagre."

"Minimalist, you mean?" he corrected, laughing at last, finding his choice of word a better one. "I have to confess that I'm after the concept in art, the idea that lies behind each piece of work that I do...and I get to finish. It's not always so simple."

"Yes! I'll have to be careful how I describe your work," Nicole went on.

"When you come over to see what else I've done...when do you think that will be?"

He had only gone and told her, if he had his way, that she would not be leaving his part of Western Australia without another meeting. They might even discuss the relative merits of conceptual and minimalist art, over a drink, but not too seriously. He had learnt quite enough of her already to know that Nicole was a kindred spirit.

"Soon, John. I'm only here for three days then it's off to New Zealand for a few days. Soon, I'll be home once more."

"Sooner than you want?"

"I can't begin to tell you, John...that'll depend on a lot of things. Why ask?"

"Oh, simple curiosity."

She gave a happy disbelieving laugh. "I'll keep you all informed...okay?"

"Yeah, it is...you'll tell me of a mission accomplished?"

"I hope so...right now there are too many ideas, new ones, buzzing around in my head to answer that with any confidence. Ballet, dance, choreography and interpretation...all of those ideas are discretionary."

"Subject to individual taste...your employer's taste or the prejudice of the time?"

"Yes, John, all of them...but not in equal measure," she said in surprise. "How...?"

"I've thought of little else during the night, Nicole...I've been comparing what you do with my art...what I do that takes up so much of my time, again...now."

"And?" She was intrigued to hear his confession.

"And, Nikki...I hope I can call you that, it's easier?" he said pausing for only a moment, "and the rest will keep until we meet again...soon, I hope."

❖

He worked furiously, his mind and the hours filled with self-critical and creative endeavour.

"It's been so long...such a long time, girl!"

He 'spoke' to Carla as memories of former times surfaced.

You understand, don't you? I've got to get on with my life again. You're near me. All that you ever taught or encouraged in me lives on through my eye for detail or that one essential moment of inspiration...and, its fulfilment by restless hands. I'm so tired, but I love it! I'm restless and edgy...I have to capture the idea somehow before it flits away into oblivion... there's one pure moment of insight...once lost any recall of that is diminished. Worse! It's nowhere near to being the same...as an artist you *feel* that it's so! Everything tells you that it's become a different piece from what you intended. Thank God, I sketched out the images brought before my minds' eye last night! I can open the pad, at any time, and see the genesis of everything that followed.

I've got to make these waking instants last! I've got to keep hold of every feeling and image that comes to my mind's eye and then, transform each *invisible* one of them into a beautifully crafted piece, make of them the best that I can do. When I've completed my work the mystique of the creative impulse becomes *visible* and tangible. From that moment on it will be for others to share, or imagine, all that I've gone through to complete the work.

I have even thought of a name for that single inspirational creative moment.

Hold onto it...really tight!

See to it, John!

The word was scrawled at the foot of the drawing, not once but several times in the same place, over-and-over, as if to reinforce their significance to him. It seemed like the pirouettes of a dancer, over and over, on the same spot.

What a poignant reminder!

◈

The visit had, to use an overworked phrase, 'been lovely'. The surroundings evoked a colonial or a recognisable past; along the street she looked out on lay the charm of Fremantle, or Freo as the locals affectionately called the place. She could almost touch the respect felt for the small harbour-side town. Perth, its neighbour could have the buzz of its highways, sky scraping beacons of light and the attendant press of the crowd.

You didn't need to live with Freo's quaintness, you chose to.

Here, among the colonnaded parts of the main street and the balconies to Victorian-age buildings with their casement windowed upper stories, she could feel a more human scale to her environment. It was an endearing contrast with all that she had seen during the stopover in the Emirates of a few days ago.

Nicole, you're getting old, or, you know what you like. Yes, that's a better way of putting it.

She sat back in silence. These pervasive thoughts quell any instinct to speak but how do I stop these intrusions into my reunion with dear friends?

Andrew and Loualla sat opposite and looked at her from time-to-time but said nothing. They had already picked up on her little habit, chatter for a while and smile happily, then, stillness once more. I'm the odd one out again. They're a couple, then there's me. She moved one hand in a swat of annoyance that their precious and all too brief moments were being disturbed.

"Away with them?" Lou asked sweetly only to be met with a nod.

You know me too well, girl, or remember the significance of every gesture that I make, even after all the years we've been apart.

She managed to smile then laughed out.

"And let's do away with these!"

The chirrup of a cheerful ring-tone on her mobile drew attention.

The number on the small screen was unknown.

"Excuse me, for only a moment…I hope?"

She saw Andrew wave at the waiter and by a simple circle of his hand over the table indicated another round of drinks was needed. Loualla glanced at her but won no admission as to who had tracked them down.

"Nicole here…Simon, this is a surprise!"

"Yes…I'm sorry for that Nicole, and for disturbing you."

"You're not. I'm with friends and thoroughly at ease. But, my thoughts do turn more than occasionally to our meeting… it's not long now."

"Right, that's good," was his slow response. "It's the reason for my call."

Simon paused for a moment too long.

"Oh…oh, I see." She gave an apologetic shrug of her thin shoulders as she met Andrew's gaze upon her. "Things have changed…is that the reason for the call, Simon?"

Her voice was calm; a phlegmatic shrug of the shoulders was for her friends' benefit.

"Yes."

"Well, at least I'm not alone." She gave Simon no time to say exactly what was on his mind. "Is the project in doubt or just my involvement with it?"

"The last bit…how'd you guess?" Simon said it with ill-concealed relief. He'd been rumbled or the lady was acutely perceptive.

"I'm reasonably in touch with the ways of the world," Nicole observed coolly. "Is that it, the reason for the change of mind, or heart? It's a new theatre and a new dance company… so younger ideas are needed?"

"Not exactly…no."

"What then? Tell me, please? I've travelled some way to be told of this now. Did someone look at the résumés and pick out an embarrassing detail in mine? I thought it would have told you all there was to know about me long before I set out to meet you."

"We looked again…yes."

"Someone could have picked up a 'phone, made a few calls…they could have been imaginative and modern, maybe sent a few emails. Whoever's asking could soon have found out all there's to know about me…professionally, and who I am, the real person. It's no secret…I live for creative dance, for ballet."

"Have you finished? Will you let me give you an explanation for the change in plan?" Simon was unaccustomed to being told what he might be thinking; it rarely happened for him to feel powerless in getting his view across early. This time he had deferred to Nicole. "The plan's changed, nothing more…"

"For now…"

"That's right, 'for now.'"

"Go on…go on, please?" She sighed and sat back to listen, with eyes closed. "I'm sorry, for interrupting you."

"Okay. We would still like to see you, to meet up and hear your ideas for a commemorative work to mark the opening of the theatre. Only…only, there will be others for us to meet and listen to."

"And to see their ideas?"

"See?" was the incredulous reply. "See their ideas?"

"Yes, of course…see and make the ideas real. I haven't come all this way merely to talk about my ideas! I'm going to show you some of them." Nicole gave a laugh. "The spirit lives on…and it moves! I do…I still dance…don't just look at the pictures of me! See all that I can still *do*…how I move and dance, even now!"

Finished, she took deep breaths and wondered if he had been moved by her passionate explanation. Her wine was left untouched in spite of Andrew's gestures to guzzle it down; he made her smile with his antics.

"Nicole," Simon said her name on a reflective sigh. "The ballet-master…our sponsors, important others, they all wanted the shortlist to be widened…they wanted a broader prospectus of ideas."

"What you've heard from me, under the stress of the moment, they're my ideas, mine alone. Please, do not forget that when you come to decide who is to be appointed." There was nothing to convince her that Simon was still there.

"Hello?"

"I'm here Nicole, I'm listening."

"And I'm not saying much more, other than…the music? What of that? Oh! And then there's the costumes…the set! What of those?" Her eyes stared as she felt the touch of Loualla's hand on her arm to still the anger that she had expressed; they had overheard her.

"All to be discussed…your ideas will be part of the assessment, the appraisal of the candidate whom we intend will fulfil our hopes…all of them."

"There's more…so much more," she whispered before silence fell between them.

The list she had given would do, for 'starters'.

I've prepared for this trip; I even dared to call it an adventure when I was invited to participate. I didn't expect it to turn into a beauty contest or a parade of all the talents. Simon told me they had done all of that before I was put through the telephone 'interview', a conference call was how they had described that little event. There I was, in a room on my own talking to people in another one, for all I knew, and way out there across the world and thousands of miles away from me. By then I was on a short list, so, what was his 'phone call really about?

I know this much, I'm seated in a pavement café while I ask myself 'what now, where to now, girl?'

I'm ready even if so many thoughts and ideas are pressing in on me. What I told Simon was only the truth. I'm with friends; what I didn't let on was that I'm also preoccupied with the piece that John Poynter made for me. Yes, all of that and I've still got room to be consciously involved with the reason for me even being here.

Simon responded but she didn't hear him, her thoughts remained elsewhere.

She sought the opportunity for one last 'hurrah', a singular collaboration if that was what Simon now intended. She wished to be part of a fine work, of ballet, of artistry in dance and movement, of tempo combined with grace and sinewy gentleness. It was to be a finale to her teaching and mentoring career, her second, because the *performance* of her craft remained her true life's work.

The day of that initial call to enquire if she would submit herself for consideration, its remoteness from the reality she had lived by, it had been the first time that the idea of retirement had taken a tenuous hold. She stepped in and out of work, or assignments, with ease but Simons' call had prompted other ideas; the day to make a hard choice could be postponed. The invitation offered a return to a former life, to become involved with a corps de ballet, not a small troupe as she came to call the able and charming young dancers that she often worked with but, invention and artistry took their toll, physically and in her emotional life. The noise of the rehearsal rooms was in contrast to the silence of a comfortable flat.

Do I accept the high of one last creative achievement or do I slip quietly away…into the mists of a comforting stillness?

I won't call it 'oblivion', at least, not just yet.

Simon induced these contradictory thoughts in me a month or so ago. Now this, I take a call retracting the original plan. There's more, just to prove the point events are ruling me and turning over my 'plans'. John has given me a tangible reminder of how my life in dance enthralled and possessed me, utterly.

Yes him, John! He's done that!

He's to blame, looking at those bloody pictures of me, those publicity snaps. But, they weren't just any old publicity snaps were they? They served as reminders…of the past, my past. Margot, the stewardess started it off by making me think my reputation lived on. Only…

Only…only Simon wouldn't even have dreamt of calling me, or have been persuaded to do so, if that reputation was unquestioned or raised any doubts. He's certainly picked his moment to tell me of the change in plans.

She heard Simon's voice once again, only louder.

"Hm? Sorry, I missed that…"

"I was saying, Nicole…continue with your trip. Come to us anyway, keep your mind free of the consequences for now? Do that, will you do that, please? Nothing has been formally decided…no one has been chosen to work with the corps de ballet. I simply wanted to tell you that we wish to see more candidates before us...to show the selection committee what they can do, if you like."

I'm not sure that I do like what I'm hearing now, she thought for an instant.

"Thank you...thank you for calling me. I'm sorry that I set off the way I did." She would try to regain her composure. "I'm rather engaged by everything I'm learning on this trip, Simon."

"Good..."

Good? She wondered about the sincerity in his remark. Is that all he's got to say, 'good'?

"I'm sure something will come out of the process, for all of us."

"Yes, thank you Simon. Thank you for calling."

I hope to God something does 'come out' of the trip I'm making, she thought. No, let's call it a journey...let's make it a journey of discovery for me, but not for me alone. I've learnt that too in the past few hours. Someone else is going through his own creative and emotional turmoil...and, he's not so far from here.

VIII

"That took longer than I expected." Nicole leant across to Andrew then Loualla. "Sorry." The glass of wine she now held was quickly consumed. "Sorry for that too! Very un-ladylike behaviour gulping that down...I needed it. That's my excuse."

"You're doing fine, no worries...tell 'em how it is. There's no sense in keeping it to yourself." Andrew held his glass up to her. "Want a top up? It's a fine vintage, comes from up there on the Swan Valley...so, it's home grown, good local stuff."

"Go on. I may as well stagger as walk back to the station."

"We're eating first Nikki, right here," Loualla smiled. "You can tell us what's what after that little exchange."

"Yes, I owe you that much after making you sit through it." Nicole composed herself. "You heard it all but the detail's this…they've changed their minds or they've decided to ask others to join the lottery of making a case…"

"Pitch for the work, you mean?" Andrew interrupted.

"Yes…it's a good word, pitch…as in, '*throw out a few crumbs of comfort*'."

"More like a throw of the dice." Loualla arched her eyebrows to make the point.

"Yes, that too. Now, it seems that anything can happen." Nicole pouted as she considered the words she had just spoken.

"Wow them…you can wow them," Loualla offered by way of encouragement. "Here, drink this…to luck!"

"I'll need a bit more than that to rely on," Nicole replied confidently.

"It's a start…"

"I gave Simon all of that, a tick list of all the things that matter, that are important. I said, listen to the dance ideas, see some of them performed or 'danced out'…I even suggested that an opinion could be given or shared on the chosen music." Nicole held out her hands and formed a cup, "there's so much to show and share with them…so many ideas to be performed! They should all be considered together."

"But by whom? You don't know anyone there and the whole dance project is one of evolution, developing ideas as you progress…you don't go there with a list Nikki, of steps, the music and so on…" Loualla spoke knowledgeably on the subject but Nicole couldn't agree.

"Don't you?"

"No…it's not how I remember it happening at all," Loualla told her. She waited for Nicole to find fault with the opinion quietly expressed.

"I've got my own ideas. I've imagined how it could go, how the session could be organised. I doesn't fit so easily into the 'habits' box."

"Habits?"

"Yes, habits. They'll say we're used to seeing things done this way…follow a routine, we're used to that…it's become a habit of ours…a recognised routine. Pass the interview, or distinguish yourself in the talent show and we'll move on." She looked at her friends for a response but received none, so her wine was drunk in silence and the menu studied with little enthusiasm.

"Nikki?" Lou ventured, "don't leave us again, please?"

"No…no, of course I won't. I'll spell it out…what Simon Attwood told me, he's the artistic director, by the way…he spoke of following a routine that's very different from how I thought we would go about this." She paused to reflect. "Yes…I gave them my own *take* on how we'd go about this little *adventure* of mine."

"Conform Nikki, bend a little…ease up…just to get through the important round," Andrew advised her. "You must have had some idea of how it might turn out? We've got our own ways of doing things round here just as you do back home." He gave a persuasive smile. "C'mon, Nikki…for your sake…and ours…we want you to succeed in your little adventure, too…just conform to the house rules only for as long as you have to, hm?"

"Sure, only I've never been the conformist, in the habit forming…traditional sense." She gave them both a wink and burst out laughing, brightly. "Do you follow me?"

"No," Andrew said staring at her. "I can understand now why they might even be a little scared of you…you're so self-confident…you just say straight out what you think and believe in."

"Nothing wrong in that," Loualla opined.

Nicole smiled. She had an ally for a moment.

"I tell them what I think and offer to let them see what I can do...I dance! I give a little performance! Is that so intimidating?"

"Possibly...or maybe, unsettling is a better way to put it. You have to study the local ways of doing things and adjust your pitch...to, uhm, suit the situation you're going into."

"If it's different, innovative but respectful of their traditions...their habits, if you like, what's so wrong with that? Pick me...the artistic director and the company...they get it all, only with me!"

"Sure, but lead them in slowly," Loualla observed in a softer persuasive voice and taking Andrew's side in the discussion once more. "They'll like their rules to be followed, *their rules,*" she emphasised, "they do it just to set an example."

Nicole thought that one over for a moment. "Okay...you mean, don't be different or rock the boat...show them that at my age I should know better. Just you behave girl! Is that what you mean?"

"For a while, and only until you get the job!" Andrew laughed before raising his glass. "We've said enough! Now...to age, beauty and bad habits!"

"Lots of them!" Loualla added as she joined in the toast.

They all laughed but deep down Nicole felt unease and recalled a single phrase that Simon had uttered, 'come to us, anyway'. She thought of it now as condescending, ageism finding muted or coded expression. Do I feel that, really, or am I conceding to uncharacteristic paranoia?

"It's me, the devoted dancer they'll be meeting!" she blurted out and pushed back her hair in trembling violent strokes. "Me! The dancer! Me, who is still creative in spirit and thought!"

"Nikki...Nikki!" Lou took hold of one arm to quell her friends anguished movements but she would not be stilled.

"They'll see how my creative instincts have brought me to where I am today, what I am able to do...even now! I'll be different and inventive…I'll show them that I've not lost faith with all the habits they might be so fond of. Mine aren't rooted in time…in history! I continually want to find new ways to express old ideas…it's what makes me feel so alive! It's all about being creative…not chained to the past."

She shuddered at the thought of restrictions being imposed upon her that would set invisible boundaries to all that she sought from her work. Loualla's softened glance upon her had been in acknowledgement that she spoke out an emotion they had so often shared.

"They may not like you pushing the boundaries," Andrew observed in all seriousness and Nicole stared wide-eyed at him.

"Clichés! What do you really mean?"

"It's a special language…Andrew's code. He's trying to tell you to conform…just long enough until you get where you want to be." Lou looked over at him and slowly shook her head to silence any further remarks.

Nicole didn't notice.

"Whatever you meant to tell me, I've just decided to think all of it through, again…all that I'm doing and what Simon was hinting at."

"Don't give up Nikki, please? Don't! Show them what you're really about…what I know of you and have seen from you?"

"Lou, it's been a while since those days," Nicole let the words go on a deepening sigh. "That's what was behind the call just now. They've had a change of mind…only, they came to their decision a little too late to stop me travelling."

"And it's to our gain…all of ours!" Loualla clapped her hands together then grabbed her glass once more. "You're here, with us…that's the best part!" She gave a smiling toast to her friend. "It's the part that really matters, right now…you're here! Our Nikki's with us!"

"Lou's right! My girl's right!" Andrew smiled at her then at Nicole. "At least you've got this far at some one else's expense."

"Yes…and, there's something else now." Nicole cleared some strands of hair from her face and looked at them both with quiet certainty. "I'd like to even up the tally. I'd like to think and talk of other things while I'm here and I still can."

Her gaze never left them as she spoke, in between nervy sips from her glass of wine.

"Do you know what I'm saying? I met someone last night that I'd like to meet again. May I ask and do that?"

"That's my friend…our friend, Nicole." Loualla gave her a softened smile. "Why conform…why be restrained?"

Nicole laughed softly and with only a trace of embarrassment. "Sorry, I've been alone too long…seeing you both so happy makes it feel more obvious."

Andrew sat back in his chair and pretended he was somewhere else. This was a moment strictly for the two women to talk through without his interruption.

"Give me your 'phone, Nikki?" Lou paused and tapped it against her chin on taking the device. "Whom should I call?" she said slowly in a pensive teasing voice. "Oh yes, John…I remember now."

"Are there more like him, then…in your lives?" Nicole asked frowning.

"No," Loualla replied with shake of her head, "and I shouldn't tease you."

"And your answer…is what?"

"No, there's no-one else like John…he's the only one…the special one."

Nicole nodded her own acknowledgement in silence. That's what I thought too; he's unique to my life; he's the only one to dedicate a piece of art to my craft and be as one with my creative impulse without a word being said.

John had looked at some pictures, nothing more than some publicity photos, and he seemed to know me.

I met a man and I thought later of its significance.

John went further, he 'told' me in the only way that he could.

Jumbled up, within me, with every other thought are enduring memories; they are of a few moments and the words that I shared, only with John.

IX

"We'll walk, Andrew."

"Okay…sure. See you both at the house…don't get lost," he chuckled and waited for them to pass on ahead of him.

Nicole watched as Loualla stepped from the car and opened the gates to the track that soon disappeared from view. The broken outline of a house could just be made out through the gently swaying stand of trees that were framed against the clear blue sky of the late afternoon. The leaves rustled on a whisper of wind.

"John will wonder where we've got to," Loualla said as she held the door open and cast a glance at Nicole's feet. "Not the shoes to be wearing for a walk on this…"

"Forest track?" Nicole was already taking in every detail of her new surroundings as she answered. It couldn't be too far to walk so the neat gold buckled loafers would survive.

"It hasn't changed in years, the old house…nothing more than a shack, had this pathway and nothing more. The bush? Well, it's still bush…left as nature and John intended."

"Except for the sculptures…they're wonderful…the setting's perfect."

"Yeah. John…and Carla, they both wanted it that way, a natural location for favourite pieces…or experiments." She followed Nicole's gaze as they walked slowly over the uneven surface. "They're works he just couldn't let go of."

Nicole could only marvel at their diversity. "They feel part of the landscape…and the others?"

"They were sold, displayed or sit in someone's garden…in a park or outside an office building, somewhere in Australia." Loualla had followed her friend's career so closely, sharing in the high and low spots over the years she had known John and Carla Poynter. "Not bad for a guy who started and struggled, then got the recognition he deserves…far too late."

"The abstract works, the figures…the representations of the human form, they all have context, they're life size…they belong here." They had almost reached the gravelled area that fronted the house. "Sorry, there I go again."

"Nikki," Loualla stopped her friend. "Don't apologise, don't say 'sorry' all the time. It's you Nikki…you speak out… what you think and feel."

Loualla set off once more but said nothing further; Carla had told her many times of the union of creative spirits that had been her marriage to John, 'my man'. They are the thoughts that John would love to hear again, only, get close to him if you can Nikki, she prayed for that now. He needs understanding, that love of his art, that unanimity of the creative spirit. It will truly make him a complete and fulfilled person once more.

⊹

Nicole felt the muscles tighten in her throat.

There's John; he has changed from how I remember him and the image I held in my mind's eye. Still, I was tired then, totally wrecked after the flight to get here. At least I can remember his smile; it's warm and welcoming; the close-cropped beard and moustache are elegant complements to his greying hair. He looks youthful; I don't care one bit that to the eye he is scarred by life. I'm attracted to the man, so I care that his soul has been wracked by loss.

She took in once more the whole man.

"Hello...welcome, all of you." John said it easily and looked at them but the squeeze to her hand told Nicole that the words were intended especially for her.

The dogs that came to her gave little barks of welcome and wagged their tales furiously; they were convulsed with interest. She was someone new to fuss over or to grant them fond attention. They sensed it as Nicole held her hands out and made a kissing sound with her lips.

"Hello...hello...hello, hello girls," she laughed kneeling down to them. "What a welcome!" They both nuzzled her face and she laughed again. "Ooooh! What a welcome!"

"Mind...mind, Nicole," John advised.

His tone of voice made her glance up; his lips were clenched tight and she perceived from the look that he gave her that other moments had been instantly recalled. She could read him; Loualla's expression was entirely different. She perceived that her friend had witnessed confirmation of another small bond being formed between her and John.

"It's all right...you can say hello to me can't you?" She remained crouched down and stroked sleek coats as the dogs pressed close and were granted equal attention.

"Your clothes...you'll get fur on them." They were banalities but John sought to wrest some calm from her visit once more.

"They're family, you make allowances...even if others don't understand why you let them get away with it." She smiled up at him. "I really don't mind, John."

"Okay...enough said. Let's have a drink?"

He waved for them to go through an archway with its beautifully crafted iron-gate decorated with arching fern leaves. John turned, waiting for the women to pass through and saw Nicole speak to Loualla.

"Yes, I made that too," he smiled, "as a small element of the setting."

It didn't matter to him if the remark was relevant or not, he spoke simply to explain the surroundings to his home.

❖

They were not a party for long; Loualla made an excuse to take Andrew away, back to their home.

"We'll soon be back," she said with a sly grin at Nicole.

"Yes, you will," John observed calmly and leaving her little room for a debate. "I've made some preparations for a meal, all of us together…so don't keep away." He looked at her over the rim of his beer glass; conventional practice, of drinking from the bottle, was for the moment forgotten.

"I'll break out a dessert, when we get back, how's that?"

"Right…see to it," John drawled. "I wanted to eat al fresco…out in the cool evening air you might say…all of us together." He caught Nicole's eye. "Will it do?"

"Yes, it will do fine"

Loualla had given no prior warning of her little stunt to leave them but Nicole was glad nonetheless for the opportunity to be alone with him. There was just the hint of premeditation in having nothing to say of her friend's plans. She wanted to be in charge of something that day and learning of John Poynter, in the few moments they might have together without others to see or interrupt, or to take account of, suited her just fine. It contrasted perfectly with the condescension that she had heard in Simon's voice that she should continue her journey anyway.

To overcome the negative feelings that conversation had provoked might take some time but she felt in the perfect company to start the process.

"Is it a dessert you made earlier?" she offered in jest and smiled at Loualla.

"You know me, girl. I'm always ready for a surprise! Won't be long…byeeee." She guided Andrew from the enclosed patio without a backward glance.

"I thought I knew the woman," John said as he offered to refill her glass with the chilled white wine Nicole had asked for. "Organised, yes...but like she is now? No."

"I've a confession to make...I put her up to calling you...to invite ourselves over here."

"And break with your usual British reserve?"

"You could say that," she confessed, laughing easily. "I may have left it behind, just this once."

"Go on..."

"I didn't stop her taking my mobile 'phone and calling you."

"Why?"

"Something happened earlier...and something was said today."

"Come, tell me as we go. While there's light I can show you where I work...my creative hideaway."

She followed him along the winding path the dogs close at heel or brushing against her legs occasionally. *What have I reminded them of, or do they recall the ways of another as I follow John?* The little house was captivating in the late afternoon light, the canopies of the Eucalyptus a glitter of greens and yellows in a bright contrast to the very straight ochre and soft brown trunks of the trees. The leaves fluttered on the breeze and offered a muted rustling accompaniment to their progress.

I feel enchanted, by everything about me here and she lightened her step.

The house and its setting were as if the trees would soon reclaim the ground it stood on but she could see John's purpose quite clearly. He sought to have the property as part of the landscape or an intimate intrusion. He led her onto an open verandah that was raised on stilts as if above a flood plain but she could see this quirk of design was but a device to keep small animals at bay. She shivered; *keep away you rodents...worse, know your place, you snakes!*

I can just imagine you out there, in the bush, watching; stay there and I won't disturb you.

"Welcome," John said as he held open the front door for her. "My haven and my cell."

Her soft laugh at his choice of words gave way to a gasp of wonder.

"Light…so much light, even now! I never would have known it."

She walked briskly to the centre of a large high-ceilinged room and twirled, theatrically. The house appeared no more than a property with a pitched roof but she now appreciated the deception of the eye. At the rear of the former woodsman dwelling the wall and roof had been removed and replaced by glass that offered uninterrupted views out onto the woods and sky.

"Clara…my wife, and I wanted it to feel like we could live in the 'open air'…it's a cheat of course, but the senses can be persuaded to feel and think differently. It felt like we could enjoy all that nature could offer…in the dry." He wanted to show off his domain, opening doors with a teasing smile. John knew what would follow, and soon she could smell the warm outside air enter the studio.

"Wonderful…it's quite wonderful. Look! The view is soon lost in the trees!" She turned to face him and realised how obvious had been her remark. "But then…you know that."

"Yes…yes I do, but I like hearing you say it."

"I'm a townie…"

"Whatever," he said unconcerned by her remark, "you know what's true. The eye doesn't deceive…not here."

"No," she replied reflectively. "No, it doesn't."

John took to shutting some of the doors he had just cast open; without prompting she had spoken of an impression of space that he could never quite grow tired of.

"I'll leave these…it's what I usually do when I'm at work. They are also the way, for some of my works, to get out of here.

It's the only change I made to the roof, apart from making it all glass…I increased the pitch by a few degrees only, mind, just to make it feel larger. When it gets too hot I can open a few panes high up there…it then becomes like a chimney…it draws the air, and smells into the room…it almost feels like I'm working outside.""

John pointed and she followed his gaze standing close to him, closer than at any other time.

"I can see why you call it your haven…and your cell," she said softly meeting his gaze upon her.

"I've never used the words before…never described the place in that way. You made me do it…and I don't know why."

"I do."

"Then tell me…tell me Nikki. May I call you that, or should I be more formal?"

"It sounds good, either way."

"You were saying?"

"Too much." She shook her head and stepped away.

"What happened…to bring you here, Nicole?" He was beside her once more but did nothing more than to simply look at her, taking in every detail of her face in the slow movement of his eyes…just on her face.

"You…and some bloody photographs that you felt inspired by. You've made a piece of art that I am quite unable to put out of my mind, that's what!"

"There was only one."

"One?"

"Yes, only one…a picture of your face, your clear eyes and just the hint of a smile…there were flowers, a bouquet held against your breast…your skin shone as if you were the happiest person on earth at that moment. I thought you wanted to burst with happiness…or fulfilment at what you had found that night."

"Date? The date? Was there a date on the picture…where was it taken?" She clutched his bare arm and recoiled with sudden shock. "I…I…I'm sorry."

"Don't mind that…and, I don't remember the date of the picture. It didn't click with me…it wasn't important…other things took me in."

"No…no, quite." She looked about her taking in the orderliness of the room. "You're very organised and tidy…I've only just noticed that about you."

"I wasn't always, my attention was on work then…I got to be that way after this." John pointed to the scarring on his arm, the one she had gripped so tightly for an instant.

"Yes, Lou Lou told me." Her face brightened and she gave a soft smile. "Don't let her hear me say that, please?"

"I'll try to remember," John chuckled.

The thing is, my mind's preoccupied with so much more! I'm like a young artist again…I want to live out all that I feel and concede to the obsession to create new work…and then, there's you, Nikki, the cause of this transformation in me.

"Both of them," he went on, "they haven't heard the whole story…of how that particular day took me, in only a few moments, back to how it once was."

It was to a former life, lost, but the experiences gained had set a new pattern, in his mind, for the future. He dared to think that, perhaps, the worst of the empty days were behind him and that once more the perceptive intensity of his art would flourish. Nicole had spoken of the insight that he may have gained from all that he had endured; she had courageously spoken, to a complete stranger, of one suffering for their art. He hadn't taken her remarks that way, then. But now, he studied every movement, the lightness of her step, the poise in Nicole's posture; he took in everything about the woman and acknowledged silently that his artist's eyes had indeed been opened still further. She was one instinctive lady and he liked her for it.

"No...I can't really begin to imagine what you went through."

Nicole fingered the heavy covers to his latest work, his night's endeavour, and John saw the unasked question in her eyes.

"Come on, we'll talk of all that later, some other time, maybe. I want to be sure..."

"Oh?"

"Later...come back to the house? It's time to set up for this meal I'm supposed to be making for us all."

"I'll help you."

"We'll see...you're my guest." He moved in the direction of the opened doors but Nicole impetuously took hold of his arm and drew close.

"I understand one thing, from tonight, John."

"Oh?" he met her gaze upon him. "Say it."

"You said something so easily, a few moments ago...but I knew that it held so much meaning."

"Oh," he sighed and knew instantly what she was referring to. "I just said it."

"I know...and here, this place, this studio...it doesn't need to be your haven and your cell anymore."

She had spoken out on a sigh in an attempt to convey her understanding of the despair that he had suffered following bereavement and how he would have felt imprisoned by memories. Being in the studio offered the chance for relief from his troubles, only a vital inspirational spur was missing. And now, she felt that the sight of a photograph, an image of her, Loualla's friend from England, had changed everything for him.

$\underline{X}$

Little remained to be done. John had made some preparations for their meal soon after the call announcing

252

that, he smiled on telling her, they were coming over. Nicole watched as he raised the lid to a barbecue neatly set into a screen wall to the main terrace of the house. The contents were unwrapped from the foil, inspected and loosely covered once more.

"These are done to a turn...yep! Perfect!"

"What's on the menu?" she asked now out of simple curiosity.

"Chicken, nothing more than that...in my own sauce, a creation that took a lot of practice to get right!"

"And patient customers, hm?" she teased.

"Yeah, but you're safe now." John beckoned. "Come? Help me get the table ready?"

"Sure." She pulled up the sleeves to her floaty blouse revealing slender wrists adorned with two thin gold chains. "What do I do?"

"We'll deck this out first." His conversation was kept brief now. John was pulling a light tarpaulin from the table and she took hold of the ends that slid to the ground. They folded it up as if they were dealing with a large bed sheet taken from the washing line.

"Is it all your own work, the terrace and the walls...the ironwork?" Nicole kept her voice light in an effort to prompt him into further conversation.

"Yes."

She wondered at the design of the turned pillars. They had been laid in narrow courses of a soft red brick that could just be made out under the glow of the wall lights. One pillar cleverly formed a flue to the barbecue; the remainder supported a tracery of ironwork against which she could see the pruned branches and tied back stems of vines. In summer she could imagine a leafy barrier, a screen that gave context to the wilderness beyond that John was so intent on keeping.

"I should have known better than to ask."

"I'm not worried by it," John answered bluntly. "I'm happy with how it turned out."

Nicole could recognise the outline of what she took to be the Union Jack flag; the pattern was unmistakable. The only distinguishing feature, and difference, were the small shields or plaques welded to the junctions of the horizontal and vertical bars. Upon them had been painted Aboriginal motifs.

"Will you tell me more?" She caught the altered stare upon her for only an instant.

"Yes, I made it…away from here, mind. I went to a foundry and twisted all the rods…I set it out to a design…that Clara had drawn." John spoke more slowly as he stood by her side looking at their work. "It had to have a distinct character… my…my wife was British, so she sought to mix a symbol of her country with tokens of my own."

Nicole noted the softer voice he now spoke in and felt unsure whether to continue. "It's an appealing combination…"

"She was full of ideas," he said quickly, "or she sparked them in me with just a few words."

"That inspired you…that set you off?"

"Yeah, she was a creative muse to me…Carla could just say something that…" he gave an expressive shrug of the shoulders on being reminded of her.

"What? What John? She offered inspiration…?"

"Yeah," he sighed as if to be freed of the intrusive thoughts. His hand touched Nicole's bared wrist for only an instant. "Let me just say…Carla helped to put into *words*, sometimes, what I could only *see* of my work…what I kept hidden inside. What she said helped to make the ideas in my work *come alive*."

Nicole now watched him remove thin wooden sheets; revealed to her gaze was a glass tabletop supported on a framework that complemented the design of the terrace's screen. There was too much to take in. She simply looked at him as John moved from the table to cupboards set into the wall of the terrace and drew cushions from their plastic covers;

they were the seats for the wrought iron chairs. Place mats were laid out, a pair on each side of the oblong table; candleholders of fluted glass were also set out. John worked briskly, certain of what needed to be done in the gathering gloom.

Before she could move to offer the smallest token of help John stood by her.

"Finished...all done. What do you reckon?"

"It's wonderful...you made it wonderful, together."

Their eyes met for an instant and Nicole saw the smallest pout of John's lips in acknowledgement of her remark and the fond recall of a memory. "Yes...we made all of this, together."

He turned away from her. Being together had changed to 'me being alone' but there wasn't that dull or numbing reality any more; absent too had been the words that came to mind only too easily, 'how the hell am I going to fill the empty hours?'

You've opened my eyes again, Nicole. So soon, so quick... can I really be so sure of it?

"Penny for them?"

"Hm?" John looked back at her. "I haven't heard that said in a long, long time! Ages...in fact."

He let the word 'ages' out slowly and with a teasing grin that transformed his face. Gone, she hoped, were the reflective looks he had given while they had attended to some basic chores.

"You were busy...your thoughts were elsewhere."

"Sorry 'bout that..."

"Don't be...what you've lived through makes the artist. It's both who you were and the person you may become that will count...again. Right?"

John stood in silence and thought over what she had just told him.

I'll be a changed man, from what I've been through and because of the few moments we've been together, Nikki.

They've been so few and yet you've still managed to understand and tell me. I made no mistake! I saw the person in those photos, and one in particular…yeah, the one with the smiling happy face. It was glorious! A happy face, the only face, the only one to wear when you've known moments of your own creative soaring fulfilment.

You're in love…in love with all that life, at that single moment, has held out to you and that you have taken to your heart.

"John?"

Without embarrassment he took her hand. "I was thinking over whether to ask if you'd do something for me…"

"And?"

"I was wondering if it was wise…"

"What? Just tell me." She squeezed his hand before letting go.

"I was wondering if it was too early to ask…ask if you'd come back here, after your trip to the Kiwis…further down under, to New Zealand?"

"Why…why do that?" She stared him down; the words used were not intended to tease but an instinctive reply uttered before any thought of their effect upon him.

"So that I'd see you again. There'd be no rushing about… watching the clock all the time. We'd take it slow and just talk…and take the time to learn some more. You say things about creative work that clicks…it clicks with me."

"John…"

Her hand touched his arm again, for only a moment, as the thought occurred to her that she would have to control the impulse to do so.

"Am I talking too much, is that it…already?" He looked at the watch that contrasted so brightly with the scarred skin of his left hand and wrist. "Jeez! We've got to keep moving…and, we'd better call Lou Lou and Andy."

John had diverted the conversation onto more prosaic concerns and walked away towards the kitchen door with a quick backward glance.

"Have I said too much?" he asked again as she followed a few paces behind him.

"No."

"What? What then? What do you think?"

He busied himself, collecting what would be needed for their meal from the cupboards and placing it all on a large tray; plates and cutlery, some wine glasses and colourful, beautifully pressed cloth serviettes. They were all carefully stacked. Finally John turned to her.

"Nikki?"

"I…I need time to think, John," she answered defensively. "Let me help, where I can, in the meantime. There's not much of that is there…time?"

"If it's right, there's time."

John could only say these few words. The dogs were barking and had rushed from the room to stand by the gateway that Nicole had admired when she had first called upon him.

"A timely interruption," she said quietly but to herself.

How long do I really need to decide that seeing John again might be the best that I can expect from this trip 'down under'? How I deal with a life 'alone' is my decision entirely. Loualla has Andrew; my friendship is distinct from the intense companionship that they share.

I've seen it in John's eyes when he looks on me. The impulse to touch him is my own admission of what we may yet find in each other, but he just speaks his mind. Certainty of what I am facing is not something I feel at all…I've fallen headlong in love with a man before.

Right now, she thought, I need some time.

XI

"You made it," John said breezily, "Nicole and I were beginning to think it was dinner for two." He took the dessert that Loaulla handed to him with instructions to 'fridge it for now.'

"It wouldn't have been a problem," Nicole added, "I just don't eat too much."

"And I know two girls who'd help us out."

"They're never far from you, John."

"Us, you mean."

"Okay, equal attention...we're friends already."

Nicole held out a glass of the local white wine to Loualla then Andrew; it was a Swan Valley classic that John had decided would accompany the meal. She had noted her friend's preferences earlier in the day over lunch in Freo and was pleased that a ready supply was available in the chiller. Only a moment's recognition that the simple act of hospitality held any significance was seen in Loualla's gaze upon her; with consummate ease she had fallen into the role of hostess and John had said nothing of it or asked that she helped.

Take care, she thought; indulging in spontaneous behaviour might draw attention if it were repeated.

It's only a small role that I'm playing, just for the evening, her look seemed to say in response to Loualla's smile and enquiring tilt of the head. It seemed to ask, how'd it go, while we were away?

"We haven't done this for a while," John said lightly as he set out the meal before them insisting that everyone took their seats as he waited upon them. It was a small gesture of thanks that the time had arrived to entertain and make a fuss over special friends.

"And my special visitor," he went on as he raised a glass to Nicole. Loualla pulled a face as he addressed her in his own particular way. 'Andrew' remained Andrew.

"Have you seen the studio or did John persuade you to help with this meal?" Nicole was asked.

"I haven't lifted a finger to help," she replied watching as John lit the candles before them; they flickered for an instant before the glass flutes enclosed them once more. "John has done it all...and I've seen the studio."

"Hidden talents, mate, you're cooking," Andrew observed. "Help myself shall I?"

"Sure...I've learnt a lot of things," John smiled. "I just stick to the recipes I know. That way it's safer...for everyone."

"Quicker too...you've learnt from your mistakes and where they can wreck all you've done." Nicole spoke of her own experiences and economy of effort to look after herself. "You've passed through the experimental stage."

"So, you know the routine?" John winked and Nicole nodded.

"Yes."

"Well, we can take on these two. They experiment all the time...new recipes, new ways to cook...new ways to persuade you to try out the results."

"New ways to feed you," Loualla intervened. "I just happen to remember an empty 'fridge and snack tins...not so long ago."

"And I won't forget what you both did." John held a hand out to her in acknowledgement. "All of that, 'camping' here on my own...it's over. Those days are gone...whatever happens now."

"Oh? What's up?" Andrew and Loualla looked at each other for an instant.

"Nothing's 'up'. Something's happened to make me want to get back to work...in a few days I'll have it all set, the finished work in two weeks or so. Nikki gave me the idea..."

"Did I? Was that the work...under the tarpaulin you kept me from looking at?"

"Yes...I've not slept much these last few days, but I really pushed on with it yesterday."

"What?" Nicole began but John stopped her by placing his hand on her arm.

"Later...I've worked on an outline, the start. It's all sketched out...I've even got a name for it."

"And?"

"It'll keep." Loualla answered for him and John nodded at them both.

"Right...it'll keep, but not for long."

"You know the special language?" Nicole laughed out looking at Loualla.

"She knows," John answered for her and he saw Loualla nod her agreement. "I don't tell it all until I'm quite ready. You'll see it if you return here..."

"Return...return?" Loualla asked sharply. "When? When are you coming back?"

Nicole gave John a silencing stare. "Nothing's settled... and he said, 'if'."

"You've talked about it?" Loualla persisted. "Have you done that?"

"Along with a lot of other things...I need to get through the next few days first. Anyway, John's found his creative spirit again..."

"It's been brought back to life..."

"We've all played a part to help you...mine's the smallest one...a few images, some photos I didn't know Loualla still had. The rest came from within you...you did most of the work yourself, John. You did the hardest part of it all."

John kissed the hand Nicole offered when the moment came to say goodbye; the gesture seemed entirely appropriate. Her stay amongst them would end the following day, in the evening, when she boarded a flight for Auckland.

"Take my number...please keep in touch?" was all he asked in a moment when they were briefly alone.

"I have it, already...I told you." She hadn't reckoned on becoming emotional after the few hours they had spent in each other's company; nor had she decided upon the words to express her gratitude for the gift he had crafted.

"Yeah, of course...well, let me take yours."

He did not press the point made earlier in the evening, that she should return to visit him. If Nicole conceded she would soon hear how he intended to complete the work that had been so carefully concealed from view under the tarpaulin. During dinner he had admitted creative endeavour would soon become an obsession, only he had refrained from telling them that the medium would be both stone and steel. The former would be roughly hewn, with some of its surfaces tellingly polished to contrast with adjacent coarsened folds; the metal would be cast, in a sculpted mould, its form and imagined surface deeply symbolic of man's experience. He had become preoccupied, possessed by thoughts of a visitor who would soon be gone; what she could say in her beautiful voice had brought the shimmer of an idea to his mind's eye, then, the clarity of creative vision. Glass! Yes, glass should also be a vital constituent of his new work; it would become the third and most telling element; it meant light, redeeming light, the dismissal of darkness.

"May I call you, in a few days...just to ask how your interview went...that you got through that okay?"

"Wounded, but unbowed?" she replied in a very matter of fact tone of voice.

"Too negative..." he began but Loualla had her own point to make.

"What she means is..."

"What I mean is...'yes, call me'. I'd like that." She spoke to him as John closed the car door. Andrew, considerately, had operated the electric window to allow them to finish before the engine came to life. "Give me a few of days…will you do that? I'll have taken in what's been going on…or has happened."

"Yes, I can do that…but, stay 'unbowed'. It's what I know about you…or I saw in the photographs."

"John…" The car moved slowly forward and he had to step away. "Take care!" she called out to him.

"I will…of everything!"

She saw him wave, and then John was lost to her view.

XII

"I'm forever looking back…that's a sure sign of ageing."

Her preparations were nearly complete for the onward journey; the stay in Perth had been brief, far too brief.

"Fifty's not old!" Loualla scoffed. "Besides, you've shown me that the spirit lives on, the flame's still bright!" She gave a little laugh. "Sorry, I can't think of any other appropriate clichés…but you get my drift?"

Nicole smiled. "Yes…all your turns of phrase, and after such a short time!"

"Go on then, Nikki? Go and show them in Auckland what you can do! I've seen it, this afternoon! You can move, beautifully! So, nothing has really changed."

The day had passed quietly; they had walked barefoot along Scarborough's perfect sandy beach, the light breeze tugging at clothes, mussing their hair and under a sun that felt unusually warm for the time of year. Nicole relaxed, demonstrating a few of the steps and moves that she hoped might persuade Simon Attwood to look beyond her life's resumé.

"I don't really have to explain who I am or what I can do… I can *still* do!" she had told Loualla; a particularly strenuous and evocative portrayal of a scene had made Loualla gasp in wonder.

"You've got it all, girl. If they don't see that then they've got no idea! It's still there…your grace, the beauty of movement and innovation! You think of beauty…and it shows on your face!"

"Lou…my dearest friend."

"They've got to see them…see your ideas. Talk's not enough. Persuade them, make them find the time and the courage to allow you to dance, to show what lives on in you… leave them no chance to think that you're not burrrsting with creative energy and ideas."

Lou gave a little laugh when she had finished.

"They're only ideas…you said so yourself," Nicole smiled.

"I didn't know then what you've been working on!"

"Come with me? Ask Andrew…we'll see if there's room on the flight? Be my cheerleader? Help me prepare?" Lou's enthusiasm had pushed those intrusive thoughts of her impending departure aside; they had even agreed that John's piece of art should remain…just in case she had a change of mind and returned for a few days more on the journey back home.

"I can't do it, girl…I just can't. I've been out of it for too long. Besides, you always had the edge."

"But you got your man…"

"Just earlier than you." They smiled at each other like two teenagers talking of their love life.

"Lou, listen?"

"I'm just telling you how I see it, that's all. Come back, here to us…just say *'yes'*? Please, say it now? Come back and see how everything's turned out while you were away? You can stay with us…we've got the space." She took hold of Nicole's hands. "Three days? It's been great having you here, but…it's nothing. We've been together no time at all after so long apart!"

Loualla's lips trembled and Nicole was reduced to silence.

"Three days! It's no time at all," Loualla persisted.

"If it's right, there's time," Nicole said and looked up suddenly at her friend. John's remark had come to mind, unbidden.

"What?"

"Never mind," Nicole said, averting her gaze. "It was something I heard."

I've been through so much; she remembered a tearful but resolute leave-taking. Loualla had been promised a call just as soon as she arrived in Auckland.

"I don't care how early it is in the morning!" she cried out as they waved each other goodbye at passport control.

And I'll want to hear a friendly voice, Nicole thought now.

It's the furthest I have ever been away, away from my friends and remaining family but I have to embark on this adventure, even if I am uncertain of the outcome.

Tea and a sticky cake, a Macadamia apparently, were carried to a nearby table of the café close to the departure gate that she needed; few people were about for her to take account of. A cursory glance at her watch indicated that she was on time, not early, so where was everyone? The airports she frequented were crowded places, a heaving mass of humanity on the move; she had seen an example in Dubai only a few days ago.

Here, in Perth, the tempo of life and the atmosphere seemed easy. She sighed; maybe it was simply another misconception of the world about her or the happy and thought provoking moments, hours even, that she had so recently experienced.

From tomorrow morning I'll be talking and dancing for my life, a life as a choreographer, an innovator, but most of all as a ballet dancer who can't quite let go of a way of life that has meant everything to me. I'm a still girl at heart, a girl in satin and silks who has lived a bit but for whom one of life's experiences remains unfulfilled.

That's how I feel.

That is how I was made to feel.

And…I'm leaving.

I'm leaving people and a place that has made me reconsider where I am going…with my inner life and all that the world sees of a me, Nicole Gorrin-Eyre, ballerina!

She shivered, jolted out of her moment's reverie.

"Now what?"

Her mobile 'phone trilled in her handbag and played a new tune. That girl! What a trick to play on me! What a tone to inflict on me, even if it is the opening bars of Beethoven's ninth symphony. Bloody tease, as only Loualla would say it! I'm not at war so why the music to announce important news?

"Hello?" She didn't recognise the number on the screen, just 'Optus' the service provider.

"Hi…I'm breaking the rules already, I know."

"John, hello."

"I just wanted to wish you the best…after this call I'll leave it…I'll do as we agreed…call you in a few days."

"I forgive you…besides, I'm alone, here." She was glad for the opportunity to talk to him.

"Not quite."

"John…"

"Okay…" His voice lifted. "I've been busy. I'm calling you from the studio…the girls are here, close by. They know something's up…I'm here all the time now."

"Are the doors open to the bush? Let me hear…?" She imagined him holding the 'phone away for a moment.

"Hear any of it?" he laughed.

"No."

"The parrots have gone for the day…or they're high up in the trees. They don't bother me much…listen, just the whistle of the breeze…"

"Oh yes!" She said it as though a new experience pleased her. It had done so; she loved the sheer simplicity of these few moments shared with him.

"I won't keep you…best way to listen to it all is to be here."

"Yes." She changed the subject. "Your new work? Tell me about it?"

John paused for a moment. "I got the quarried stone today," he said at last. "I'm working on it now."

She would have to get used to the clipped way of speaking he often used to communicate. "So soon?"

"Yeah, there's no time to lose. I'll have that part of it done in a day or so…there's no distractions, for the moment any way."

"Don't overdo it." She said it in an almost motherly tone and pressed her lips tight shut, in annoyance. I'll have to stop that…at once!

"I'll know when it's done, the stone work that is. The rest of the piece is where the real hard work lies."

"Mine's to come…from late on tomorrow, then the day after. I'll know something pretty soon after that."

"Well, go to it…my best wishes, again. Lou told me…you can dance and give expression to your creative inner self." He gave a chuckle. "Know what I mean? I'm not sure where that little speech came from."

"It's okay, I follow you…when…when did Loualla tell you that?"

"Oh, a few moments ago…she told me what you did today."

"Oh?"

"Yeah…I called and asked her straight out."

"Hm!"

"Yeah…only she said I should ask you myself. So, it's another reason for me calling you."

I'm never going to be too far away from this place, she thought listening to him. She heard the voice of a man who had affected a change upon her in the short time they had known each other. Too much has happened by simple deeds, so much has been said in a few words, and I've been touched, but by unseen caring hands

"Nikki?"

"Yes? I'm not far away…I'm not going to be too far away from any of you. Let's just see what the next day, then the day after that, brings. Can we do that, John?"

"Yes. Go safely."

"Thanks…you too. Work with care, John."

"I will." She thought he had gone. Then, she heard his admission.

"I want to see you again, Nikki."

It's enough that I know. Don't say any more, John, please? If it's right, there's time.

"Soon John…maybe soon."

Maybe.

Her parting words had sounded so indifferent to the circumstances and in contrast to how she felt.

I'll have to say something, the next time John calls…to make up for the way I spoke to him.

The hotel was comfortable and lacked any overt ostentation. It was modern and the furniture a pastiche of tastes that could not be made acceptable to her eye by the use of brilliant colours in the fabrics covering chairs and settees to the public areas. She had been confronted with the clash of modern style and a more recognisable street scene from home upon her arrival in Auckland's city centre. Now she stared for a moment at the cover to the large bed in her room.

Forget all that; it's a place to sleep and nothing more. The view's good. I can see the harbour and the islands beyond. The map inside the hotel's guide was helpful. I can see all that I need to from up here even in the gathering gloom. At least the lights are on and show someone's at home.

Unrelated thoughts came to mind as she took in her new surroundings.

Below was the busy street. She didn't care to look for long or to judge just how far below the double glazed window the pavement was. It was far enough to make her uneasy. Flying 'was fine'. Standing as if on a ledge and looking straight down conjured up different fears entirely and were quickly blotted out.

The curtains were closed with a noisy flourish. However, she could not close off her mind to the thoughts of a few days she had spent with friends.

They had all wished her well…and they had all asked her to return.

I want the parade to be over; then, I can enjoy myself and just let go. I want to stay in one place for a while and live normally. Silly to expect that when I'm on a trip, a 'business trip' some might say. The journey's about me…the *'inner me'*. Yes, we're back to that again! I've travelled alone but now I'm to be 'alone' amongst strangers while I convince them that my skills and passion for dance can produce what I believe they are looking for.

While I embark on that particular journey I have helped a man step out onto a new life's path. I didn't plan any of it; Loualla couldn't have intended anything by it other than to introduce a friend who had come to stay.

And yet, her efforts had wrought their own effect upon two people who had each entered another's life so unexpectedly.

XIII

"Is the hotel okay?" Simon started off the proceedings with easy chatter. "We thought it best to have you close to the city centre…that way you can see the sights and be nearby, to the theatre...not far from where we intend to open our new centre for dance."

The introductions were over.

She had scribbled the names of the interview panel in her neat leather bound notepad with its slip fastening. It had been a prized possession for many years; it held many memories of co-operative endeavours or creative inspiration that maintained links with a world that she loved and tenaciously clung to.

Nicole clutched at the comforting suppleness that the leather offered. The notes she had made as a means to prepare for the meeting had been drafted and redrafted, then summarised until a few sheets of paper were neatly pressed within the folds of the notepad.

The faces before her were youthful, the men were casually dressed; the woman had paid more attention to her appearance. But, Nicole noted the hard set to her features, as if she had intruded upon their world, whereas the men had open expressions.

I'm here for an interview, a discussion of ideas, not a grilling...well, that's what I thought until I saw you, lady.

"Everything's fine," Nicole replied and dismissed the moment's other intrusive observations. "I even plucked up the courage to go to the top of the Sky Tower..." She offered a smile.

"And?" Simon asked.

"Oh," she went on lightly, "I merely took in the views, as best as my fear of heights allowed...but I forsook the chance to do a skydive and see the city suspended from a wire harness." She had seen others undertake the experience and could only wonder what they gained from it; the activity seemed utterly foolish.

The panel members gave a collective smile as if to say let's all get the opening formalities dispensed with.

Simon Attwood gave the appearance of chairing the meeting and after a look at his two colleagues nodded to one of them. 'Amber Jardine' was the name on the label pinned to the woman's jacket. They had been introduced upon arrival but initial impressions lingered.

Proceed with caution…is that what I do? Nicole asked the question of herself once more. She had seen, instantly, the aloofness in the woman's character through all the polite introductory words.

"What do you understand by the phrase *'conceptual dance'*?" Amber asked it straight out and Nicole met an unblinking riveting stare.

She took a moment to compose herself. I've done this too many times, she thought. I'm not going to be intimidated by such an opening shot.

Amber waited, twisting a pen between her fingers as she did so.

"The idea of the work," Nicole finally answered, "what lies behind it is more important than its physical representation… the choreography…the steps."

"It's not just the idea, but how it is performed that should matter? Is that it…is that what you mean?"

"It is what your question invites me to reply…yes."

"Does it?"

"Yes, in my opinion it does. 'Conceptual' is a word borrowed from the art world…like 'minimalism'. For me it means no more than *'what you see is what you see'*. There's no depth, no recognisable content to the emotions you are seeking to recreate on the stage…" she paused. "Or on the canvas, for that matter."

John Poynter suddenly came to mind and the piece of glass so wonderfully created.

"It could even apply to sculpture…certain works of that nature," she said as an afterthought.

"Do you disagree with the idea of 'conceptualism' as it is applied to dance?"

Nicole looked at Simon who had asked her the question.

"No," she answered on turning to meet Amber's look upon her once more. "I simply believe that you should create something, a dance piece if you will, that endures in the memory."

There would be no concession to the tactic of speaking out any ill-considered answers. She had enough experience to know that some used the technique to discover the foundations of her artistic beliefs and whether she was truly an innovator. The world of ballet had its conformist elements; some called them 'conservatives'; disrespectful others called them 'conservationists'.

The one word response had the desired effect. Amber, what a name, persisted with the simple but invasive line of her enquiry.

"How is 'conceptualism' applied to dance...to modern ballet? How would you see your role as a choreographer in a company that espoused such values...those ideas?"

"We're looking at ideas...your ideas." Alistair Dyson, a hitherto quiet panel member, spoke up at last. "We're wanting you to express...to put into words, your mind-set and how you believe you would fit in with our aspirations for the company. May I put it that way?"

If he had sought to be helpful Nicole could only think that Alistair had failed with his contribution to the discussion so far.

"I understand the question perfectly, thank you." Nicole looked at all of them in turn with a quick unblinking scan of her eyes. "The honest answer can only be given by an audience...not the creator of the piece or the dancers."

"Oh?" Amber asked. "Perhaps you can explain what you mean by that?"

"Certainly," Nicole answered calmly. "To me the whole notion of 'conceptualism' is dated...it is rooted in an art movement whose ideas came to the fore sixty...seventy years ago." She waved a hand as if to indicate the date was of little consequence but the ideas were.

"Meaning?" Amber tilted her head in enquiry before she caught the eye of the other two.

"Meaning that if art, or dance, is to survive and appeal to all tastes it has to have a unique yet recognisable physical representation...the art form has to be portrayed and executed...whether in paint, dance or sculpture in an innovative but still recognisable manner. The art," Nicole said heavily, "lies in the execution of the work as well as the idea behind it...be it by a painter, sculptor or choreographer...or the dancers themselves."

"The dancers," Amber said, "let's keep to them, them only."

"Sure...I'll limit my answers to how the ideas may affect a company of 'dancers'.

She said it heavily as other thoughts came to mind. She recalled vividly now...now of all times, the beginnings of a conversation with John. It was that piece of work, small and genuine; it was breathtakingly simple yet beautifully crafted. He had called it 'minimalist' but she had sensed that the remark had only applied to how the work had been executed. The idea and its significance were profound; the observer's mind had to be provoked by the image before them. None of those thoughts, others might say, could have been stimulated unless the beauty of the idea had been recognised by the artists' eye and wonderfully transformed by his, or her, hands.

Simon prompted her once more with a smile. "You were going on to say something...Nicole?"

She nodded. Minimalism, that was it! I spoke to that man about it, to John.

"Yes," she resumed, "I was going on to say that the idea at the core of any ballet piece is important...the audience needs to recognise that quickly and associate with all that the work seeks to portray. They need to identify with the dancer's movements, what they show of their feelings and how they may express the deepest emotions demanded of them in the piece being danced. The audience needs to be certain of their interpretation of all that they see before them…the movements of the dancers, their hold on each other…the meaning that lies within every step and turn, leap and pirouette. Everything has to have a unity of purpose…it can not be 'abstract'."

Nicole sighed slowly. *I can't deny how I still feel about dance…the expression of every emotion through movement.*

"Hence, if I understand correctly what you've just told us, dance is not conceptual…" Amber spoke in a reflective tone provoking further comment.

"Or minimalist," Nicole said as if to finish the sentence for her.

"What does choreography mean to you now?"

"Drawing inspiration…being motivated to learn from the past and being informed by it. An audience likes to see some work re-interpreted, others like to see it performed in a classical manner…others may care nothing for tradition and are sold entirely on the new."

"Is there something wrong in that…in the last part of your answer?" Alistair asked.

"No, but tradition has to be married to the new and the innovative. You don't study history by simply looking back to what happened last week…"

"And yet," Simon prompted, "even what happened last week may inform what you do this week."

"Agreed…I agree," Nicole suppressed a sigh. *This wasn't the discussion I had hoped or prepared for. Is that the reason others are involved in the process now? Creaky ideas of yesteryear, let's hear them from Nicole?*

"But!" she said in a strong clear voice to stop them interrupting again, "as I told you, in my view tradition informs the new…be it in the music, the costume, the movements to the music scored or even to associate with the title of the piece. 'Swan Lake' trips off the tongue…as do other fabled works."

"They don't always fill theatres," Amber observed sharply.

"No…although that may also be a reflection on who is performing the work." Nicole arched her eyebrows in reply for an instant. "The company should be associated with a range of work…variety, in styles and ideas, helps in the technical development of the company for other still more demanding work. I have done both, modern and traditional…so, I believe I know."

I may as well tell them I've been only too involved in ballet for some time. It's in the papers before them so why should I make a secret of it? I'm not ashamed of my past, the ballets I have been a member of…an *active* member…I'm not ashamed or going to be coy about any of it. She felt that Simon had been watching her closely as she spoke and instinct made her look at him.

"And if I told you," he was prompted to say, "that the company being formed…it's well on the way incidentally…was to devote itself almost entirely to modern work? What then?"

"Nothing more?"

"That's what all of us here, us talking to you…believe in for the ballet company." Amber spoke but Simon nodded in agreement.

She didn't answer immediately. Instead, Nicole scribbled in her notepad and looked up from time to time to indicate that she would answer soon.

"I'd say that there might be tensions between the sense of personal creativity that the chosen choreographer felt for their work, what an audience might expect of the company and how the artistic direction of the new company co-existed with commercial reality."

Yes, quite a mouthful Nicole admitted to herself but she had known of a company that had been avant-garde and had soon gone out of business.

"Wow!" Amber laughed, but in disagreement with the opinion expressed. "Is that a general comment on the choreographer's role or merely your own opinion?"

"Both," Nicole answered bluntly. Have I travelled all this way to listen to this rubbish?

"Please explain," Alistair asked her calmly, noting that the tension between the two women was now evident in their exchanges. "Please, explain…say what you mean? Tell us what you were thinking of just then?"

"I'd be concerned for my own work and its reception as well as the success of any company. I'd be wondering if I'd be adding to the conflict that would arise between being popular and the real future…a sustainable future of ballet."

"We want to fill the theatre," Simon observed.

"Yes," was her slow reply, "we can agree on that, but if you as a new company are relying on persuading someone to commit first…to put together a programme of unseen pieces of modern dance…"

"Yes! Yes!" Amber felt compelled to interrupt. "We have every intention of being innovative…forward thinking!"

I'm getting the hang of this now, Nicole thought. Ill simply say what's on my mind and make my own observations of their plan.

"Sure, be creative and innovative…only, you won't succeed if you're hoping to persuade people to attend performances on that type of programme alone. You're a new company, so…if I may so, you're taking a gamble…a huge risk, if you rely solely on what you think may be ballet's future."

"We're not competing with any European ballet company…or to be like them, trying to compare with the Kirov or the Bolshoi." It was Simon seeking to justify their company's direction.

"No-one does," was Nicole's succinct reply. "They're in a class of their own."

"And the Royal Ballet, hm? What of them?" Amber had to bring that into the conversation.

"I never once sought to outdo their work…I watched and learned from them. I carried on with that instinct after I stopped being a company member, and I do so now…still!"

Nicole fell silent.

"Go on, express your opinion," Simon encouraged with an even tone of voice. "I think we're now speaking of the meeting…or the clash, of traditional ballet with the modern. We discussed the project in an earlier conversation between us Nicole."

His companions agreed with a single nod of their heads.

"I remember talking of established ballet works interwoven with new and innovative pieces, Simon. Your call to me of a few days ago seemed to indicate a change of mind."

"The edges have blurred," he replied, adding, "that's true."

I'm tired of this wordy jousting, Nicole thought suddenly, but she stared at them all, the three judges of ability and passion for their art, with unblinking eyes. I've done everything possible for a dancer, loved the life and the people…well, some of them.

"No, it's not a clash but a working together, hand in hand… literally. It is in the dancer's training, in the development of technique and the portrayal of the innermost thoughts of the character…their emotions…their hopes and fears…their joys and sadness. They are skills founded in tradition…you gain that from the study, and performance, of all that has gone before and you apply it with a new layer of richness to the present."

Nicole paused but she could see that for once there would be no interruptions.

"All of that is what the audience asks each member of the company on the stage to portray...to convey in every step and look, in every touch or outstretched hand. It comes...all of it, from study...a deep and open study of their art, of all that has gone before. If tradition, the history of steps and the deeper knowledge of their calling is absent, well...it's just *an act!*" She tapped her hands together in a soundless but evocative clap to reinforce her point. "It's little more than a circus act set to music, gymnastics to a background tune."

She fell silent. I had to say it! God only knows where it all came from but it did!

The note pad, held so loosely and placed on her lap as she made a point of view known was now closed with a definitive slap before clutching it tightly. She gave a toss of her head and felt the bundle of soft, plaited hair caress her neck.

I've said it all too clearly. I've danced with the best, learnt from experts...the ballerinas of the day and the doyen of their craft, my craft! I'm not going to compromise on my past to secure a fractured future.

The silence that had fallen was broken.

"You told me when we last spoke that you wanted to show us your ideas."

Simon smiled at her to win some concession, or was it in acknowledgement that they had reached a crisis point in their meeting?

"Yes, I did Simon...but that was a few days ago."

"And now?" Amber asked. The tilt of her head and the teasing smile could provoke the direct response that Nicole felt it deserved, but, she controlled an all too natural instinct to react, almost.

"I may be older than any of you before me but ballet can have a future, even if it has to compete with so many other distractions that pass for entertainment...even bloody computer games!"

She gave a soft laugh. Loualla would be proud of that little 'bloody'!

"Right now I think my devotion to traditional art forms, their influence and portrayal as a source of learning is going to be out of favour here. For me there's a place for well-known work in the repertory of any company…any company."

I'm walking away from this, that's what I'm doing talking like I am, she thought. I can't keep hold of my opinions or feelings about my work any more.

What the hell, it's my life…and I'll do what I want to!

"Rely on modern creations alone…just being innovative… will not fill your theatre."

She said it in a disembodied voice, as if speaking out her deepest feelings and Simon was prompted to respond, at last.

"That's for us to say, Nicole…for us to decide and talk through, with the chosen choreographer."

"And I wish you good luck with that!" Nicole stood up. "It's been interesting travelling to see you here…and, thank you for the invitation to consider the options."

"Steady," Alistair observed. "We will want to see you for a follow up talk, to investigate some more all the ideas the candidates have put to us. We'll be doing that over the next few days."

Nicole shook her head and gave him an understanding smile.

"I'm sorry, but I am withdrawing my candidacy. Conceptualism, popularism, whatever it is you care to call the genre of ballet work you seem to be intent on pursuing…"

"We haven't begun to talk of it yet!"

Amber flared angrily only to be met by an apologetic shrug of Nicole's shoulders.

"No, but then you didn't have to say too much. I got the drift very early on in this meeting, from you."

"So, you're going?" Simon said needlessly.

"Yes…I'll settle the hotel bill myself. I feel it's the least that I can do."

"And then?"

"I think I'll go back to Australia, to my friends from ballet and of sculpture…to talk of the true meaning, for me at least, of the differences between art forms. I've made a mistake. The concepts of innovative dance and ballet, I've devoted time and study to them both, are so very different. Maybe ideas that have a home in Europe don't travel too well."

"I'm sorry that you feel that way." Amber stood up as if to confirm that the decision not to waste any more time in each other's company had been reached.

"Oh please, don't be." There was nothing to be lost now. "Meetings like these help the creative process, you gain confirmation of your deepest creative instincts or you agree to think again. Innovation can only follow the analysis of recognisable traditions and practice. You perform well-known pieces in order to learn and develop yourself and the company. Our views differ…the meeting has made that clear to me." Nicole gave a soft smile of recognition that their animated discussion had served its purpose. "Give thanks for that."

"If I hadn't read your resume', or spoken to others about you and your work, I'd describe your remarks as conceited."

"I'm sorry for that Simon. I believe in my art, what it was, what it has become…in all of its many guises, and…what it may become. It's passionate and emotional, it changes over time but it never forgets its origins. Somewhere and at some time it pays homage to what went before…that way the past continues to live on and gives hope for the future." She sighed. "Sorry, it's just how I see it…more important still, how I *feel* about my art and all that I have learnt from it."

"We too," Amber hissed. "We don't need to be talked down to, the old speaking…or lecturing, the new!"

Nicole stood up, proudly. "I'm not ashamed of what I believe in."

"Thank you, I'll take that in the meaning I think it was intended, a comparison between ballet and mere dance."

Nicole held onto her things and checked that she had them all.

"I'll see myself out. Good luck with your venture. If you can bring your selves to send it to me, I'd like to see the opening night's programme."

XIV

"Wait! Nicole, wait!"

"Simon?" She said it on a sigh.

He had admired the confident steps that she took. Nicole possessed beauty, a fine posture and ease of movement that her training and life's experiences had bestowed. She had dressed simply but radiated style; it seemed effortless. To him it was as if she wore a crown, her hair a beauteous contrast to the black outfit she had chosen for the occasion of meeting them.

"Quite an act," he went on, "what we saw back there."

"Was it?"

"Don't mess with words, Nicole. You know what I mean. The meeting was to see how deep your commitment to the art was…it still is."

She looked about them. Standing out in the street was hardly the place for this conversation. Simon seemed to pick up on her thoughts.

"Yes, it still is," she said with a quiet emphasis in her tone. "My commitment remains as strong as ever. The new fashioned from the old…the youthful from the elderly, if you like."

Simon managed a smile at that.

"Don't mind her! Amber has her ways," he laughed. Nicole simply looked back at him. "She tests everyone, just to see what they're really made of."

"I'm bound by and to certain traditions so I'm made differently from what you, she, and Alistair may expect. It's not going to work, Simon. I learnt that very quickly and I don't want to waste anyone's time debating it any further. You click with people or you don't. It's very instinctive…conceptual even."

She gave him a smile as Simon stood before her, mute.

Strange, she thought as they finally said good bye and walked in opposite directions, he hadn't reckoned on female intuition at all.

Nicole strode purposefully, unconcerned that she might become too warm; the sun gave a welcoming cheerfulness to the city's streets as she tried to clear her mind of intrusive thoughts.

I could have dragged the whole meeting out a bit more, just to see if discussion would persuade them to see the project a little differently…not in my way alone, but a blend of ideas on modern and traditional forms of ballet. She sighed. Oh well, I can't help believing what is right or appropriate to the circumstances as I see them.

"This looks like the place to unwind!"

She stood before a welcoming fully glazed façade that simply could not be ignored; it gave brilliant distinction to a modern sunlit interior that soon caught her eye.

The words painted on the glass said 'Gastro Bar'.

"This looks right…it's what I need, given the mood I'm in."

She said it under her breath and pushed open the door, glad to have encountered a place for an early lunch. She took in her new surroundings quickly. Square tables were haphazardly arranged over the highly polished mahogany floor, its deep brown a wonderful contrast to the beech wood table tops. Rattan chairs complemented the colour of the tables. Assorted photographs of surfers, bikini clad girls, yachting types and wide sandy beaches covered the walls.

"Just the place to have a drink and make some plans…or rather, to change them."

"Can I help you?"

"Hm? Oh! Oh yes…yes please." Nicole had taken the menu from the porcelain holder that stood on the table and had been scanning the drinks listed, unaware that a waitress now stood close by. "Can you recommend anything?" she asked smiling.

"The salmon's always very good, here…" The waitress pointed it out on the card. "Look, there's even a speciality."

"I'll have that then, on your recommendation…the salmon en croute, with a side salad, nothing more…please?" Her mood had lightened from their very simple exchange.

"Let me get that on the go…I'll be back to take your drinks order in a minute."

"I know what I want."

"Okay," the girl replied in a sing-song voice as she made to leave.

"Champagne, that's what I would like…a glass of champagne. May I have that, no more or less?"

"I'll ask…" Nicole couldn't help but notice the interest that the waitress took in her.

"Is that okay?"

"Are you dancer?"

"I…" Nicole was momentarily lost for words. "Whatever gave you that idea?"

"I watched you…as you walked up to the door…I also noticed you walking on the pavement outside…your footsteps are precise…trained."

"Yes…yes, I see."

"Are you?" The questioning persisted.

"And, are you?" Nicole asked it herself now knowing that to delay her reply would not succeed for long.

"I'm studying ballet."

Nicole beckoned to the girl and she bent a little closer. "Don't tell on me will you? Yes…I was a ballerina once."

"Oh!"

"Don't look so surprised," Nicole laughed. "I thought you recognised it in me!"

"I did." The girl looked embarrassed. "I don't know what made me ask."

"Never mind, I certainly don't. Now, can you fetch me some champagne...otherwise a glass of your dry house white wine, please?"

Nicole gave a reassuring smile and tilted her head slightly on making her request.

"I know we do that." The girl left.

Whatever next, she asked of herself. First on the aeroplane and now here. Nicole took some more time to consider the surroundings of this fashionable meeting place. The atmosphere seemed relaxed and downbeat, the pictures on the walls nearby in carefully co-ordinated frames. She found it a welcome contrast to the heady, even intellectual, rigours in which she could have become embroiled.

The ideas I've got won't go to waste. She took the notepad from her valise just to make sure that nothing had been left behind. Good, all present and correct. Her bag was fastened once more yet the recall of events continued.

Only, I didn't have the chance to tell them, or, the truth is that I walked out on the chance. Still, their loss is someone else's gain. I'll be okay; I've survived these little setbacks before...after all, I'm not in it for the money.

The girl was by the table once more; a glass of wine stood on a small paper mat set out at the centre of a round polished steel tray. Nicole paid closer attention. 'Sylvie' the name badge said. She hadn't seen it before, neatly pinned to the crisp white blouse.

"There you go," the waitress announced without a trace of formality.

"Thank you."

"Gladly done...your lunch won't be long." Sylvie held the tray against her chest.

"Fine. Now, please tell me…if you don't mind? What sort of ballet are you following?"

"I'm taught classical style, but…I prefer to apply it to modern dance."

"You can't do one, properly, without the other."

"So my tutor tells me."

"A woman after my own heart."

Sylvie smiled at that and gave a giggly laugh. "She's…she's a man!"

Nicole took in the girl's youthful elegance as she turned away.

It is how I was, once…how I still feel deep within myself only I can't carry it off so convincingly anymore. It's just as well that I followed my instincts in that room…the Amber room! Proceed, with caution; I read the signs.

She gave a chuckle and sipped on her wine.

I have a choice; maybe it's been made for me already, in some respects.

As one door closes, so another opens.

How appropriate the cliché now sounded.

The mobile 'phone was soon to hand; the speed dial number made the connection as if it was no more than a local call.

"Hello?"

"Hello," Nicole continued in a softer conspiratorial tone, "it is I."

"Nikki! How'd it go?" Loualla paused. "It's early, I've just checked out your time!"

"Done and dusted, girl."

"What?"

"It's over, sorry…that's what I meant to say. Over and done with."

"Already?"

"Yes, already. There wasn't a meeting of artistic minds. I'm learning today all sorts of things. Maybe what I do, or still want to do is all a bit passé."

"Rubbish! Did you show them? Did they see what you can still do?" Loualla's voice sounded incredulous.

"No."

There was a moment's pause. "It's crazy! Why...you've only just got there! You've travelled for days...across the world...and for nothing!"

"I wouldn't say that, Lou...I came for other reasons, remember?"

"Yes...yes! But the ballet that's what matters at the minute."

"Some things are quickly decided, like the conflict between popular dance and classical ballet. I've learnt a lot on this *short* trip."

"I'll have to think on that one," Loualla replied. "You had your say at least?"

"Oh yes," she chuckled ruefully, "only they didn't quite agree with what I had to tell them."

"So?" Loualla sighed, "What now?"

"Well," Nicole replied hesitating, "I've got a few days free, I was wondering..."

"Of course! Don't give it a second thought! Book a flight and come back here...get on a plane and just come back here! I've not touched your room."

"Just in case?" Nicole said lightly.

"Not exactly...but things happened while you were here."

"Meaning?"

"Get on a plane!"

"Loualla..."

"Do as you're told, girl!" was the laughing reply. "Others will say the same, you can count on it."

"Don't know who you mean."

"Don't tease, not now." Loualla's tone hardened.

"No."

"John's a dear friend, and…he's a changed man."

"How…" Nicole couldn't begin to ask the question before Loualla spoke once more.

"I know, so does Andrew, because we've seen it in him. John's hardly stopped working…day and night it seems. He's doing it to the point of exhaustion. We called in to see him… the man's possessed with energy…determined to get close to finishing his new piece."

"But…but why?"

"To show it to you…you, Nikki! The work he's totally absorbed by! It's all because of you!"

"Why? He did that before! Why again now?" She was speaking like her friend in short, almost shouted out conversation.

Sylvie placed lunch before her and all Nicole could do was nod her thanks in acknowledgement.

"Don't you really know Nikki?" There was a moment's pause as she let her thoughts sink in. "You've got to him."

"How am I supposed to know that?"

"Jeez…" Loualla didn't correct her outburst. "Just come back here, girl. I'll ring John and tell him."

"No…no, you won't. I will. I'll do that, hear me?"

"Okay…see that you do."

"It's my life…"

"Yes, I know, sorry…we all need some help occasionally. You matter to me, both of you. That's all I meant by it, Nikki."

XV

"You're in luck. Two seats have come up on the afternoon flight, tomorrow."

"Good, perfect timing." It's something else I've learned over the years. Nicole scrabbled for her pen and notepad.

"Don't worry, I'll print out the details."

"Okay, thanks…at least it's not an early start."

"No…the flight's at fourteen twenty, or thereabouts. You may even get good weather, anything's better than that."

The agent pointed and Nicole turned. The sunshine had quickly faded and heavy rain now lashed the windows of the airline office, whipped along by a gusting wind.

"I may have to fly through that!"

"Oh," was the easy answer, "that's just a shower for these parts at this time of year."

"And more like a gale where I'm from."

"That's the wonder of travel…you may see the same things, only differently."

Oh well, the conversation passes the time. Nicole watched the girl as she stood casually waiting, one hand at the outlet, before a slender form issued from the ticket machine in virtual silence. Neatly pressed and folded the salient details were read out to her - the flight number, the departure time, the destination and the date of travel.

Nicole gathered it all up and pushed it down to the bottom of her handbag.

"Thank you."

"No problem. You've got a last night to see Auckland." The girl engaged in friendly small talk as Nicole made ready to leave. "You haven't stayed long…it's not a place you pass through…more like the end of the line."

"That's true, but I'm glad to have visited you."

"Well…enjoy the rest of your trip." The girl moved to other administrative chores.

"Thank you, I will."

I will, now that I can think of other things and salvage some private moments from this expensive little jaunt.

She stood by the window and watched the downpour create rivulets of water on the pavement outside. Those that braved the weather kept away from the pavement's edge as cars swooshed by seemingly indifferent to the spray their wheels threw up in their wake. A flimsy unflattering but entirely appropriate fold up travel mack was pulled from her bag together with a headscarf.

There's nothing else for it, Nicole told herself, I'll have to walk to the hotel, dodge in and out of the shops whenever I can until I get there.

"John" she gasped hardly reducing her pace as she grabbed at the mobile 'phone she had put in her jacket pocket; it had trilled against her. "How nice of you to call."

The words sounded much too grand.

"Are you okay?" he asked cheerfully.

"Yes…I'm breathless, that's all."

"It's that exciting is it, in Auckland?"

"Possibly." She loved his teasing sense of humour. "If I was to stay here for long I'd find out. Right now I'm trying to get back to the hotel through a storm." The rain showed no sign of abating and now she heard a loud rumble of thunder. "Did you hear that?"

"Just…you keep fading."

"I'll call you back…there's things to tell you. I'm not going to be long…the hotel's not far now. Okay?"

"Yeah."

He was gone.

Nicole stood by the hotel's entrance doors and remained perfectly still. The water dripped off her thin coat onto the polished terrazzo floor, her shoes and the sodden ends to her trousers; they were filthy. The unflattering rain hood was pulled free and she shook her head before fussing over her hair. Finally, she unbuttoned her coat.

"Made it," she said brightly under the watchful gaze of the doorman who stood close by with an umbrella, ready it seemed to go out and meet any new customers that might arrive by taxi. He merely responded with the hint of a smile and a nod of the head.

The duty receptionist told her no messages had been received.

"There's two people here to see you, though…they arrived just before you did."

"Really?" Nicole adjusted her jacket and blouse before turning to see whom the receptionist was pointing out. "Simon! Hello, Amber!"

"Hello, again," he smiled. Only a brief glance was exchanged with Amber. "We thought we'd come to see you once more…hoped you might be in, seein' how the weather's changed".

"Yes…"

"You've travelled a long way," he went on.

"Only, for us to part the way that we did," Amber said in a conciliatory tone. "I'm sorry for that now."

"I see," Nicole acknowledged what they had both told her with a slow nod of her head. "Shall we go for a drink in the bar? It seems like the best place to go…and, I need to dry out after a walk about in the rain."

"Right," Simon held out his arm to direct her, "it sure isn't walk-about weather."

"No." Nicole cast her things onto a chair in a cosy corner of the bar and looked at them both. "The least I can do is buy you a drink…white wine okay for you? It's what I'm going to have."

"Yeah…yes, please. It'll help put an end to the day." Amber spoke out her feelings.

"Has it been tough?" she was asked.

"Yes," Simon answered for her, "you could say that, Nicole…for all of us." They fell silent and the three of them waited until the wine was served. "To…to tomorrow,"

Simon raised his glass. "Will you stay and talk to us again, tomorrow?"

"Direct, and to the point," Nicole smiled but there was no ill intent.

"Yes."

"May I ask, 'why'?"

"Sure, we haven't heard it all from you Nicole…and, we've thought over what you had to say to us." Amber spoke out calmly. The bluster and aggressive certainty she had displayed earlier had gone.

"The others we saw seemed malleable…conformists to the brief we had set and thought, then, that we would stick to," Simon explained some more. "You had other ideas…"

So, they had come to realise that what she had so honestly expressed and argued for had touched an artistic nerve in them after all. Maybe they hadn't wished to be reminded of it quite so honestly and without deference to their positions or status.

"I was too bloody minded," Nicole confessed.

"Yeah, you were!" Simon had to laugh. "At least you made us think, again."

"I didn't say that much…"

"Or, nothing that we wanted to hear just then. But…after we had listened to all the candidates we agreed that we wanted to listen to your ideas some more." Amber spoke with practised ease now. "Can we meet, will you come over again tomorrow, as Simon's asked?"

"Us alone, again?"

Her guests looked at one another and came to a decision.

"Yes." It was Simon who spoke up for them.

"I…I fly out tomorrow afternoon." She had acted in haste and realised that all too clearly now but other impulses had also been at work within her.

"That's quick." Amber said it as if to confirm her own conclusions. She reached for the bottle and topped up Nicole's glass then her own.

"Yes…but I'm not going far."

"What time does that leave us? When's your flight?" Simon brought the discussion down to practical levels once more.

"Just the morning, say until eleven…no later. The flight's at two twenty…and I wish to be on it." Nicole spoke softly; her tone held more of a plea than an unshakeable intention.

"So, shall we say eight thirty until ten…ten-thirty?" Amber looked at her then at Simon. He simply shrugged his shoulders in assent.

"Fine…I'll show you some ideas."

"Show us?" Amber stared at her. "We talk…think over some ideas, like we usually do in these situations." She looked at Simon but he remained impassive.

"No, I thought I would demonstrate my ideas, rather than simply talk about them. I've got the music with me…on a CD."

"You came to us prepared to do all of that, Nicole?" Clearly, Amber had not been told of earlier conversations with Simon.

"Yes…if it's no trouble I merely need a rehearsal room and a player. We can talk there and I'll dance…I'm in shape."

"It'll be different!" Simon smiled on meeting Nicole's look upon him.

"Yes…it's why I came all this way to see you. Ideas also need an honesty of expression. I choose…no, I offer to show you. That way the talk, or expression, of ideas is confirmed by action. It is how I would want any relationship to be."

Nicole looked down at the tabletop, startled. Her mobile 'phone's screen flickered.

"You'd better take it?" Amber looked down in amusement at the contraption that played a well-known piece of music.

"Okay…please excuse me for a moment."

291

The number was only too recognisable.

"Hello...I'm sorry but I can't talk now...something unexpected happened when I returned to the hotel." She stood in a quiet section of the bar and spoke softly.

"Oh...right." Something in John's tone prompted her stinging response. He did seem to want things to go his own way.

"I'm trying to salvage something here!"

"And I'm interrupting that, Nicole...sorry. Does what's happened matter?"

"Yes! All of it matters! I simply need to bring some order into everything. Now please, let me get on? I'll call you."

"Okay."

It was his phlegmatic ways of reply that irritated her. Something else that I may have to get used to, she thought, if that's what I want.

"I hope it will be. Now, I've really got to go. I'll do as I've just said...I'll call you when there's more time to talk."

"I'll wait on it. Mind how you go."

"Yes...and John?"

Her intention to take the heat out their all too brief exchange was met by the hiss of the broken connection between them.

She quelled the frisson of irritation that passed through her once again. That man!. Easy...think easy.

"Thank you...thank you for waiting. It was someone asking me about my plans. I'll get back to them."

Nicole took up her glass of wine and slowed down her thoughts in time with each sip that she took; they were more the touch of lips to a communion bowl than large gulps. That John! He says so little yet demands a unique devotion to the moments when he calls.

"Where were we?"

"Sorting out a plan for the morning." Amber said it in a tone of voice as if to suggest it wasn't that difficult to recall.

"Okay," Simon chipped in before the two women could start any needless debate. "We're through with all that. We meet…at eight thirty. I'll arrange a rehearsal room…at that time it shouldn't be a problem. What else do you need, Nicole?"

Some peace of mind would be welcome.

"A cleared floor in the rehearsal room…six small and light chairs…I'll put them out…and a CD player." She thought on it. Yes that's all I need. "Oh! I almost forgot. I'd also like a small hand basket nothing heavy mind you. It's nothing more than a prop."

"Sure?"

"Yes, thank you. That'll do."

Simon smiled at her. "What's it all to be about?"

"You'll see. It's talk and action…only about five minutes of the action bit. I'll have to try and make it enough."

And make it convincing she could have added, but of her ability and devotion to her craft she had no doubts. She merely harboured a concern that the minds of the interviewers had truly been opened and that they would give her ideas the consideration that she felt they deserved. It's down to me again to prove who I am and what I can do, I can still do.

Simon and Amber took their leave. Try as she might, being at ease in Amber's company could well be the hardest part of any creative relationship that ensued between them. She remained only too aware of the difficulty in finding the balance between her instinctive allegiance to the heritage of dance and the risk attached to new choreography.

I'm not stuck in a rut. I can still create new work, so, while I'm able to do that the art of ballet and formal dance lives on in me.

"Hi, John?"

"Hello, how's it going?"

She couldn't feel annoyed with him or his way of speaking to her for long. His manner suggested that honest emotions were at work within him. If she dared to admit to it she could liken his frequent calls, obeying her wishes, as a profound interest in her and the display of due consideration for what she sought herself.

"Fine now. I was with people from the Dance Company that's why I couldn't speak to you. Now, I'm alone...in my room. I've got to prep for tomorrow's session. Then, I'm gone from here."

"Well...I seem to call at the wrong times...and wind you up, or so it seems. I'm not happy about it at all."

"You're sorry you mean?" she teased.

"Yeah, okay. I'm sorry about it."

"I am too. We just need time, the right time to talk."

He agreed. "So, what now? What's happening tomorrow that's got you wound up like a spring?"

"It's not quite how I feel, John," she said defensively.

"Put words to it then, Nikki. Do that for me?"

"I've got a second chance. I gave them my ego to think on for a while the first time we met. Afterwards, I went for a walk...it became lunch...I met a girl, a waitress who does ballet...modern dance more like. We had a chat and I came round to another way of thinking."

"You came round? Came round from what?"

"From thinking it was either to be done my way or not at all. I just spoke it all out too strongly. But...I was lucky or the people doin' the interview had no clear idea themselves just where they were going or wanted to do."

"So you're going to show them? Call it...a meeting of minds?"

"Or a compromise on my arrogance and creative conceit."

"Maybe. You don't have to give up on your own creative beliefs; you can always try to learn from others so it helps you grow some more. That's what I tried to do…when Carla was taken from me."

"It may help…to carry on with life?" she said hesitantly.

"Yeah, that too. It's not all about work though, that doesn't give you everything you need, does it? Not in my book, anyway."

"No…no John, it doesn't."

"Are you coming back this way?" he asked in a low voice. He wasn't going to beg for her to return but she noted the restraint in his voice.

"Don't you know that?"

"No," he said in surprise. "How am I supposed to know that? Are you?"

"Yes."

"That's good."

"Is that all? Is that all you've got to say?" she laughed.

"Yes…we've got to start somewhere."

There he goes, being obtuse again. "I simply thought you'd know, or have heard of it."

"No, I haven't. Anyway, who'd I hear it from except you?"

"Quite," she replied taken aback by the direct question, "yes, quite."

"LouLou cares about her friends and what happens to them. I know that much of her but she doesn't meddle…not directly so that you had to tell her to back off."

"People have to find their own way, for themselves. Is that it?"

"Yeah, that's just what I mean, Nikki."

"Lou told me you've found your way with your work…she told me that much."

"Yes, I'm putting in the hours just now. The girls are with me…they're wondering what's up. I'm almost living in the studio at present."

"What's up, John? Tell me?"

"I saw a picture of you."

"Do I have to guess the rest?"

"You know the rest."

"Not really…or, not yet."

"Then come back here, Nikki and really see me and my work. Will you do that for me? Do you understand what I'm really getting at…what I'm telling you?" His voice held no condescension only the admission of a discovery.

It took a moment for her to consider what John had truly spoken of and to recall words spoken years ago, absolutely years ago, at ballet school. She had been told that to overcome introspective individuality and for the soul not to become isolated required love. For her, love, art and creative endeavour brought the individual truly to life or restored a lost soul. Love and a human's creative fulfilment, by their own hand, offered renewed hope and purpose.

Fancy me being reminded of all that so many years later!

I've only just met the man but we seem as one already…in our thoughts.

"Yes, I'll do that for you, John."

"And yourself."

"Yes, and for myself. First, I need to get through tomorrow morning. Then, I fly back to Perth…I'll be there in the early evening, I suppose." She hadn't checked the time it would take and it didn't seem to matter much at that moment, the decision had been taken.

"Come over the day after. I'll have something special to show you that I couldn't have made unless I'd met you…what you inspired in me."

"Easy…easy, John."

"No, it hasn't been easy but it's the truth."

296

"John…" she sighed out his name. "You saw a few photographs, that's all."

"No, it was much more, you know that and…now I've gone and told you." Nicole heard him laugh softly. "Maybe, it's an admission you didn't expect to hear?"

"No." It was all that she could bring herself to say.

"Leave it for now. I won't bother you again with words…at least not until you're here. What we've spoken of? It's been on my mind over the past few hours…since you were last here, with me."

"John…John, I…I…" She stamped her foot, irritated to be so uncertain of her own reply.

"I needed to say it, Nikki. Now, I can get on with my work again. Take care; make it all work out, tomorrow…and, see you, soonest."

He was gone again, that quirky man.

'Goodbye' wasn't a word that John seemed to use very often, if at all. Somehow their conversations ran their course and simply closed, whether she was ready for them to do so or not. The sound of his voice remained with her and the image of his smiling face, the look of his laughing eyes, came easily to mind. Lou had even told her that she had noticed the change and thought she recognised the look of a man smitten; oh yes, she'd spoken of it.

"I don't fully understand the way it is with him now," Lou had said.

"Oh really?" she had laughed in her own gossipy way. "Do you expect me to believe you?"

"Yes! I've not seen him like this before…John's usually so considered, so careful or pre-meditated in all that he does…except for his art, of course. That's instinctive and, uninhibited"

The notepad and her CD player were pulled from her bag and she reviewed all that had been written in preparation for a display of dance. She thought her ideas would be deferred to another time or consigned to a portfolio of ideas that she kept at home, never to be seen.

"I'll call you...tell you the final arrangements, Lou. I've got to prepare...bye."

I've got to find my inspirational source for one last time or admit that someone very different has entered my life and that inspiring creative moments still await me. I'll also have to admit that I may have found a sought after and longed for distraction.

But, Im so very far from home.

<u>XVI</u>

The rain showers had passed; the sun lit up the countryside with its stark coastal fringes far below her. The Economy Class seat was reclined and she closed her eyes, overcome with tiredness and relief that the mornings' 'interview' or 'display' had not only been endured but also given pleasure.

I'm old...older, but still capable of sustaining my art.

I'm not the least bit nervous. The setting is perfect and the floor polished; the light through the high level windows is clear and bright. It's lifted my spirits. Even the sun has come out, all too briefly, to illuminate the proceedings. Maybe it's an augury of what is to follow, for me, for the Dance Company, my dear friends close by and for that man, John. Enough now, he's in my thoughts.

The members of the interview panel, my inquisitors, have settled down. There are more of them than I thought would be present so early in the morning. What of it? They are a momentary distraction. I'm in my own world now; when the curtain rises and the introductory bars give way to the passage that draws me in I am set free. I am now among the characters of the piece portraying a festive dance. Chairs that I have so carefully arranged in two lines on the dance floor represent my companions. I am the only living soul but I have to breathe life into all of them, inspire or provoke the imagination of those who watch every move and step that I make.

It is autumn, the dancers are also the reapers; the harvest's safely gathered in and now there is to be a celebration. You might think it was a religious, or votive, piece and liken the dance to a hymnal only it is being acted out.

You know? 'They plough the fields and scatter, the good seed on the ground'.

You may believe that to be the sentiment that I seek to portray, but you'd be wrong.

There's no religious intent behind my portrayal, whatsoever, merely an all too human response. It tells of pleasure and relaxation being sought after the hard work gathering in the harvest, the fruits of labour you might say. Yes, there is gratitude but the overriding feeling is one of relief that the toils of the season are at an end.

Money's to be earned and the coming winter months provided for.

All that! I've got to convey the range of feelings in every step, in every movement of my body and by the expression on my face and in my eyes.

If I can manage that, at my age and with my unwavering belief in myself, and all that I have been taught or discovered, then others more youthful, with vitality in spirit and form should be able to follow me.

I'll show you!

The heritage that is ballet can be given new life or reinterpreted by the fullest expression of all that moves people in the present day.

Ah! It's starting. The music's wonderful, simple and evocative. I've danced to it many times and never grow tired of its melodies and the harmony of sound and instrumental expression of sentiment. The piece is joyful and encourages the belief that thanks are indeed being offered for the harvest. It is music of the time, a distant time but it resonates with human sentiment even now.

You don't have to be told everything; you have simply to listen and watch how another is moved by sound and to form your own impression.

'Dancers and Reapers'; it's a piece of music by Sullivan. Who?

Yes they, those watching me, may well ask themselves that. Wait and see; watch me perform and act out a part that I know so well! When you've done that then you can decide if the music and the ideas I bring to life should remain hidden, nothing more than a piece of ballet's history, a fragment from earlier times; it's an informative heritage but it should be laid to rest.

Wait a minute! Everything that is ballet's heritage and informs me on how to dance and move, twist and spring, pirouette and step precisely…all of it, that history, has made me who I am.

You can't become a dancer of the present without paying homage to the past.

I told them that many times. Now, I'm going to show them.

Then, and only then, will I travel to confront another or an altered life.

John, can I dare to believe that your hand is held out to me? Dare I take hold of it and all that is promised if I do?

◈

They were polite and respectful, considerate too, making available a small changing room with its own shower. I could look my best for them and feel easier when the words of rejection came. You never quite get used to it, to being told that you're great or have good technique and enthusiasm but, sorry to say it, the magic ingredient that will forge an enduring creative bond between us is missing.

It was succinctly spoken out, in their opinion. To me, creative individuality for the good and benefit of others was not acknowledged or the possibilities understood. Oh well, there it is.

I'd been persuaded to go against my instinctive rejection of the first meeting between us. What a vain girl I am to have believed them last night, only Loualla wouldn't agree with me if I told her. So, I've learnt something else on this trip or I had confirmation in new surroundings of what others have often said of me.

A few meaningless pleasantries were exchanged; I say 'meaningless' as all I then wanted to do was get out of the place.

And I did, but not before I spoke to a few of the people who had taken the trouble to watch me through the glass; they were my mute audience and an appreciative one at that. They'd heard a rumour I might be coming to be the company's choreographer and were shocked to be told it wasn't going to happen. They were polite in their expressions of amazement that I wanted to 'show' the interview panel what I could do.

I told them of the words one of my teachers often used and that remains with me.

'Listen and always wonder; show and really teach; watch and really learn.'

Very dated…outdated even, but it's message has stood me in good stead, until now or so it seems.

So, what I have been through is an episode, brimful of interest and not short of intrigue. I was told, or did I misunderstand them totally, that I was the one they sought. But that woman, Amber, yes the one to proceed with cautiously, she had her own ideas and allies in the room.

They held sway, so I left them.

We all put on quite a performance. I stuck to the truth of my art as I saw it, and I will continue to hold on to it, fast. The pain of rejection will ease and I'm not going to face that alone, not this time.

XVII

The trip was over.

Auckland had been a place to visit more in hope than expectation. Deep down within her soul she had been prepared for the outcome. Now, another stage on her real life's journey could begin.

I'm still unsure how long I will remain here. I simply can't answer the immigration official, even if she is looking me squarely in the eyes, waiting. I'm living it, day-to-day. Would she really want to hear that? No, much too personal. So, what is it to be?

"It's a stopover…say a week, yes, seven days."

The smiling answer that she gave was meant to reassure the official and confirm her own decision.

Yes, put that in your records. I'll know long before then where I'm going and where my final destination is to be.

I've recalled all that I have lived through many times. The dream or sleepy stupor I was in for most of the flight allowed me that. Now, it's time to clear my head, to sweep away recurring thoughts of the past and to look to the future and only that.

She strode purposefully, found her luggage on the carousel and swept, almost imperiously, through Customs and out into the Arrivals Hall once more.

"This could become a habit!" she laughed as Loualla greeted her with a happy noisy laugh.

"And I wouldn't mind that one bit!" She was alone and so they could talk to each other without Andrew to consider. "Well?"

"I'll tell you all about it, sometime," Nicole said fondly in reply to the first of many questions that she knew would come her way and that would need an answer to satisfy a concerned, an almost devoted, curiosity.

"Okay, girl. When you're ready. I guess something needs to be attended to first."

Loualla didn't look at Nicole but kept her eyes on the road as they left the airport parking area, so conveniently placed directly in front of the terminal.

"Tomorrow's a special day."

"I know, Nikki. Others…another, might say each day has been special…ever since a miracle happened and creative genius was rediscovered."

"We'll see," Nicole answered.

"No, you'll see. Now…welcome back." Loualla moved her hand from the steering wheel and, without embarrassment, Nicole grasped it tightly for an instant.

"It's as though the years in between us seeing each other never happened. You're such a dear friend."

"Drop me here, by the gate, please Lou? I'll walk the rest."

"You sure? You'd better call him and tell John you're here. He'd expect the ute's noise to announce your arrival."

"Well, this will be different. Say…enter stage left, in silence…or to music molto but allegro, so to speak."

"I'll leave you to explain that to him," Loualla laughed brightly, watching as her friend made ready to leave. "So! See you…when I see you?"

"Yes, and thanks." What would I say, she wondered now? Of course, soft but with a happy lilt; yes, that's how I would explain the music, so appropriate to the circumstances of two people meeting each other again but with a palpable sense of pre-destination.

Nicole had spoken as she fumbled for the mobile 'phone before stepping from the car. With a quick happy wave Loualla left her.

"John? I'm…I'm here, by the gate. I'm going to walk up to the house."

"I know…I can see you."

Nicole scanned the trees and undergrowth that dotted the parkland, as they might call it at home; here it was the bush. It offered a wilder image to the mind's eye and made the house and its immediate surroundings seem like a little oasis within a wilderness.

"What? Where?…Where are you?"

"I'm walking through the scrub…the bush to us here. See me now?"

"Ah!" She saw him step onto the track and raise one arm in greeting before his pace quickened. "I'm not very observant," she said and frowned. Her gaze took in his weary but handsome features. Not every detail had been remembered after all and she looked closely for an instant at him.

"You look done in."

"And you're here." John took her arm, gently relieving her of the bag that she had clutched to her side. "You're here, that's all that matters to me now. The rest doesn't matter a bit…it'll pass." He now took her hand. "Come."

"Yes, show me what you've been up to."

She fell into step beside him and felt at ease, in spite of the hold that he kept on her. It was as if he had no doubts on how it would be between them and her instinct to be restrained in the circumstances now deserted her.

"What have you done? What have you done? What have you done?" She almost screamed out the words but they reduced in their dawning intensity. Her eyes had flitted first to the sculpture then at John. The work had been exposed by the drawing away of its shroud for her to gaze upon and as a blinding surprise.

"My very best…to express what I have been through, in those few life breaking moments in Bali, and what I finally woke up to when I saw you, for the first time."

"All that, from a few photographs?"

"No, I've just told you." He took in her shocked expression and stood by Nicole's side. "Pictures…then meeting you."

"John?" She looked at him and could not suppress the tremor in her voice. "John?"

"I want you to be near me…joined to me, in time. I've mourned and I've come to terms with my life then and how it was ended. Anger and hurt are put away but not forgotten…it can never be."

"Never forget!" She shook her head as if to reinforce the depth of feelings his words had provoked in her. "No, never do that."

"I'm through my quiet phase, isolated and being alone. I've come through and can now work again, thanks to you, to the few words we've spoken and how I feel when you're near me."

"You're so sure," she whispered as she felt him draw so close to her.

"Yes, it's how I see the future…the piece tells of it."

"It speaks of you, the man…"

"No…it's of us, man and woman, human kind in spite of all that we do to one another. You can't stand in its way…life continues. To be human lives on."

He had spoken with an impassive expression on his face but she knew it was an act, a deception; it was steely resolve pitted against the emotion that she knew would burst from him and that lay within her.

"What name have you given the work?"

"I'm reborn…"

"What is the name?" she interrupted.

John persisted and gripped her arm for an instant that silenced her. "I'm reborn. Yes, the work has a name…I came to a decision soon after I saw the pictures, heard you were coming here and when I met you…then, when I saw you again just now. Then, I was certain."

"The name! What's it called?" she cried out, now taking hold of his arms and shaking him with every breath that she took. "Tell me, John! Please…tell me?"

"Resurrection."

"Resurrection?" She spoke the word slowly, then wondrously. Her hands slumped to her sides and Nicole seemed to fall in upon herself until she finally put both hands to her face and uttered in a sobbing voice, "yes…yes, of course."

I'm with a kindred spirit. I can't explain it, any of it. I simply know it. She stood quietly and her silence provoked him to speak.

"It means so much…"

"Yes…yes it does, John. It means everything."

The hand that she now held out was taken and she felt drawn against him.

"Can you understand it, any of what I've been through?"

She nodded and turned to look at the piece of sublime craftsmanship upon which he had devoted all his time and energy since she had last seen him.

"Resurrection." She whispered it again in a voice that avowed its full meaning for her.

"Yes…the body at the spirit's feet is marble. I carved the face and the outline of the body's shell. It signifies 'earth to earth'…"

"Ashes to ashes…"

"Yes. The shaft of glass by the side of the spirit represents heavenly light…or symbolises the words, 'lighten our darkness'.

"And the steel?"

"It's iron resin…I have shaped it to make the human spirit, rising…of a life renewed or transported to another place. It's also meant to signify…'out of death, life'. And…it conveys man's strength and resolve. It should speak of a commitment to make out of the old something very new…and hopefully, better. The wonder for me, of steel, is that you can melt it and reform that liquid into a new shape to suit a purpose or to convey its' own message…it has been resurrected…*re-formed* into a new life."

Nicole looked at the wonderfully crafted risen spirit. It was again likened to a slender dancer, rising from the folds of carved marble and a darkened contrast to the shaft of light in the glass, captured by sunbeams that streamed in from the windows high above them.

"From death springs life…from bereavement or disappointment springs hope." She leant against him, her face to John's chest and gave way to gentle tears. "I understand… the work and everything else that has happened."

As Nicole looked up at him she knew.

"Too soon?" he smiled down at her.

She shook her head. "No…it's taken me a long, long time." She gave a broken laugh, softened by the emotion in her voice. "I didn't believe it could happen quite so quickly…or in such circumstances…or find expression in the way that you have told me."

"Or here?" John gave a teasing laugh but she silenced him with her first kiss to his lips.

"'Where' doesn't matter."

"The mystique of the moment?"

"Yes!" she cried out loudly, "yes!" He was the only one to hear or witness her concession to profound feelings of relief. Love and a devotion to art had found her.

"We're not alone anymore."

"No John, no." She met his kisses and clung to his neck in a crushing embrace of gratitude and profound joy. "Neither of us need be alone any more."

UNDER BLUE SKIES

A story of family, love and restoration in the aftermath of the Indian Ocean tsunami, Christmas 2004.

1

A bedside telephone rang in the quiet, lonely house.

"I'm calling to you! I had to tell you…I love you, Mama!"

"I love you too, Josie!" was a mother's sleepy reply. "Is this my Boxing Day present, Josie?"

"Yes! I also wanted to hear your voice!"

"That's nice."

"Jaaymieee!" Anya heard the plaintive call before Josie spoke with renewed urgency. "I had to call and speak to you…I had to!"

"What ever's the matter, darling?"

"Something's happened! The sea's gone out…it shouldn't have! I've got to go Mama and find Jamie. He's out there, swimming and fooling about…Jaaymieee!"

"What is happening, Josie?"

"I'm very frightened, Mama," the girl now confessed in a small childlike voice. "Jamie! Jaaaymiee!"

"Tell me, please! What's happening? Stay, stay there! Keep talking to me…tell me Josie, what's happening?"

"Oh no…oh no, Jaaaymieee!" A fearful distant shout was heard as the mobile phone was held away. "Mama! It's the prelude to a wave…I learnt about it…long ago…at school. It's…it's a tsunami! I can see it!" Josie was running and her voice came on gasps of terrified breath. "No one seems…to realise…the danger!…Jaaaymie!…Oh God! Jaaaymiee!."

"Josie…Josie!"

"I'm going Mama…I'm leaving you," she exclaimed on each anguished breath. "I may be leaving you Mama…I love you! I love you! Sorryeee…sorry."

"I love you!" Anya screamed out now in her own remote terror. "I love you! Josie?…Josie?"

She closed her eyes and imagined the scene, of people running and crying out for loved ones, their appraisal of what they confronted informed by all that could be seen and heard about them. A choice had to be made, in an instant, between flight and self-preservation or placing your self at risk in the caring for another's plight. Josie's cry of tremulous relief jolted her.

"Mama! I see him! Thank God! Jaaymieeeee! Thank God! Jaaymieee! Come here! Run...run...ruuun! Thank God! Be with me! Oh please, stay by me!"

"There's no time...there's nowhere else...up the tree...up you go!" Anya just made out a young man's commanding voice. "Quick! Breath in deep...hang on tight!"

"Yes...and you?"

"I'm close by, babe...I always will be."

And then, the transmitted sounds were the terrified despairing sobs of an only child and shrieks in the background accompanied by a frothing roar that increased its thunderous noise. And then...and then there was silence, an unfathomable empty space and the absence of a credible reality.

Anya's trembling hand clutched the 'phone to her ear, pressed it to make out any sound at all and to abate the realisation that intemperate nature, providence or, to some, a God's will had been exercised.

Josie, her lively tousle haired slip of a girl had gone.

The first shiver of comprehension took Anya stumbling into the darkened hallway as she too ran or scuttled like some frightened beast. She crashed into a chair but felt no pain, just the overwhelming urge to collide with any object that might restore all visceral sense of feeling, of a love unconfined and the joy from knowing that another made of her own flesh was again close by. She cried out for Josie in a voice to reassure and wrest from her the tremors of panic that she was irrevocably separated from her child, her only one, by nature's reaping circumstance in a sunny oriental haven.

Life wasn't meant to be like this.

A clever, pretty girl had been waved goodbye, no, it was seen as an 'au revoir' or 'we'll meet again' moment, a tearful parting of only a few days ago. Josie's trip was a gap year experience before she began a university degree. Jamie, the love of her life, was in attendance acting as a dutiful and devoted consort. They had become passionately inseparable.

And now, what now? Now, there was silence and incomprehension, the gnawing doubt that accompanied so many draining, immediate wishful prayers; they were recounted out of a conviction that her girl would survive nature's onslaught, somehow. Josie was too young to leave and her mother was so far away, safe and still of the world they had so joyfully shared.

'Anguish' was no longer a word that Anya recognised as belonging in her Book of Life, nor 'torment'. Until the moment that her bedside telephone rang those debilitating emotions belonged to the past, to her own and Josie's lives.

There was no where to go, no means to close her mind to invasive thoughts of Josie's terrified calls to Jamie nor the recollection of her girl's months of work to accumulate the funds that made her journey possible. Josie had craved greater independence and as a devoted, loving but possessive mother she had granted consent and helped out, telling her girl that Christmas on the beach in Thailand would be an exotic start to her Australian journey. They had waved to each other in farewell and controlled bravely, for the others' benefit, the heartache that their separation would cause, but Josie had her companion and the thrill of an adventure would overcome a moment's sadness.

"And me?" Anya asked of herself as the sting of tears gave way to weeping, her steadfastness in any circumstance finally broken. "What is to become of me now, without you, girl?"

She took a dressing gown, wrapped it tight against her shaking body and went to the kitchen telling herself all the while to summon up her courage, to pull herself together and believe that Josie, with her James, would survive. Josie would be cared for; that was the prevailing thought that she clung to…she had to do that, had to. The turmoil of emotions that she had experienced in the days leading up to Christmas had left her exhausted and it was with some relief that she had not endured a hectic Christmas Day.

A day spent with close friends, who lived across the common, had been the perfect antidote to intrusive thoughts of being on her own.

Any further thought of sleep, even at this hour of the morning, were dismissed. She filled a glass beaker with hot water and made a fruit tea, seeking to understand now the moments of a profound inner stillness that overcame her the previous evening, in spite of being in good company. Had they been a premonition of an awful event that she had just listened to?

What the hell can I do from here?

A voice inside her screamed out the question and the answer was quickly given; nothing, it's futile to think of it, I'm too far away. I've got to count on others, on Jamie if it's in the least possible, or whoever remains after the water withdraws.

I'm not going to lose her…I'm not…I'm not!

I'm so far away from you, but we're together in spirit! Even Jamie told you that, the sweet perceptive young man that he is. No wonder you love him.

She sipped at her tea without much interest but clutched the mug to her throat seeking some comforting warmth from its touch to her skin. I need that now, another's consoling caress.

"You're away…but you're not taken from me! Do you hear me, girl?" She screamed it out, quite indifferent to how irrational the words might sound after all that she had listened to only minutes ago.

"Are you hurt? Where are you now? What's happened in the few moments since I last heard your voice?"

Reality intruded upon her tumbling thoughts. The television, a programme like Sky News, anything on satellite

TV, might give another world perspective. That's it! She rushed into the sitting room and opened the cabinet that concealed the unseeing eye she thought the screen represented, when it was stilled. Now, it burst into colour, into sharp relief and she found the station.

They were preliminary reports, talk of devastation and the magnitude of the earth tremor, its epicentre and the effects such a seismic event would have on coastlines nearby. And yet, she reflected for an instant, the cause was an event so far away…so far away to the south and yet the waves, there had been several, affected the resort in Thailand where Josie had called from.

"You're born of me," Anya whispered, as she tried to imagine the devastation that lay in the wake of the turbulence so calmly and graphically displayed on the TV screen, in the comfort of her home.

"You're not to be taken from me, not there under those blue and cloudless skies! No! No! No!"

The screen became lifeless once again by her simple touch of a button.

No!

"You're there girl, but you are not of nature's harvest!"

There was nothing else to do but make a nuisance of herself. She was a mother and like all parents and relatives, friends and loved ones, she would make enquiries of her own government; they would know or find the ways and means to help. We're all of one world, isn't that the repetitious mantra spewed out until the words don't register or we begin to doubt the sincerity of the speaker?

Show me, prove to me how it is!

Before then, and in spite of the hour, a telephone call had to be made.

2

They had vowed to each other to keep in touch and exchange any snippets of news that the 'children' might send. Josie and James were old enough to make the word, 'child', redundant but the label never quite left their parent's fond recall.

Josie, or *'Josephine'* as Susan insisted on calling her, had charmed Edward and Susan Hounsome; it seemed she had done so from the moment that James had first brought her home. This concession to old ways had endeared Josie to them and confounded their opinion on accepted practice amongst the young, or teenagers. Parents belonged in another life, an existence somewhere beyond a carefully guarded border; oh, they were human but had ways alien to those of younger folk.

Parents were a source of funds, a safety net if ever it were needed. But, a hell of a lot had to happen to their 'independent' existence before a call was put through to them on the 'mobie' to confess that extreme circumstances required their help and intervention.

Anya pressed the speed dial number, stored in her own 'mobie', and waited.

Engaged.

Do they know already…at this time of the morning? She asked herself before pressing the keys once again.

Still engaged.

"Doh!"

The handset was tapped impatiently but it sprang into life without any further need for her to fret.

"Hello?"

"Anya?" began a cheery voice in spite of the hour. "It's Edward…I'm sorry about the time…I…"

"I know! I know why you've called, Edward!" she exclaimed.

"Do you?"

"Yes! Josie called me…not twenty minutes ago."

"And?" he said on hearing the news.

"And…she was with James."

"Thank God…that's a weight off our minds!" Anya heard the laughing sigh of relief. "We've seen the news. Someone in the village called…said we should switch on the tee vee. They said there'd been an earthquake…and…and…"

"Yes…yes! A tsunami!" Anya answered impatiently and mispronouncing the word. "Sorry…sorry, Edward! I know all about that!"

"Are…are they okay?" he asked softly, unsure if he wished to hear the reply.

"I don't know…I simply don't know! I thought it might be Josie on the 'phone again…we were cut off…I…I heard it happening." Her voice trembled but what she had to say failed to fully register with him.

"Where were they? Susie and I began to wonder…already, whether they would stick to their plan…and have Christmas on…"

"Yes! They were on the beach! Jamie only just managed to find her. I can't tell you any more other than they scrambled up a tree…it seemed the safest thing for them to do…I guess…I really don't KNOW!"

She yelled out her anguish.

"Oh God!" he gasped. "They were actually caught up in it?"

"Yes! That's why I called you…that's what I'm trying to tell you!"

She had no wish to relive the moment, not even to help them come to terms with all that may have befallen their boy.

"We had no idea…none. All we can do is hope and pray for them."

"More! We do more than that! We have to!" Anya replied loudly in her own efforts to bolster her failing resolve. "We

317

ring the Foreign Office...anyone in authority there who may be able to tell us what they know or have heard. That's what we do, Edward."

Anya now heard concerned questioning in the background and wondered if Susan would speak to her as she sought her own take on the situation that confronted them all.

"We'll come over to you," Edward said quickly.

"Yes, do that!" She was distracted for a moment then continued talking of her own concerns. "They were together... they had found each other."

"Thankfully."

"Yes, Jamie was caring for her." She conceded to the moment's anxiety. "I can't bear the silence...the helpless feeling...at the moment at least!"

"We'll soon be with you, Anya...then we can decide what to do, who to pester for news...the government for a start... anyone, just to get some news on what...what to expect."

"There won't be any. It's chaos out there, just think about it!" Anya said forlornly as a more rational 'take' on what had befallen her took hold but she was interrupted; the telephone had been taken from Edward's hand.

"We'll see," Susan told her firmly wishing to have her own say on events. "At least they're together...and we can be company for you. Is that okay or have you got other family with you?"

"No...I'm alone here. Josie is 'my family'!" Anya drew some comfort from the thought that James might be with her girl and clutched the 'phone tightly, in both hands, hoping to quell the return of her tears. "Come for breakfast," she went on. "I'm in no mood for sleep and Christmas is already over."

That didn't take them long, Anya smiled to herself. She had seen the approaching headlights and gone to the door to greet them. The Hounsome's BMW came to a stately halt on the gravel driveway to her cottage. The Downs were but a murky outline and the village in complete darkness. Her cottage lights were the only one's to illuminate the scene.

"Hello," Susan said in a reassuring voice as she stepped from the car; she still held out her hands to gain some emotional support from a woman she barely knew but who shared in a mother's anxiety for a child.

"Hi," Anya replied and making it sound as if she had a grip on her tumbling thoughts.

"We found you…we got here as soon as poss," Edward told her. "I was worried I'd get lost."

He took hold of Anya's hands and squeezed them as he gave an understanding smile. All she could recall of him was a gruff man, but that had all changed in the circumstances they now faced together.

"Come in…the coffee's almost brewed…or I can offer you tea, if that's what you'd rather have?"

The Hounsomes looked at one another.

"Coffee's fine," they said in unison.

The car's alarm beeped as Edward locked it before following the women into the house.

"Come in…go on through."

Candles flickered and the Christmas tree lights gave off their own homely glow in a sitting room festooned with cards; all served to add poignancy to the news that had brought them together so unexpectedly.

"Let me help you…through there…the kitchen?" Susan prompted.

"Yes…yes, do."

"And I'll look out for the latest news, on the TV."

Edward would leave the women to their own discussion, so it seemed to Anya. She welcomed the opportunity to have some female company, of one so directly involved in their frightening circumstances.

"It's far too early to know of anything," Susan volunteered kindly and in a reassuring voice as she watched Anya lay out some cups and saucers on a tray and in a ritual more suited to an afternoon tea party. She took the milk bottle that Anya offered absentmindedly and filled the small crystal glass jug that was already set out before putting it back in the 'fridge.

They heard an excited cry and met Andrew as he rushed into the hallway.

"It's ringing out! Jamie's mobile is ringing out! It's something we can hold on to while we wait! He won't answer!"

"Or he can't," Susan replied brusquely, but she drew closer to him and seemed to stand tall as if invigorated by the news of their boy.

"I'm not going to give up! I'll try every so often. I...I..." He stuttered now out of embarrassment the effects his words were having on Anya.

She looked back at him unblinking but her lips began to tremble.

"Where's your 'phone?" Andrew now asked her, kindly. "I'll also try to get through to Josie's." He looked at his wife once more then at Anya. "I'm sorry...I forgot what I was saying...or doing."

"Looking after your own," Anya answered directly as she met Andrew's look upon her.

"Yes."

"I mean nothing by it, Andrew." Anya came to his side. "I...I'd do the same. I'm sorry for what I said...how I said it."

She gave him her mobile 'phone having found Josie's number upon it.

"Try this...and jot the number down. I can't...I can't bring myself to hear it ring only for it not to be answered," she confessed in a soft but clear voice.

"We'll all go into the sitting room," Susan suggested in a bid to calm their frayed nerves, "maybe we should consider what to do?"

"It's too early to call the authorities…even our own," Anya told her.

"Yes, agreed," Andrew studied the screens of the mobile 'phones in turn. "The scale of the thing…the extent…it's not something many people will have experience of or know how to deal with."

"We're on our own…with our thoughts and memories."

"Shush…shush now…Anya?" Susan asked of her.

"There's hope." She met the Hounsome's looks upon her. "Isn't there? Andrew?"

"Yes…let's hold on to that. Now," he continued purposefully, "I'm going to try Jamie's 'phone again…then Josie's."

"How is it that Jamie's 'phone rings?" Anya asked.

"Silly as it may sound," Susan said giving a thin smile, "Andrew told him to wrap it in small plastic bags…like those sandwich ones you can get…two of them…and in a special way. You never know…"

"What may happen, or come at you?"

"Something like that."

"What a thought!" Anya laughed in nervy disbelief at what she had just been told. "Be prepared? Is that it?"

"Yes…it's a simple remedy, taking precautions, and the amazing thing is that the idea seems to have worked, even after all that we imagine may have happened to them in the last few hours."

"A signal has got through?"

"Yes…it's a miracle."

Susan was interrupted by Andrew's shout. "Jamie? It's you, Jamie!"

He rushed into the room his eyes wide with excitement and pointing with his free hand at the 'phone held close to his ear.

"Thank God! Thank God I can hear you! Mum's here! And…and Josie? Are you together? We're with Anya…with

321

Josie's mother!" He stopped gabbling, finally making allowance for the time delay in the speech transfer to such a distant and remote location. "Oh! Oh!"

"What? What?"

Susan restrained her. "Anya…"

"What's he saying…what have you been told?" Anya cried out.

Andrew turned to her, his lips pressed to quell an immediate reply and he closed his eyes for only an instant then stared at her.

"Jamie's in tears…Josie's not with him…she's not with him."

"Ooh…ooh!" Anya swayed before turning away from them. She slumped into a small armchair and lent forward, resting her head in clenched fists. "Oh! My poor, darling girl," she whispered. "My lovely girl…my poor girl."

"Let me speak to him," Susan said holding out her hand. She beckoned for the 'phone to be handed over after a quick glance to check that that Anya had not fainted from shock.

"Jamie?"

3

"Mum?"

"See that you keep safe," she ordered and, glancing only at Andrew, continued in a whisper. "No more heroics…the rescue teams must get to you soon."

"You're not here, Mum," was his blunt reply. "Just take a good look at any of the TV coverage there may be…you'll see what a shit hole it's become here! It's totally wrecked and the sun's still shining!" Jamie didn't wait for her. "Let me speak to Dad again."

"Hi."

"What's with her, Dad?"

"Worry."

"Okay," Jamie conceded. "So am I…and, I'm alone here… for the moment. I'm hoping and praying for Josie."

"We're doing that too."

"I got pulled off the tree we managed to climb. I couldn't stay with her, Dad…the waves were too strong! Then…I lost sight of her!"

"Okay, son, okay."

"But it's not 'okay'!" he cried out in a trembling voice as the events he had lived through were recounted. "I lost her! I swam with it, best ways I could…I yelled out for her! I hung onto any lumps of wood that came my way and there were plenty…and all the other crap! I just prayed I wouldn't be smashed to pieces somewhere…and lose my girl too."

"Not now, son, don't tell me now, please. Not now."

"When can I, then? I couldn't stay with her…to help Josie! I got yanked away and lost sight of my lovely girl! She was so brave…she waited for me…she knew what was going down before I did, but she stayed! And now…and now I've lost Josie…but I'm going to look for her. Tell Anya for me, will you?…Dad?"

"Yes, I could do…but, do you want to speak to her?"

"Speak to Anya? Is it wise?"

"Yes."

"D'you think it's right?"

"Yes…we're with her. Your mother thought it best we came over to her place, until we heard from you…from you both."

There was a moment's pause as the mobile was handed over.

"Hello? Mrs…?"

"Anya…I'm Anya. I heard all that you managed to say to Josie before…before it happened."

"I care for her, more than that…you know?"

"Yes, Jamie….I know. Hold onto it."

"Yeah," he said ruefully. "I…I couldn't stay with her…I'm sorry…so sorry. The wave, then the others…you know?" He finished in a whisper and it became so still she thought he had gone.

"Hello? Hello...Jamie?"

"I'm still here...sorry."

"Don't ever say that, 'sorry' for you being there. It really matters...to all of us, to me and to Josie, when you find her."

"I know."

"If you can, stay there...stay close to where you last saw her." Anya looked from Andrew to Susan but they gave no sign that they disagreed with what she had to say. "Please, be near to her, somehow."

"She's in my thoughts..."

"Yes..."

That's very deep and meaningful Anya felt like telling him but she kept from doing so. Instead, she drew some comfort from the genuine concern and devotion to Josie that he had expressed so simply.

"I'm coming out...I'm not staying here," she told him now. "I want to see it all for myself and to find her, to see her...Josie, one way or the other. I've got to do that, most of all for myself."

"I'll be here, Anya...count on it."

"Thank you."

"It's okay...I'll wait. I won't leave her. I'll tell my parents where I am...and, I'll meet you. Who knows? We may both meet up with you."

"Yes...yes. Let's hold onto that idea...let's hold on to it, real tight."

"Yeah."

"I'd better go now...leave you with your parents. Thank you for looking after her...thinking of Josie...before...before yourself." She had no doubts; it was an overwhelming impression that she had formed from the few words she had managed to hear spoken to her girl before the call faded away.

"We travelled out here together, so, it couldn't be any other way."

"No, Jamie. I realise that now…and I heard it too." Her daughter was a lucky girl…IS a lucky girl to have him as a consort, a partner and, she hoped an attentive lover. "She's a lucky girl."

"Yes, she IS!"

Jamie's voice sounded brighter but Anya could hear, in spite of his gallant efforts, the tremble of deep emotion in his voice.

"Bye, James…rest and look after yourself. Pray for her?"

"I do…believe me, I do."

"Thank you, and…if I may say it, that's a comfort to me. Bye, James."

She had no qualms at the expression of her feelings of relief at having heard him and knowing that he was there to find the jewel in her own life.

The 'phone was handed over and finally Anya's resolve broke. She burst into tears as she fled from the room not noticing Andrew's restraining hand to his wife's arm to keep her from following.

"Leave her. She has to come to terms with what may have happened. We can still be of help…by being here." Andrew now spoke to Jamie. "I've got to go, son. Take care of yourself…we're so glad to hear your voice."

"Okay…just tell Anya that I won't stop looking for her… for my Josie."

"I will."

"Give my love to Mum."

"Hang on…" It was all that Andrew could say before Susan took the 'phone from him.

"Take care, James," she said once more in an authoritative voice. "Keep safe…make sure that you do."

"I'll be fine again when Josie's by me…not before. Bye!"

Edward saw Susan's mouth set in a moment's annoyance.

"That was abrupt…Jamie's goodbye," she told him.

"He's been through hell…what do you expect?" Edward replied with little sympathy in his tone. "Leave him be…the girl, Josie…she means everything to him."

"I know that!"

"Then leave it, make some allowance, for a change."

"Not so loud!" Susan hissed.

"Okay."

"That's right…we're okay."

"You just remember, Susie…we're a complete set again. It's Anya we should help and feel sorry for…she may be quite alone now."

4

"I'm quite clear in my own mind what I've got to do."

Anya spoke to them as Edward and Susie came to her in the small kitchen that was kept in pristine order. "I'm not going to wait here, I'm going out there…as I told Jamie."

"Wait a few days…" Edward began.

"No!" Anya shook her head vigorously to dispel intrusive thoughts of what had befallen her and Josie, but it really wasn't so easy. "No…I can't sit here and just…wait.""

"Jamie's out there, he will let us have any news, somehow," she was told.

"I need to know of it, there…I need to see the place and find out for myself."

She had discovered a fragile source of renewed hope, in Jamie's voice, and would cling to the belief that his few words had instilled in her that Josie might yet be found, alive.

"It'll take a few days to arrange a flight…and a place to stay," she continued, preventing any interruption that Susan felt inclined to make in an attempt to dissuade her. "So…I've got to wait…I've no choice."

I'll go up to town, to the Foreign Office and be there… finding out what they know. I won't be the only one, so they'll have to put someone up to tell us…or answer any questions we have. She had thought it all out in an instant.

"It'll be chaos…" Susan spoke out.

"So why add to it, by being there, you mean?"

"That's not quite what I meant, Anya."

"Okay," Anya had already moved on to another pervasive thought; where was her girl? "You've just heard your reassurance, but I've got none. I'm not going to rely on Jamie for everything…he's torn up by what has happened to them and I'm not going to sit about and wait! I've got to dooo something!"

She expressed once again all of her motherly instincts, feelings that she had suppressed or not given voice to, as best she could, while her girl…her only child made preparations to leave. The void in her life that she felt opening up before her was not to be filled so easily by the comforting words of the young man Josie had fallen in love with. The pair of them had so little experience of real life, an adult life that she took for granted at only forty-two years of age.

"I want to go out there and find my girl," she said now. "I want to see Josie and hug her, be a help to her…and Jamie, nothing more. Then, I'll see them on their way again and I can come home." Her voice fell away as she conceded to her emotions and thought of the comfort to be found on seeing her girl once more. It will put my mind at ease and I'll feel more settled than I am now. She stared at Jamie's parents through tear filled eyes.

"I'm so far away from her!" Anya screamed out, overwhelmed at last.

It felt the most natural thing for her to do; without any restraint she noisily expressed the anguish that she felt was taking hold of every nerve and sinew. But, she felt quite alone with her turmoil as the distraught emotional outburst was met by an embarrassed and perplexed silence. She met through her tear-filled blinking eyes the looks of parents that had received a reassuring touch from the voice of their son so far away.

I'm alone with you girl, my spirit is with you and I'll soon know your comforting touch once more. Josie? I'm going to pray that it will be so. My hands are held out to you, so, wait for me.

5

Anya collapsed onto the bed, conceding to the exhaustion that the rendezvous with the Hounsomes had brought upon her. They had been restored by the sound of Jamie's voice, but she feared for all that the young man would have to endure on his own and as a consequence of a natural disaster on an unimaginable scale; they would have to rely upon him for any news of Josie.

"We're not going out there...only to add to their troubles," Susan had confirmed very quickly. "The locals have enough to contend with."

"Fine," was her own direct response to a stern voiced observation, then she added, "I'll let you know when I intend to travel." They had been guided to their car as she felt weariness overcome any further interest in talking through their different circumstances. "My mind's quite made up," she had finished, just for Susan's benefit. "It's no good trying to tell me otherwise."

The woman had shrugged her shoulders. "Here, I've written down Jamie's mobile number, just in case you don't have it."

"Thanks." She would store it away in her 'phone's memory.

"We'll keep in touch on anything that we hear, Anya... be assured of that." Edward had again shown a softer and considerate side to his nature that she had failed to notice before the evening's events unfolded.

"Thank you. I've got to salvage something from this, quite literally…and being there is my only hope."

Yes, that was just about all she could remember saying to them. Her eyes fluttered and she was overwhelmed by the need to sleep that an hour or so earlier she had believed to be quite beyond her.

"When is Papa Frank coming back?" Josie called out in her small high-pitched voice. "I want to swim…over there!"

Her little fingers pointed beyond the gentle swell that flopped lazily onto the glaring white sand that the hotel kept in a pristine raked over state of attentiveness. The speed boat that had taken Frank, and other scuba divers, out to the reef bobbed at anchor and was clearly in view.

"Soon…then we can all have some lunch. How's that?"

"Goody! We can see the men climb the coconut trees again, can't we?"

"Yes," she laughed and beckoned to her daughter. "Come, sit down here with me, just for a minute."

Josie was intrigued by the agility and easy grace of the men who soon returned and offered their harvest to the guests that were seated on the terrace or at the tables nearby, shaded by large colourful parasols. Once a choice had been made, the tops of the fruit were neatly sliced off with a machete that hung loosely at the men's waists as they set about their business.

"Look, Mama, I've found some more shells."

She said it with little interest in her voice and threw a collection onto the towels spread over the sand before flopping down to sit close, a small hand on her mother's thigh. They stared out to sea in silence hoping to catch a glimpse of Frank, or 'Papa Frank' as he had been nicknamed.

"Show them to Frank, he knows so much more about them…he may even bring you a special one…when he comes back." She kissed her girl's hair in an easy show of affection. *That man's my daughter's father and a companion, a lover but not a husband to me. It's an arrangement that suits me, perfectly.*

"Can you see him?"

"No darling...but he's safe, don't worry. He'll soon be back with us."

"For a while," the little girl's soft and reflective voice said all too clearly.

"Yes...it's a lovely time."

When I discovered that we had made you I said that I'd never lose you; your father had his life and I would have mine, with you my girl. Papa Frank cared and stayed with us whenever he could or when he was able to draw free from other arrangements and duties. He never forgot you or how important you were to him. He was often remote but your place in his life was assured; Papa Frank maintained a bond with his English girls, as he often called us, in the early years, until illness kept him away and finally took him out of our lives, forever.

Anya stirred in a restless sleep and dreamt.

Frank, you cared for her, for my Josie, and you cared for me. We found happiness and peace under blue skies; we sought our own way of loving and a joyous warming contentment from all that we could then share and chose to give to each other.

And now?

And now?

And what do I have now?

There's been no tempest, no raging wind or a turbulent sky above, 'just' a wave under a brilliant azure heaven...below a place of solitude. No! You're not there! You're not, Josie...you're not! Jamie's near to you, he cares for you and looks for you until I am by your side once more and I can feel your hand to my skin, as before, as it was just a few years ago. Renew the bond. Let me know that of you, my daughter, once more! Let me know your touch again! Presence offers its own consolation!

"Josie!" she screamed out.

The room was in darkness, still, and a heavy lonely quiet enveloped her. All she could recall was the hazy outline of a dream.

Frank had gone from them and her Josie was away…she was only away, away…not gone. No, her girl had not gone from her to be with their Frank, her Papa Frank. No, you will see her again, Anya; in your heart you know that your life will not be broken by the loss of the girl you made and brought into the world. Christmas is about new life and spiritual renewal. Your faith and inner resolve is being tested, cruelly, but this is but a page in your Book of Life; continue in the belief that torment will give way to joy once more.

<u>**6**</u>

You're on your own in this, Anya. She observed the rough rubble strewn and untidy embankment speed past the carriage window.

The train was busy with shoppers heading up to town and the end of year sales. The happy faces and the laughter contrasted with all that she imagined of those caught up in the aftermath of the wave, their homes and familiar surroundings shattered and unrecognisable. She shared in their anguish as the search for loved ones began. At least they had a tangible reality whereas she could only endure remote emotions or attempt to imagine all that arose within those dispossessed people.

Soon, she would be there amongst them.

Yes, I've got to be there, closer to her.

Everything could change; there was so much uncertainty; there are so few people to call on for information that we can rely on; getting in touch with authorities in the affected areas would take time, the place was in chaos; communications were badly disrupted; so, please, bear with us.

Yes, I've thought through all the answers that I might receive to questions I've got racing through my mind and that a civil servant has to deal with. The Foreign Office, the crowd that deal with the Commonwealth as well, they would know what to do. I'm not the only one who will be there...at least, I hope I'm not. I hope I'm not the only one banging on a door with a little sign that says, 'Closed, for Christmas.'

Yes, it's that time of year.

If no one's there they will have a call centre or an emergency room, somewhere, that I can ring...if I ever got through. I'll visit them all and anyone else I might be told of, to hear what they know or who can tell me what I should do.

And...I'm going out there; they won't dissuade me. The flight's booked...a 'special', what a relief to have that chore out of the way! I'm certain of my plan and I'm going! I've kept my inoculations up to date and the passport's only just been renewed...same time as...my Josie's!

Where are you, my darling girl? Where? Where? Where?

I can't stop thinking of you...and of all that we've shared in our life together.

It's not been so long!

I want to be there and see for myself what's being done and to help Jamie find you!

Oh, how I want to be reassured and to know you're still in my life!

I want to 'know', somehow, that everyone's being looked after as best as it's possible, that is, everyone who's exchanged a routine festivity in all too familiar surroundings, with their kith and kin at the hearthside, for another world's seasonal, seasonal...seasonal maelstrom!

Oh God! Where are you, Josie?

Tell me, somehow! Give me a sign!

"Tickets please?"

"Hm!"

She was jolted out of her destructive debilitating reverie and searched for the Travelcard in her coat pockets before looking at the conductor. A twist of glittery tinsel hung from his uniform jacket's buttonhole and a small sprig of holly had been casually thrust into the hatband.

"Thank you," she said on taking the ticket from him and in acknowledgement of his remark that they were on time. "It's a shame for you to be working on a Public holiday."

"Yeah," he shrugged. "Still, it's not the weather for doing anything else."

"Yes…I guess so." Their exchange was at an end.

She had passed the time of day, made out as if life was normal and that she was merely a day-tripper on her way to London. *A different person's inside me, living on her hopes and fears for a loved one.*

Help!

"I regret that I'm unable, at present, to offer you more news that may be of any comfort or assistance, but…the circumstances are unique and…we're trying to deploy more staff to the areas worst affected…"

The Foreign Office spokesman couldn't finish. His audience in the briefing room waved papers that set out much of the information that would be of use in their personal quest for relatives and friends who may have been caught up in the tsunami and its aftermath.

"They all are," someone called out, "they whole Indian Ocean coastline's affected somehow."

"Yes," the official began but was interrupted once more.

"Our relatives or our kids are out there…they're all affected!"

"I know ladies and gentlemen. My colleagues and I, here… we know of and understand your concern and the anguish no news may cause you…"

"I doubt it!"

"Is causing us...IS causing us!" another yelled out.

"If you had people there...on the spot, you'd be better briefed!"

Anya listened and studied the faces of those nearest to her or glanced at those who had spoken out so vehemently. Fatigue, the result of anguished hours spent trying to find out about their relatives, was clearly to be seen on their faces. Do I look like that? She couldn't help thinking on it.

"Ladies and gentlemen! My colleagues and I are here to offer whatever assistance we can in circumstances that are clearly beyond anything we or the affected region have experienced before on this scale. There are help-lines...the Metropolitan Police are manning a large call centre...we will do all we can to assist you, but..."

"We're on our own in this...and, so far away. Is that what you're telling us?"

"No! That is NOT what I or this department means!"

The FCO official toiled in the face of constant interruptions and he struggled to keep hold on a clear train of thought that would convey information of use and yet of limited comfort. He referred to a list that Anya took to contain all the items that he was ordered to disclose. So far little had been said to offer any reassurance. Instead, routine administrative information was spoken of and reference made to web sites that contained details of how relatives might be traced, all of it conveyed in cold bureaucratic tones. They were told of the steps to be followed that would assist relief agencies in the grisly and heart-breaking task of identifying loved ones...lost ones...the only ones who mattered and featured in a life that passed for family and community until the waves struck.

Why did I bother to do this?

Anya shut her eyes for an instant sitting very still and upright before she opened them once more. I'm just going to travel out there rather than rely upon others...save for young Jamie.

The information she had gathered would be of some use even if it dealt with the 'worst case scenario', an appropriate phrase for those who faced the prospect of irreparable loss and the identification of a loved ones' remains. She shuddered at the thought.

That's not for me. I'll take the information and some items of ID, say some of Josie's hair off a hairbrush or a sweater... but...but they won't be needed. She lives. My girl LIVES! I know it! Otherwise I would have felt a sign. It's like that with me and for all I know in all mothers. I'm never going to explain it and I certainly won't confess to it, the fact that as a woman you feel a bond, only too physical...it's like the umbilicus, it's never quite severed. The child born of you is with you forever, in body and soul, unless...unless you've felt a rending change.

I haven't felt that Josie's 'gone' from me, departed, not in that earthly fleshy, sensual and emotional sense. She's lost, not gone. There's a difference and I'm holding onto that thought and belief, real tight.

She made to leave but a plaintive whisper made her turn in the seat.

Z

"We'll find them, won't we Dad?"

Anya heard the softly spoken wish and she now looked at a young girl who clutched her father's hand and pressed it to her cheek. She appeared small against him and stared up into his strong face for a sign that her wish would be fulfilled.

The man pouted in a gesture of restrained reassurance in circumstances that Anya recognised only too clearly; his eyes betrayed a despairing recognition of their relative's fate. From that fleeting moment's glance she also took in a tall well-dressed man, bulky but of a fine physique, with hands that clasped his girl in what Anya took to be a consoling touch. It

335

contrasted with his evident strength and the soft-eyed look of tenderness he had given his daughter.

"We'll do everything possible, Kate darling…everything, but…" He merely glanced at Anya for an instant as he spoke.

"But…we should be ready?"

Anya gasped upon hearing the girl's confession of an inescapable truth that could confront them all. She turned away, averting any further eye contact with them. I can't speak out as they have of all that may await me, she thought. For that, if it's true, I need to be there, close to my girl. The officials now answered any questions that the huddle of inquisitors dared to call out to them but she felt no compulsion to be a part of that; instead she turned in her seat to check the best route to follow out of the crowded room. Kate's Dad had given a direct heart breaking reply, so honest and unsparing of his daughter's deeper feelings. How could he to one so young? Easy, perhaps, for one who knows his fate and that of others. I don't believe it's like that for me; she repeated it to herself as the scene before her was taken in once more, with unseeing eyes; instead she felt an almost serene spiritual bond to her daughter.

She half-turned in the chair and felt compelled to look up at them.

"Yes," the man said to Kate, "be prepared."

The girl met Anya's gaze upon her once more as her father spoke and the unrelenting stare that she now gave could not be held for long. Anya fidgeted, adjusting the silk scarf at her neck as she contemplated pulling it over her long auburn hair. It would keep it from being blown about and mussed in the breeze during her walk along The Embankment, the chosen route back to Waterloo Station, and the train home. Yes, home…that quiet and seemingly lonely silent house.

"Excuse me?"

Anya felt the gentle tap to her arm.

"I'm prepared too," she blurted out, unprompted, as if the revelation of a suppressed emotion or the acceptance of 'no news' from her girl or Jamie being expected was normal from such a remote place. "I continue to believe that many people have been spared…that they're safe."

"Yes…I hope so too," Kate replied in a precise even voice.

"Her name's Josie…Josephine. That's my daughter's name."

"Mine's Kathryn…my friends call me 'Kate'…Kate Richardson."

Her father remained silent as Kate looked at him, seeking acknowledgement that she could talk to a stranger. Her eyes darted back to Anya as he nodded his consent and she felt emboldened to talk to the smart but casually dressed woman who offered some recognisable reassurance on the predicament they both faced.

"I stayed with my Dad…my Mum…my sister and brother left us…before Christmas. We're separated."

"Kate," her father spoke out slowly; he had remained close enough to hear what she spoke of. A deep commanding voice restrained her from any further revelations of a family matter. Yet, his intervention had only a moment's effect.

"Yes…Dad?"

Anya suppressed a smile on hearing Kate's impudent questioning.

He would have none of it. The look he now gave his daughter showed all too clearly that no explanation would follow his request for her to exercise caution; he had ordered silence on a separation that even Christmas had brought no end to.

"Perhaps…it's time we went, Kate," he said slowly before looking away.

She gave no answer on seeing that an official, who happened to be free of the pressing throng that had engaged him, now held her father's attention.

"I'll show you where my mother...my sister and a brother are," Kate said now, resuming her confessions. "I looked it all up on the Internet this morning, before we came here."

"And I'll show you where my Josie is...with her boyfriend."

"You had Christmas alone?" Kate asked so directly that Anya couldn't help but laugh softly; she was not irritated in the least by the girl's manners. Her company was a small and distracting comfort, their conversation somewhat surreal; their loved ones were missing yet lives continued in their particular and fragmented ways.

"Yes...or rather, with friends."

"I stayed with my Dad," Kate repeated. "His name's Dennis."

"Yes...thank you." Anya looked over to where he stood but 'Dennis' was deep in conversation; he glanced only once in their direction to check that this daughter remained close-by.

"He and my Mum are divorced..." Kate gasped and held a hand to her mouth before looking round. "I shouldn't have told you that!"

"No...I'm sorry for you...for both of you."

Anya looked at her; she couldn't be more than twelve or thirteen but had spoken with calm assurance. She felt compelled to wonder whether the Richardson family's break up had imbued Kate with this attitude. Divorce or separation, the testing and straining of loyalties towards two parents whom you loved, affected children in a multitude of ways. She knew of this through her own painful experiences with Josie and the death of Frank, her daughter's father. The girl's emotions could so quickly become ragged and unpredictable from the recall of loved ones who had brought her joy only, in the blinking of an eye, to be confronted with the vaulting sense of loss.

"My Dad's a lovely man. I didn't want him to be alone, 'specially now, this first Christmas...with us all bust up."

"Kate…" Her name was spoken in the same manner that her father had done to restrain an impetuous talkative streak. Anya offered solace. "He's lucky to have you with him, to hug and to hold."

"Yes…I'm glad I stayed."

The questions and answers spoken out by others on trembling voices enveloped them as they stood close to a display stand with a large map tacked upon it. Anya turned to look at it more closely and pointed to the place where she knew Josie had flown to at the start of her adventure. She sensed that the young girl's eyes had never left her.

"Phuket, this is where Josie…my girl, this is where she flew to only a few days ago…where she is, with her boyfriend. He called…Jamie called me."

Speaking of them helped her to cope with her own gnawing disquiet.

"Are you frightened?" Kate interrupted, blurting out her question as she sought a kindred spirit in their plight or a mother's reassuring words.

Oh God! It is what Josie often asked me when she was so much younger. Anya felt a moment's loss of control before she gave a deep sigh. She met Kate's look upon her once more.

"Yes," she sniffed and pulled a hanky from her coat pocket, just in case she gave way to her emotions. "But…but, I hold onto the belief that Josie will come through. So, I'm going out there…to find her…to make sure that…that she's got through," she went on, haltingly, "and to help her boyfriend. I've heard his voice, but not my girl's."

"We had an e-mail…before it happened…from here." Kate stabbed a finger onto the map and Anya noticed that her little hand shook. "It's gone…there's not much left of it."

"Kate…" Anya now saw that she had pointed to the same spot where her own daughter had called from, a small tacky resort that she simply had to visit.

Kate suddenly turned away, looking for her father.

"I've got to go," she said quickly and in a tearful voice, overcome at last by the confessions they had made to each other and what possessed them. "Thank you for talking to me."

"It's the least I could do."

"Goodbye."

"Yes…goodbye." Anya held out a hand as she replied and Kate was inclined to take it, only for an instant. "Be strong, for your father…if you can. Keeping thinking of them, light candles to keep your thoughts of them alive. That's what I'm doing…all of the time I'm at home…lots of candles lit up for my girl…for Josie."

"Yes…but it's hard to keep believing."

"I know, Kate…I know," Anya replied in a gentle tone. "I know. It's something that few people can help you with. It has…it has to…"

"Come from inside me?"

"Yes." She gave Kate a nod in recognition of an astute observation made by one so young. "Who told you that?"

"My mother…when Granny died."

"Oh!"

"I'd better go."

She left to rejoin her father, a hand slipping easily and quite naturally, without any affectation, into his and in search of a familiar restorative touch. Kate turned only once to wave, as if to acknowledge the concern and comfort that the few words exchanged between them had bestowed upon her.

And, Anya thought, I'm making preparations to travel, in my heart and mind, for my own particular reunion.

Fastening the headscarf Anya strode down the steps and crossed the road to walk along The Embankment, stopping occasionally to look at the drift of The Thames in its own serenity. There was time enough before the train left Waterloo.

Only a brief glance had been exchanged with Dennis as she left the briefing room. He had said nothing; he simply pursed his lips in a mute sign of thanks for having spoken to Kate. She could not deny that she found him a handsome man, attractive for the resolve and attentive comfort she had seen in the look upon his daughter, from the touch of his large hand to her cheek and consoling clasp as she renewed her bond with him.

The young girl, prescient in her way of speaking of all that she would have to confront, had need of him now. Anya had taken in the tokens of love from a moment's glance and noted the absence of any reserve in the man. Her Frank, for that was how she regarded the one true love of her life, had been like that too. Frank had told her, and Josie, what counted most for him when they had been together and a public venue no hindrance to giving a small sign of love, care and attention. It had been the most natural thing to do, uninhibited and spontaneous.

But, Anya thought as she walked purposefully and memories of their meeting crowded in, Dennis' calming demeanour for his daughter's sake also betrayed, in the fleeting look they had exchanged, the acknowledgement that a life changing event had befallen him and, now, his only child.

"I hope, for that lovely girl's sake, that I'm wrong."

The carriage doors hissed shut behind her. The unremarkable train journey to Haslemere had passed; she could recall little of it. Instead, she felt overcome by exhaustion brought upon her by the myriad thoughts that could not be dispelled...of Josie, how she would be found, how Jamie withstood the uncertainty that also gripped her, so far away from them, and his own sense of loss.

8

Anya dispelled any further frivolous thoughts of driving home with the roof to her coupe' neatly stowed; a light rain fell as she walked to the car park where the Peugeot had been left earlier in a day that had dawned clear but cold. The mobile phone was taken from a jacket pocket and the coat slung onto the narrow seat behind her.

She drove over the quiet roads and felt no inclination to adhere, too closely, to the speed limits imposed. Instead, she opened the car's windows and breathed in the damp evening air with the scent of pine trees from the dense forest that lay on either side of the road and encircled the Sanatorium. She had just passed the junction that led to that Edwardian property which overlooked the landscape about the town beyond, Midhurst. Her home lay close-by that endearing place. The local radio station played a recognisable tune and she hummed along, absentmindedly, until flashing lights from a car travelling towards her raised a curse and made her look at the speedometer.

"Ay!" she exclaimed as the screen to the mobile twinkled in the darkness and her foot eased off the accelerator. "Hello?"

"Anya! It's Jamie! I've…I've found her!"

"And?"

The car scraped the bushes that lined the roadside and Anya cried out again. "Ay!"

"She's in hospital…poor thing! I searched all over the place…all day, then, I found her!"

The car had slithered to an abrupt halt against the Gorse bushes and their spiky foliage pressed against the passenger window. Anya felt herself shake, uncontrollably, and was lost for words; she breathed deeply through barely parted lips.

"Anya? Anya?"

"Yes," she whispered as tears of relief trickled down her cheeks. I must keep hold of myself, she thought, until I'm home again…with my anxiety. "Yes! I'm here."

"She's hurt, Anya...sorry...she's hurt."

"She lives..."

"Yes...just, Anya." The young man's voice faltered. "I had to ring and to tell you."

"Yes...thank you for your concern."

"Anya?" Jamie said at last to break the moment's silence that had fallen between them once more. It also seemed that he was dismayed at her calm replies to his news of Josie.

"I'm here...I'm in the car. I've been to London to find out about things. I met some people...people waiting and listening, just like I have been, for news of loved ones."

I've met a father and daughter who might not receive wonderful news like I have or hear the words to end so many fearful moments as I have endured, for far too long.

"Anya?"

"I'll soon be home, Jamie...where are you?"

"A hospital, near Phuket. Josie was brought there. It's relatively untouched...compared to where we were and where I nearly lost her."

"I'll call you...give her my love...tell her that and that I know."

"I...I can't...I can't, Anya."

"Jamie?" She had picked up on the change in his voice.

"Shock...her injuries...she barely knows the what...or where, of anything."

Anya now switched off the car's engine and put on the hazard warning lights. A few cars appeared and sped past; where she stood was not ideal but Anya felt overwhelmed by inertia, an unwillingness to do anything, as the news of Josie took hold.

"I've got to get home...somehow," she heard herself say.

"Mum and Dad don't know yet."

"Right," her reply was breathed out slowly.

"I'll be here, for however long it takes, Anya."

"And I'll call you soon, Jamie…maybe I can speak to Josie?"

"Okay…maybe. I'll see…I'll ask the nurse."

She again noted from his answer that Jamie was surprised at her low voiced reaction to the news.

"I'm very, very…happy!" Anya whispered now and in a trembling voice. "I'm so relieved that she is with you again, Jamie. You're so close…tell her, that I'm with her too…all of the time."

She ended the call then burst into tears, slumping over the steering wheel that she gripped fiercely and oblivious to everything except the intensity of thoughts that now possessed her. No one stopped; she was rocked gently in the air-stream of cars passing by as she thought of her Josie, so far away from her…

I'm a mother,
Thank God! Again!
I'm a mother!
Thank God!
I'm a living mother,
A loving, living mother, and
I'll know my world, again!
I'm a mother,
Who's mercifully been spared,
A mother's true loss and pain.
I'll always be a mother,
A mother who's known pain,
But, I'm a happy…happier, mother
And,
I'll hold my only girl,
My one and only girl,
I'll touch that warmth, again.

She felt light-headed, shivering with relief at the thought that in two days time she would be in Thailand, in Phuket, the distant location that had become the centre of her new world, for now. The journey would bring to her a blissful reunion with Josie; physical and emotional wounds could heal, for both of them.

There was no rush to get home, she told herself, as the car moved off; she would drive slowly, safely, as the few words exchanged with Jamie were recalled. Others too came to mind, of young Kate and her dad, Dennis. Would they, after all, have any news to complement her own that brought joy, and renewed hope, out of the despair that she had seen on their faces and that the silence of estranged but cherished ones still provoked?

"Hello…hello, Anya?" a sleepy voice spoke out.

"Hi…I've only just taken in the time, where you are! Sorry! I've woken you."

"I'm dossed down, in the passageway of the hospital, near to where Josie is. They let me stay close…for tonight, at least."

"For what's left of it."

He managed a rueful laugh on hearing her reply.

"Yes."

Her mood had lightened.

"I'm so glad you're there with her. Don't worry about the time…whether it's okay to call me…just do it! Tell me how she is. Our girl's going to be okay…I believe it's going to be so."

"They say it here, too."

"Good. Now, you rest up, Jamie. In two days I'm going to be there with you both…just two days. I wish it were sooner!"

"I'll let Josie know. They won't allow outside calls to the patients, at least for now. Where…where are you going to stay?"

"Nothing's settled, for certain. I'll text you…I should hear tomorrow."

"Today, you mean."

"Yes…don't remind me of the time difference." She laughed and felt at ease for the first time in two seemingly endless days.

"Please…call my folks. Tell them how it is…how I am now?"

"Of course. Are you okay, really?"

"Yes…it can only get better now."

"And Josie?" Anya would continue to talk on, after all.

"Bad cuts…I heard, all over her body but not on her face, thank God! Came from wood and glass debris…she's grazed and 'all shook up'. Josie was lucky…she's a very, very lucky girl. Someone fished her out of the water…quite literally…as she washed by on the wave."

"Who did? Have you met them?"

"No…they're locals…folks that had lost just about everything and everyone, so I heard. And yet…they still helped out. The folks here have been brilliant…ace."

"I'll have to make it up to them, somehow…and to you, Jamie."

"Not for me! I care for her…Josie means everything to me. I found her! I've got her back…that's what counts!"

Jamie made the words sound so heartfelt and simple that Anya fell silent and thought of them, together again.

"Take care, both of you," she said at last.

"Yeah, count on it," he laughed with evident relief. "Bye, Anya."

They rang off.

There had been no fuss, no feigned politeness or reticence in his dealings. Anya was struck by the maturity in the young man, the devotion to Josie that had at first been acknowledged as 'young love'; it had changed into an enduring and deep affection. She felt touched by the feeling of responsibility they held for one another because of the circumstances that they had so recently confronted, as a devoted couple, together.

She did as had been asked of her; she rang the Hounsomes and recounted all that Jamie had said at such a late time of day. Jamie had done as she had heard of it from him, he had told them, but only after his happy call to her. Anya now waited for the Abbots, her closest friends to answer the 'phone.

I'm so tired, so thirsty…so hungry. I'm so happy and relieved!

"Tom? It's Anya!" She spoke out her name on a tremble.

"Hello…what's the news, Anya?" He spoke warily and his voice deepened as if to prepare for the worst.

"The best, Tom!" she cried out. "The very best! She's been found…alive! My Josie's been found…alive!"

I must stop being so weepy, keep from giving in to these emotions so openly, she told herself. Oh! What the heck! They're my friends, Josie's Godparents…I can show them how I feel. She heard him call his wife.

"Mary?" It sounded as if the handset was held away while he called out her name. "I'm so glad, Anya…we've been so worried…for both of you."

"Oh…I'm okay…I am now."

"Sure?" he asked. "It's news…the best we could have," she heard him tell Mary.

"How wonderful, Anya!" Mary Abbott shrieked it out as she took the 'phone from her husband's hand. Anya was once again possessed by her tumbling emotions of relief and gratitude that her Josie had been spared. "We've suffered with you."

"I know…I know. Come over, Mary? Please, come over? I want to see you, both…to tell you what I know and of my plans."

"Plans?" Mary sounded surprised.

"Yes, plans…I'm going out there…the day after tomorrow."

"We'll be right over, Anya," her friend said purposefully. "I suppose you'd like me to look after the horses while you're gone?"

It was so like Mary, to be so practical, even at a time when she was deeply moved to hear the news. The offer to help had been made without a second's thought.

"Please…yes. I'm sorry to ask…at such short notice. I have to…I just have to see my girl again."

"Don't say anything else," Mary said softly. "Josie's special to us…it's no trouble at all. We'll bring something for you to take to her. Our Godchild lives." Mary's voice fell away to a whisper. "We're all blessed…again!"

"Oh, Mary! Come over…be quick!"

"Have you eaten anything, Anya?"

"No…not a thing…my mind's been on so much else."

"I thought so. I'll bring something over."

"Thank you," she said tearfully, "you're so good to me."

"We're together in this Anya."

"Yes," she replied on a whisper before giving a feeble wobbly laugh. "I'll get out the wine."

"Good idea. We've got something to give thanks for, and…Tom and I can watch you eat," Mary joked, in a lighter tone. "Okay?"

"Yes! Now…what's keeping you?"

Anya put down the 'phone, slumped into the hall chair and expelled a long sigh. In Tom and Mary she had the most wonderful and compassionate friends. They were childless and seemingly untouched, so they ensured to all about them, by this emotional void in their lives. She had been ignorant of their circumstances until Mary had embraced her and given thanks for being asked, chosen perhaps, to become a small but vital part in Josie's early life. A Godparent existed in so many guises but Mary and Tom, Mary especially, fulfilled this solemn assignment with devoted dignity.

Reflecting upon their recent conversation, she realised once again that Mary was a very close friend to Josie. Her duties had as their counterpoint a blessed and natural capacity to make Josie laugh and share thoughts with someone who had grown close but who was not of her own flesh and blood. They saw each other almost every day, mucked out the stables and the three of them often rode their horses on Heyshott Common thereby maintaining a deep yet easy bond. Ritual seemed to have no place in their dealings with one another.

2

Here I am, alone.

The journey to the airport had been timed perfectly. The suitcase handle was pulled free from its neat stowage point and she began her walk to the Thai Airlines check-in desk that she needed. Time would be spent in the departure area gathering her thoughts once more before the flight was called. Driving her to Heathrow was the least that Tom and Mary could do to be of help. Anya felt heartened by their company; her resolution not to concede to the emotions that attended their leave-taking had been broken. She'd hugged them both and they forgave her for the tears that she shed.

"Sorry! I'm such a mess…my nerves are all over the place! I don't know whether to laugh or cry! I'll soon be myself again."

"You're forgiven," Tom smiled as he hugged her in farewell. "You've been through hell."

"We all have," she smiled back, feebly and in recognition of their tumult.

"Call me, as soon as you can, please?" Mary had asked, her own womanly instincts aroused by the thought of a reunion with a precious only child. She had looked at Anya through tear-filled eyes before they had finally spluttered a farewell.

"Yes, it's the least I can do."

Tom smiled reassuringly. "Give Josie a hug, from me? Now, go on, don't worry about anything here, Mary and I will look after things…horses and all."

She had nodded her thanks.

"I'll think of you all, Anya. Give Josie my love and a big hug from me with best wishes for her trip…from now on. Tell Jamie too, please?"

"Bye…thank you, for everything."

She had stood back from the kerb before waving goodbye as they left her. Thank God! What a couple to have as my friends; how fortunate, blessed even, they are to have each other to talk to and share life's burdens…as best as they could.

Here I am, she thought, alone.

In a few hours I will be with my daughter and I can speak to her, at last.

Soon I will be complete again.

She regained her composure by checking her makeup and brushing out her tangle of hair, all the while giving thanks that she wouldn't have to endure the noise and bright lights of the Duty Free Area for too long. Waiting around was so wearisome when longing for a reunion possessed you. Her hand luggage contained only a small bag for toiletries and make up permitted in the cabin, a change of clothes, a blouse, in case it was needed, a book, and Mary's tiny secret gift, neatly wrapped, for Josie. Her small suitcase contained floaty tops and swirly skirts, sandals and more restrained evening wear and shoes, all of them suited to the warmth and humidity of her destination. She would have to judge the mood carefully, in her chosen hotel, before conceding to frivolity in what she chose to wear. Still, away from areas devastated by the waves everyone and everything looked to be taking up with their lives that had been momentarily interrupted.

You couldn't help but admire people's resilience and will to resume normal lives as soon as decently possible. She reasoned that respect for local people who had lost loved ones would be her guiding principle; no painful contrast would be made, consciously, with her mood of elation at seeing Josie and James.

Her moment's reflection was interrupted. She heard running footsteps before an exclamation.

"Anya! Hello, Anya!"

"Kate!" The name was spoken out in surprise.

"You remember!"

"Of course I do. We had a special chat, didn't we?" she answered before noticing Dennis' gaze upon them. "Hello."

Anya held out her hand to him. Did they have any news of their relatives she wondered?

"Hello," he said rather formally. "I'm sorry…I need to apologise, straight away, for not thanking you when we last met. You were kind enough to speak to Kate and so…be of great help, to me."

"When we last saw each other would be a better way of putting it."

I could have said that in a softer voice, she now thought, knowing that the circumstances at the time were emotionally charged and social niceties soon overlooked. At least he was making up for it.

Dennis still managed a wan smile, to acknowledge the truth in that very direct reply; he now met her gaze. No one spoke. They just stood in silence for a moment staring from one to the other until Kate tugged at her father's jacket sleeve to draw his attention only to her.

"We don't know anything, do we Dad?"

Anya watched him close his eyes and purse his lips for an instant. He now shook his head.

"No…no, we don't." He said it as much to state the obvious to his daughter, once more, as to inform the woman before him. "I gave you some money, Kate. Go and buy something to read…or to amuse yourself on the flight, if you want them… I'll be over there."

Dennis pointed to a cafeteria.

"Will you join me?" he now asked Anya. "There's enough to keep Kate occupied for a while here...isn't that so?" Kate met his look before nodding.

"Won't be long then...both of you!" She hurried away without a backward glance.

"Kate has her mother's direct way of telling you things... no finesse or consideration for the moment." Dennis began to walk and said to her, "I need a drink, a Brandy perhaps and a coffee..."

"I...I can be company for her, if it'll help you, on the journey?" Anya said it on impulse as she considered his very matter of fact statement.

"We'll see...thanks for offering. What will you have?" He had chosen the spot for them, his case was already 'parked' and now Dennis drew a chair away from the table for her and waited until Anya was seated.

"Thank you," she smiled at the small courtesy just offered to her. "I'll have the same as you...only, bring a few packets of brown sugar, please? I need the sweet and the sour."

"Done."

She couldn't keep herself from following every step that he took, his bearing...he must have been in the military she decided, how smart but casually dressed the man was and Dennis' control over what he said to his girl as she blurted out family news. Still, Kate may have taken to her and the understanding that had been shown at the only time they had met. It was as though they were embarking on a very particular and poignant journey, together.

Dennis noted the woman's flamboyance, the easy smile that never quite left her face and the bright eyes that simply stared straight back at him. If I didn't know better, he told himself, in the circumstances, I'd speak a lot more to Anya rather than be wrapped up in all that Kate and I have to face. The lady did offer to keep her occupied, not something that I'm an expert at but I'm learning…in the hardest way imaginable. The Service prepared me; well, you accepted what had befallen you and your men, got on with things and prepared to meet the new day. Such mental adroitness was all very well but when events involve your wife…ex-wife, and two of your own flesh and blood, you never could prepare for that…not quite.

"There you are, Anya…a filter coffee with a tot, a large one in my case."

She'd decided on it as he neared their table. "I have something to tell you."

"You've had news…good news?"

"Yes…how did you…?"

"I noticed it in your eyes…they weren't so haunted, like the last time I met you."

"Yes," she replied with some relief that no detailed admission seemed to be called for. "Yes…I see."

"You're travelling to make sure…to see what can be done to help her out?"

"Yes…that too."

She gave a sighing smile. He didn't say much, clearly, but Dennis said what he needed to; she'd learnt that of him already.

"So am I. I have papers and documents, some items of clothes…things…to help with ID. It'll serve in the process of confirmation…of what Kate blurts out so openly. They've not been heard of is what she means. Finding them?" He gave a shrug. "That's different and unanswerable, until I get there."

He drained the measure of brandy in a single swallow, quite unashamed. An index finger slid over the lip of the empty glass in slow mesmerising circles as the purpose of the trip took hold of his thoughts for an instant. Anya felt closed out.

"I can still help," she ventured in an attempt to break the silence between them.

"Don't push." Dennis pressed his lips together in annoyance. "I could have said that differently…I'm sorry."

"Accepted," she told him; he had meant to say it, that much she knew from the look Dennis had given her. "At the risk of annoying you, again...she's young, forgive Kate for having to grow up a little quicker just now."

"I do."

"I'm sorry for you both...very sorry."

"Thank you." Dennis swilled the dregs of his coffee around in his cup. "I may get another brandy...no particular reason."

"Let me?"

"No," he shook his head. "Thanks." His thoughts had moved on. "I'm tempted that's all...it won't make any difference. Kate and I will have to deal with whatever awaits us...in my case I don't need the help of the drink." He slid an index finger along his lips in a moment's reflection once more. Anya recognised it as a little habit. "She wanted to travel with me once I'd told her I'd decided to go. She said that there was nowhere else for her to be. Kate told me about the chat you had with her...later, when we were in the car going home."

Anya looked at him and suddenly remembered her tearful confession to the girl, a stranger, that she had resolved to travel and find Josie. A few hours had changed her world on that night, again; for them the agony of silence was being prolonged.

"She's very close to you...she needs to remain so. I offered to help, just now, if I could...and if I'm nearby, because I learnt so much of your daughter from the few moments we were together." Anya paused. I may as well tell him what I felt that night. "Kate sought a mother's touch and...I happened to be there."

Not quite true, Anya, she thought. Motherly instincts were provoked. You wanted to be there with Kate, to stay and talk, for as long as you could.

"Yes, I appreciate that." He said it on a sigh, then looked at her directly. "It was a conversation to suit the circumstances… maybe like ours is, now?"

Anya didn't avert her eyes. We meet again, Dennis…

I may have to help you both, Dennis, only I'm still not sure I'm ready for that, just as being engaged by Frank, so long ago, caught me unaware…so unprepared for all that followed. The only difference now is that I'm not alone, just as you're not 'alone' in one heart-breaking sense…you've got Kate to love and care for while you come to terms with your loss. We've both got to pick up the pieces in our own ways, put it all back together, somehow, and live on.

"If I can be of any help, with Kate…just ask me, Dennis? Josie's got her boyfriend to care for her…and I'm going there for reassurance…and to help restore her."

"How is she, Josie?" He'd side stepped giving any response to the offer of help.

"I can't speak to her…shock has made her close in. She's almost a mute, for now. What I hear…I hear second-hand, from Jamie…her boyfriend. He's devoted to her…and that's been of great help, to me."

"I see," he now replied in a voice that seemed certain of a cure. "Love and reassurance, care and attention…above all some patience. Together, they will help to mend her."

"I hope so, yes." She was pleased to receive his fleeting smile in return. "If I can be of help, ask…please, just ask me Dennis?"

He simply nodded his acknowledgement before standing up.

"Another brandy, after all. May I get you something, Anya?" He pronounced her name properly, with a harsh sounding beginning and end.

"No…thanks," she added as an afterthought.

Their dealings were hard work; she had to concede that it was so, but it would not quell her quiet mood of optimism.

The light jacket she had chosen to travel in was shrugged off and hung over the back of the chair beside her; loose-fitting tan trousers, matching pumps and a long-sleeved wispy flowing blouse made her feel at ease. She had to be certain, of course; the overwhelming need was to be physically reassured by the touch of Josie's skin and the sound of her bubbly chattering to confirm that she was complete once more.

And Dennis, what of the man she had looked at and now continued to follow by her attentive gaze upon him? He possessed a commanding physical presence but there was no pretence; he could not keep from her the turmoil that held him. When he smiled she sensed that a lively spirit dwelt within him but his eyes betrayed his true emotions; they were still and she imagined that intrusive thoughts or images of loved and lost ones had briefly taken hold.

At such moments she could not dispel the image she had of herself as a new person in his life, and Kate's, someone with a hazy outline, someone who was becoming part of their transition from one way of life to the next. They were bound by a common experience only for her the genesis was so very different. Kate and her father had to confront the awful physical truth, the magnitude of loss before they could start the process of gradual restoration.

She saw a proud man; Dennis stood tall with shoulders squared back and with his head held high. He grieved, she had seen it in his eyes but he also displayed resolution; not even his girl, young Kate, would see the proud man break down before her on having the awful news finally confirmed. That was for him to endure alone somewhere, his mind possessed by memories of all that had gone before, while his presence assuaged the grief that his only child would soon have to confront. A word, a look of love and above all a touch, many consoling strokes of the hand or embraces would be their salvation. And...

And…it was early, far too early to consider other pervading thoughts, too seriously.

And, I should know better.

And, I'm a woman, not a youngster or the young girl some said that Frank had met and wooed. He had been older but none of that had mattered. At the time I had found my life's one true man, true in the sense of being so perfectly companionable and loving. I wasn't looking for a soul mate and yet I still found him, or rather, he met and found me. Together, we made Josie and we lived our lives. Our union may have appeared dysfunctional, to some of a more conventional disposition, but we believed that we were the luckiest people alive.

In the years since his loss to me I haven't sought another's touch, but…circumstances change you or someone is met who opens your eyes once more and you see that maybe, just maybe, a different life beckons or an unseen hand is there, guiding you.

I was meant to meet and fall in love with Frank. It was unexpected, I was unprepared and, wonderfully, it 'just' happened. When I last saw her, I told Kate that I was travelling out to Thailand to find my girl; at the time I never expected that we should meet again. And…now I'm wondering why I'm so pleased that we have and I'm thinking…is our meeting here really such a coincidence?

Kate returned and stood by her father's side making Dennis look up and smile, only for an instant, before he put an arm about her waist. She leant against him in a casual familial pose.

"Found something?" he asked.

"No…there wasn't anything I fancied, or need."

"Do you need something to eat or drink?" Anya volunteered.

"Yes, I fancy a hot chocolate…and a biscuit, please. Is that okay?"

"Sure."

Anya left them.

"We've found a friend," Kate told her father as she flopped down in the seat beside him and looked over to Anya. Dennis followed her gaze and took in the understated elegance that he liked about the woman, Anya. He didn't even know her surname.

"Have we?"

"Yes…we share something."

"Oh?" Dennis had grown accustomed to his daughter's thoughtful observations but sought her explanation nonetheless.

"We've lost people. That's why we're going out there… together." Kate took hold of her father's arm and he felt her shaking.

"Darling…darling," he whispered as he bent his head to hers. "She…Anya, she's had some news."

"Of…of, Josie?" she faltered.

"Yes, she lives," he told her gently.

"Oh!" Kate looked straight-ahead before following Anya's progress towards them, clutching a tray. "Mum said I would learn from moments like this," she went on.

"When was that?" He said it quickly realising too late that it was with misplaced irritation in his voice.

"When Granny Graham died." Kate was crying now and made to leave the table. "Things change, so quickly," she sobbed. "I'm just not ready for any of it, when it happens…or when it's our turn to find out."

"Stay? Stay by me, please? Help me…to help you," he whispered. "Will you do that for me, please?"

"Oh Dad, yes."

She loosened a moment's embrace upon him and settled down to think over what had just been said, sweeping back her hair with nervous thrusts of her hands; under her father's watchful devoted gaze she pressed her lips shut; only, the anguished tremble upon them could not be controlled.

"Oh Dad!" she wailed.

"Should I leave you both, for a moment?" Anya asked gently as she took in the scene before her.

"No…no," Dennis beckoned for her to sit down before he embraced Kate's shoulders. "Stay, will you do that, please…for us both?"

Anya nodded and simply held out her hands across the space between them as she gave Kate a soft smile.

"If it helps," she said to her, overcome by a mother's impulse to offer comfort, but possessed by the anxiety that she might be too forward in showing such concern for the girl. The tightening hold on her slender hands gave some reassurance that it was not so.

Anya felt the young girl shake as, with her head bent down and hair all a tumble once more, Kate wept, uncontrollably.

"We're together," she said at last, tearfully, and looking only at Anya. She clutched the hands of a woman who had entered their lives, her life, when she had least expected it.

"Yes…yes, I think we are," Anya replied taking in all that she believed this young, precocious and intuitive girl had said. She held Kate's gaze before she felt drawn to meet Dennis' own look upon her.

My life, our lives, she thought…everything's being altered. I can't do anything about it, or so it seems to me. The effect of all that has befallen us is too strong to resist. I'll simply have to live for each of the next few days and nights as best I can. There will be Josie to tend to and now an enchanting and captivating young girl. I've got to discover my place in her life as she comes to terms with all that awaits her.

And, if that wasn't enough, I've got my attraction to a strong man, a handsome man, but a broken man to contend with.

10

"There aren't many left to call," Anya observed with some relief. She couldn't disguise the impatience to start their journey.

They sat close to the departure gate waiting for their row numbers to be announced. The Thai Airways flight would depart on time, the announcements told them, with a stop over in Dubai; otherwise it was routed direct to Phuket where its airport had been spared the worst of the devastation from waves that had smashed into resorts further to the south.

Anya tapped her feet and fidgeted. I want to leave the uncertainty behind and rediscover companionable times even if I'm going to be in strange and trashed surroundings. At least, I'll be reunited with my own flesh and blood. Josie will be there!

Kate had used the very descriptive word, 'trashed', often enough to convey her innermost thoughts and fears of what awaited them upon arrival. She had not been stilled, or restrained, by her father as she spoke of the graphic Internet images that conveyed the scenes of devastation, all of them in glorious colour and with a blue sky to emphasise the debilitating sense of unreality. In her case, the pictures had done their work of informing, provoking the imagination and frightening the observer.

The poor girl; she was travelling along a life's path that many would have chosen not to step out on, but, Anya had followed Dennis' example, offering soothing and comforting words at appropriate moments and became reconciled to the thought that he alone would not be his daughter's comforter.

I'm not going to allow them to distract me completely, Anya affirmed to herself. I'm possessed by other emotions, those of thankfulness and gratitude that Josie has survived. She anticipated a tearful reunion and, no doubt, a mother's clucking concern for her offspring. A scene was easily played out in her mind but she realised that when the vital moment came she would once more become a model of self-restraint. People, folks you didn't know, strangers, would be all about you, so you couldn't simply let go, yes, really let go and holler out your own thanks for being spared a mother's, father's, husband's, wife's or a precious child's loss.

That's how I have usually behaved or kept hold of my feelings, she thought. Will I be so restrained in a few hours from now? Maybe not…so, what then?

She sighed audibly. Later, all of that is for later…let's get going!

Who am I kidding? The emotions are welling up inside me, right here!

"Hi."

She felt Kate's hand grip her arm.

"Hi," she replied and met the unflinching perceptive gaze upon her before she looked towards the departure gate. Travellers, maybe people just like her and Dennis, were patiently handing in boarding passes and passports for a final check.

"Not long now," Dennis muttered.

"No."

"You're nowhere near us," Kate broke in as she studied Anya's ticket.

"Maybe not…but it's not such a big plane. I'll find you," Anya smiled softly. "Maybe you'll come and find me? Will you do that…if it's okay with your Dad?" She looked from one to the other.

"Yes," they answered almost in unison and Kate giggled.

"Good." Anya suppressed a smile. Another girl still shone through in spite of everything that had befallen her and Dennis.

"We may be able to swap seats…if we ever get on that thing!" Dennis finally expressed his own impatience at the time it was all taking and clutched a bag under one arm tighter.

"When needed," Anya replied curtly. Dennis understood the coded message quickly enough.

"Thanks…it's all I seem to be saying to you." He saw her gaze upon the scuffed brown leather travel case. It provoked a confession. "I've got papers…and certain items, things from my wife's house that may help me with anything they…the authorities out there…have to ask of me. Apart from meeting you…it's the only other thing that I remembered from the briefing at the FCO…what I needed to bring…for making ID's."

Anya touched his arm, relieved that for an instant Kate was out of their hearing.

"I want to help, I've told you…in any way that I can."

"And yet…we hardly know anything about each other."

Anya only shrugged, as if to say, 'that's how it goes'.

"At last," she said relived that they were called.

He looked back only once at her before walking past the departure desk, draping an arm about his daughter's shoulders as their footsteps echoed all about them in the narrow walkway down to the aircraft's forward entry door.

"Now?"

Anya gasped. Her mobile 'phone trilled intrusively as she fumbled in her bag for it.

"Sorry," she mumbled and looked at the flight attendant for only a moment.

"You'll have to switch it off, before you board the aircraft," she was told.

"Yes, I will."

Anya stepped to one side and studied the screen. She had received a text message.

"Oh! How I want to c u! I'm so pleased that you're coming here! C u soon Mama. Love you! I can tell you again, soon! My voice's is coming back. I had 2 let u know."

She had signed off as 'Josie girl'. Anya sighed, hoping that she would not give way and become tearful.

"Oh, darling Josie girl."

The words, 'Josie girl', had usually preceded a rebuke when her daughter had been so much younger. She was surprised at how they had seemed to fall into disuse without it being noticed or remarked upon, until now.

Trembling fingers pressed the keys as she composed a brief reply.

"C u soon darling, Josie girl…v soon. I'm not alone anymore. Mama xxx."

Anya knew exactly what the message meant. She had put into words an emotion that was taking hold, inexorably.

The 'phone was switched off. Fortunately, she had the presence of mind, long ago, to buy the little contraption that worked it's own particular magic, wherever she might find herself in the world. It had restored her bond, a life's line to her Josie girl.

The aircraft rose and fell in a drifting majesty high above the thin cloud layer that shrouded from view the earth's surface far below. Anya read her book of short stories in relative calm; she had made her choice on impulse deciding, as she packed her remaining things, that she had no inclination or patience for an intense wordy piece to pass away the time.

It's just as well, she thought. I'm not going to settle into anything with all the turbulence we're encountering en route to our destination. I don't need these bumpy, uneasy and queasy moments, even if Dennis makes light of them. 'Angel's flatulence' he had observed at one point, much to Kate's amusement, as the fasten seat belts signs had come on again. During one of her exploratory sorties around the cabin Kate had found three seats that would do as a venue for them to have a meal together, the stewardesses obliging and making no comment when, later, they returned to their allotted places.

They weren't far from each other and in moments of boredom, or intrigued to know what she might be doing,

Anya would catch Kate's eyes upon her as she looked around the back of her aisle seat.

'Trying to read' she would mouth, smiling, and pointing to her book only for Kate to turn away, discouraged from doing the same or listening to any of the in-flight entertainment that kept her father in an apparent state of torpor. It seemed to her more likely that Dennis sought a distraction from all that awaited him in a few hours.

Anya shut the book, made certain the page was clearly marked, and placed it in the seat pocket close up to her knees. A touch of the button on the armrest reclined her seat for a few degrees and she dozed.

Dubai's been left behind; we now skirt the trouble spots and then head south east across the oceans, their surfaces untroubled by any cataclysmic surge. I'm on my way to renewal; others, that I'm being drawn close to, will confront the further desecration of normality. Dennis and his girl have lost a settled family life but now...?

"Anya?" a soft voice asked. She felt warmth to her cheek and turned her face to the source before opening her eyes. "Sorry..." Kate whispered without moving away. She leant on the armrest.

"It's okay," Anya replied and raised a hand to touch the girl's tear streaked face. "Want to sit close...in our special seats?"

Kate nodded. "Mind?"

"No...no." Anya closed her eyes for an instant.

I was thinking of us all, so, no, I don't mind.

She left her place and followed Kate.

The girl simply raised one of the arm rests making room for Anya to sit down close up to her.

"Help me...to sleep?"

"Yes...I know how to." Anya broke the cellophane wrapper that contained the thin veil of a blanket that had lain on the seats. She draped it over Kate's shoulders and then embraced her. "Closer…someone's by you…I'm by you…I'll help you… rest now."

Kate nodded before nestling against Anya. She tucked her legs up on the seats beside them. Stilled, they both fell asleep.

11

"You have my hotel number don't you?" There seemed no easy way to being reassured.

"Yes, Anya," Dennis answered. "You've already asked me…earlier. I've also got your mobile number…"

"Oh," she feigned forgetfulness, "yes, of course."

She noticed how he held Kate's hand, tight. The poor thing, she looked so pale and fearful and stood close to her father, staring, with a blank expression on her face as the tumult, a chattering language and the strangeness of their surroundings pressed in on them.

They had arrived and the purpose of their visit held them in thrall.

"Call me…please?" She now looked at Kate, once more. "You too?"

"Thank you…for just being with me," she said somewhat formally and without giving Anya the reply she had hoped to hear.

"Yes," Dennis nodded in agreement. "It's been of enormous help and comfort to Kate. I'm grateful for your friendship and company."

"But…but," Anya stammered as she failed to control the surprise in her voice, "it doesn't end…here, does it?"

"No…but our relationship…and our dealings will change."

"Oh?"

You've been working this out, Dennis, while I tended your daughter, Anya thought. Or, it's that military training of yours, that part of you that I know nothing about…I still know so little of you…maybe that's made you distant. You're here now. Face the reality, deal with it, then mend yourself. Is that the side I now see of you, Dennis?

"Yes," he said in a voice that told Anya some explanation would follow. "Our circumstances are different, Anya. We have our own situations to deal with. Mine…ours," he continued while he looked at Kate, "ours…ours is different."

"And I offered to help…I know only too well how…"

She was irritated but restrained herself from further comment as she thought through, in an instant, whether it was prudent to say anymore. I've got to get to my hotel and meet Josie…that's why I'm here, only I care for him and Kate, about what they have to confront and deal with. They will need another hand to hold…someone else to talk to…and draw comfort from a few words of understanding that may be spoken.

"Don't push," he told her now. It was direct but he spoke without malice or in rebuke.

"I gave you my answer to that in London," she reminded him.

"Space…and some time…that's all I ask of you."

"You have it…I never meant my concern to seem like… like…I was interfering."

"I'll call you," Dennis met Anya's unflinching stare. "I'm sorry to put it like this…but, I need to get through the next few hours, day or so, in my own way. Kate will be looked after."

"I know, Dennis. I've seen that of you."

People swirled and jostled about them in the noisy baggage hall but they seemed oblivious to these distractions as they conducted their low voiced conversation, with Kate a silent onlooker.

"Okay," he acknowledged with some resignation in his tone. "We need to get through the next few hours…or days as best we can. I wish you the happiest of reunions with Josie…

that you find she's not hurt, too bad." He touched her arm for an instant. "Seeing you will be the best present of all…"

Anya nodded, quite unable to think of anything appropriate to say in reply to his expression of a heartfelt understanding of what the reunion would hold for them both. He also saw the need to recognise the void between her joy and their sorrow.

"I'm nearby, Dennis…that's all I've tried to say to you… someone else to talk to…be with." She said the last on a whisper. It seemed so forward, so direct, expressing her feelings like this.

He's said the kindest words and yet Dennis leaves me to wonder how I can correct the mistaken impression he's formed that I'm offering to take responsibility for Kate. I've stayed silent on how she is to be cared for while he's engaged in the grim task of calling on the authorities and, for all we know, put himself through the ordeal of identifying the remains of his and Kate's loved ones, if they've been found.

I sought and offered company, and a woman's…a mother's help for a young girl.

I'll do whatever is asked of me, to help them, while I restore my Josie. I thought I'd shown him that I could help… that I wanted to help?

"Anya?"

"Yes?" She answered in a distracted tone as she continued to think of Josie, who would soon to be in her arms, and the contrasting intrusive imagery of what Dennis would have to confront and relay in carefully chosen words to Kate.

I can't help it, she told herself. I'm drawn to them, both of them…in spite of everything else I have to face right now. I've got hope, certainty…

Dennis stood before her and held out his hands. "I will call you, we both will…I promise…Anya?"

"Yes?" She allowed herself the briefest of touches as he kissed her hands.

"I need to do this…Kate and I need to deal with family, you understand?"

"Yes…yes, I do."

Dennis turned to his daughter.

"Thank you, Anya." Kate spoke to her now. "I hope I will get the chance to meet Josie, somehow? You've told me so much about her."

"Yes. Soon, I hope…at the hotel." Anya shrugged. "Sorry… there I go making plans again."

The siren on the luggage carousel wailed silencing them for an instant; the belt began its jerky journey and soon bags tumbled onto it encouraging passengers to draw near.

"We'll get through, one day at a time…that's all we can manage right now," Dennis told her directly but with concerned honesty for the effect the words might have. She saw the flicker of his eyes upon her as he gauged her response.

"And, I'm living for today…soon, I'll see Josie again," she felt obliged to confess and blinking back tears. "Oh dear, I don't need this right now."

She felt Kate's tug on her hand; they each took her attention in turn; Anya bent to receive her kiss.

"Thank you for being a friend…"

"Oh, Kate!"

"I need to be with Dad." Kate told her as she maintained her grip. "Thank you for helping me out, for keeping me company."

"I know…and I was glad to have your company, Kate," she replied forcing a weak smile to her lips. The girl before her was so articulate and she had drawn some comfort from her company too. "At least we know a lot more of the world, don't we?"

"Yes," Kate smiled on being reminded of the quiz they had made up.

The maps found at the back of the 'in flight' magazine had provided amusement and helped to forge a bond. Even the fashion pages had served to prompt questions, 'where's this made?' or 'where do the fashion houses find the materials to make these?'

"Dad told me, he's been everywhere," Kate had responded to Anya's congratulations on her knowing many of the answers. "He reads…a lot!"

"Well, clever you…for remembering it all. That's what I think."

Yes, they had found a distraction and passed away the time.

"Bye…Anya."

Reality intruded with Kate's few words.

"No…see you. I'll be thinking of you, Kate…both of you."

Anya noticed her one piece of luggage making its way towards her on the carousel as they parted but not before a final look had been exchanged between them all. Then, they were lost to her view.

"See you soon," she whispered. Another boundary mark in their relationship had been passed…

With Josie I had to face the overwhelming loss of our Frank, Papa Frank, and I the heartbreak of being alone once more, with no special man in my life. Soon, what joy! I will see my Josie and her James but I don't want to lose contact with Kate or her Dad, that lovely man, Dennis. They've become a part of my life too, so quickly.

Our worlds have touched…and yet…and yet we've been preoccupied with our own hopes and fears. We've controlled our emotions, some of the time at least. Even the landing, that clunking rattling bounce we felt, seemed to be in shocked harmony with our thoughts of the days ahead.

What a mess I'm in! My nerves and emotions are all a jangle.

Josie, I need to see you and know your touch. Dare I to admit…that your Mama can only manage so much?

369

12

There's so little time to gather my thoughts but I have to, my daughter awaits me and I have to be strong for us both... I have to be.

The little suitcase moved silently over the polished floor as she made her way to the exit and the Arrivals Hall beyond. Avoid the tuk-tuks had been the advice offered, they charged too much. Walk a short distance, it'll be worth it, and the yellow cabs would be found.

Switching on her mobile 'phone she put it in her jacket pocket, absentmindedly, thinking that any messages could be looked at in a moment or two. There was too much to take in, the noise and bustle, the foreign voices so discordant with the sharp nasal expression of local people. Life here seems to have settled back, into what passes for normality, after a devastating hiatus boldly portrayed on the newspaper stands.

You don't look like a tourist the control man's look seemed to convey in a quick dart of his eyes over her face and then at her passport. She had agreed; I'm here for one reason only and offered little more explanation. The crisply dressed official could ask.

Move on, he had waved, but not in dismissal and before saying 'good luck'.

I'm here to be reunited with a loved one, a lost and found one, a lost to sight one, but not an every waking thought one, a dear one, but one who's silence brought another into my life, another one whose family loss I have been spared.

I've been distracted but I feel no guilt. Some may even say I'm selfish, or possessive. My girl lives, she's not alone, but I need to see her, now, soon! I have to be physically and emotionally reassured that Josie's with me again. Oh yes, I have to see her and feel her touch once more.

She stood quite still simply to take in new surroundings, jostled by the throng of passengers and those greeting them. She heard her name yelled out.

"Anya! Anya! We've found you!"

It was a young man's voice, clear and happy.

Before she could take in where the call had come from she was embraced, her arms pinned to her sides, and all she could do to control her surprise was to meet the kisses to her cheeks.

"Mama! Mama!" was the hoarse cry that she heard. "Jamie called Mary…she told him the flight you were on…we found you!"

"Yes…yes, my darling."

The almost suffocating yet restorative embrace eased before she could respond with her own silent clasp. They simply clung to each other.

"Oh Mum!"

"Oh Josie! At last!" It was all that Anya could say as she pressed her face to Josie's cheek and shivered at the sense of touch and the renewal of a physical bond to her own girl. She held out a hand to Jamie. "I'm so glad to see you, both of you."

She pulled on James' hand and embraced him for an instant.

"From your parents…from your mother," she told him without embarrassment.

"Don't move for a moment…Mama, don't! Stay still, like this, please?"

Anya did as was asked of her. It seemed as if the years fell away and those intense, not forgotten, moments shared between a mother and her young child were revisited. For herself, for Josie and her man Jamie, she felt no cares. The burden of anxiety and anticipation had been lifted. She felt overwhelmed, drained of all strength, and now yearned for sleep.

"The hotel, we need to get to my hotel," Anya murmured and gently broke free from Josie's embrace.

She nodded, smiled and looked to James as her hand was held out to him now. "Yes, we're together again."

"For a few days, darling," Anya confessed. "I'm not going to interrupt your journey for too long...or cramp your style." The cliché sounded odd coming from her.

"You won't...you aren't." Josie held onto her arm to fiercely make her point.

"I'll take this." James grabbed Anya's suitcase handle and watched his girl and her mother link arms as they began to walk towards the exit. They had all found a unity of spirit.

"Everything's going to be all right now," Josie whispered. "We're together again."

"Yes, for us it is...for us," Anya replied as her thoughts drifted and the plight of others came intrusively to mind. We've each got a role to play and can draw strength, comfort and understanding from one another. Kate would have company and succour from Josie and James, if they met, while I can offer my own support to Dennis...if he would only allow me into his world.

"There's no rush, is there?" Josie asked.

"No, we've only just met...again."

Her girl's remark complemented perfectly her own wayward thoughts. Our whole 'take' on life and relationships would be changed by our unique and shared experiences.

A solemn promise made to Tom and Mary was kept. They were told of a joyful reunion that she had given way to once she was alone with Josie, for a few moments, in her hotel room. Tears had been shed in private and relief that they were reunited laughed out. It was no more, she told Mary, than her instincts had told her to expect.

"I gave Josie your lovely, thoughtful gift," Mary heard from her.

"She was looked after...I asked for that, Anya. I sought it for her before Josie left us."

"She's been spared…your prayers were answered and my belief confirmed. Our girl's bruised and scratched, thankful for all that has been done for her, and…she's madly in love."

"She seemed so before, Anya."

"There's been a change…it's grown deeper. I see it in her eyes, in the looks she gives and receives from her James. They're so young but have endured so much already…separation from a loved one and then being sought for. Josie told me she was overjoyed, so happy and thankful that they had found each other again. She regained the will to speak…it was as if the shock of being parted so violently from each other had made her a mute. I also saw something else…the confirmation that nothing would separate her from James now."

"They're so young." Mary repeated Anya's earlier observation.

"Yes, but that's what makes all that I saw between them so wonderful. I can sleep now. I've seen my girl. I really know that she's cared for…I'm at ease with that, at least."

13

"I can hear a mobile. It's not mine…I lost it."

"It's mine…Josie, it's mine. I didn't hear it above the din…you're getting better by the day," Anya smiled at her as she took the thing from a patch pocket on her linen blouse. "Oh! Oh!"

"What? Who is it?"

"I'll tell you in a minute." Anya left the table they had been seated at on the noisy hotel terrace. Dennis' number was displayed on the small screen and as she sought a quieter spot considered what to say to him.

"Hello…I've been thinking of you both. How…?"

"We found two of them…" There was no preamble to his reply.

"We?" Anya felt a small shiver pass through her. She'd seen for herself how the temporary mortuaries, in the grounds of a temple or shrine were regularly sprayed with disinfectant, by a hose played upon the rows of recovered bodies wrapped in plastic sheeting.

"I did, Anya, I did," he corrected now in a clipped voice. "I found my boy Alex and his sister, Rachel. My wife," he said on a trembling sigh, "my, uhm...ex wife, Laurel...she's not been traced...lost...presumed dead."

"I'm very...very sorry."

"It's been a tough couple of days...I wished to say a proper goodbye to Laurel, not this."

There's an understatement; she kept from blurting out her opinion. He sounds so closed in on himself, so in control. For God's sake...your own sake, let go! A voice seemed to shout it out, in her head.

"And Kate, where is she now?" How is she, poor thing, getting through all of this?

"She's here, in an adjoining room...at our hotel. She'd like to see you, Anya...would that be possible?"

His voice remained flat, emotionless. She had to wonder just how the man had learnt or developed the skill to erect such barriers, defences even, to all that must be consuming him but that he would not confess to or disclose to any one else, or at least, a comparative stranger.

"Yes, of course...I'm with Josie. When?"

"Today...now," he added quickly.

"And you? Will I have time to see you?"

"I'll be bringing her over, Anya...I'll see you then."

"And...and then, Dennis?"

She spoke out like an inquisitor, purposeful and in control of her feelings whereas she felt an irrepressible need to express compassion for them both and to offer comfort, to embrace Kate, to hold Dennis' hands and thereby assuage the feeling of guilt that now overcame her. I've been spared what others have travelled so far to confront was the pervasive thought that took hold within her.

"Where will you go, alone?" she asked now.

"I return to some temple grounds, where my boy and girl are kept…I make arrangements…they're coming back home… I'll bury them in our local churchyard…close to us…close to me and Kate."

His voice finally broke and Dennis fell silent. Anya heard him clear his throat and give a deep sigh.

"Sorry," was barely to be heard from him

"Dennis, I'm so very, very sad for you both."

"I've no one else to turn to, out here…while I deal with this."

"I can help…I offered to do so, Dennis…may I, now?"

"Yes…thank you. I need that…Kate needs it too. She's been wonderful, a darling, so strong. I'm very proud…but, it's got to her…just being here, but, not seeing all that I have had to."

"Come here," Anya gushed, "just come over, both of you…be quick, please?"

"It's a lot to ask of you."

"I've a lot to give," Anya replied and wondered if she should have done so in those words. Too late, she admitted to herself. Any way, I'm telling him how it is, for me.

"Why?"

You do ask me the most direct questions, Dennis. I guess I've asked for it.

"You meet someone…or, someone comes into your life and it changes…"

She couldn't finish or express all that now came to mind. You can't do anything about it…no, not really…you can deny many things or pretend that something important never really happened…but it has… the timing wasn't the best…but, you've got no say in the matter. It's happened and now you've got to face up to whatever confronts you.

"Sorry, Dennis," she went on with a break in her voice. "Sorry."

"Sorry for what, Anya, for being who you are?"

"Who's that?"

"Someone special, you're honest and direct."

"Oh! I've said far too much…far too much."

"No, or time will tell."

"I'd better go, Dennis. Please, just come over whenever you can. I'll look after Kate…and, things will just have to happen."

She stood alone by the railings to the terrace, staring at the palm fringed pool and the sea beyond that provoked fond memories of another time and place. I've lived through moments like this before…saying something special to one special person.

"Mama? Mum?"

Her daydream was interrupted as Josie took her hand and drew closer, staring into her eyes in search of some explanation for her mother's withdrawal from her.

"Who was that? What's happened?"

"I've met someone…"

"You're upset…"

"Yes…yes, or a bit weepy. It's become a habit just lately."

"It's okay…I only remember one time."

"Sh!" Don't remind me of our Frank, not just now, she kept herself from saying.

"We met a day or so after I heard you were lost…then rescued. I've met a man and his daughter…a girl like you…of your age…it was like the last time we were in a place like this…with the sun, the blue skies…the trees…the beach."

"Papa Frank's time?" Josie interrupted.

Anya nodded. "I didn't think it could happen again…not in the same way. Papa was special…as this may be."

"Oh, Mum!" Her lips quivered as Josie heard her mother recall shared memories.

"I have to tell you…"

"What?"

"He's here, Dennis is here…he's just called me. We travelled out here on the same plane…he's with his daughter…he's told me that he's lost two of his children…they're dead. His wife… his ex-wife, she's gone…lost without trace it seems…not found. He needs help…he asked if we could meet…so that I could help him…and his girl, Kate."

"The poor man."

"Yes, poor Dennis…poor Kate." Her voice fell to a whisper for an instant before she looked into Josie's eyes. "It had to happen. I never expected it to happen and here…in these awful circumstances but in a beautiful place."

"What? What's happened?"

Anya met Josie's stare and gave a weak smile. "I…I think I've met someone who I care for. It's been a while…a long time since I felt like this."

"So quick…and so soon?"

Josie cried out her disbelief and hugged her mother oblivious to anyone who cared to look at them as they embraced.

"It's happened only once before…there weren't any complications then. I was alone…now, I have you, wonderful you. He…Dennis, has his only girl now, Kate. We barely know each other but we're close…getting closer." Josie simply listened, with a soft smile playing at the edges of her lips. "I hope he realises what he's gone and done…he's trying not to admit it may have happened, now of all times…but he said something to me, a moment ago."

"You barely know each other…"

"No…or yes. Depends on what you want me to admit to."

"But you know, just as you knew how you felt when you met Frank…my papa, Frank?"

They had spoken of her first meeting with him and the certainty that had possessed her thoughts from that moment on. Anya nodded.

"Yes...that's how it seems."

She fell silent and held her daughter in a tightening clasp of love and gratitude that she had been spared. *I can let you go on now, with James. You've been restored to me, Josie, and I know that others ask for my help now.*

I can't tell him, or confess to Dennis how I feel, until we find the right moment to talk. Our paths have crossed and re-crossed; everything that's happened to bring us together, the wave, has changed my perception of the future; that's how it is for me. It wouldn't be seen as proper, it isn't the time or the place to think of a new life...or, not yet. The present, for Dennis and Kate, has to be confronted and dealt with, memories of loved and lost ones secured and a period of mourning observed. Social niceties and respect for the departed have to be given their rightful place before I can consider, no longer on my own, how an altered and renewed life can be pursued.

ᘓ

Strength of Character

It was the first thing she noticed about him, about Frank.

He had beautiful hands, large fingered and yet, gentle.

An impression was gained that he could coax a response from inanimate objects; it did not seem like compliance to the will of a strong impulse. She sensed it upon being introduced to him and acknowledged that Frank had provoked this response from her. Even then she felt a compulsion to know him, to acknowledge his touch on her and confirmation that she had met a man who could help her.

More importantly, he appeared to be a man to help her ailing daughter. Oh, those hands!

They were so open and expressive. You could not look at him without sensing that he wished to share his contentment with life as he encountered it, daily; she saw that he could bring tranquillity to a troubled mind. Frank gave every indication of not being closed in on himself, crumpled by life's travails into a smaller person, cowed by circumstance. He stood tall and had a directness of gaze that did not intimidate; he seemed to say quite simply, I am Frank Ahrends, you should take me as I am.

And she had.

Frank entranced her with his long stride; the lightness of foot, even the swing of his arms seemed to be in sympathy with a secret rhythm that beat inside him. He portrayed such a casual outward appearance that she had been forced to stop and stare and then to ask the lead consultant who he was.

"You're going to meet him. That's Frank, and he will be Clarissa's counsellor...he will talk everything through with her, support her and offer comfort as the memories come out from the shadows."

"But...but he's a man!" she had said, foolishly.

"Why, yes Mrs Bloom." They both looked at him for a moment before they continued with the tour of the small private clinic. "May I call you Rebecca?"

She received a nod of assent. "I prefer Becky"

"Call me Margaret...we believe informality and a homely atmosphere helps our 'visitors' best."

"Visitors?"

"Why, yes...Clarissa will only be visiting us, to be helped and cared for. It depends upon the circumstances, but she will leave as a renewed young person."

Becky looked at Margaret in response to her use of words.

"She's nearly fourteen...on the brink of young womanhood. That's how it is now...you leave youth behind so quickly."

Margaret nodded. "Frank will help her with that, given the circumstances that brings you to us."

The case notes recorded the details of Becky's experience and how she had struggled to help Clarissa deal with an event that would shake a mature person to the core. Becky's own admissions had laid bare once more the common misconception that age and life's experiences fully equipped a person to deal with tragedy. Such a human being never truly existed. Honesty with what you had to confront was the best means to come to terms with your lot and live on.

"I'm pleased to meet you. May I call you Clarissa?"

"Yes...but not Clarrie. Don't forget that." Her reply was direct, her voice firm and unthreatening. Frank smiled.

"Thank you, and I won't. I'm Mr Frank, for now."

Clarissa looked amused and repeated his name. "Mr Frank."

"That's right. What does the word mean?"

"Frank?"

He gave a nod and met her gaze upon him with an unflinching but softened stare.

"Honest...that's all I can think of."

"Good. In Holland it would be very different…you make it sound lighter." He smiled again and studied her eyes carefully. "Hold out your hands to me, please?"

She did so. "Why?"

Frank pressed one finger to his lips and studied her hands; they hardly shook; he did not expect that, yet.

"Good, thank you."

"You're polite…is it like that where you come from?"

"No…at least not with all young people, but they learn."

"Do they call you Mr Frank there?"

"Oh no…or if they do it's a rarity. It sounds very formal but how we are together will soon change, after we've got to know each other and talked. You will share thoughts with me…you know that don't you?"

"Yes," she whispered.

"Well…when that's done and we are happy with each other we will be like friends just talking."

"Just friends?"

"Yes…not any old friends but two people who have shared something very important."

Clarissa did not allow him to continue and sat very still in her chair looking intently at her counsellor. She had also heard him described as a "mediator", someone who would help her by listening and comparing all that she spoke of and he had learnt of her from others.

"I do that with my mother! We've shared everything over…over…over again these last few weeks…even hours and days." Clarissa's voice wavered.

"Yes, I know and that is very important too. But…I will try to help you in a different way and I hope that you will help me to do that. There's no rush, Clarissa. We just talk and share what comes into your mind. You are in charge…"

"Not you?"

"No, not in the way you might mean…or think." He spoke slowly and maintained a softened eye contact with her.

"I will say, or ask you something, and you will do your best to answer me...but you will answer me with the first thing that comes into your mind when you hear the question." He paused and Clarissa looked down for an instant at her slight clenched hands. "Do you understand me?"

"Yes, okay." She nodded flicking away her hair as she did so.

"Good...thank you. It is most important to me that you answer me in that way."

"Will I have to do it, Mr Frank?"

"Yes...you will. But I will see to it that you come to no harm."

"It will hurt," Clarissa now told him in a subdued tone. "It hurts now...even now, just thinking about it."

They fell silent contemplating the moment.

Frank gazed around his small consulting room. He had made sure that it felt like any room at home with comfortable chairs and a coffee table with magazines scattered over it. A very modern turned metal standard lamp stood in one corner and cast light up to the ceiling, like a halo. Sunflowers on long stems and with crumpled leaves brightened a corner by his desk. His laptop computer was on a shelf, in the cupboard; that was 'the office'. Where they now sat was where joy and pain would be found or tearfully disclosed. There wasn't a single photograph of him or any companions anywhere to be seen. He had made sure of that. Instead modern prints, one a Picasso, hung on the walls; he sought some informality and a counterpoint to what he sought to achieve with a young mind.

"Mother will be nearby," Frank said breaking the silence. "But...there are some thoughts that only you and I can help each other with...do you understand what I mean?"

"Yes...I need to go back...so that I can go on."

"That's right. You have already learnt an important lesson...Clarissa. Well done." He held out one hand to her. "Just shake it, please?"

She looked at him in puzzlement but did as he asked of her. "Why?"

"Because I think you will be calling me Frank, just Frank, very soon." She met his smile with a weak one of her own and gently slipped her hand from his grasp. "Good...that's the deal we're going to make, Clarissa, right now...right here... today."

"I must ask you not to interfere, however upsetting the cries are. Clarissa has to let go and what you believe you hear are the very ties to her past experience being cast off. She will remember but she will also feel enlightened. It will dawn on her gradually and that's when she will need you most Becky."

Frank spoke to her in the small observation room some parents or guardians sat in to watch him at work. They could only see, and not hear, what his consultations provoked. Becky attended them all, she regarded her unseen presence as a mantle of comfort, both for her and the only child she had borne.

"She will need you most as the emotional anchor to her new found reality. I know...you've been there all the time but you will soon have your girl back, not wholly as she was before the traumatic event, but she will have overcome the worst effects and she will be able to recognise that a different future awaits her."

"She will remember." Becky's tone was frigid with the purest knowledge of the legacy that the consultations would bestow; they had attended the clinic for three weeks and progress was heartbreakingly slow for her as she watched Clarissa speak to him.

Frank waited before replying.

"Yes...but she will also remember the coping strategies that I will have taught her. Until now these have simply been to close off the terrifying images that spring up and are prompted by the memory of a few heart breaking moments."

"Yes," Becky's voice fell to a whisper. "Yes."

She had been through the ordeal but no one had helped her in the compassionate way that Frank had hitherto shown Clarissa. She had seen it in his hands, in the way he had simply held one out to Clarissa at their first meeting. She had noted the hesitancy on her daughter's face but the purest belief in what he had to do for her on Frank's.

When Clarissa conceded to all that his gentle questioning or prompts provoked in her febrile mind and her loud sobs filled the room he simply held out a hand in a moment's unselfish sharing of her daughter's turmoil and as a means to restore some tranquility.

"If I have done my work properly you will soon see the spontaneous lovely girl that you know her to be. The very essence of Clarissa as a human being will be there for you to see once more...the wonder and the beauty of that essential strength of character that makes Clarissa...Clarissa!"

Becky couldn't hold back the first tears and shook her head. It was not in disbelief of what he had said but the expression of a glaring truth from a man who had come into their lives.

"Are you sure?" she asked.

I don't deserve a look like that. She observed how his eyes followed her every move as she ran the fingers of one hand through her long curly hair. Look at me! The veneer that covers all my emotions is cracked and I can't hide it from you, Frank.

"I...I can't guarantee anything that I do, but, Clarissa has an inner spirit that shines through, even now. She wants to overcome...she wants to, but is still too young to cope with it on her own. She has turned to you for help and you have lovingly given it. You have come to me...to this place to help you, to help you...both."

"Yes...both."

"I know. So…what I am able to do for your daughter will relieve some of the hurt inside you and that you live with and have to cope with…somehow."

"Yes…somehow." She breathed out slowly between parted lips. "As her mother I'm supposed to know it all…even how to deal with…with…" Her voice trailed away.

"No…no one does, entirely. The circumstances of each case are different and so personal, truly unique to the personalities involved. You ask for help or turn to other loved ones who can listen quietly while you pour out your heart at the loss of someone you both loved…and at the manner of his passing."

"It wasn't my fault!" Becky's eyes widened in a recalled terror as she screamed out her reply. "What happened to her was not my fault!" She hit his arm with the side of one hand in a furious chop. "Oh Christ! Save me!"

She broke down in a gasping flood of tears and Frank rose from his chair, to give her some *'space'*.

"Becky?" Frank held out a glass of water. "Here, take this…and drink it slowly."

"Thanks." Becky wiped at her nose.

"You'd better take this as well." He offered a clean cotton handkerchief before sitting down again. Frank made a joke of what had passed between them.

"You pack quite a punch, lady."

Becky gave a stifled laugh. "I guess you get a lot of those?"

"No…there's always a first time." He gave a rueful smile. "No two days…none of the people I meet and help are the same. Every experience is unique."

"Oh!" Becky moved away in her chair and stared at him. Frank stared back. "What now?"

"This," he replied emphatically.

"Don't, don't Frank." She looked at his lovely hand and the strength she just knew could be drawn from his grasp as he held it out to her. "You're not supposed to."

"What? Touch…or care too much?"

"Yes…both."

"You may be right, to both counts. What I've been asked to help Clarissa with…and you, is outside…on the margins of my usual experience."

His hand was still held out to her and Becky took it. She watched as if in a trance as it closed over her own, only for an instant in a reassuring clasp.

"Don't worry…it's easy for me to say, but…don't."

She held his gaze now.

"I'm not *'worried'*. Clarissa and I have found a man to help us with…with our loss, the absence of someone through… through…" Becky stopped and took breath. "Through suicide…he did that through his own choice…by his own hand," she whispered.

The words drifted off on the air between them.

Becky clung to his hand wracked by tears and disbelief that this man, Frank, had opened the door to her own restitution. Is he supposed to do that? Is it permitted, to hold out a hand and to help in the way that he does?

She didn't care what the rules might say. What he did…it felt? Well, it felt quite natural.

His touch seemed to her to be life sustaining; it neither pushed nor drew her on to respond to his will. He offered comfort, understanding and time. Oh, how she needed time! He gave them space for an exchange of sentiments and suppressed emotions and quiet engaging moments to deal with them as they resurfaced.

Irrational and fanciful?. Maybe, but she realised that they both needed his strength. Her daughter had expressed it suddenly and without prompting after her first meeting with him. His character would sustain them on a journey the course of which only Frank seemed capable of directing. They had tried, but Clarissa needed another's touch.

Frank had remained quiet, leaving Becky deep in thought. Now he loosened her grip on his hand.

"You both have to trust me."

"Clarissa's more important."

"No, you both are and to each other." He watched as Becky sat back in the chair and listened with her eyes closed. "She can tell me one version of events and I will counsel her. You have to be strong and help her to understand that she was not at fault..."

Becky opened her eyes, provoked once more and now looked at Frank in a blaze of fury.

"Neither was I!" she yelled. "It wasn't my fault either! Do you hear me?"

"Yes...yes, I do."

"My husband had his moments...when he closed in on himself and neither I or Clarissa could reach him."

"Okay!" Frank stood up suddenly. "Okay."

"We both tried...oh, so hard...we tried to help and let him know that we were there for him...when he came out of those spells."

Frank listened. He had used the wrong words and cursed to himself for doing so. Becky watched him as he reached up to the ceiling in a tension relieving stretch. Finally, Frank turned and looked down at her.

"Can you...do you want to tell me about it?"

"How...how do I do that?" Becky asked. It was a lost voice that he had not heard from her daughter. "Help me, Frank? Help me too...I...I need that."

It was not in the plan but neither was it in his nature to refuse a call for help.

"Close your eyes," he said soothingly. "Take some slow breaths...slow and easy. Good...that's it. Now...tell me... where are you?"

"You can see the effect the whole experience has had on me."

Becky spoke curtly through barely moving lips as she dispensed with any acknowledgement of his pass. Yes, that was what Frank had done; he had given the first sign of his attraction or was it merely a deeper attentiveness to her? She had told him everything and he confessed her tone had been icy cold and detached.

"It's beautiful," he had said on touching her long lightly curled hair. The compliment had been heard from only one other man, long ago before he had changed unseen and deep within himself. On seeing herself, really studying her image in the mirror, could she acknowledge the transformation that she had undergone?

"It's not! To a woman it's a sign of ageing or trauma. It can only get worse."

"What? Greying hair? They are so few and you are too young to be concerned with that. To me it lends distinction…a worldliness even, that others might envy."

"What?" Becky laughed derisively. "What?" She gaped and pushed him away. He had stood close to her and simply talked; but really, what nonsense! Only, his look had conveyed a different sentiment. "What are you saying? Have you taken leave of your senses?"

"No."

"Clarissa found him! Hanging from the stairs! I came to her screeeam! You think that's worldliness? Seeing him there changed me…changed us and how we looked, in an instant!" She gave Frank a dismissive glance. "Christ Almighty! And here I was thinking that it was going so well."

Frank stepped in front of her and made Becky look at him. "It is…Clarissa is a wonder! Don't you dare say it isn't going well! You see it yourself. Right now…we're talking about you, YOU!"

"Oh?"

"Let me explain, let me do that at least!" He spoke softly, the flash of temper had gone. "Please?"

There was no sign that Becky's angry words had any other effect than to bind him to her situation more strongly. Yet, she looked at him haughtily.

"Why?"

"Because it may help."

"Huh! So *you* say!"

"Listen to me, Becky…will you do that, please?"

She had seen the persuasive tilt of his head often enough, through the mirrored glass when he had counselled Clarissa. Now he was trying it out on her.

"Get on with it! Explain away what you've just said…make some excuse for it."

"No, I won't do that…and you should know me well enough to know I won't do that."

She settled quietly into the chair with her legs crossed and her hands folded on her lap. Only once, under his ever-watchful gaze did she run the fingers of one hand through her hair.

"What?" she asked unable to prevent a weak smile coming to her lips. "What is it now?"

"You too can rebuild your life…you're beautiful, and yes… even with a few distinguishing grey hairs."

Becky pulled at the curls.

"Hm?" she asked pointing a finger at the strands of hair she now clutched. "Like these, you mean?"

"Yes, like those…they're a sign of worldliness and I mean by that so much more than you think I do."

"Go on," she said, "don't keep stopping."

"I want to be sure you'll listen."

"I am listening…go on," she urged, her look upon him softening.

He was impossible to stay angry with, signalling for her to stay calm with an almost graceful movement of his hands, downwards, as if to suppress all of her bitter feelings.

"Okay…by beauty in a worldly sense I mean you have seen how life truly is, that you have really lived and not existed just in a softening comfort that leaves you unprepared for the harsh realities we must all face. It's not something you can learn from books or endless TV dramas. They still sweeten the emotions…they have to, to get the viewers. Real life can not be read about…it has to be lived and learnt from. Nothing is fair in this life."

"I didn't *want to learn* about life from that terrifying sight!" Becky almost snarled as she sat up once more. "What you're telling me? It's so banal, so lightweight…so…so…"

She gave up trying to explain herself and slumped back in the chair.

Frank met her gaze upon him once more and held it. She's alone with me, so I'm the one doing this to her, provoking those mood swings, the anger! He sat still, facing her, and simply stared before sighing. Maybe he was too involved with the case, drawing too close to the mother when it was Clarissa that needed his help most. Becky was a distraction and her attitude was provoking him to disclose what lay at the root of his whole approach to life counselling.

"Let's leave it here," he felt prompted to say, suddenly.

"No…you haven't said everything that's on your mind. I'm the one needing some help at the minute…remember?"

Oh yes, he thought, I remember that all too clearly.

"So? What are a few grey hairs compared to what you have really learnt? Tell me that!"

"Frank…"

"No, don't avoid answering! Tell me! You're an enlightened soul…you've seen, lived and endured. You've brought another precious soul to me, but now you seek my help. I'm not about to smooth it all over with soft words and leave either of you to live on somehow. I just know that by saying what I do I might make a *real* difference to how a life progresses…maybe two."

He breathed slowly and looked with unmoving eyes at her. Becky finally met his gaze and held it.

"My God! You're…"

"Arrogant? Sure! Do I believe in what I can do?" He gave an unexpected laugh. "You'd better *believe* it!"

They both stared at one another and Frank gave her a wonderful smile.

"Sorry…I'm sorry. I don't know why I put it all so deeply."

"Yes you do," Becky answered. Her lips trembled as she looked across at him.

"Yes…I'm sorry if you don't want to hear it in quite those words. Tough as it is…heartbreaking and sorrowful as all that you go through may be, you have to learn and live through it. In the end, we all have to face a situation that tears us up. I'm sorry that I didn't put it in a way that you wanted to hear it."

"I didn't at first…but it's okay. You mean what you say and believe in what you do…I have seen your effect on Clarissa… others have too…she's coming back. I knew you were so very different from the moment I first set eyes on you. I…I knew it from the moment I first saw your hands…yes, those large open healing hands."

"And it took me so long to understand," he smiled before taking a moment to stare at his hands.

"The chief of staff here, she told me that it's not been a problem. Holding someone's hand is a comfort, your patient draws some strength from it. Others here have said that it's your way of finding a way into the mind of the person you're helping. It's…it's as if you want to suffer what they're going through too…in order to learn and understand…"

She paused for breath and Frank spoke out.

"It's my way…"

"I know…I know Frank. I've seen it! You're so engrossed in helping, all of them in your care…and Clarissa. She has changed so much. I don't know where or how you could have learnt so much…all those little tricks to help young people."

Frank's eyes became very still. Becky felt completely under his spell and could not, then, look away. She had momentarily lost the instinct to do so and she suddenly felt that they were completely alone with each other.

"I have experience…from recent times and in another place."

"Don't look at me like that," She could no longer endure it, the unwavering stare that provoked her into speaking out.

A buzzer sounded twice, softly in the room. Their consultation was over.

"I don't mean to frighten you," he said at last.

"You don't. I suddenly get the feeling that something special brought you here…"

"Oh yes." He replied without any sign that he would divulge his story to her. "It is something for another time…and another place, altogether."

"You're alive! You can dance and sing! Shout it out! You are you…Clarissa! Clarissa the beautiful and the strong! You will survive and come through all that you have experienced to become a better person…so much stronger! You know how precious life is, how much love you can find when you look closely, deeply and with understanding. You're not alone!"

He watched her as she danced and moved in a sweet rhythm to the music, it was loud and enervating and no one could hear it. The room was totally sound proofed. She had style and the intensity of her stare had lessened, she was letting go; the music was the primary impulse now, but he had coaxed from her a more receptive attitude to what had befallen her. The actions of another that precipitated her loss and headlong fall into a seemingly fathomless abyss were being overcome and reconciled to a more personal reality.

He was helping Clarissa step out onto a path to a future, her own but altered life.

"Okay?" she shouted and began to smile so broadly that he called out to her again.

"You're not alone! Say it!"

"I'm not alone!"

"Again…again!" He shouted and laughed with her too; he began to dance, not closely, but in recognition that the fact of Clarissa's assimilation into a more comforting world awaited her.

"I'm me! I'm not alone!"

"That's right! Say it again…yell it out!"

As he spoke to her Frank's mind raced and intense thoughts of all that Clarissa had endured overcame him. It may have been your instinctive response, provoked by the realisation that someone you loved had still undertaken a self-sacrifice that denied all love and companionship. But I have shown you the unique place that you occupy in another's life; others love you or have come into your life to help you. Each one of us is unique; we deserve all the love and comfort we can find to sustain us.

"That's right! You're not alone." His ecstatic words died away and Frank's face changed. The broad winning smile had vanished.

Clarissa stared back at him in shock. Her man had never shown anything except a devotion to help out, unaffected by what she had yelled, often screamed, out at him.

"What is it, Mr Frank?"

She first eased in her flowing rhythmic movements, then stopped.

"Frank, just call me Frank." He shook his head to deny to himself the answer. "Remember the words, sing them out… never forget but learn from what you've been through. Use the techniques I have taught you...you're alive...and you're kicking...just like the words of the song."

"But we aren't '*simple minds*', are we?" Clarissa held out a hand to him for the first time; he took hold of it touched by her concern.

Frank felt gladdened by this small display of maturity; he regarded it as a sign that his message was registering and that they were as one, for the purpose of healing.

"No...no. None of us are, and that's why I wanted to be the one to help you...and your mother too. You both deserve special attention and I'm glad to be the one to offer it."

Talking like this with a consultee was quite outside normal practice. But then, he had never worked in these very particular circumstances before, of helping a young person confront the tearing and numbing realisation that someone you loved and whom you thought loved you in return could do such a thing. That precious and unique person, *for her*, had performed a calculated and brutal act of deliberately and irrevocably leaving her, forever. What conscious turmoil in that saddened person had brought them to that final traumatic moment?

"Frank?" Clarissa turned to look at the mirror and then at him. He sat before her with his eyes closed. "Frank?" she called out again only louder.

"Hm?"

What am I doing he thought opening his eyes with a startled twitch. Clarissa's hand was on his shoulder.

"You hurt too...I see it now."

She had tears in her eyes.

Frank put his hands together, to his lips, as if in prayer, and felt a moment's detachment from his surroundings

"Don't worry...it's you who is important. The real Clarissa is here again...I've seen it. Hold onto that and make yourself so special again. You won't forget but you can grow now and live your life as a whole person. Go out and show me and your mother that you can do that."

"And you?" She had taken hold of his hand again as he stood up, towering it seemed, over her. They simply stood still.

"I'm good...I'm strong. Please, don't worry about me."

He gave her a smile and a nod of the head as if to acknowledge the confession that had been made.

Becky met them at the door of the consultation room.

For the first time she had witnessed the expressive and lively personality crumple. It had immediately become apparent from his movements; the sudden hollowing of his cheeks and the look of his eyes through the glass had told her everything. Frank had lived with Clarissa's agony to help her pass through the veil that had fallen between two stages of her life. Becky realised at that moment that it had taken its toll on him.

"We're all here now, Frank."

"Yes. But you've begun a new journey. Take care." He gave them an abrupt smile to match the brevity of his response and then, guiding them to the door, he closed it.

A sharp knock brought him out of the short nap that he often took to unwind before the next appointment. Frank looked at his watch; it was late, gone six thirty, so there was no other appointment scheduled, after all. The knock was persistent.

"Hi...forgotten something?" he asked on opening the door. "Where's Clarissa?"

"She's okay." Becky brushed past him. "She said she would go to the reading room."

"So...so, what can I do for you?""

"Yes, so...so who did I see with Clarissa for a few moments, earlier? Who was it that you became?"

"Someone..."

"Yes, yes! The last time I was in here alone with you I got the strongest feeling that something brought you here."

"Someone...someone did."

"Oh!" she answered flatly. "Oh!"

There was a hint of resignation in her tone now. So, in spite of her hopes she now knew that there was another woman involved after all...someone who filled his life.

"Don't say '*oh*' like that."

"Then, how should I say, '*oh*'?"

"Don't think about it." Frank reached out to her and Becky reluctantly took hold of his open hand. It seemed the thing to do but she felt so unprepared for the spontaneous expression of what seemed to be at work within him.

"Say it...tell me, Frank."

She bit her lip. Her words sounded so harsh and unfeeling. Until that afternoon Frank seemed in complete control of himself and everything he seemed to touch.

"I have two daughters," Frank said in a softened and wistful voice. "My wife...my '*ex*' wife has turned them against me and I can not begin to understand why."

"There's not a single picture of them here." Again, her tone was coolly observant as she made a gesture encircling the small consulting room.

"No...I have them in a private secluded place. At home... and up here." He pointed to his head.

"Frank!" He had taken hold of her hand and squeezed so tight for only an instant of declaration that she had to cry out.

"Yeah?" He stared down at their clasped hands.

"You're..." She followed his gaze and said in wonder, "You're *holding* my hand, *holding* it now."

"Yeah, should I be careful? It's been a long time since I did this...and with either of my girls too."

"I'm not going anywhere Frank...I know that now."

"You know that, so soon?"

"Yeah." She gave him a little smile. "You?"

"Into the darkness shone a great light," he said profoundly but with a smile and a look on his face that prompted a reply.

"You!"

But they said it together, spontaneously and pointed to one another, laughing.

She felt at one with him. "You found me, Frank and…you brought back my Clarissa."

"And I'll be in trouble for this."

He embraced her, his lips touching her eyes and mouth in soft lingering kisses.

"Who's to see?" she murmured, thinking that at last his strong hands held her. From the first glimpse of him she had known that she was meeting an unusual man, one whom she had known from some raw instinct was destined to come into her life and make her feel complete once more. A tremor of recognition ran through her; both she and Clarissa could make Frank the complete person again that he so ably and tenderly sought for others.

"The mirror," he whispered, too late.

They had heard a loud knock on the door.

"Clarissa!"

Becky answered happily, remembering all too clearly the moment that they had arrived home on that first night after meeting him. Unashamedly, she had confessed that a saviour had been found for them. 'Mr Frank', as he was known to them; the man with a laugh and a caring word; above all there was the strength of character to sustain another in spite of all the difficulties he had concealed and borne so well. And then…those lovely hands that by their expressive movement bestowed the reassuring belief that he would help to restore an inner calm. Oh yes! He had worked a miracle for them both, maybe for them all.

A smiling girl stood in the doorway.

"Special! Special!" she cried. "We're alive again!"

"And kicking!" Frank added and held out his arms to them. They hugged each other and performed a little jig.

"We're all alive again and kicking!" Becky sang out.

Why should they care who saw them?

Into the darkness had shone a great light; someone had written it, somewhere, some time ago.

ॐ

You and Me.
Myth and Reality.

_1_

"What are you doing here?"

"I might ask the same of you, Jen."

Martin looked away, towards the door of the café, feigning cool indifference. What had they to say to each other now? A brief and passionate affair was over.

She stood before him, one hand casually resting on the back of the bamboo framed rattan chair that complemented the glass topped table he had chosen. Martin was snappily dressed, of slender physique and well groomed. So, nothing had changed the man, outwardly, too much since she had last seen her lover. The anger and resentment that had consumed her in the days, no weeks, since she had been in his charming company, ebbed away. Jen had been his name for her from the moment they had met, in similar surroundings. 'Neutral ground' they had called the setting for a nervy first rendezvous and she remembered how his laugh at the very moment of them meeting had lifted her spirits and dispelled any concern at their age difference. Reality had overcome perception.

"You look very well, Martin."

"Thanks."

"Meeting someone?"

"Yes…you know this part of town is way off my usual beat."

"And mine."

The door to the fashionable café and bistro remained resolutely closed. He could talk, for a few moments at least, to the woman who had entered his life as a "hit", someone sourced or discovered via the internet, not a dating website but a message board. The circumstances of their first meeting felt tawdry but the cliché was very apt, 'the ends justified the means'. He had enjoyed her and the company she offered. Both parties had sought pleasure and companionship as consenting adults engaged in a game that others might frown upon but for many was an accepted consequence of a modern busy life.

Put in those terms a convenient excuse or explanation could be found for their meeting.

Jen, or 'Jenny' as she preferred to be called, had made nothing of the twenty or so years between them. She admitted to being lonely, let down and diminished by some of the relationships in her life, and that someone with charisma and an 'old world' attentiveness to her womanly needs was now sought. Sure, she was younger and vivacious, but that was a skein to all that worked within her. She'd let that slip during their time together but Martin reassured her; it was of no concern to him and they'd devote time to creating a fulfilling relationship. A flurry of emails and 'phone calls between them, when work meant days apart, only prolonged their languorous reunions.

"So…?" he said, pausing, to signal that some explanation from her for lingering was expected.

"So?" she teased in reply and pulled at a chair before taking her place at his table.

"I'm meeting someone," he said pointedly.

"Like me?"

"There's only one of you, Jen…"

"You always did have a way with words…"

"I've been around for a while…as you kept reminding me."

"I said quite a few things…before we split up."

"Yes," he said calmly. "Words and the expression of an emotion, they're an important part of living my life…and a livelihood."

His eyes flicked down to his watch then scanned the door once again. Anna was late, by ten minutes or so, and his mobile 'phone hadn't chirruped. Has she changed her mind and stood me up? He pursed his lips as the phrase came to mind.

"Well, our differences didn't matter…not for too long."

"So you said," he replied without irritation on being reminded of what he had taken, at the time, to be a casual and insensitive remark. Martin pulled at the short coat that had been cast over one of the chairs at an adjoining table. His mind had been made up.

"Well," he sighed, "if you'll excuse me, Jen? Take care of yourself…you look wonderful by the way."

"Thanks," she answered slowly as if her manner might delay his leaving.

"Yes…I have to go…it seems that my appointment's been cancelled. I'll have to leave you to wait on your own. A date is it?"

"You could say that, Martin."

A moment's silence fell between them.

"Anna's not coming."

Jen spoke without any emotion in her voice. A lively teasing look of her eyes now kept him in thrall.

"So, you're unwounded and unbowed?" The only sign that he gave of being duped was the clench of his lips after he had spoken and an unflinching stare upon her. "Is that the meaning of this drawn-out trick you've played on me, Jen?"

"No…quite the opposite," she answered softly, noticing that his hands did not shake as he now put on his coat. The display of calm assurance was at odds with what she had seen in him before and what she had expected in the circumstances of their rendezvous. They had both declined the offer to look at a photograph posted on the *'friends'* web-site; as before, they would wing it and be surprised by their first encounter.

"What? I didn't quite hear you. Wounded but unbowed, then?" He leant down to speak to her. "Had to make your point, did you? That Martin, he's older but no wiser!"

"That wasn't the point of me making contact…which you fell for."

"I fell for you, Jen, the first time…I fell for you, only to be told things that ended it all, everything we had. You did that, to us. That's what I remember of that time…the words you used then."

Jenny looked away. "Martin...I..."

"Don't tell me you're sorry for them...not now. You said that you'd put all that we had shared behind you and move on. That's what I'm trying to do too."

Martin sat down heavily beside her and simply stared at the woman who had kept him spellbound for such a short moment in time.

"Why rake it all up, again?" he continued. "You said that you'd get over '*us*' soon enough...it was fun while it lasted, nothing more...I think I got that right! Well...am I?"

He uttered the last words in a voice that hinted at the rawness of feelings on being reminded of the emotional intensity that Jen had aroused within him and she had discovered for herself. To make the point, he stared into her eyes.

"I didn't expect you to pick up the 'phone and talk to me...that's why."

"You could have tried." Martin thought over how petty and charmless he now felt, the rejected man who couldn't take the humiliation of it, again.

"Yes."

"Instead, you resorted to this little trick?"

"It was mean..."

"You said it...you planned it."

"You fell for it..."

"Yes," he shrugged quickly acknowledging her remark. I was taken in completely. He met her discomfiting look upon him. Now I'm behaving like...like an old fool. "You were clever in disguising who you were...it was quite an act. Still," he reflected, "you've had some training in that, playing a part...on the stage. I even fell for the voice...over the 'phone when I called you...just once."

"Martin?" She tried to moderate the plea in her voice. Yes, she'd tried every trick to make him believe in her, in Anna.

"No, forget it! Try your games on someone else now." Standing up suddenly he gave the chair a purposeful shove to make his point. "I hope you find the person who can take these games you play. Make it soon, will you...please? Then the rest of us men will be safe."

How theatrical he told himself on leaving her, without a backward glance. Pathetic 'old' git that you are! Oh Christ, I thought I'd get over that woman!

Some hope! Look at me!

She's bloody well got to me, again!

And, she knows it.

The clack of heels on the pavement made him stop.

"My e-mail address hasn't changed, Martin."

He looked at the hand that clutched his arm as Jenny stood close.

"You changed enough, on the message board...then the emails, to hook me, again. Let it be now, Jen...move on." There was no malice in his tone.

"Over the last few weeks I've had time to regret what I did...what I said when I last saw you even more."

"Me too...I've felt that way too. But, it can't...our meeting again won't change anything."

"Are you sure?"

"Yes," he said, uncertainly, and in a voice that he now recognised carried little conviction. "I've got work to attend to...being distracted once before was quite enough."

"You came to meet Anna."

"She stood me up...the woman who seemed like someone who might make amends or be different...she stood me up."

"Maybe she, the real person, can still make a difference?"

"Leave it...leave it, for now."

Jenny renewed her grip on his arm to restrain him from leaving. He did not demur from allowing her the moment's show of intimacy.

"I'll remember that, what you've just said, Martin, 'leave it, for now'."

"And I'll wonder why I said them. They're only words, Jen."

"Are you sure? The look you've just given me…as you said them, it shows me something else, Martin."

"Appearances, and a few choice words…they can mean anything you want from them, at the time. You know that better than most."

"And I've had time to think it all through," she said looking at him directly. "Everything I've said and done."

"As I did, Jen…at the time and again a few moments ago. Now, please? Excuse me."

2

He knew Jen's eyes were upon him as he strode across the road.

I don't have to make anything up or imagine the outline of a story. I'm living it, right here and right now. The idea didn't have to come out of the blue, out of a clear blue sky. It arose in my creative imagination while I sat with the woman and heard her tell me how it had been since we were last together.

Stepping onto the platform of a Routemaster bus, a comforting red contraption, he was reminded that some things didn't change. He took his seat on the lower deck just as it moved away. Any bus will do he had thought, anything to win some space.

I didn't need to be reminded of what we had, Jen, or to show so clearly how I had been taken in once again. I spite of the circumstances, your trickery and duplicity – are they the right words? – I can't deny how I felt, how glad I was to see you. I took in once more that lovely svelte figure and that crop of black hair. It's so short, almost manly, but it suits, it complements perfectly, beautifully, that unblemished youthful face and is entirely in keeping – no, in harmony – with the clothes you wear!

You're a lass, a modern girl, I can use the words when I'm in my own company and locked away with my thoughts, of you, of us together. I loved the clothes you wore, those silvery slacks and the black blouse, the silken scarf at your throat. It all screamed out at me, of elegance and vitality, but…but, that's on the outside.

And what of you, who is the woman on the inside? Well, it was your other self, duplicitous, cunning and selfish.

That's how I was made to feel and think of you just now, only, did I get that right?

Bloody hell! I don't know, not any more, not after I saw you again. I never saw that in you before.

If I feel this way now why didn't I ring you?

Good question!

I know the answer but I won't go there. I told her when we were in the café, I'm an oldie only it didn't matter then, too much, and it sure as hell doesn't matter to me now.

I don't feel like…like an old fart!

Fifty odd isn't so old and I've got my wits about me and have more than enough vitality to keep it up. She found that out soon enough and never complained, not once. I gave her some 'satisfaction' often enough, I remember.

Leave it!

No! Credit where credit's due!

Anyway, I showed up at that café, that's how desperate I am to be in company again, associate and mingle, linger over someone different from the usual crowd I'm in touch with, work for, rush about for to earn a living, a good one that's true.

I sought a woman's touch, maybe the prospect of that Anna's touch, who would captivate me just like Jenny did…only a few months ago.

Great times went by, but so quickly, that I never thought there would be an end to them.

I thought I'd found it with her, that Jenny, only she told me how it was for her, towards the end of her little 'fling' or 'intermezzo' as she laughingly called our time together when she left me…abandoned me to the memories of us together, more like.

Leave it, you sentimental git!

No.

I saw what we had together, even as an unlikely couple, so very, very differently.

What was it she said? Oh yes, she told me what she thought, how bizarre or 'freaky' – yes, that was the word – how freaky being with an oldie like me had been. They're not the kind of words or memories that make you want to call her and ask if there's anything to be done to salvage the times we had lost. Still, I took her to places she hadn't been to before, that made her feel very different…in and out of bed.

At the time, I thought we'd found an emotional and physical union. How wrong could I have been? Was I…so wrong?

He looked out of the window, over the throng of pedestrians shuffling and hustling along the pavement that passed by so slowly.

What a mass of people, all those lives connected or separate, enclosed within their own bounded little worlds or maybe they're just like me, wanting to break free of certain stifling bonds and share a life with others, or, one in particular.

Jen, I thought we'd found each other and all that we needed from another compassionate soul. No, I don't believe it was just a matter of fleshy friction that kept you by me…in spite of what you said then, when we parted. You said so yourself…only a few moments ago, you'd lost something.

For God's sake, no mine! I wasn't ready for it, being…being… what's the word? Okay, reunited, I wasn't ready for it!

I said what I did because I need some space. How does it go? Oh yes, I need to get my head around what's happened again, with you.

How we came to meet wasn't so unusual.

I've read about people who seemingly exist in solitude, the world passes by while they tap away at a computer keyboard

*surfing the web, they post messages on an electronic message board
or read what others have posted there. If one such message, or
muted cry for help and attention, chimes with another, as it did
with me when I first 'met' you, at a distance, what's so wrong
with that?*

*It's the opening of a door to another life, to companionship
and, if you're fortunate, to a life of love.*

*Where did I go wrong in hoping for that and thinking I'd
found someone just that little bit special? Tell me that, will you
Jen? I haven't figured it out, not at all, but then the words you
used on me in those last days made me lose sight of all that we'd
been through, together.*

"Piccadilly, please."

The conductor gave him the ticket.

*Yes, life's a circus. I can't help it if the cliché fits the situation
I'm in.*

3

The days passed, then a week, and still nothing had been
heard from Jen. She had taken his parting words as affirmation
of how it was to be.

The flat, an apartment that he owned, near the Paddington
Basin, was home. Buying the leasehold interest had been one
move that he had never regretted. It had been bought with
the proceeds, or profits, gained after a very successful year
when two plays and a book had found commercial and critical
favour. Sustaining that streak of good fortune had been the job
of a lifetime and he had been modestly successful ever since.
Financial prudence had been born out of necessity and a fear
of growing old, or older, in strained circumstances.

The likelihood of that now seemed remote and he was
thankful for all that had been achieved over a lifetime's
work.

He rose early, exercised for half an hour undertaking Pilates and Yoga exercises before a light breakfast and a reading of the daily newspaper that had to be collected from the post box in the block's entrance lobby. He took the stairs on the way down two-at-a-time in a light –hearted skip, whistling occasionally to match the mood he was in. On the way back the tempo slowed but his efforts made the heart beat a little faster and he drew some reassurance that he was still able to follow this simple, singleton's routine.

The daylight hours were fine, they were accepted as part of the writer's life that he sustained. He would devote hours drafting and redrafting work-in-progress, in promotional work that a publisher or commissioning company sought of him, or attending literary events that kept his name on the public's lips and in a publisher's overtaxed mind. The evenings and nights were the problem; company that would fill the dark hours and relieve the silence was the antidote to a pervading loneliness.

Useful these computer things, aren't they?

He would break the silence. A message was sent and he now turned to the pages of a proof that was in its final draft.

Ping! That was quick!

Yes, Martin…I wondered if I would hear from you or I would have to ask, remotely and out of your sight, how you were. Are you ok?

Yes, Jen. Are you, okay?

Yes…I'm still sorry for how it is.

You've taught an older man how silly he's been. I should have known better than to sit at this machine and make out that another life was to be found out there, by this means. It's a poor substitute for face-to-face contact and…the sharing of a touch. The real thing counts for so much more!

Oh, Martin!

He imagined her sighing out his name, as she used to when they were so close.

Yes?

I prefer seeing you! I'm not obsessed by reading what you've got to say, or hearing your thoughts spoken out by someone else, hearing them in a radio play, or looking at some TV piece that you've written.

Jen? What's happened between us…all this scribbled internet 'shit'…it's utterly wasteful of time and emotionally draining. So, yes, it is infinitely preferable to be with someone and know that their look is upon you and to feel their touch and breath on your skin.

Let me see you, please? Let's meet again?

Sorry, no…or, not yet.

Why ever not?

I'm older…one too many in your life.

He remembered that jibe as he tapped out the line.

And there's only one of me, Jen…you said so yourself.

Or…there's only one Anna?

Don't!

Don't what?

Mess me about!

Me? Mess you about? Why would I want to do that?

He waited, allowing his conscience to speak to him of his baseness, his own cruel teasing of her, before he relented.

Sorry…I never wanted to mess you about, Jen, or take for granted how you felt. Forgive me?

When?

When…when? What do you mean Jen? I almost typed in 'girl'.

He avoided any answer on when she might have an opportunity to forgive him in her own way.

I'm not that, a girl. I'm not that, Martin, not even to you.

Not even to me…an older me?

No, and pleeease? Don't go on about age!

Ok. Our meeting, a few days ago?

A week…to be precise.

413

Okay, sorry, a week ago...that meeting set me thinking and it had one important consequence...

Only one? Why don't you ring me and talk...speaking is better and more, hm! Intimate!

I've learned to take things a little easier, Jen.

Ok.

As I was trying to type out, our meeting had one consequence... a particular one if you want me to put it that way.

Just one out of so many others?

Yes...yes. I'm trying to type out that I've outlined some ideas. It's the nascence of another piece by the old, but sometimes great, Martin Scrivener (what an apt name someone in heaven above will say).

May I read it?

Why do that?

Do I have to say 'sorry' to you again?

No, I know who you really are now. Once burned I'm twice shy...

You weren't shy, never that...never, once we knew how it went between us, Martin.

I was myopic...I could say it comes with age, for some.

Not that again! You may have noticed, I've stopped referring to the "age thing".

Oh yes, that again! The eyes only see...

But the heart yearns for something else? Is that it...is that what you mean to tell me?

In a manner of speaking, Jen...no, in my way of writing!

Meaning?

I'm not going to expand on the theories of mythical love and the reality. The words blitzed out over cyberspace tricked me...into confronting reality, or your perception of it.

I wanted to be in contact with you again, Martin!

Well, you have been, in a curiously frightening and modern way. I'm off on my travels for a few days and I'm going to try and restrain myself from prompting or replying to these remote contacts we have.

See me…agree to meet me again? You've contacted me this time…I feel a little easier, just, that I'm not chasing you…or a hopeless cause.

I'm never that…hopeless…or helpless, for that matter.

I know…I know, Martin. Ring me? Please, let me hear your voice again?

I've been ensnared twice, Jen…you know how it could be.

Yes.

I've…I've had to learn a lesson.

From me?

Yes, in a way. What I'm attaching to an e-mail I'll soon send to you may give a clue to what I'm tempted to write about. I may try and make a film script of it…I've lived through some of the episodes myself…I've crashed and burned as a result of them.

I'd like to find you again.

Hm?

Never mind. In the meantime I can think of myself as your muse…I'm Martin's inspiration!

Please! I have enough to contend with, Jenny.

Mind how you go, Jen? In spite of everything before…and what we've written just now, I still care.

I know…even if you've got a strange way of showing me.

This is now…you know how it was between us before. I think of those times only too often, girl.

Girl? Girl! I'm really happy you've written that, now! I have some hope…that I still matter.

There you go then.

Yes, I will, Martin.

Good.

I'm not sorry…not one bit, for making contact with you again in the only way I know! Is that what you're minded to think when you read this?

No.

It's pushy but I'd be showing my older side if I told her that.

Good.

Jen, you mattered a great deal to me…I could even have admitted to stronger and deeper feelings, with an intensity that I found only with you.

You lovely man!

Not lovely…just a man!

You know what I mean to say, Martin.

Do I?

Yes.

Let me think on it some more. Read the attachment, if you're interested. Our short reunion has sparked a few creative ideas in me, so, THANK YOU, Jen!

You know where to find me, Martin. Absence…fond recall and memories…then seeing you? They've all changed me.

I won't be away for long.

He signed it, 'Yours, Martin'.

An email was quickly typed out.

Sparkly Jenny, (I loved the slacks you wore the other day!), I wonder what you'll make of this, the notes I made following our meeting and the ideas I had playing around in my head before we did so. The web's got a lot to answer for! Please, read it and tell me what you're provoked into thinking. Will you do that for me?

Yes, I will Martin, I'll read it, but on the understanding that these remote hands-off and out-of-sight exchanges are at an end, or soon will be…okay? I would like to see you…want to see and speak to you again, be in your company and revert to a normal way of life.

Not live a closed off existence?

Exactly. Why are we going through this torment of separation?

Is it like that, Jen, torment?

Yes! You know very well what I mean…you know me well enough, Martin, just as I know you.

You knew me and still said the things that you did?

I've said sorry.

I don't recall the word, 'sorry', crossing your lips, girl, or the exact context when you said it. He erased the text before he re-considered a reply.

What else were you going to say?

I know that presence, companionship, a touch or a smile…a kiss, a caressing embrace, they're all tokens that make you live, Martin…they're what make you the man.

Live again?

Yes, they make you live again…

Read my email attachment, a voice cried out inside him.

Go on, say it, Jenny!

I know that all those little things make you live…make you feel alive. I know that, I knew that of you before and I want to see, feel and hear it from you again.

Steady, miss!

Okay…okay! I'm smiling at that, Martin.

Good. Just go steady for a while.

No! I want to tell you everything.

Was it all in the plan when you hooked me, as Anna?

There was a long pause and Martin waited. He wanted to read or recognise the truth as Jenny expressed it.

No, it wasn't. I fell to pieces, deep inside, when I saw you again. Are you satisfied now?

He imagined the tremble of her lips, the emotional response he had provoked within her by the economy of language he had used. He wrote scripts, told a story and described as best that he could the human condition. His characters expressed all that they endured through his words. To adequately portray all that moved them, and transfer those emotions onto a blank page, he felt compelled to act out the parts, in his mind. The problem remained, he couldn't quite carry off the full range of emotions himself, in real life and with a passionate woman as his companion, nor could he remain indifferent, or callously ignore, the effect of his own spoken words and look upon her.

Jenny had sought him out and to perversely wreak retribution upon herself for the dissolution of a relationship effected by her own words and deeds. He had to admit that it took some courage and cold premeditation to create the scenario where she would place herself in his company once more without any assurance of the outcome.

I'll believe that you're sorry for what became of our relationship, Jenny. Recognition of the fact came to him as his e-mail was typed out.

Dear Jen, don't break. Please read what I've written? I'm sorry that it's cold and studious but I felt obliged to be rigorous in my approach to the subject. The trick is going to be in the writing of it, to give the story that's developing in my head the sympathetic treatment the reader or the observer, if it's to be a TV play, expect. It's only an outline of a deeper, hidden and emotional journey that many people have to make. In my opinion, it could be the outline of a story about a single soul looking for another person, just like them. They search for someone to have and to hold...

And? Go on...continue, Martin?

I'll call you, Jen...in a few days, I promise. Take care of your dear self. Martin.

4

He scanned the text once more looking for any 'spell check' or grammatical errors, but there were none.

Modern relationships, or how we find another to be close, or closer, to. These are the ideas that have been provoked within me, Jen, after meeting you so unexpectedly. Speak to you soon? Martin.

The pages of text were attached to his email.

Send.

There's no hurry to reply, Jen. I said I needed some space.

He logged off, shut down the laptop, put it into his case in readiness for the journey the following day and went into the living room. There, he poured out a glass of white wine and settled back in his favourite chair.

I need a few days away, from all of this emotional turmoil and disclosing my susceptibility to her charms. An interlude may will help me see things clearly again.

He felt reassured and drank a little toast to the prospect.

CYBERMYTHS & REALITY

Relationships at a distance, sustained by the Internet, seem to be growing in number. The world's biggest cities are now filled with "solitaries", single people, of all ages, maintaining a relationship with many others but all at a distance instead of face-to-face. Reports would have us believe that the phenomenon is growing at an alarming speed.

Company is fine. Being in close proximity to one another, or body to body, is not rejected but young people today follow a different life from those of their elders, their parents, or from those that care about them and how they adjust to the new ways of the world they live in. Parents only have their own experiences at such an age to inform them of how their offspring should live. Only, the world has changed since then; they don't recognise it from what they themselves lived through.

And why restrict the findings to the young alone? Old people are lonely and isolated too, from their kith and kin, someone they could love, or are in love with but lost to them, or from friends and former colleagues too.

Some commentators have called this isolation, or solitary existence, as "hyper-individualism", a phenomenon that was first brought to the attention of social commentators at the end of the 20th Century. The voices of concern have been silenced by those that argue for the growth of "interconnectivity" between these individuals, that some refer to as single souls, over the Internet or cyberspace. Relationships are sustained but at a distance and often without any idea what the other person, or people you are in contact with, may look like or where they live. An image can be portrayed that, for all anyone knows, is that of the person projecting it. Discovering the truth, or physical reality, is very difficult. No one, unless the two "individuals" concerned meet face-to-face, will really know the other.

Hyperspace allows the hidden/distant/remote individual to project an impression that has been created by their own hand, at the touch of a keyboard and mouse, and under the disguise of a "nickname"; games can be played upon each other without fear of any physical or vocal retribution. Like the creation of the image, the outcome is in the writer's hands, in his or her gift. Virtual space can now permit an individual, in solitude, to create a new person, a stranger to the reality they are or grew to become.

Some might say they are "aliens".

Fortunately, the maintenance of solitude or separation can not entirely replace the joy and pleasure of company, of another's touch or the sound of the spoken word from a loved one. However, for some, a sad minority it is said, the electronic hyperworld offers its own peculiar solace. Like a prisoner in solitary confinement, or in the Gulags of the Soviet era, the individual turns in upon him or herself and finds a life, remotely, with other like-minded or *'captive'* people. Little of enduring substance may be exchanged in those written words, or blogs, but they matter to those who created them on the screen.

What has so far been written may be contrary to the primordial sense, in humans, to deal with each other face-to-face, by word, deed and touch, body-to-body. Those who try to explain the modern era's apparent obsession with solitude point to the dozens of contacts anyone can make, enjoy, endure, suffer and reject, all of it pursued or inflicted remotely. What you can affect upon a person's heart and mind, as the sender, you write and convey at the touch of a button; others can inflict their treatment or abuse upon us too, in an instant, without any satisfactory means of redress. If you don't want to respond or continue with the "relationship" you restrain yourself from answering or delete the message as unread, by a keystroke and in a microsecond.

The screen is cleared – the thoughts provoked, they endure.

Stated like that there is something sinister, cold and alien to the real human condition and needs. It is said that in South Korea cyberspace relationships, if they can be called that, outnumber those of face-to-face contact. Elsewhere, it is reported that the construction of dwellings or apartments for single people is driven by this impulse in modern men and women to be alone – en soledad, or, in solitariness, as the Spanish would have it.

Fortunately, there is another view on what has been said so far.

The problems of solitude and the closing off from others have an all too human solution and continue to offer hope. Humans can not do without each other; physical contact is a pre-requisite for a full(er) life and a sense of belonging.

Accordingly, we prepare ourselves, mentally and emotionally, to meet the troubles and setbacks we encounter in our daily lives. Having someone close-by, physically, is of enormous help and comfort. The proven solution to solitude and isolation is to convince yourself, and others, that interdependence is paramount to the continued well being of the individual and society.

We are, as humans, both individuals and companions, independent citizens and a member of a wider society. Reconciling these opposites is not made any easier by the electronic age; you don't have to be in the same room/country/ hemisphere to be able to communicate at an instant. The paradox is that the virtual world has supplanted the real and companionable physical world for many and out of their own choice.

This is a sad commentary on where we have travelled.

It is comforting, however, to realise that in all humans it is a matter of personal choice on how far we allow ourselves to be isolated, live in solitude and away from others. We have not become so affected by the virtual world that we can easily be 'alone' like dogs, cats and horses often manage to live. And, it is all too human to think these animals deserve company and are the happier for it...ours.

Fecit – *M. Scrivener©, London – Jan 2008*

5

The doorbell rang and Martin rose wearily from the chair.

"Hello?" he said over the intercom.

"I've read it! I've read the piece you e-mailed!" Jenny exclaimed, her crackly voice echoing through the small hallway.

"You came here to tell me that?" He chuckled before remembering his good manners. "I'll be right with you."

"Open the door, Martin...press the release!" Jenny cried out on a laugh. "Quickly!"

He did so.

They met on the stairs and faced each other, awkwardly.

"Jen?"

"Are you looking...are you looking for someone to have and to hold?" She cried out the words brushing the drips of water from her hair and rubbing her hands on the sodden jacket she was busily unzipping.

"Come here," he coaxed, taking hold of her hands before tentatively embracing her. "I didn't expect this at all...or you coming over to see me, so soon. Everything's changed again, has it?"

Jenny nodded. "Yes! I had to come over and see you, forward of me I know after all you've said recently."

"It's a la mode and I don't mind, not a bit." He smiled at her. "You *had* to come over?"

"Yes! I read the piece and remembered what we had written to each other..." She looked about and took in her surroundings. "Can we go to your flat?"

"C'mon on." He tugged on her hand. "It's...it's not so far, as you know."

"I remember the place had a lift. Is it out of order?"

Martin laughed. "No...I took to the stairs."

"I heard you."

"I took them, two at a time..."

"At your age?"

"Well," he shrugged, "I'm having to stay fit and youthful, and I've got to adjust...to being with Anna *and* Jen."

"One never existed...the other's changed. I told you, I'm not going to carry on with remote contact, it's cold and utterly lifeless."

She made him stop on the half-landing.

"C'mon girl, what is it now?" He smiled cheekily. "I want to get to the flat where I can hold and talk to you...up there, not in this echo chamber."

"Just hold me? No more talk...no more space and no more empty times in between, please?"

He kissed her wet hair, her face and eyes then settled a lingering kiss to her parted lips.

"I only ever wanted one person, not the cyber miss but Jen...or Jenny, the real woman. I've learnt about the real woman...the one here." He touched her breast, at her heart, and Jenny clasped his hand to keep it against her.

"I became someone else," she confessed, moving to embrace him and whispering into his ear. "I got lost…from you."

"I was lost too…only for a while, for a few seconds after you said Anna wasn't coming."

"You were angry."

"Yep! For not calling you, you Jenny, and for believing what you'd said when we split up. Is that how you say it?"

He gave her a quizzical stare before loosening their embrace upon each other. They resumed the climb of the stairs.

"Martin?"

"Jenny?"

"To have and to hold?"

"Yes? What of it?"

He turned away only for an instant to unlock the door to the apartment before pushing it open impeded by her renewed clasp upon him. They shuffled giggling into the apartment before Martin kicked shut the door.

"From this day on?" she reminded him.

"Yes…yes," he replied through a moment's deepening kiss. "I meant you to think what the words really meant."

"I do."

"Then, welcome to your other home, Jenny."

"Jen," she mumbled against his lips.

"No," he corrected.

Martin cupped her face in his hands and kissed softly, just once, before he pushed the sodden jacket off her shoulders and heard it fall with a thud onto the boarded floor.

"You're Jenny to me now, the real woman and no-one else. Got that? I'm all through with make believe and cyber love."

"Only the real thing will do?"

"That's right, only the real thing." Martin pulled on her hands. "Now…what's keeping you, girl?"

෴

Printed in the United Kingdom
by Lightning Source UK Ltd.
135202UK00001B/7-18/P